DANCE TO YOUR DADDY

Dance To Your Daddy

A Novel

Gail Levy

Elliott & Thompson
London

To Aubrey Gordon (1924-1962)

Dance to your daddy,
My little baby,
Dance to your daddy,
My little lamb.

You shall have a fishy
In a little dishy,
You shall have a fishy
When the boat comes in.

Traditional nursery rhyme

In ancient times people believed that the soul of the deceased haunts the grave for a long time. Because of this fear, prehistoric men rolled great boulders in front of graves so that the boulders should prevent the dead – or rather their souls – from escaping and plaguing living relatives. ... The psychoanalytic insight into the origin and significance of the practice of putting a number of small stones on Jewish graves is that the many pebbles are a substitute for the one big boulder. The small stones become substitutes for that primitive custom once essential for the burial. It is as though the survivor who visited the grave of a relative protects himself from their envy or hostility by putting these stones on their abode, preventing the dead from escaping...

'Stones on the Graves of Jewish Cemeteries – a Psychoanalytic interpretation' – Theodor Reik, *Pagan Rites in Judaism*, 1964.

Prologue

November 22nd. 2004
London, SW6. 4.35 am.

The body was face down on the floor, next to the toilet. Legs spread wide, arms up around the head, lips and nose flattened against the white toilet base. It was hard to tell what colour his hair had been. Now it was a matted red.

He was naked. A pair of pyjamas soaked with blood were draped over the edge of the bath. On the window above the sink was a bloody handprint. Beneath it four smudgy lines dragged down the glass, colouring the raindrops on the other side a bright orangey-red. He had fallen with the violence of the first cut, raising one arm to ward off the next blow and trying to steady himself with the other, then slid down to the floor. On top of the lavatory lid were three fingerprints in a brown sticky pool where he had briefly rested his hand.

Bloodstains covered the walls, arched over the doorframe and fanned out into long splash marks across the ceiling. There were rust-brown streaks on the floor and across the white tiles round the bath; the silver taps were speckled with tiny dots. And down the slatted wooden door of the fitted cupboard, three long, broken stains, like an angry row of exclamation marks.

He had been dead slightly over three hours. Rigor had started in the muscles of the neck and arms – he was slowly stiffening from the jaw muscles down. By four-thirty the heavy rain which had started in the early hours of Monday morning was just beginning to stop. His body would lie in its blood and excrement for another two hours. Then the people would arrive, collecting, measuring, counting – the murder investigation would start. Meanwhile he would grow cold in the bathroom painted with blood, his lips pressed in their death-kiss against the smeared white toilet.

London, NW1. 4.36 am.

She blinked open her eyes. Something had woken her.

A click, a tiny noise, hardly anything. But she was already awake when the phone began ringing. She lay in the dark, eyes open wide, staring at the innocuous grey plastic phone by the bed.

Silently she counted. One, two, three... The room was still and unbreathing around her. The ringing seemed incredibly loud. At the third ring she slid upright, her eyes still on the phone. Her vision had become more accustomed to darkness. She reached out her hand and picked up the receiver and whispered, 'Hello?'

Nothing. Silence. Not even breathing.

'Hello? Who is this? Who is this speaking? *Hello?*'

A second imperceptible click, then she was listening to the familiar whirring of technology. Slowly, she replaced the phone.

She looked at the bedside clock. 'Shit,' she said, seeing the time. 'Shit, shit, shit.' She took a deep breath and exhaled sharply. Frowning, she lay back down. Pulling the duvet up to her chin, she closed her eyes. Behind her lids she could see nothing, only more and deeper circles of darkness. Brown to purple to whirling black... The silence was as violent as the brash sound of ringing. She nestled her face into the pillow, trying to relax, trying to go back to sleep, hearing her breath beginning to grow gentler... more regular...

Someone's here, she thought suddenly, jerking open her eyes. *Oh, God, someone's here in the flat with me.*

She sat up, the duvet slithering down her body with the sudden movement, heart hammering, eyes wide, ears sensitive to the slightest sound. She could feel a presence. Where? Perhaps hidden in the shadows thrown by the open door? Her eyes flickered over. A movement? No. Just shadows, that was all.

Eyes. Unfriendly eyes.

Someone was watching her. She was sure of it. She had never been more certain of anything in her life. A man. It was a man's eyes on her. 'Shit,' she breathed again, like a mantra, to calm herself. But the hairs on the nape of her neck were prickling, her skin felt clammy with panic. Her heart was thumping so hard it hurt her chest, her throat felt constricted. It was hard to breathe. She began to imagine she could see him, crouched and still, waiting, half hidden behind the door, his murderer's eyes turned into black, burning sockets... I'm just spooked by the call, she told herself, swallowing. It's nothing, I'm being absurd.

But, run, run! a voice inside her was screaming.

Slowly she swung her legs out of the bed. The room seemed suddenly larger and filled with unearthly shapes. She sat on the edge of the bed, breathing deeply, her eyes straining into the darkness. Those weren't shadows, of course they were not, she could see – What? *What?* Her heart stopped, then began to thump harder than ever: nothing. She saw nothing.

Keeping her eyes fixed on the dark corner, she leaned back on one elbow to click on the bedside lamp.

An empty bedroom. Within the small circle of light thrown onto the bedside table, a clock, three paperbacks, half a shell used as an ashtray. An open packet of Drum tobacco. Cigarette papers. Matches. Under her bare toes, the rumpled edge of the rug. Over by the door, a pile of clothes. Two hastily kicked-off shoes. She released her pent-up breath. Clothes. Shoes. Not the face of a murderer. Everything normal. Everything perfectly bloody OK.

In the morning you'll be laughing at this, she thought, trying to smile at her own foolishness, but her mouth was too tight and twisted. It took an effort to cross the room. *Eyes on her... Malevolent eyes...* Slow, easy movements... She tried to move casually, like it was the most natural thing in the world to go down to the kitchen in the middle of the night and make herself a hot chocolate. Which it is, she reassured herself, it is. She wasn't wearing much, just a long white tee-shirt. She felt uncomfortable, with those eyes on her, wearing so little. She bent down and picked up the pants and jeans which were lying in a huddle on the floor. Stepped into them quickly. Then, buttoning her flies, she left the bedroom without looking back.

She poured a generous tot of whisky into a mug and quickly swigged it down. So it was only half-past seven in the morning? So she hadn't eaten yet? So what? Seated on the sofa downstairs, she swirled the whisky over her teeth and stared at the phone. *In the morning you'll be laughing at this...* Oh yeah? Well, ha bloody ha, she thought grimly to herself, sipping ferociously.

One

ONE YEAR LATER

YAHRZEIT: n. a Yiddish word meaning 'a year's time'; the anniversary of a person's death. A Yahrzeit candle, symbolic of the soul and spirit of the deceased, is burnt for 24 hours. [Yiddish, *anniversary*, from Middle High German, *year* (from Old High German; see *yer–* in Indo-European roots) + *zlt*, time (from Old High German; see *da–* in Indo-European roots).]
The American-Yiddish Dictionary of the English Language

At three o'clock on a cold, bright November afternoon there were only two other people at the top of Primrose Hill. Susan and Nina strolled past them and gazed out across the park. The long grassy slope, criss-crossed with paths, led down to a deserted playground and, on the other side of iron railings, to a busy road. At eye level in the distance they could see the tall buildings of London.

'Nice view,' Nina commented.

'Yes, isn't it?'

Susan shot her a quick sideways glance. She opened her mouth to speak, then changed her mind.

Nina turned to her and smiled. 'You were spending the weekend with Paul, weren't you? Well? How did it go?'

Susan pulled a face. 'He cancelled.'

'You're kidding.'

'Right at the last minute. I had my bag packed and everything. He couldn't get away,' Susan explained, squinting a little in the winter sunlight.

'He'll never leave his wife. Whatever he says. He will never leave her.'

'She isn't his *wife*, Nina.'

'As good as. You're as bad as he is frankly. Do you realise, people who are involved with someone who can't make a commitment, *can't make a commitment?*'

Susan sighed.

A man and a woman with a child in a carrier strapped on her back appeared on the hill behind them. The man moved her plastic cape so that the toddler could see over the woman's shoulder and pointed towards the city.

'Surely you want to be in a proper relationship?' Nina was saying when Susan turned back. 'Because you won't be while you're still seeing Paul, you know. You think you're available but you aren't, not really. You compare everyone else to him. Though God knows why. He's not exactly an oil painting.'

'He grows on you.' Susan frowned at the horizon.

'What about that man from work I introduced you to?'

'Who? Roger Simpson?'

'Yes. Did he ever phone?'

'Oh, Nina, he was boring.'

'He was keen. Keen and single. *That's* what bored you.'

'And bald,' Susan muttered. 'Don't forget to add that to the list.'

'He has nice, fair, curly hair that is thinning very slightly,' Nina corrected her. 'The point is, he's forty and he's looking for a wife.'

'That's what I mean. How can you look for a wife? You meet someone, you fall in love. You don't wake up one morning and decide – ah, now's the time. Not unless you're a total creep.'

'To you, he's a creep. To me, he's a rich, successful, available, good-looking lawyer. Which you only don't see because you always fall for men who are involved with someone else.'

Susan pulled a face. 'So you go out with him then.'

'I don't need to,' Nina responded smartly. 'I'm not the one who's looking for love. I'm already engaged. Remember?'

Susan hunched her shoulders as protection against the wind and Nina's words. She's a nag, she thought despondently, digging her hands deeper into the pockets of her leather jacket. An amusing, well-meaning nag, but still a nag. Why does she always speak to me like my mother? It's because *I ask too many questions*. Should I do this, should I do that? She loses all respect for me and thinks she can talk to me as if I were a child. I must remember never to ask those kinds of questions again. Mental note: don't do it.

A sudden wind whipped her hair across her face. Holding a dark strand back with one hand, she thought of the promise she'd made to herself earlier that day. To tell Nina everything. Looking at her, it was even harder to do than she'd expected. Those clear blue eyes, now turned on the soaring shape of the bird cage across the road in the Zoo, that blonde hair glinting in the sunlight, hands deep in the pockets of her black cashmere coat… Come on, Susan, she told herself. Tell her. Talk. She took a deep breath.

'I've been getting these funny phone calls,' she blurted out suddenly.

Nina turned. 'Funny ha ha or funny peculiar?'

'Peculiar. When I pick up the phone the line goes dead.'

'They're computer generated. Very irritating. Happens all the time.'

'Actually, I don't think these ones are… They come late at night or very early in the morning. *Very* early – I mean, four or five. And sometimes – sometimes there's a faint sound on the other end.'

'Of what?'

'Almost like breathing.' Susan thought for a moment. 'But not quite.'

Nina pulled a face. 'Have you phoned 1471?'

'The number's not logged.'

'I presume you've informed BT's nuisance calls section?'

'Would they do anything?' Susan asked doubtfully. 'I mean, the calls aren't abusive or threatening or anything. They're just – silent.'

'If they're a nuisance, yes, of course they would. Malicious calls of any sort are a criminal offence.' Nina frowned. 'So what happens exactly? The phone goes. And?'

'I say hello, then there's silence. Sometimes this sort of rasping sound. But he doesn't say anything.'

'He? How do you know if the calls are silent?'

Susan stared up at the grey clouds that were grouping above their heads. 'I don't. It's just a figure of speech.'

The sun had gone in. The day seemed suddenly cold. The sky was so grey that it made the grass look greener. By unspoken consent they began walking again.

'There was a woman at work, ' Nina said, as they took the gently sloping path down the side of the hill. 'Caroline Pringle, remember her? *She* had the same kind of calls. Heavy breathing mostly, like yours, but apparently he'd also leave on the answering machine once or twice a day the sound of water pouring into what she could only imagine was the lavatory. This was for three months only but at the end of that time she was about ready to have a nervous breakdown. She lost over a stone in weight, couldn't sleep, became an, oh, what's the word?'

'Insomniac?'

'Yes. Dark bags under the eyes, twitchy, thin. The doctor put her on Prozac. Well, Barry Jackson – you know, in conveyancing? Lives in Holland Park with brown curly hair? He arranged for BT to intercept her calls, and that was that. She was a different woman in no time. A *different* woman, Susan. She said she couldn't act herself, she felt paralysed. So Barry sorted it for her. A couple of weeks later she met this man, they fell in love and now she has two children, maybe three, I forget. Unfortunately she's put all the weight back on, but nothing in life is perfect. The point is, the solution to your problem is very simple.'

'Prozac?' Susan murmured.

Nina frowned. 'Do you want me to help you or not?'

'Yes, Nina.'

'So listen then. Ring BT and get your calls intercepted. Have you bought a new answering machine yet? No? Well, get your act together. Do it.'

A group of tourists were pressing up the hill towards them. Susan fell back slightly, stepping onto muddy grass to avoid them. Nina's voice floated back to her as she hurried to catch up. 'This can all be sorted out quite easily,' she was saying. 'These kind of calls are quite common… which, of course, doesn't make them any more pleasant… ' She stopped, half turning. 'Do you want a coffee? Otherwise we could keep on going.'

'Oh, a coffee I think. It's getting a bit chilly.'

Nina smiled agreement. 'The Polish café?'

'OK.'

They turned left towards the gates and walked without speaking for a while. Tell her the rest, Susan thought nervously. Tell her. Her heart was suddenly beating fast. It seemed to be banging against her rib cage as if it were planning to escape out of her mouth. I'm in trouble, she considered beginning, but she could already imagine Nina's response to that: 'You're pregnant. By Paul. Oh my God.' And her own hurried: 'No, no, it's nothing like that.' Perhaps she should say, very seriously – there's something I want to talk to you about, something rather bizarre… No. Slightly worrying? Fucking shit scarey? Oh, come *on*, she told herself. For God's sake, get on with it. Just tell it straight. Don't piss about any more than you can help it. She took a deep breath. 'Another thing,' she said horribly casually.

'Yes?'

'I'm being watched.'

'You mean – What *do* you mean?'

'Just that.' Susan pulled an apologetic face. 'Someone's watching me.'

'I don't understand.' Nina slowed down. 'You're telling me that – ' She stopped dead. A man walking behind almost bumped into them. She apologised to him and turned back to Susan. 'Let me get this straight. Someone's stalking you? That's what you're saying?'

'Yes.'

'Of course you've informed the police?'

Susan hesitated. 'No. I thought I ought to talk to you first.' Which was true. More or less.

There was an empty bench by the side of the path, the wood still dark from the morning's rain. Nina seized her arm and, dodging out of the way of an oncoming couple, pulled her towards it. 'I suppose you've told Paul?' she asked, sitting down.

'No.' Susan sat down next to her. 'No, I haven't actually.'

'Because it could be his wife, you know. That's the most likely scenario, isn't it? Julia's hired a private detective. She's found out about you and decided to get her own back.'

'Not unless she's psychic. It started before I began seeing Paul.'

Nina looked shocked. 'But you've been seeing him for *months*. How long's this been – '

'Eleven months.' Susan smiled tightly. 'Give or take a day.'

'Bloody hell, Susan. Why didn't you say anything before? Is he – ' Nina glanced over her shoulder, unable to suppress the flash of excitement in her eyes. 'Is he around now?'

'I don't think so.'

'You don't *think* so?'

'I'm not sure.'

'Well, what does he look like?'

Susan fixed dark, troubled eyes on her. 'I have no idea.'

'I mean roughly.'

'Not even roughly.'

'You must have *some* idea. Or else why would you think you're being stalked?'

Susan shifted slightly on the bench. She could feel the damp seeping into her jeans. She waited for a moment before answering. 'It isn't anything I've actually seen,' she replied at last, 'except perhaps a fleeting glimpse out of the corner of my eye.'

Nina frowned. 'Of what?'

'Oh, I don't know really… A shadow where there shouldn't be, the sense of someone turning the corner too quickly for me to catch sight of them… Nothing specific.' Susan clenched her hands in her pockets. 'Mostly it's just a feeling. A very strong feeling. I probably haven't made myself very clear,' she said a little desperately, seeing Nina's expression. 'It's hard to put into words. It sounds so – ' She took a deep breath and tried again. 'I just have the feeling, pretty much all of the time, that someone is watching me. I say, just. But that doesn't capture what it's like at all. It's a very powerful feeling. *Very* powerful.' She looked at Nina anxiously.

'A feeling.'

'Yes. I know someone's eyes are on me.'

'Just – watching?'

'Yes.'

Susan stared at the sodden grass at her feet. She shot a glance at Nina, then looked quickly down again. 'In the beginning it was only the faintest of impressions,' she explained, trying to ignore the small, patronising smile she'd seen on Nina's face. 'I just had the sense, somewhere in the background, of these eyes on me. You know, a little spooky but nothing much more. I didn't say anything because it seemed so weird. I carried on living normally. I even got used to it, in an odd sort of way.' She grimaced. 'I suppose you can get used to anything. But after a while, the feeling grew stronger. Much stronger. And much more *persistent* somehow…' She stopped, looking up, straight into Nina's disbelieving face.

'When does this feeling come over you?' Nina asked, her tone dismissive.

'It can happen anywhere. On a bus, in the street.' Susan faltered. She took her hands out of her pockets and gazed down at them thoughtfully, running the tip of two fingers over the knuckles of the other hand. 'At home.'

'At home?' Nina echoed incredulously. 'That's impossible! I mean, that really *is* impossible.'

'Not impossible,' Susan suggested gently, eyes still down. 'Not strictly speaking impossible.'

'Where do you think they could be watching *from*? It's a second floor flat. I mean, do you suppose they – I'm sorry, *he* – has hidden a camera in your bedroom?'

Susan hesitated. 'No.'

'And you haven't actually seen anyone?'

Susan shook her head.

'Has anyone else?'

'I'm always alone. It only happens when I'm alone. That's why it's so –'

'Why it's what?'

Again Susan shook her head. Already she realised she shouldn't have spoken, but it was too late. I should have kept my mouth shut, she thought. She couldn't really blame Nina for mocking her. A strong sense of being watched? Nothing more? It sounded ridiculous, even to herself. Especially to herself, she thought bitterly. The trouble was, seeming ridiculous didn't change anything. It didn't make it go away. She said helplessly: 'I knew you'd just laugh at me. I don't blame you really.'

'I'm not laughing, Susan.'

A golden retriever raced up to the bench, tail wagging, and began sniffing round their ankles, then lifted its leg and peed on a patch of short grass. Susan shifted her feet out of the way just in time. 'Drummer! Dru-mmer!' someone called. Drummer scraped at the earth with his back paws a couple of times and gave their ankles a last friendly sniff before dashing back to his owner.

'Look, I know it sounds crazy,' Susan said. 'I don't need you to tell me that. I've told myself a million times. But the feeling of someone watching is overwhelming, it's –'

'But it's still nothing more than a feeling,' Nina interrupted her. 'You can't have an idea someone's watching you without any evidence. Not if you want to be taken seriously – I'm sorry, but you can't. I really don't know what to say to you. You're normally so –' she searched for the right word, 'so reasonable. I mean, apart from the Paul thing. How can you have a *feeling* someone's stalking you? It isn't the kind of thing one has a feeling *about*. If you had seen something I would support you totally, of course I would, but otherwise –'

What did I expect, Susan thought, for God's sake? She said hopelessly: 'There's nothing definite.'

'Otherwise it's absurd.'

'And if it was you?' Susan asked after a moment. 'What would you do?'

'Me?'

Susan glanced sideways at her. 'It sounds completely bonkers, doesn't it?'

'Frankly, yes. Clearly *not* a matter for the police.'

I don't get it, Susan could see her thinking. One moment we're having a perfectly normal if slightly predictable conversation about the usual romantic fuck-ups in Susan's life, the next we're talking about – what? Unseen stalkers? Hidden cameras? The bogey man? Spies? It was always like this, she remembered too late. Talking to Nina was never quite the same in reality as it was in her imagination. There was no comfort to be found in those gentle blue eyes. No comfort at all. 'Let's get a coffee, Nina,' she suggested wearily. 'I'm cold. And my bottom's getting wet.'

They walked through the gates without speaking and waited to cross the road. Susan looked down miserably at her feet on the kerb. The leather round the tips of her shoes were stained a darker brown.

'Are you taking anything?' Nina asked suddenly.

'What do you mean?'

'Are you taking any drugs?'

Susan smiled. 'Why? Have you got any?'

'Well, are you?'

'No, I am not!'

'Well, there was a time – '

'Oh, you're not going to bring *that* up again. Besides I was only sixteen.'

They crossed the road.

'You sound very upset,' Nina said accusingly, once they were on the pavement.

Susan looked at her in amazement. 'Wouldn't you be?'

The air inside the café was warm and smelled of other people's smoke. They sat at a table by the mirror that ran along one wall. Nina shrugged off her coat. Underneath she was dressed in elegant navy blue trousers. A grey cardigan with a pattern of pale blue and red flowers was buttoned to her neck showing a glimpse of a white lacy collar, her shoes were polished, her shining blonde hair tied back in a ponytail. Besides her, Susan felt scruffy. She hadn't really bothered that morning, just pulling on the clothes she'd worn the day before – jeans, a big black jumper and the leather jacket. She'd barely brushed her hair. Hunching awkwardly over the round marble-topped table she let straggles of long dark hair fall over her face. 'It's been a rotten year,' she sighed to herself. 'An absolutely all time, rock bottom twelve months.' And she needed a cigarette badly, she decided, fumbling in her bag. When she found the packet, she lit one with a match, pretending not to notice Nina's disapproving frown. Nina ordered two cappuccinos and a tuna sandwich for herself. Susan wasn't hungry.

'Well, it's obvious what this is about, isn't it?' Nina said, turning back to the table.

Susan raised dark and anxious eyes. 'Is it?'

'You're still suffering from the effects of concussion, my dear. I hadn't realised it could carry on for so long but – ' Nina shrugged. 'That was a pretty nasty crack on the head you gave yourself when you turned the car over, wasn't it? When you returned from France at Christmas you couldn't see straight. You couldn't drive, you couldn't even walk easily down the street – remember?'

'I remember.'

'As I recall, you had to go around with one eye permanently squinted. You were seeing double for ages. These delusions are – well, they're obviously a more long term reaction.'

'I don't think it's concussion. It doesn't seem the same kind of thing at all.'

'What else could it be?'

'I don't know.'

'Have you even considered the possibility?'

Susan frowned moodily down at her hands. 'Of course I have.' Still frowning, she took a drag of her cigarette, turning her head and blowing smoke in the air, away from Nina.

'There *is* no other rational explanation. I mean, do you really believe that someone's been following you around for almost a year remaining completely unseen by you or anyone who knows you? It's a *delusion*, Susan. You've been imagining all this.' Nina smiled at her pityingly. 'Look, I know it isn't a pleasant thing to accept but once you do – well, I'm sure things will get sorted out quite quickly and easily.' Her smile was patronising, her voice gentle and understanding. It was almost worse than her impatience had been. She gave a little laugh. 'You're such an odd mixture of realism and gullibility, Susan, you really are.'

Their cappuccinos had arrived. Susan picked up her cup and took a gulp of coffee. 'And the phone calls?' she said, staring into the cup. 'I'm not imagining them. The phone calls are real.'

'A coincidence,' Nina replied promptly. 'But they've probably made you more vulnerable to these kinds of fears. You know,' she reached for the sugar bowl, 'it's quite likely that these experiences are connected to your father passing away – '

'I *hate* that expression,' Susan said, more violently than she intended. 'He didn't pass away. He *died*, Nina.' She lowered her eyes. 'He's dead.'

Looking a little startled, Nina stirred sugar into her cup. 'Well, however you want to phrase it,' she said, recovering. 'You were terribly shaken up afterwards, weren't you? Quite naturally,' she added quickly, seeing Susan's expression. She gestured. 'You've got froth on your top lip.'

Susan licked the offending froth away with her tongue. 'Gone?'

Nina nodded. 'Look, let's think about this rationally for a moment. When did these feelings of allegedly being watched first begin?'

'This isn't a court case, Nina.'

'When? You said about eleven months ago, is that right?'

Susan hesitated, thinking of the first time it had happened. That night in the flat. She'd been in bed, it was late, the phone had rung. She'd listened for a moment before replacing the receiver. She'd been angry – to be woken so early in the morning for no good reason. And then the sudden certainty – someone was in the room with her. Even the memory made the hairs on her arm stand on end. The sensation had disappeared the next day and, relieved, she'd dismissed the whole thing from her mind. It had only been a passing impression, she decided. Until a few months ago. She'd been in the kitchen. It had been broad daylight at three in the afternoon. She hadn't had a drink and she was wide awake. The feeling of two invisible eyes staring at her, intense, curious eyes, had slowly overtaken her, making her skin creep, her breath come quickly and her hands grow clammy and cold. She'd turned off the gas under the onions she was frying and hurriedly left the room, run down the stairs right out of the building, leaving her coat behind in her haste.

'More like eight or nine,' she said, deliberately vague. 'I'm not quite sure.'

'Ah,' Nina said, looking pleased. 'So it was after the phone calls began?'

'Yes.'

'And the car crash?'

'Also a bit beforehand,' Susan admitted.

'How much before?'

'Two months, six weeks. I forget exactly. Except for the first time. The very first time was before the smash-up. Not long. About a month. But it was only once. Then the feeling disappeared.'

'So to all extents and purposes it was only after the crash that you started having the feeling you were being watched?'

'I suppose so, yes.'

'Is that the order in which things happened or not?'

'Yes, it is.'

'Well, that's conclusive then, isn't it.'

Nina leaned back in her chair and stretched her arms in the air above her head. 'Ooh, I'm so *stiff*! I've been sitting at a computer far too long.' She dropped her arms and wriggled her shoulders a few times. 'Do me a favour, will you? Forget the feelings. Your imagination's not only working over-time it's taken on a second job.' She rotated her head slowly twice before sitting up straight. 'Let's stick to the facts. Fact one,' she held a finger in the air, 'you've had a number of unpleasant phone calls. And they're frighten-ing you. Right?'

'Well, right.'

A second finger. 'And because you're frightened, you imagine, you *feel*, as you put it,' a third finger went up, 'that you're being watched. The car accident, plus your father passing away, I mean, his dying,' she corrected herself quickly, 'have combined in a pretty short period to make you rather more – ' she hesitated, searching for a word, 'let's just say, it's made you more nervy, shall we?'

'How many facts are you holding up now, I've lost count,' Susan said irritably. 'Four? Or three facts and a thumb?'

Nina pulled a face. 'Don't be sarcastic.' She curled her fingers into her palm. 'I'm only trying to help.'

'Oh, I know… I'm sorry… Thanks, Nina. Really.'

Perhaps it was that simple. For a moment Susan let Nina's matter of fact tone convince her it might be. She was disturbed by strange phone calls, concussed by the car crash, thrown by her father's sudden death… She gave pale smile. 'You're probably right.'

'Of course I am.'

'Tuna sandwich?' the waitress announced, holding out a plate.

'Oh yes. Yes, thanks.' Susan swivelled round, glad of the diversion, and handed the plate to Nina.

They didn't speak for a moment. Nina ate the sandwich. Susan drew a circle of ash with the tip of her cigarette in the ashtray. They could hear the two women at the next table rather irritably discussing the merits of a pen-sion over an endowment mortgage. 'Didn't you see the Panorama pro-gramme the other night?' one was saying. Susan turned the circle into a square. Nina wiped her fingers on the thin paper napkin on her plate. 'Why do they always put the napkin *under* the sandwich?' she grumbled. 'By the time you use it, it's *covered* in mayonaise.' She gestured impatiently towards the ashtray. 'Look, if you're not really smoking that would you mind putting it out? At least while I'm eating.'

'Sorry.' Susan stubbed out the cigarette.

When she'd finished the sandwich, Nina crumpled the napkin into a ball and dropped it onto her plate. 'There you are,' she said with a sigh as she did. 'Problem sorted.' Looking over, she smiled. The way you smile when a problem you've been asked to solve turns out to be really easy, Susan thought irritably. A smile for the easy-peasy. Sometimes I really dislike Nina.

'You should have told me before,' Nina said. 'I don't know why you didn't tell me.' She sounded a little put out.

This is why, Susan thought. Because I already knew what your reaction would be. I don't need Nina to tell me it all sounds like nonsense. I'm perfectly aware of that myself already. She fished in her bag for the packet of cigarettes, ignoring Nina's pained expression when she found it and extracted another cigarette which she put between her lips. She could have predicted exactly what was going to happen, almost word for word, incredulous emotion for emotion. So why had she bothered? Unless this is what I wanted to hear, she thought. Disbelief. Reassurance that it's all make-believe – the cause, simply a bump on the head and my overwrought imagination. That I've lost my perspective – I've lost my *grip*... Nina was right – concussion was the only rational explanation. It was certainly the one she had given herself over and over again. Except...

Except she wasn't convinced, she decided, striking a match with quick, nervous fingers. Because she knew something which Nina did not, and could not, know. She knew what *it felt like*.

Eyes down, she held the match's flame to the cigarette. Talking with Nina hadn't really changed anything. The dread in the pit of her stomach was not dispelled, nor was the strange, disquieting sense she'd had for the past week and which she could only describe as – expectancy. In the steamy warmth of the cafe, she shivered.

'You've bottled it all up, so what is actually a smallish problem has grown into a monster,' Nina explained kindly. Smiling brightly, she squeezed Susan's hand. 'Feeling better?'

Susan gave a suitably grateful grimace. 'Oh, much.' The knot in her stomach tightened.

'I'll get the bill.' Nina gestured to the waitress. 'Doing anything special this afternoon?' she asked, turning back to the table with the same bright smile.

'Only if you count food shopping as something special. Though I did have some notion of driving to Dancer's Hill... I'd like to see the house again. I haven't been there in years. Do you think it's strange wanting to see it now?' Damn, Susan thought, biting her lip. I've asked one of those questions again. 'Have you ever gone back to the house where you grew up?' she said hurriedly, trying to recover lost ground.

'Oh, I go all the time – my parents still live there. As a matter of fact, Daddy grew up there himself.' Nina was still smiling, rather smugly Susan thought. She looked like someone whose parents had lived in the same house for donkey's years with her round, almost plump face, lustrous fair hair and those serene blue eyes. She still calls him daddy, Susan thought, embarrassed. Daddy? At twenty-six? But she felt a little envious.

'Now Susan,' Nina said, when they were outside.

A cold wind blew Susan's hair into her eyes. She held it back with one hand. 'Yes?' Her face must have shown some of the anxiety she was feeling because Nina said simply: 'Don't *worry*. Sort out what's tangible first and I'm absolutely sure everything will be alright. See your GP to start with. He'll know what you should do.'

Susan looked at her. Smug, she thought. Very, very smug. She sighed. 'Are you heading back home?'

'Yes. What about you?'

'Oh, I don't know. Sainsbury's, I suppose,' Susan said, deciding definitely as she spoke. She didn't want to go back to the flat yet anyway. What for? More delusions? And she had a couple of hours to kill before her mother arrived. Impatiently she pushed a lock of hair behind her ear. 'You are coming tonight, aren't you?'

'To Nick's birthday party? If you still need me for moral support.' Nina looked amused. 'Sure. What time will you pick me up?'

'My mother's coming over to my place at seven… Um, would eight be too early?'

'Eight's fine. And contact BT!' Nina called as she was moving away. 'Start dealing with this sensibly and everything will be alright, you'll see!'

Susan dropped her cigarette onto the kerb and flattened it with a twist of her foot. 'Yes,' she sighed, letting her hair whip over her face for a moment before catching it back. The wind almost snatched her voice away from her as she said, 'Oh, yes, I'm sure it will.'

Susan walked slowly up the street. Before she reached the corner she had stopped and looked back and seen Nina's pitying smile and cheerful wave. She had nodded curtly, not waving back.

The car was parked at the top of Gloucester Avenue. Susan unlocked the battered blue Mini and climbed in, chucking her bag onto the passenger seat. She sat for a moment without moving, going over the conversation with Nina in her mind.

Frowning, she stared ahead into space.

Concussion... The car crash...

She sighed, rubbing her forehead. An image rose before her as she lowered her hand. She lit a cigarette quickly, hoping to block it out. But it was no good. Boxing Day, 2004. France, the auto-route. The ruined silver Audi, upside down... grey smoke coming from the wreckage, wheels spinning in the air... smashed glass on the snow...

She rolled down the window and blew smoke thoughtfully out the crack.

There had been hardly any other cars on the road. Everyone had been home with their families celebrating Christmas. As she had driven down the auto-route keeping an eye out for signs to Rouen, Susan was congratulating herself on her decision to travel on Boxing Day. She was going fast but not too fast, just enough to get to the farmhouse in time for supper. And humming along to the radio, a French cover version of *Hotel California* – she'd been tapping a finger on the wheel in time to the music. She'd felt almost happy. At any rate, it was a relief to get away from the looks of sympathy and commiseration and be on her own for a while. In the back of the car, beneath a bag of her warmest clothes, was a frozen pheasant, carefully wrapped in plastic, which she'd reckoned would survive the journey without defrosting too much – the following night's supper. It was very sudden, the way the car went out of control. One moment she was driving along, wondering how the French could get it so right with food and wine but so very wrong with music, the next she was on a skating rink. It was snowing, under her wheels was only ice and slush and she couldn't stop the car from skidding across three, luckily empty, lanes onto the wrong side of the road.

She took her foot off the accelerator desperately hoping to slow the car down – she didn't dare try to brake, it would only make things worse. But she was right in the line of any oncoming traffic. Someone, perhaps as out of control as she was, might come hurtling towards her at any second. She had to get back to the grass verge on the other side of the road. And fast.

She turned the steering wheel to the right. Gently, very gently, resisting the urge to frantically wrench it round. The car looped in a long, crazy S. Steering wheel? The wheels of the car were not gripping, there was nothing to steer with. She was not driving, she was *dancing*. Doing the loop de loop. La la la de dah, la la la-la la la-la de dah… She felt strangely calm. But underneath, fear. She had known, as she slid crazily across the road, that she was going to crash the car. There was nothing she could do to prevent it. The only question was, how badly? Could she avoid total disaster and get out of the way of anyone else in time?

The car veered to the left. She twisted the wheel, trying to straighten. But on all that ice, going at the speed she was, she simply couldn't keep the car steady. She was, at least, heading towards the grass verge on the correct side of the road, going slightly slower now, but not slow enough.

Oh, God, this is it, she thought. Here goes… It all happened very quickly. Quickly and slowly at the same time – in a way, it seemed to take forever. There was a great jolt. A jolt and a sickening crunching sound. Despite the shock of the movement she had not expected what happened next. 'Hold on!' she cried aloud to herself, just before the car turned over.

It took Susan a whole minute to realise she was hanging upside down, held in place only by her seatbelt. She was completely disorientated. Her mind wouldn't work, she couldn't find where the seatbelt unfastened. When she did, it seemed to take ages to actually undo it. The window next to her had shattered on impact. As soon as she was free of the strap, she crawled out on her belly, using trembling legs to push herself over broken pellets of glass and icy slush, and sat in soaking trousers by the side of the road, in the glass and snow. Her whole body was shaking, shuddering from shock and cold. The car, her father's old, silver Audi which she'd borrowed for the trip, lay upside down beside her. She couldn't bear to look at the wreckage. It was her own fault. She'd been going much too fast for the icy road, she hadn't stood a chance. But there had been no warning, no indication of what lay ahead.

Two cars drove cautiously past, slowly, very slowly, probably not doing more than ten miles an hour, perhaps less. Clearly they'd had enough time to register the changed weather conditions. One of them, a small, white van, pulled over carefully a little further down the road. A man in a bomber jacket and jeans got out and hurried through the lightly falling snow towards her.

'*Y a t-il autre personne dans la voiture?*' he asked urgently, gesturing towards the vehicle.

She looked at the wrecked car. 'No, I'm alone,' she answered in English. *'Comment vous sentez vous?'*

When she looked puzzled, he tried again, *'Etes vous gravement blessés?'* Then, haltingly, with a strong accent, 'You are OK?'

Susan looked down at herself. Amazingly there didn't seem to be a scratch on her. 'I *think* so.' Her head was throbbing though. There was a large lump under her hair on the crown which felt very sore when she touched it. 'I just seem to have bumped my head,' she said slowly. 'Nothing much.' She shook it slightly to try and get rid of the fuzziness in front of her eyes.

The man clearly did not understand her. *'Vous voulez vous asseoir dans ma voiture?'* he said, and she, in turn, did not understand him. All her French seemed to have deserted her. 'What do I do now?' she asked, aware of her shaking hands and the icy wetness of her trousers. Aware, too, of how shocked the Frenchman looked. Somehow his concerned face made what was happening seem horribly real. 'Will the police come?' she asked through chattering teeth. 'The gendarmes? *Ici?'*

She knew that her money, clothes and passport were all trapped in the car. Even her jacket – she'd taken it off for ease of movement when she'd started driving. Now she was very cold. On the other hand, she thought, looking up, dazed, at the man in front of her, if I hadn't taken it off, it would have been much harder to squeeze out the broken window, perhaps impossible. And her warm clothes? And the carefully wrapped presents? The frozen pheasant? All the things that had been so important a few moments before. None of it seemed to matter much now. Because the car was a write-off. And sitting in the softly falling snow at the side of the empty road in only jeans and a thin black check shirt, she could only be glad that she wasn't. Except for a slight throbbing in her head and a sore knee, she was unharmed.

The car had begun to smoke. A thin, grey stream that blended with the horizon came from its upturned belly. She wondered if it were going to catch fire. 'Perhaps we should move,' she suggested after a moment, wondering if she could.

The Frenchman nodded and pointed to his own van. He said something which she knew, more from his gestures than his words, meant he was offering her his jacket.

'That is very kind, *mais non. Non, merci,'* she replied, shaking her head. A mistake, she realised immediately. The world started spinning. She recalled putting her hand to her head and saying faintly, 'If I could just – '

And then she passed out cold and nothing more for some time.

Of course her mother had come up with some typically cock-eyed theory afterwards. That it had been a death wish because it was her father's car. A not-so submerged longing to join him – he'd been dead then only a month. All of which Susan had dismissed as ridiculous, as she always did her mother's crude attempts at psychoanalysis. Stick to acting, she'd said irritably. That's what you're good at. It was bad luck, a freak accident. How does wishing come into it?

Perhaps that was why she'd never mentioned what happened just after she'd crawled out from the shattered side window to a soul. Never said a word about the few dizzy seconds before she'd passed out beside the car in the snow. He was smiling at her, beckoning from the overturned car. He was wearing a stained black checked shirt, rather like her own, and an unbuttoned raincoat. Dried blood was on the collar. His expression was welcoming but weary. But she could tell from his smile that he had missed her as badly as she'd missed him. She felt the tears pricking behind her eyes, as she felt them now, sitting in a stationary car, parked at an awkward angle in Gloucester Avenue. Tears of happiness and relief. A vision. Amongst all the snow and slush and broken glass. She opened her mouth to cry out to him, to tell him to stay or something, she was not sure what. To call out to her dead father, waving at her from the wreckage.

Her father for a blinding flash, the house in Dancer's Hill shimmering before her eyes, then out for the count.

Her mother was sheltering on the doorstep under a large green umbrella when Susan arrived back at the flat.

'Aren't you a bit early?' Susan asked guiltily, unlocking the street door.

'Only five minutes.'

'I'm really sorry. The traffic was terrible, it just crawled along.'

'You're soaking, darling.'

'I couldn't find a parking space. I had to park on the other side of Primrose Hill and it started absolutely bucketing down. Come in.'

Isabella followed Susan up the narrow hall stairs covered with rough beige coire matting and through the door to the flat. In the tiny hallway, she handed her daughter the dripping umbrella, then removed her coat. Underneath she was wearing a low-cut black sleeveless dress and a fitted velvet jacket. She took off the jacket, too. 'It's very warm in here.'

'Too warm?'

'No, it's fine.'

'You look lovely, mum.'

'Do I? Thanks.'

Isabella ran a hand over her glossy black hair, smoothing it into place. Susan pressed aside some jackets to make space on the peg, then hung up her mother's coat. She propped the umbrella by the front door, dumping two plastic bags filled with shopping beside it, and hung her own leather jacket on top of the other coats. Her mother stared down at the pool of water forming round the umbrella on the wooden boards. 'Hadn't you better put that in the sink?'

'Oh. Yes.' Susan bent to pick up the umbrella.

'Did you take this?'

When Susan straightened, her mother was examining a framed black-and-white photograph of a woman's bare feet walking in sand hanging near the living-room door. 'Oh, that. Yes.'

'When?'

'About eighteen months ago, I suppose. But I've only just got around to hanging it up.'

'You've improved. It's very good.'

'I'm glad you like it,' Susan said, pleased. She held up the dripping umbrella. 'I'll just put this in the sink.' With the other hand, she picked up the bags of shopping. 'Would you like a coffee, mum?' she shouted from the kitchen.

'No, thanks! Perhaps a bit later.'

There was no room in the sink. She hadn't washed up that morning – for a week is actually what it looks like, Susan thought with a sigh, scrutinising the stack of plates and cups. She piled some of the plates on the draining board and stuffed the umbrella on top of the others, fitting it under the taps. 'Actually, I was contemplating driving over to the house in Dancer's Hill this afternoon,' she said, coming back into the hall.

'What on earth for?'

'Oh, I don't know really. I suppose I just wanted to see it again.'

'I wouldn't have thought you'd be interested. You were only nine when we moved.'

'Seven actually.'

'Were you? You were sweet when you were seven. I'd just got my first big part.' Isabella smiled reminiscently. 'I was playing Olga in *Three Sisters* and we moved to that lovely house in Hampstead – Oakdown Road, do you remember? The garden was bigger than the whole house in Dancer's Hill. If you want to see somewhere we used to live, go and see Oakdown. Of course, we never should have sold it but your father wanted to move further out.' She sighed. 'It would be worth a fortune now, an absolute fortune.'

'Didn't you like Sussex?'

'Oh, it was alright, I suppose. The house itself was nice enough and we were very near Brighton. But I was glad to move back to Hampstead again.'

'Was Dad?'

'Was Dad what?'

'Pleased to move back to London too?'

'Not as pleased as I was,' Isabella replied, a faintly annoyed inflection in her tone that implied – He's dead, what does it matter now what he did or didn't like anyway?

But even when he was alive what Dad wanted was never as important as whatever you liked, Susan thought, scooping a pile of newspapers off the sofa in the living-room so that her mother could sit down. She switched on a lamp in the shape of a curved silver shell, seeing the room through her mother's eyes in its soft glow. A mess. There was a sofa with a red striped throw flung over it and a low Indian table piled high with paperbacks facing a small TV. A stack of old newspapers, more books and a pile of glossy prints were heaped untidily beside it on the rug. A large, framed poster of a Robert Rauschenberg painting was propped against the wall. It was the only present Paul had ever given her and she'd never got round to hanging it up. Now she'd got used to it there. Her mother didn't say anything but Susan could see from her face what she thought of the room. She was good at emanating disapproval even without words. Hopefully she wouldn't look in the kitchen at her umbrella propped amongst a pile of dirty cups and saucers.

Susan picked up an old newspaper and a mug of cold oily-looking coffee from the jumble on the table. 'Are you sure you wouldn't like a cup of coffee?'

Isabella glanced at the mug. 'Oh, don't bother.' Crossing long, slender legs in sheer stockings, she tugged her skirt a few inches over her knees. Her nails were painted the same red as her lipstick. She held one hand in front of her, tilting it slightly from side to side. 'So,' she said, admiring her manicure, 'what have you bought Nick for his birthday?'

'He's fifty. It's about time he stopped expecting presents.'

'You won't say that when you're fifty,' her mother said crossly, letting her hand drop. 'He's your uncle, Susan. You could at least have got a card. Luckily,' she gestured towards her bag, 'I've brought one with me, just in case. You can sign it when you've finished dressing. Have you decided what you're wearing tonight?'

'I really haven't thought about it.'

'What about the black dress?'

'It's a bit tight, isn't it?'

'It's supposed to be. You've got a lovely figure, you should show it off more. Remember, if you've got it flaunt it.' Isabella gave a little light, fluting laugh, running her fingertips down her sides. 'Aren't you going to do anything with your hair, darling? Brush it, or put it up, or something?'

'It was raining, mum. I got wet.'

'You'd better have a bath, then. You might use a few drops of the Floris jasmine oil I gave you. Please, darling, make an effort this evening. Look nice.' Her mother added, with a brilliant smile: 'For me!'

'I'll have a bath,' Susan said wearily.

The feeling came back as she was running the water. The door was shut and she was alone in the bathroom but she had that feeling.

Someone was watching her.

It was worse than it had ever been. She could feel two eyes staring intently at her. She checked the blind: it was pulled right down, and anyway there was only a high brick wall opposite. There wasn't anywhere to watch *from*. Susan tried ignoring the sensation as she got in the bath. Pretending to be an ordinary person, having an ordinary bath, which Nina would insist was true, she told herself. Adding more hot water, pouring in a few drops of jasmine oil, she lay back and tried to concentrate on the evening ahead. She would wear the short black dress as her mother suggested, with which shoes?

But the sense of being watched only grew stronger.

Eyes. Dangerous eyes.

It was a man. Looking. She was sure of it. For God's sake, get a grip! she told herself fiercely. What's the matter with you? There isn't anyone watching! There can't be! You've been over this with Nina! Be reasonable! But now she was alone, reason didn't seem to help. She began to feel uncomfortable lying there naked. She stood up, fighting her rising panic, controlling the urge to grab her things and get out.

Conscious only of invisible eyes boring into her back, she slowly got out of the bath and wrapped a towel round her, slowly picked up her make-up and the dressing-gown she had earlier dropped to the floor. Then, still dripping wet, she opened the door and left the bathroom, forcing herself not to look back.

She sat shivering on the bedroom floor, the damp towel still wrapped around her. Come out, wherever you are! she cried silently. Who are you? Who? *Who?*

She could hear Nina's calm, matter of fact voice speaking: 'Susan, it's impossible, there isn't even a window for someone to be watching *from*.' Heard her own miserable voice in reply, 'I know.'

But whatever anyone said to her, whatever she knew, or thought she knew, she wouldn't have stayed in that ghastly presence for anything.

Where is it now? Behind me? The hairs on the back on her neck prickled: she swung round on her bottom. Nothing.

It's all in your imagination, she told herself weakly, flopping back and lifting her knees, resting her forehead on them. It has to be. But in that case imagination made the hairs on the back of her neck stand on end, her body tremble and her legs feel weak. She felt physically sick. From her huddled position, she opened her eyes wide and stared at the wall.

This is it, she told herself. The end. I can't even have a bath anymore. This flat has become the setting for a bizarre emotional collapse – Is that what's happening? A nervous breakdown? Concussion has unhinged me – Nina was right about that, too. And on the surface I carry on as usual. Pretending. Pretending everything is normal. Underneath are horrors; on the surface, things go on as before.

From downstairs, her mother called: 'Are you ready yet, darling?'

Susan crawled to the bedroom door and croaked, 'Almost.' How strange that she could shout down the stairs fairly normally, 'Make yourself a coffee, Mum! You'll find some beans already ground in a glass jar in the fridge.'

Dressed. She must get dressed. She unwound the damp towel and pulled a pair of black tights out of a drawer. The tights had a ladder. She was rummaging through for another pair when she heard the phone. It rang three times and then stopped.

Susan froze. Her mother must have answered.

Hunching, naked, over the banisters, she could hear her mother's voice murmuring gently but couldn't make out any words. She didn't dare pick up the bedroom extension. Perhaps her mother was saying, 'Hello? Hello? Who is this?' at that very moment.

Susan grabbed the dress from its hanger. Where were her shoes? Where were her bloody shoes? When she found them under the bed, she squeezed them on quickly, hopping on one foot to pull on the second shoe.

Downstairs, her mother was replacing the receiver.

'Who – who was it?' Susan faltered.

'Nina.'

'Oh.'

Relief flooded through Susan. Her hands were sweating. Surreptitiously, she wiped them on her dress. Why did she have such a burning urge to keep this all hidden, especially from her mother? Surely there was no need to be so secretive. She could say simply – I've been receiving these anonymous telephone calls, Mum. Also, I have a strong feeling that someone is watching me… Perhaps this time her mother would be helpful and comforting, you could never tell, she occasionally was. But desire fought against caution. 'I'm sure someone is following me!' Mentally she shouted the words but something stopped her from saying them aloud. She cleared her throat. 'What did she want?'

'She wanted to know when we were leaving. I told her, five minutes.' Her mother touched the delicate diamond drops hanging from her ears and frowned. 'What shoes are you going to wear? Those?'

Susan looked down at her feet, hoping she wasn't wearing an odd pair. 'What's wrong with them?' she asked, when she saw that she wasn't.

'Nothing. They're just a little – unflattering.'

The familiar tone of the conversation brought Susan back to normality. For once she was glad of her mother's critical comments. 'What do you think? Boots instead?' she asked, managing a smile.

'Yes, perhaps… I only want you to look your best this evening, darling. Oh, much better,' Isabella smiled approvingly, when Susan came back downstairs. 'And your hair looks lovely now you've brushed it.'

As she hovered on the stairs, one hand on the banisters, a foot poised over the bottom step, Susan again considered confiding in her mother, at least about the string of anonymous phone calls. She took the last step and walked into the living-room. Isabella bent to pick up her jacket from the sofa. 'What is it?' she asked, straightening. 'Why are you looking at me in that peculiar way?' She lifted a hand to her face. 'What? Do I have lipstick on my teeth?' To check, she pulled a small mirror out of her black beaded bag and examined her teeth carefully, running her tongue across their white surface.

Susan shook her head. The moment had passed. 'You look perfect, Mum,' she smiled, hoping her mother would not notice how shakily. 'It's just that I miss Dad being here, that's all. It's feels strange going to Nick's birthday party without him. Don't you find it hard without Dad at times like this?'

'Of course I do,' her mother replied briskly, pulling on the jacket. 'But I try not to dwell on it. Anyway, it's not a party exactly, it's just dinner with a few friends. We'll take your car, shall we, darling? I came by taxi. Nick will drop me home.'

But Nick was not driving anyone anywhere tonight, Susan thought as soon as she saw him. He was drunk and, in the way that drink often took him, in one of his dangerous moods. It was not obvious if you did not know him well. His speech was not slurred or his movements clumsy, but Susan could tell from his eyes. They were very bright and there was a nasty glint in them they had only when he'd been drinking heavily. Probably whisky, she decided, and a lot of it. They were having dinner at Julie's restaurant, in the private room downstairs. The floor and walls were stone-flagged and candles cast a flickering light over the great oak table. Nick was sitting at its head in a high-backed oak chair, his hands resting on its carved arms. 'Like he's sitting on a bloody throne,' Susan thought, handing him his card and the present which she'd been nagged into buying on the way. 'Happy birthday, Nick.'

He tore off green tissue paper. 'Ah, whisky and one of my all-time favourite brands. You remembered. Thanks.'

Most of the other guests were there already. Nina was seated next to a thin man with a moustache; Susan sat beside an old friend of her mother's. He introduced himself to her as Raymond – she didn't catch his last name even though he said it twice. She thought, Rivet. Or perhaps Illet. She felt she couldn't ask a third time.

'I directed the first play Isabella ever starred in,' he told her over the fish soup. 'My dear, she was enchanting! Terrifically talented, of course. You look *so* like her at that age.'

They both looked across the table at Isabella, who was sitting on Nick's left. Unusually for her, she was smoking though when she put the cigarette to her lips she barely inhaled, tilting her chin and blowing out a stream of smoke vertically at the ceiling. Despite her calm, rather theatrical movements, it struck Susan that she looked troubled, her dark, glittering gaze hardly moving from Nick's face. He was talking without stop to whoever was around him, and drinking without stop, too. One hand held a glass which was kept constantly topped up by a nod from him to the waiter. The other, under the table, was at a slightly odd angle. For a moment Susan had the impression that... But she instantly dismissed the idea.

'Of course, she was exquisite in everything she did,' she heard Raymond saying.

Susan turned to him. Surely Nick's hand couldn't be... 'Sorry? What did you say?'

'I was saying that your mother was an immensely talented actress.'

'Oh, yes… yes, I believe so.'

'I say, was, though the tense may be incorrect – is? But sadly, she left the stage so young… When she married and, of course, had you.' He smiled to take the sting out of his words. 'It was such a terrible loss to the theatre though I expect that sounds frightfully pompous.'

'I believe she did do a couple of plays after I was born,' Susan said, watching her mother and Nick out of the corner of her eye.

'Oh, but she wasn't really serious anymore.' Raymond smiled wistfully. 'Love changes everything, I'm afraid, even if one does not wish it to.'

'Yes, I suppose it does,' Susan agreed, distracted.

'Are you an actress, too?'

'No, I'm a photo-journalist. Actually, an out of work journalist,' she added.

'I should think that's a jolly sight better than being an out of work actress,' responded Raymond politely.

'Yes… yes, I should think that it is…'

Nick's hand couldn't be on her mother's knee, Susan thought. This I *am* imagining, she reassured herself. Though how reassuring it was to admit one was living in a haze of paranoid delusion she wasn't altogether sure.

She watched as Nick lit a cigarette after the main course had been cleared away. The flame of his heavy gold lighter was turned slightly too high: it flared up, a two inch flash of blue fire, briefly illuminating one side of his face. How different he was to her father, Susan thought critically. Physically there were similarities, though her father had been taller, generally heavier, less obviously good-looking and yet, she thought, so much more of a man. But, in every other way, they were totally different. It's funny how two brothers could resemble each other yet be world's apart. Nick was wearing a dark linen suit, well-cut enough to be deliberately crumpled, and a shirt without a tie. God, I miss Dad, Susan thought, taking a gulp of the wine that had been set down in front of her. How I wish he were here. She couldn't imagine her father getting pissed like this, especially at his own party.

But perhaps she wasn't being very generous, it occurred to her suddenly, looking across the table at Nick's dark, drunken, smiling face. Perhaps he was missing her father, too. It was his birthday, after all – the first one since her father had died: he must be thinking of his older brother. Maybe that's why he's got so plastered, she thought, impatient with herself. What a bitch I am. Poor Nick. Underneath, he misses Steven.

The group of people around Nick laughed suddenly at something he said. Smiling broadly, he leaned across her mother to re-fill her glass. As he did so, his face seemed to brush against her hair. It was a very slight movement, hardly noticeable, but Susan saw the look that her mother turned on him. It was an expression she recognised from her own face in the mirror when she was with Paul – admiration, hope, adoration. Her heart skipped a beat. Oh no, she couldn't be… It wasn't possible…

The room seemed suddenly stifling. Susan unfastened the top two buttons of the jacket she was wearing over her dress. Her throat felt stiff; she needed some cool air. 'Excuse me,' she muttered to Raymond, standing abruptly.

Outside, a little mirrored hall led into a corridor and, at the end, to a door marked Ladies. Pushing the door open, she walked into sudden quiet. She sat down on a red plush stool and, without really thinking, more to do something to still the feverish workings of her mind, opened the clasp of her bag and pulled out the first thing she found. A white lace hankie. Looking at the delicate thing crumpled in her hand she realised she'd picked up her mother's bag by mistake. They must have swapped over in the car without realising. At her mother's suggestion, she'd used the same one as her, a little black beaded clutch Isabella had given her for a birthday. Lipstick, perfume, a tiny eyebrow brush. She frowned. Did her mother possess a comb or did her hair stay perfectly in place by magic? Probably. Black magic, if so. A small mirror in a silver case shaped like a shell, another hankie… Also a postcard. The picture was the *Mona Lisa*. On the back it said simply in small type – I'm back from New York but I can't get in touch. Will you ring me on Thursday? And at the bottom, beneath a row of typed x's, simply: thanks. There was a stamp but the date on the postmark was too smudged to read.

Frowning, Susan examined the card a bit longer, then slid it back into the bag. Without really thinking, she opened her mother's lipstick and sprayed on scent from the tiny bottle of perfume. A woman came out of the cubicle behind her. Susan stuffed everything back into the bag and stood up.

Coming back along the corridor she saw them. In the brightly lit mirrored hall, at the bottom of the stairs. His arms around her, his mouth on hers – her mother and Nick from all angles. His hands, both reflected and real, were moving slowly down the curve of her mother's back. Susan stood, frozen to the spot. She couldn't move her gaze away, couldn't escape seeing them. It was like a dream, a bad dream… their bodies pressed together, his mouth over hers…

Gathering her wits together, Susan walked quickly on numb legs back the way she'd come and pushed open the door. Mercifully, the cubicle was still empty. She sat on the lavatory and bolted the door, her heart pounding, breathing hard as if she'd been running. It was true, true... not only in her imagination... He was kissing her, it had happened, it was true...

Oh, how could she? she thought, when her body had begun to calm down. How could she, with *him*? Her husband's brother! Her dead husband's brother, Susan reminded herself. Her dead-for-a-year husband's brother. Angry tears slid down her cheek. It felt as if she'd swallowed her heart, swallowed it whole, it was stuck halfway down, a hard, aching lump.

My poor father, she thought, my poor, poor father. Dead and buried; he is dead and buried. And what did that mean? Forgotten. They have triumphed over you simply because you are dead and they are not. They have won. There was something so awful about being dead, not just the obvious, brute fact of it, but the sheer helplessness of everything going on afterwards, without you. It was a moral victory simply to live longer than someone else. Looks, talent, all the things that mattered when you were young, faded into insignificance besides this, the final success – longevity. Her mother and – Nick. Oh, he would be her father forever but her mother's husband? Not for long... not for very long...

A sob broke out uncontrollably. Oh, it was horrible, horrible! She couldn't bear it, she just couldn't! She would march straight up to the head of the table, stare her mother in the face and tell her, in front of everyone, exactly what she thought of her and then – But the plan was not finished, even in her mind, because she knew that in reality she would never do anything like it. She couldn't seem to stop crying now she had started. This was real, it had happened, she couldn't do anything about it – it was beyond changing.

Susan looked at her hands, clenched in her lap. Black with mascara where she had dashed away tears, there was also a smear of lipstick on her thumb. Carmine red: her mother's colour. My God, she thought, I could be trapped in this toilet for hours. Someone, probably Nina, would eventually realise they hadn't seen her for a while and start looking for her. What a fool she'd seem, sitting here on the loo, a bag between her knees, snivelling. It wasn't even her own bag, it was her mother's. Somehow the thought made her cry even harder.

The door of the Ladies swung open. Susan stiffened, pressing a hand over her mouth to stifle her sobs. There was the clatter of a brush on the table, the sound of a tap running, the scent of a lemony perfume filled the air. After a moment, the door slammed again. She was alone. Susan breathed out, realising that fear had dried up her tears.

Cautiously, she slid back the lock of the cubicle door and stepped out. Examining her face in the mirror, she saw that the damage wasn't too bad.

When she'd wiped the black from under her eyes, there was a bit of puffiness around the lids, that was all. She blew her nose hard on some toilet paper and took a deep breath. How could she go back into the restaurant and face them? How could she act as if everything was normal when her life lay in a dirty, broken heap at her feet? But she had to – she drew a sobbing breath – there wasn't any choice. *Underneath are horrors; on the surface, things go on as before…*

In the stone-flagged dining-room, coffee and brandy were being served. There was a hum of conversation. The smoke of cigars and cigarettes formed a thick cloud above people's heads. Susan exchanged the little black beaded bag she was holding with the one lying on the table and sat down, as far away from Nick as possible. It was not far enough: she could hear everything he was saying. People had placed their chairs at angles round the table, chatting in small, relaxed groups, so that the seats between her and Nick were now mostly clear. Nina was on her other side, talking animatedly to the man with a moustache. Her mother was nowhere to be seen.

'Imagine everyone has a box with something in it,' Nick was saying, pouring himself a drink with exaggerated care from a bottle of Couvoisier which had been set on the table in front of him. 'We can all look into our own box but we can't see into anyone else's. No one knows what's in anyone else's box. It could be absolutely anything, or even nothing at all – we just have to take their word for what's inside. Now,' he opened a box of cigars that had also been placed on the table and chose one carefully from it, 'suppose I have a beetle in my box. It could be a diamond or a screwdriver or fucking *anything* but, as a matter of fact, it's a beetle. Of course you can't *see* it's a beetle but you can tell something's in there all right. And you want it, just because it's what I've got. No other reason – that's human nature.' He lifted his glass with the hand holding the cigar and swallowed the brandy in one go. 'So as it turns out, you want that beetle real bad. But you didn't even know it *was* a beetle till I told you. The beetle drops out of the picture, see? It's irrelevant to your desire.'

The waiter placed a brandy glass in front of Susan and, when she nodded, filled it. She took a long, warming gulp. Nick looked up at Isabella, who had just returned. 'Hello, darling,' he drawled. 'I'm just explaining to everyone present what Wittgenstein really meant.' He held out the cigar. 'Want one?'

Isabella shook her head. 'I'm not that brave.'

'Oh, I can't believe that,' Nick replied with his lopsided smile. 'Something to drink?'

Isabella sat down with a smile. 'A cognac, please.'

Seeing them together, Susan felt tears threatening again. Her throat felt

GAIL LEVY

suddenly swollen, her eyes hot. She looked down, searching hurriedly for a cigarette. But when she put one in her mouth, her bottom lip was trembling too hard. Quickly, she took another gulp of brandy. When she thought she could safely speak, she leant sideways and said in Nina's ear: 'I've had enough. Are you ready to leave?'

'It's a bit early, isn't it?' Nina said. Then, staring at the glass in Susan's hand: 'Do you think that's wise?'

'Very.'

'You're supposed to be driving.'

'I've just had a sip.'

'It's big glass for a sip.'

'Please, Nina, I'd really like to leave.'

Nina glanced at the moustached man and sighed. 'Five minutes?'

Susan nodded.

'I was just saying, Isabella,' Nick said loudly, his voice thick with brandy, 'that it's human nature to want what other people have got.'

It's your nature, Susan thought, glancing over with dislike.

'Though, of course,' he added, 'we can never really get it.'

'Can't we?' Isabella asked lightly.

Nick shook his head solemnly. 'Impossible.'

Christ, he's really very drunk, Susan thought, noting the sudden swing into melancholy. He's not simply pissed, he's *sodden*.

'Why impossible?' asked the man with the moustache, taking a cigar out of his mouth.

'Because when you desire something you want to possess it,' Nick replied, talking slowly as if he were explaining to someone who was especially stupid. He did not light his own cigar, just continued rolling it slowly between his finger and thumb. 'You want to possess what you don't already have. That's what desire *is* – wanting something.' He slurred his words slightly – *possesh*. 'But as soon as you get what you want, it's no longer the thing you don't have. The object of desire changes.' He examined the cool dark leaf of the cigar he was holding for a moment longer, then put it back very deliberately in the box which had just returned from round the table and closed the lid. 'Completely.'

He looked antagonistically around, daring anyone there to disagree with him, deliberately, it seemed to Susan, avoiding her mother's eyes. He had not looked once at Isabella while he was speaking; he had totally ignored her. It was almost worse than if he'd been addressing every word to her. Because Susan – and God knows who else around the table, she thought suddenly, perhaps everyone – everyone knew exactly who he was talking to. *You've changed Isabella – completely*. Eyes cast down, Isabella sipped her cognac. Susan felt she was almost holding her breath, waiting for something to happen.

She's playing a part, it occurred to her suddenly – the object of desire, waiting for the blow to fall. Nick, she used to say lightly, was a little *difficult* when he had been drinking. Difficult? He becomes a bloody monster, Susan thought. As a woman, he's your biggest nightmare. 'If you'll be Mr Hyde, then I'll be Mr Seek' – it only took half a bottle of whisky to find the Hyde beneath Nick's charming Dr Jekyll. Only a few glasses of Glenfiddich to break a heart. But after a few months Nick's women always looked like rats who'd just started their electric shock treatment. Under different circumstances Susan would have felt very sorry for her mother. She could see that she was suffering. It wasn't as if playing the part of a hurt woman made her feel it any less. But so long as she's the centre of attention, for good or bad, that's the way that she likes it, Susan reminded herself coldly.

Her mother's dark eyes were glittering unnaturally brightly in the candlelight when she lifted heavy lids, the lines of her face were watchful and tense. She looked very beautiful: she sat differently, ate differently, every movement she made seemed to scream out – I'm having an affair with Nick! I'm sleeping with my husband's brother!

They hadn't waited long to jump into bed with one another, had they? Susan thought bitterly. What had Isabella expected? Did she really think she would be any different to all the rest? Perhaps that was Nick's magic trick, how he always managed to pull it off. *This time it'll be different, this time you're the one – Oh this time, yes!* Different to the long string of unhappy, discarded women reaching back into his past, beginning with his ex-wife. Beautiful, cool, tall, blonde Inga, as she'd been at the time. Now, alcoholic, devastated, desperately unreachable Inga. At least you could say that for him – he'd never made the mistake of marrying again.

'So we only want something because we haven't got it?' a woman in a low-cut silk blouse asked, reaching for the bottle of Couvoisier. 'Is that it?' The blouse fell open slightly, revealing a little too much cleavage and the lacy top of a bra.

Nick slid the bottle across to her. 'By definition.'

She took the bottle, tucking a strand of highlighted hair behind her ear. 'And once we have it, we don't want it anymore?'

'That's not the only reason. But, yes.'

'That's a bit strong, isn't it, old man?' the man sitting next to Nina said, with an uneasy smile. 'Jolly fine cigar, but not at all sure I agree with you on this one.'

'Well, Mark, old man,' Nick replied, 'you'll bloody well have to agree.

It's my birthday, isn't it?' He laughed, and the man called Mark laughed too, rather nervously Susan thought.

Taking a packet of Lucky Strikes from his shirt pocket, Nick put a cigarette in his mouth straight from the pack. He leant over and, without asking, took the cigar out of Mark's hand and used it to light the cigarette. When he'd finished, he handed it back, saying insolently, 'Thanks, old man.' There was an embarrassed silence, then Mark began talking rather too loudly to Nina.

Susan couldn't bear any more. She stood up and walked over to where her mother and Nick were sitting, asking abruptly: 'Have you any idea where we can find our coats?'

Isabella put down her glass. 'Oh, darling, are you leaving?'

Susan scowled down at the floor. 'Yes.'

Nick raised his brows. 'Already?'

Susan nodded sullenly, not looking at him either.

'And Nina, going too?' Nick asked. 'Do you two always travel in pairs?'

Nina had said her goodbyes to the man she had been sitting next to and followed Susan over. She replied with a polite smile, 'Thanks for a lovely dinner, Nick. It was really delicious. The *carpaccio* – fantastic.'

Nick rose unsteadily to his feet. 'But we've barely spoken.'

Nina's smile grew apologetic. 'I have to be up really early tomorrow. Six-thirty actually.'

'Oh God, what do you do for a living? Deliver milk?'

'I'm a solicitor and I'm in Court in the morning.'

'A solicitor? Are you really?' He took the hand Nina was offering and held it in both of his. 'You don't look like any solicitor I've ever met. Nina's a solicitor – she doesn't look like one, does she, Isabella?'

'Oh, no, much too pretty,' Isabella replied, with a vague smile. She turned to Susan: 'I'll find your coats, shall I?' But she didn't move, standing possessively by Nick's side.

'What kind of law?' he asked, without letting go of Nina's hand.

'I'm a divorce lawyer.'

'Oh, what a shame! I'm already divorced! What made you choose that?'

'I don't know really. I found it more interesting than conveyancing.' Nina licked her lips and curved them prettily into a glossy smile. 'And I like working with people, I suppose.'

'Oh, dear, I'm always willing to buy a new house… But that's no help. I'll just have to marry again, won't I, Isabella? You must have one more drink before you leave, Nina, my sweet. No, no, I insist! She must, mustn't she, darling? It's my birthday – just one.' He smiled at Nina, with a big flash of charm.

Susan saw Nina responding. 'Well, just one, then,' she said, returning the smile. 'After all, Susan's driving.'

She's *simpering*, Susan thought incredulously. Did she have to fall so easily for Nick's tricks? After all, she was engaged.

'Susie?' Nick was holding out a glass to her.

When Susan took it from him and saw the look in his eye, she knew. He'd seen her in the hall, watching them.

Nick raised his glass. 'Long life.'

'Happy birthday,' Nina said, raising hers.

'I'm glad you could come tonight, Nina,' he said. But his eyes, dark and shadowed and slightly amused, were all the while on Susan.

'He's a bastard,' Susan said violently to Nina in the car.

'Yeah. But a good-looking bastard.'

'If you like that kind of thing.' Susan gripped the wheel, thinking of the mocking light in Nick's eyes as he'd handed her the drink.

'Oh, come on. You can't deny he's attractive. How old is he anyway?'

'Fifty.'

'Yeah? He doesn't look it.'

'He *looked* pissed out of his mind.'

'It's his birthday. You're allowed to get pissed on your birthday, especially your fiftieth. Anyway, you can talk.'

Susan glanced at her but did not respond. 'And so bloody patronising. Oh, you're much too pretty to be a solicitor Nina,' she mimicked mincingly. 'What does he expect a solicitor to look like? Sixty with a long white beard?'

'It's not a quality that's totally off-putting in an older man. Gorgeous but patronising I could deal with.'

'I thought you didn't approve of affairs with a twenty year age gap?'

'I don't normally but there are exceptions that make the rule. You know who he reminds me of?'

'I'm afraid I don't.'

'Marlon Brando,' Nina said dreamily, 'in what's it called. What is it called?'

'I have no idea.'

'You know, with what's her name?'

'Vivien Leigh?'

'No, the other one... Oh, *Last Tango in Paris*! He's like Brando in *Last Tango*. Don't you think he's a bit Brando-ish?'

'Not in the slightest. More like Jeff Goldblum at the end of *The Fly*. The very end,' Susan muttered.

'I don't mean exactly like Brando. But he's got the same charismatic, sexual quality, except slimmer.'

'Unfortunately I don't have your powers of imagination.' Susan turned the wheel sharply. 'You should have been a novelist not a bloody divorce lawyer. Which way?'

Struck by the anger in her voice, Nina looked at her. 'You know which way.'

'I don't, I've forgotten. Is it left here?'

'Right. Then straight over at the next set of lights. You've done it a hundred times.'

'I know. But I can never remember.'

'He's divorced, isn't he?' Nina remarked, as the car swung round the corner. 'Though I notice he still wears a wedding ring. Has he got a girlfriend?'

'Who?'

Nina sighed. 'Oh, you are being difficult this evening. Nick. Your uncle. Has he got anyone special in his life?'

Susan shot her a glance. 'Why do you ask?'

'No particular reason,' Nina answered innocently. 'I just wondered, that's all.'

'I really wouldn't know,' Susan said roughly. 'And can we please stop talking about Nick?'

There was a short silence. Susan broke it by fumbling with one hand in her bag for her cigarettes and asking as pleasantly as she could manage: 'Do you mind if I smoke?'

Nina wrinkled her nose. 'I'd rather you didn't.'

'It was smoky all evening.'

'That's why.'

The lights by *The Gate* cinema were red. Susan looked grimly ahead, the unlit cigarette between her fingers. Nina was a prissy little bore sometimes, she thought, drumming her fingers on the steering-wheel. Don't smoke, don't drink, don't have affairs with married men… Well, she was probably right about that one. 'God, she disgusts me!' she burst out.

'Who?'

'My mother, who else?'

Nina glanced at the unlit cigarette between Susan's fingers. 'Oh, light it, go on.' She watched as Susan pressed in the lighter on the dashboard. 'Sorry to bring the conversation back to you-know-who, but was it also my powerful imagination or were he and Isabella getting on extremely well? I mean, rather better than in-laws usually do?'

'It wasn't your imagination. He's in love with her.'

'In love? I thought you said – How do you know?'

'He's so bloody cruel to her,' Susan yanked out the lighter and pressed in the cigarette's tip, 'he must be. Oh, he'll move in with her soon, I know he will.'

Nina looked out of the window. 'Pissed and patronising and lives in Pimlico... Where does he live, anyway? I thought his house was in Fulham.'

'It is, but he's renting a flat in Notting Hill. Said he couldn't bear to live in the house where his brother died.' Susan gave a short, humourless laugh. 'That's a joke. He doesn't seem to have any problem about moving in with his widow.'

'Well, he hasn't yet.'

'No, but he will, believe me.' Susan thumped on the steering wheel, once, a quick, angry movement with the flat of her hand which made her palm sting. 'My God, my father hasn't even been dead for a year and she's having an affair with his brother!'

'Do you think they were having an affair when your father was still alive?' Nina asked curiously.

'No. My mother's not the type.'

Nina raised thin eyebrows. 'Everyone's the type. You of all people should know that. Even one's parents. Except for mine, of course,' she added quickly. 'They really *aren't* the type.'

'They were so *happy* together. It wasn't a pretence, she really seemed to love him. And Dad adored her. Eleven months!' Susan gripped the wheel. 'Eleven months and she's forgotten him already.'

'Because she's having an affair with Nick? *If* she's having an affair with him – '

'Oh, she is,' Susan said grimly. Her stomach lurched when she thought of the passionate kiss she'd witnessed. She recalled her mother's expression as she was leaving the restaurant – reproachful and sly.

'It doesn't mean she's forgotten your father,' Nina said, in what Susan thought of as her wise voice. Although she couldn't see her face, she knew very well what it would look like, lips pressed flat together, eyebrows ever so slightly raised.

'I bloody well hope not! The stone setting's in three weeks!'

'People do strange things when they're in pain,' Nina said, still wise.

'Pain? Her? Eleven months and she's dancing with her dead husband's brother – that's a little too strange for me.' Susan squeezed her eyes tightly shut. 'Oh, Nina, it's not just anyone – it's Nick. Dad's younger brother. That's what makes it such an insult to his memory. That's what hurts so much. It's like – it's like they're laughing at him. Oh, if she had to have an affair, why couldn't she have chosen someone else?'

'The lights are green.'

'What?' Susan opened her eyes. 'Oh, yes, sorry.'

'What's a stone setting?' Nina asked, once they had moved off.

'A year after the burial a headstone is put on the grave. The stone is set.'

'Really? There's no headstone for a year?'

'Not in the Jewish religion.'

'How do you know where the grave is then?'

'You put something there, I suppose. A piece of paper or card. Maybe it's marked down in a book.'

'But that's all?'

'That's all.'

There was a hollow in her chest but at the bottom of this emptiness, a weight, heavy as a stone, which pressed down on Susan's stomach and made her feel sick. Her mother and Nick... A kiss, cold and empty as a grave... 'When you visit the grave you leave behind a small stone or a pebble,' she said quickly, to rid herself of this image.

'Not flowers?'

'No, a stone. I'm not really sure why... except that stones last forever and flowers soon die... And I suppose there weren't many flowers in the desert... You know, where the Jews would have been living when the religious traditions began... I expect you'd easily find lots of sand and stone but very few flowers.' I'm babbling, Susan thought. I'm talking complete crap. She indicated and pulled out, overtaking the car in front.

'I see,' Nina said, but as if she did not.

A car came towards them, headlights full on, horn blaring. Susan swerved in again.

'Hey,' Nina said nervously, clutching the dashboard. 'Watch it.'

'Sorry. It came from nowhere.'

'Yeah, well.' Nina laughed nervously. 'I hope your mother wasn't right about that death wish. How much did you drink tonight, anyway?'

'Nothing much.'

'You had a brandy.'

'One brandy. That's nothing.'

'Tell that to the police.'

'Oh, Nina!'

'Oh Nina what?'

They didn't speak for moment. Susan slowed down. Nina resettled herself in her seat. 'What were we saying?' she asked, smoothing her coat over her knees. 'Oh, yes. That in the Jewish religion there's no headstone on the grave for a year.'

'Putting down the tombstone is symbolic. It's meant to mark the end of mourning,' Susan explained. 'There's a Jewish expression – to put a stone on it.'

'Which means?'

'That it's time for things to come to an end.'

They drove along Bayswater, then turned into the bright lights of Queensway. Nina lived just past the tube station on the right. Susan double parked outside the building, leaving the engine running. Nina opened her bag and fished around for her keys. 'Have you phoned BT yet?' she asked, when she'd found them.

'Haven't had a chance. Mum was already waiting when I arrived home.'

Jingling her door-keys, Nina leant over and brushed her lips against Susan's cheek. 'Thanks for inviting me this evening. Actually I rather enjoyed it.'

'Oh, Nina, thanks for coming! It made all the difference. I don't think I could have faced it alone. Though as things turned out – Well, thanks for coming anyway.'

When the front door had closed, Susan let off the handbrake and drove up the street. It was twenty past eleven when she got home. She would get into bed and try to sleep, she decided, stumbling wearily up the narrow stairs. Try to wipe out for a few hours the image of her mother and Nick. Kissing… holding each other, their bodies pressed close together… wrapped tightly in each others' arms… Or perhaps she'd have a glass of wine and watch some TV before going to sleep, get a bit blotto, that might do the trick.

Inside the flat, she collapsed onto the sofa. She didn't need to pretend any longer; she could let her emotions have free rein. But, strangely, now she was alone and free to react as she wished, she felt nothing, just a blank. She tried to think of Paul and her own life, the sex they'd had last time they'd met. He'd pulled up her skirt, bent her over the table and… But it was no good, at the crucial moment her mind kept reverting back to the kiss she'd witnessed. In the end she didn't even turn on the television. She just sat downstairs in the dark, hoping against hope that if the phone rang, this time it would be Paul.

She was crawling through the ground. She couldn't see anything – it was pitch black and her eyes were caked with mud. It was as airless and stuffy as a coffin. Warm. Like a box closed tight. She could hear something though, some muffled thuds far off.

She rested for a second, trying to wipe her eyes clean with hard, scaly fingers. When she tore at her hair, she clawed out dark, decaying leaves in handfuls. But after a while she had to move on and crumbling earth soon swelled her eyelids again. Soil dragged at her hair and clogged her ears and nose. She could barely breathe – when she snorted, brown snot, like a worm, shot out of each nostril. She spat out earth, the sick-brown taste of it.

She knew why they'd buried her father. Why they'd piled earth over his body, then slammed down a stone on top of him. They had known. That the dead are not really in the ground and their caskets contain only the rattle of bare bones. Pile on more earth, hammer down the stone hard, harder! But however long she searched, she couldn't find him.

She pressed forward, seeking the dark scent of decay, searching desperately for the stink of reality. She would not give up, she would not! She battled through the thick muck using her only weapons – nails, teeth and fists. Water seeped out of her eyes and nose, mud turning the clear liquid rust-brown. Like blood. Like sad, mouldering leaves. Clay stiffened the backs of her knees, she breathed grit into her lungs, her spit turned black. And still she hunted…

– 6 –

Even before she opened her eyes she knew something was wrong. She felt cold. There was a cold feeling in the pit of her stomach. And the dream… Oh, my God, the dream…

Susan was lying in bed, her face cradled in her hand, her legs curled up to her chest. She lay staring at the white wall in front of her for a minute or two before she knew where she was and that she'd only been dreaming.

She was in bed at home and she'd only been dreaming.

Slowly she swung her legs to the floor and sat for a moment, staring down at her bare feet on the rug. She sat like this, breathing deeply, till reality had sunk in fully. Then she got off the bed. Awake now, but still with a cold feeling of foreboding, she stood, naked, before the long mirror in the bedroom.

'Oh shit,' she said. She stared at her reflection in disbelief, trying not to panic. 'Oh shit.'

She walked quickly through to the bathroom and ran the taps. Bending over the sink, she splashed lukewarm water on her cheeks and forehead. When she looked in the mirror nothing had changed. Her face was still deathly pale, her features frozen into a stiff, white mask. There was a peculiar twist to the left side as if a thread had been pulled through too tightly, making her eye droop and twisting her mouth up into a leer. Her mouth was dry as if it was filled with cotton wool. The whole left side of her face felt like she'd been to the dentist and had her mouth shot full of Novocaine. However hard she tried, she could only move the right side. Over the other half, she had no control – whatever she did, it retained its stricken lines, hardly changing at all, like the face of a stranger.

Susan stared at herself in horror.

'My face,' she whispered, touching it. 'My poor face.'

Her left cheek was completely numb. The only feeling was in the tips of her fingers.

She dressed quickly, pulling on jeans and a black V neck pullover without bothering with underwear. She tied back her hair, then thought better of it and left it loose, letting it fall over her face like a long, dark shadow. Lipstick only emphasised her mouth's ugly grimace. She wiped it off hurriedly and pulled dark glasses and a long silky black fringed scarf out of the drawer. As she drew the scarf on, she was struck by something else. It wasn't only her face – her memory was blank too. She couldn't remember a thing about the evening before – nothing between arriving home last night and waking up

49

this morning. She remembered the dinner-party, of course, and dropping off Nina on the way home. She recalled walking up the hall stairs, getting out her keys and opening the front door of her flat, yes – but after that, nothing. Not taking off the black dress and boots that she could see lying in a heap in the corner, not washing off her make-up or getting into bed.

That's ridiculous, she told herself, tucking the ends of the silk scarf inside the jumper. You must remember *something*. You can't simply erase several hours of your life from your mind. Frowning, she tried hard but there was just a yawning black hole in her memory. Surely she hadn't been that drunk – had she? A glass of wine, a couple of swigs of brandy… Had she drunk much more once she was home? Because, if so, this was one hell of a hangover. She felt a chill down her spine. *She didn't know. She couldn't remember. Not one single, little thing.* She grimaced, and it hurt like crazy.

Bloody hell, she had better get to the doctor's fast.

Her Filofax was by the downstairs phone. Susan looked under D for doctor and S for Spelling and finally found Dr Charles Spelling under M, for medical, she supposed, dialling quickly. A recorded voice told her the surgery would open again at three o'clock. Three? In the afternoon? Her heart gave a thump. What time was it now? She dialled again. Another recorded voice told her it was two thirty-four and twenty-nine seconds. Twenty five to three? That meant she must have been asleep for – she did a quick calculation – about fifteen hours…

She took two deep breaths trying to calm herself, then went through to the kitchen.

On the kitchen floor was an empty wine bottle. Around it on the lino, a dark purple stain. She'd opened a bottle, it seemed. But hadn't drunk much, she thought, examining the floor – it looked like most of the wine had been spilt. When? Susan had an odd feeling. It was like walking into a strange room and feeling that you'd been there before. Or a name which you couldn't recall but were certain began with an A. Except in this case, rather more worrying, she thought, glancing at a silver corkscrew placed neatly on the counter-top with a cork still twisted in it.

She picked up the bottle and dropped it into the bin. Again, as the lid slammed shut, the disturbing sense that there was something she ought to remember, something important. Not about the bottle of wine itself but something linked to it… Perhaps the person she had been drinking with? The mysterious A? But there was only one glass on the table by the telephone. She'd been drinking on her own when… What? The phone had rung? She shivered, staring down at the lid's white metal top.

The drive to the doctor's surgery only took five minutes even though she had to crawl along behind all the other cars over Primrose Hill. She was lucky. There was a parking space right on Elsworthy Road, almost outside the surgery. Keeping her scarf wound high and her head down, she ducked quickly into the small path at one side of the house.

'I'm afraid I haven't got an appointment. I was hoping for an emergency slot,' she said loudly into the intercom.

'Come up,' the nurse's voice said over the crackle.

Susan pushed the door open quickly before the buzzing stopped and climbed the stairs.

There was no one else in the waiting room yet, but she kept on the scarf and dark glasses anyway, pretending to read an old copy of *Hello*. A very old copy. Jennifer Lopez was marrying Marc Anthony in a twelve page colour spread. She turned the pages, growing fascinated, despite herself. Everyone looked so beamingly happy in the photos it made you wonder what was really going on behind the scenes. She was engrossed in the pictures of Anthony's smiling family when the nurse called: 'Miss Savage?'

Susan looked up sharply, then feeling a pain in her neck, regretted the movement. 'Yes?'

'You're in luck. The doctor can see you now.'

Outside the doctor's room Susan took off the dark glasses and muttered a short prayer. 'Please don't let this be permanent. Just don't let it be permanent.' She stood for a moment, eyes closed, hands pressed together, thinking that she prayed an awful lot for someone who wasn't even sure she believed in God, then knocked on the door.

The doctor continued tapping the keys of the computer on his desk as she entered. There was a photograph of two smiling blond children in school uniform on the grey filing cabinet, probably his grandchildren. Out of the window she could see white sky and the bare tops of trees. She sat down on the chair besides his desk and unwound the scarf. After a moment, he looked at her over the top of his glasses.

'It's my face,' she said forlornly. To her dismay, her eyes suddenly filled with tears. She blinked them back. 'I woke up like this.'

'Oh, dear,' the doctor said. 'Let's have a look, shall we?'

He moved his chair forward and tilted her face to the light. 'Feel anything?' he asked, touching her left cheek with gentle fingers.

'No, nothing.'

He swung round in his chair and chose a wooden stick from a metal container above the sink, then swung back again. He pressed her cheek lightly several times with the stick's sharp point. 'Now?'

'No.'

'And this side is fine?'

'Well, fine-ish.'

'Do you have any other weakness anywhere?'

'No, I don't.'

'What about ear pain or anything like that?'

She shook her head. 'No.'

'Had a cold lately?'

Again she shook her head.

'Are you on the contraceptive pill?' The doctor consulted the computer. 'Yes, I see that you are. You've been on Nystolyn for,' he frowned at the screen, 'two years?'

'Could it have caused this?'

'I shouldn't have thought so. Married? No, I see not.' He glanced up from the screen. 'Been under any stress at work lately?'

'Actually I'm not working.'

Spelling typed this in. 'At home?' He glanced at her over the top of his glasses and repeated: 'Under any stress at home?'

'Well,' she cleared her throat, 'my father died almost a year ago.'

'Did he?' With two fingers Dr Spelling tapped this information into the computer. He was obviously new to technology. His typing was laboriously slow. 'When was this exactly?'

'November.' She cleared her throat again. 'The twenty-second.'

'And it's now,' he consulted the calendar standing on his desk, 'the third.' He looked at her with clinical coolness over the top of his glasses. 'Was it a natural death?'

'No. He was murdered,' she answered as calmly as she could.

'Murdered?' Spelling looked startled. 'Do you mean, a car accident?'

'No. He was stabbed to death at home. In his brother's house, actually. The police think it was a burglary and the burglary went wrong. It was just bad luck he happened to be there at the time.'

'Good God! In Primrose Hill?'

She almost smiled, the question was so absurd. 'No, Fulham. Does that make it any better?'

'No, of course not.' Embarrassed, Spelling busied himself with the computer keyboard before asking, 'Have the police found out who murdered him?'

'They have no idea. They seem to have given up looking.'

'How do you feel about that?'

His voice had resumed its usual smooth, professional tone. He watched while she considered this question. Her face throbbed, especially the left side. 'I suppose I mind rather a lot,' she admitted. The doctor waited, not speaking. To fill the silence Susan found herself adding, 'It makes me feel so helpless.'

He pounced on the word: 'Helpless?' then waited so that she was forced to explain. She spoke haltingly, struggling to find the right words. 'It makes Dad's life seem such a big *mess*. I mean, all of it, not just the very end bit. Because how you die changes everything. If Dad had died peacefully in his bed at eighty his life would appear different from the start. His childhood, his teens, his working and marrying. They're all altered by what happened to him later. Murder has destroyed not just his future but his entire past too. And now they've even given up looking for the culprits. No one's even trying to find out who did it. No one seems to care about it anymore. Least of all me,' she finished bitterly.

'What could you do?' Spelling asked gently. 'Nothing's going to bring him back, you know.'

'No-o. But if we knew who his murderer was then we could at least give his life a proper ending.' She stopped, expecting the doctor to speak but when he merely stared, she pressed on. 'At least we'd be able to repair some of the damage that's been done to him. There'd be some sort of res- olution to this mess. Wouldn't there?'

Her confident manner cracked. She'd been in Fulham that evening, when her father was being beaten to death, just a few miles away. After the funeral she'd looked up the route in the *A to Z*. If she had taken Trawley Avenue, then crossed into Musgrave Court and turned right into Kempson Road she would have been nearby in his final moments. 'You probably know this already,' she said with a tense little laugh, trying to regain her calm veneer. 'About the way you die... but I didn't... not until now... Does this all sound very silly?' she asked, when he still didn't speak. 'I'm not even sure if knowing who his murderer was would make any differ- ence really. But I wish –' She stopped. She'd been going to say, I wish Dad could tell us who did it to him.

Spelling removed his glasses. 'Yes?'

'I wish I knew that whoever killed him was being punished,' she fin- ished instead. 'It's horrible to think that they can go on living happily and Dad can't.' She looked down. 'I suppose that sounds very childish, too.'

'Perhaps they aren't living so happily,' Spelling suggested.

'You mean because they're consumed by guilt?' Susan grimaced. It made her face ache even more. 'That's not very likely. They're probably having a good laugh about it as we speak.' She added morosely: 'Anyway, it looks like we'll never know.'

'There's a support scheme for victims of this kind of crime, you know. It's called, um, Victim Support After Murder, I think. I could put you in contact with them, if you'd like.'

She shook her head, rejecting the idea. 'No thanks.'

'It can be helpful talking to people who've been trained to help.'

Again she shook her head.

'Well, shall I get them to send you some information through the post?'

'OK – yes,' she said, more to shut him up than anything.

Spelling fiddled with the stem of his glasses. 'What did your father do?'

'He owned a shipping company.' She looked down at her hands, clenched in her lap and added: 'His real love was photography though. And he still liked reading philosophy. He did a degree in the seventies. He always intended retiring early to read a bit more and take pictures full time.'

It's all so bloody unfair, she thought fiercely. Why couldn't it have been Nick at home that evening? Or no one? Why couldn't her father have stayed in Fulham on some other night? Two nights earlier and he'd still be alive – hoping to begin the life he'd wanted to enjoy for years. He didn't have a chance, she thought. Everything was snatched away from him before he could even begin. Now it seemed like he'd always be waiting, just waiting to start the life he'd always planned. And herself? Wasn't she not living but simply waiting, too? She didn't even know what for.

Spelling's fingers were moving aimlessly in the air above the computer keyboard, perhaps thinking, too, of his retirement and of whatever he intended to do then. Play the piano? she wondered listlessly. Discretely, he examined his watch then settled his glasses back on his nose and asked more briskly: 'What was your father's name?'

'Steven. His name was Steven.' She had trouble getting it out. Her face ached badly as she said it. 'Steven Savage.'

'Are you sleeping?' the doctor asked, searching for S on the keyboard. 'I could give you – ah, there it is – I could give you something to help if you're not.'

Susan hesitated, recalling the dream she'd had earlier. Perhaps sleeping pills might blot the images out. But niggling at the back of her mind was the feeling there was something important she ought to remember. Something vital… Mightn't pills blot that out, too? 'No, I'm fine,' she replied. 'In fact, I slept for about sixteen hours last night.'

'Really? Well, that's not so strange under the circumstances. Is there anything else that you wish to talk to me about?' the doctor asked, without looking up.

Susan stared at the balding spot on top of his head. Anything else? What more did he want, for God's sake? She could tell him about her mother and Nick's love affair… Or perhaps her own futile, probably going nowhere type of relationship with a married man… Even her memory loss of several hours. Was that what he wanted to hear? At the very least she could describe her almost constant feeling that she was under someone's careful scrutiny though without the faintest idea whose or the slightest solid reason for thinking so. That would give him something to put into his computer. That would really turn him on. She almost smiled at the thought. Go on, Dr Spelling, reduce me to a few cold lines of black and white type – turn me into a series of ungrammatical sentences filed in a cabinet under S. Contraception: The Pill. Status: Unmarried. Reason: Unsatisfactory affair with Married Man. Father: Murdered. Name: Steven Savage. Status: Dead. No, thank you very much. It would be even worse than talking with Nina. He'd think she was barking. After he'd recorded everything on a floppy disc he'd pack her off to a psychiatrist pretty sharpish, and who could blame him for that?

'Not really,' she murmured. 'I do feel a little sick though.' Sick? Was that the word for this deadly nausea which chilled her bones? And when Dr Spelling carried on typing: 'Look, I'd prefer it if you didn't put this on file.'

Spelling looked up sharply. 'It's much easier if I do. It is all confidential,' he added.

'Even so, I'd rather you didn't.'

He shrugged, looking put out. 'Very well,' he said, a little petulantly. 'But of course, I can't promise to remember any of this on your next visit.' He turned back to his computer, perhaps realising this wasn't an appropriate thing to say under the circumstances. 'It looks like you have Bell's Palsy,' he told her, typing with a sudden spurt of speed, even with two fingers. 'It's an inflammation round a facial nerve, between the skull and the brain.' He stopped for a moment to draw an imaginary line down his cheek. 'The nerve gets pinched, if you can imagine that.'

'Is it – ' she hesitated. 'Would you say it was psychosomatic?'

'Not entirely, no.' He considered her over his glasses. 'But nobody's entirely sure of the cause of these things. It has a psychological element.' He began typing again. 'I'm prescribing prednisolone. It's a steroid and should reduce the swelling. Avoid alcohol until you've finished the course.'

'Nothing at all?'

'I wouldn't drink too much if you're on steroids. I mean, a glass or two of wine in the evenings is fine but I wouldn't drink much more. A thought occurred to him. He looked up. 'Do you normally drink more than two units a day?'

'Oh, no,' she replied, looking a little too straight into his eyes. He's taken a course in the psychology of alcoholism, she groaned inwardly. These are questions he's been told to ask. It's just as well I didn't say anything else. He'll only assume I've been drinking too much. The computer began spilling out paper. She cleared her throat. 'How long will this take to go away?'

'Hard to say. It may clear up quite quickly.'

'How long is that?'

'A week.'

'That's *quickly*?'

'Of course you may be lucky and get rid of it in a day or two. On the other hand,' the doctor said, ripping a sheet off the printer and handing it to her, 'it could take a few weeks or even months. And some people, I'm afraid, don't get better at all. If this hasn't cleared up by the time you've finished the pills come back and see me again. I am sorry about your father,' he said, as she was turning the door handle.

Outside it had begun raining. Susan decided to fill the prescription later. She couldn't see anyone looking like this. If necessary, she'd stay in forever, her face softly hidden in a scarf. The traffic lights on England's Lane were changing to red as she drove up. Susan considered driving through but braked at the last moment. Adjusting the rear mirror she tried smiling at her reflection. A flicker of hope shot through her. Surely there was a faint movement? She ran her tongue along her top lip. There was a slight tingling sensation where her warm tongue touched skin. The numbness was beginning to disappear. Relief coursed through her body. Dr Spelling had said it might go in a day if she was lucky. It appeared, for once, she was. She raised her hand to her face.

As she watched her hand in the mirror she had a strange distancing feeling, as if her reflection had receded far into the distance and then come instantly flying back again. It was like a jolt running through her body. Her hand was moving through air. Her head felt empty. She was touching her cheek. At the same instant that her hand made contact, skin to skin, the events from the night before came back to her. She remembered. Not going to bed or how she'd got home again, but everything else. Dropping off Nina after the party, arriving back at the flat, the telephone ringing... Now she understood what had happened to the left side of her face. Now she knew why she hadn't been able to remember – she hadn't wanted to. *She hadn't wanted to.*

Susan didn't move as the lights turned to green. She remained staring at her startled eyes in the mirror, the half smile frozen on her face. She did not move as memory flooded back, even when the man in the car behind began ceaselessly pressing his horn.

7

The phone had gone at eleven twenty-five.

Susan had opened a bottle of wine and was slumped despondently on the sofa, glass in hand, hoping Paul would call – he occasionally did when he was working late. She jumped at the sound of the phone but let it ring several times before picking it up. What if it weren't Paul, what if it was another of the silent calls? It was neither. She was both disappointed and relieved to hear an unfamiliar male voice, clear and pleasant.

'Is that Susan Savage? I'm sorry to call so late, but there's no answer on your mother's number. My name is Alex Emmerich – I live at 59 Keyes Court.'

''59?' she repeated blankly. 'The flat below my father's studio?'

'Yes, immediately beneath it on the fifth floor… Look, I was wondering, was anyone using the studio this evening?'

'Oh, no! Nobody's been there for some time.'

'I thought not.' There was a note of triumph in his voice.

Susan carefully set down her glass and sat up straighter. 'Why?'

'I heard a bit of a racket up there earlier. Sounded like someone shifting furniture about, banging doors, that sort of thing. To be honest, at first I assumed it was exactly that – you were moving out. But then I wasn't so sure – I knew the flat hadn't been sold and, anyway, it seemed rather an odd time to be moving. So I thought I'd better check. I went upstairs and – Did you know that Steven had given me a spare set of keys?'

'No, I didn't. No. I don't think he ever mentioned it…'

'About a year and a half ago, when I first moved in. We had lunch together a couple of times and he told me he wasn't around much in the evenings, asked if I'd keep an eye out when he wasn't there. Anyway. I went up. I thought I'd better let you know as soon as possible. There'd been someone in there alright.' He must have heard her sharp intake of breath for he added quickly, 'Nothing's been taken, as far as I can see. TV, video, cameras – still there. They'd shifted things about a bit, that was all. Opened a bottle of whisky, rolled a couple of cigarettes. One was still smoking in the ashtray so they couldn't have been long gone. Oh, and the phone was off the hook. In the end, I decided it was probably a friend of yours, after all. I'm just calling to – well, to make sure.'

Her hand on the receiver gripped hard. 'It wasn't any friend of mine.'

There was a second's pause. 'I see. Does any one else have a key?'

'Apart from you, only me and my mother.'

'Your mother then?'

'I was with her this evening. We were at a dinner-party.'

'Perhaps a friend of hers?'

'But she wouldn't give a key to the studio to anyone else. Not without telling me first.'

Susan's heart was pounding so hard she thought he must hear it on the other end of the line. Her skin felt clammy. She leant across and switched on the lamp next to her. The warm circle of light enclosed only her, the small table with the glass of wine, and a section of the sofa. Someone in her father's studio, drinking his whiskey, smoking his cigarettes… Unable to keep the tremor out of her voice, she asked: 'Have you called the police?'

It was his turn to hesitate before answering. 'No, it didn't appear to be a break-in on the face of it. I thought I'd better contact you first.'

She took a deep, quivering breath. 'Well, thank you for calling Mr – '

'Emmerich. But please – call me Alex.'

'Alex. I'll be round first thing tomorrow morning to – '

'Actually I did think of calling the police a few days ago,' he interrupted her. 'About the man I saw outside the flat.'

'A man?'

'About twelve-thirty last Tuesday night. Man in his fifties. He was wearing a raincoat. Kind of shabby looking, well-built. I didn't think anything of it at the time because he had a key. Well, I assumed he did – it looked like he was sort of fumbling with it in the lock. I saw him quite clearly, closing the door.'

'*Closing* it? I don't understand. He'd been inside?'

'I realise I should have contacted you straight away.'

The phone felt suddenly slippery in Susan's hand. She had to wipe the other one on her dress and swap the receiver over. 'Do you think you could have mistaken the floor?' she asked, her voice hoarse. 'I mean, they all look pretty much the same. You could easily think you were on the sixth floor and be on the seventh or the eighth.'

'It was the sixth floor alright. He was definitely outside number 69. I'd taken the lift up too far, you see, and had to run down a floor to my own flat.'

'But with a key?'

'He was coming *out* of the flat. I just assumed – The lock didn't appear damaged when I went in this evening,' Alex Emmerich added as an afterthought. 'It was one of the first things I checked.'

Someone with a key to the studio? It didn't make any sense… 'I suppose it could have been Nick,' she said slowly, considering the possibility. 'He may have gone over last week, for some reason. Of course, that doesn't

explain the noises you heard this evening. And he didn't mention it but – '
But there are a lot of things that he hasn't mentioned lately, she thought.
Aloud she said: 'Perhaps my mother lent him her key.'

'Nick? I think I met him once. Tall chap, slim, dark?'

'That's him.'

'I only met him briefly but – Has he recently grown a beard?'

'No. He's clean-shaven.'

'Perhaps he's grown one since you last saw him.'

'I shouldn't think so. I was with him this evening, too.' Unfortunately,
she nearly added. 'And he definitely did not have facial hair of any kind,'
she finished instead.

'It couldn't have been Nick, then,' Alex Emmerich said firmly. 'He had
a beard the man I saw, I'm sure he had a beard. Of course, he was partly
turned away from me but at the time I could have sworn… I said to him – '
He stopped. 'You aren't going to believe this. It will seem so ridiculous to
you.'

It sounded like he was smiling slightly. She could imagine the smile –
embarrassed, self-deprecating. 'Never mind how its sounds,' she said
impatiently. Then, more politely, 'What did you say?'

'I said to him, Good evening, Steven. I spoke without thinking, he was
just closing the door and that is what I said to him – good evening, Steven.
He never said a word in reply, he ignored me completely. I didn't call the
police because, for a moment, I thought it was your father up there last
Tuesday night. He looked just like your father. When I reached home of
course I realised it couldn't have been. Not on Tuesday night. Well, not
any night really. Whoever it was, I said to him, evening Steven, but he
went on turning that key like I didn't even exist.'

8

The block of flats where Steven Savage had had a photography studio was a large 1930's mansion block on Kensington High Street. The creaky wrought iron lift Susan remembered from childhood was now a quiet mirrored box with harsh lighting. She looked drained in its white light. She was still wearing the short black dress from the dinner-party though over the top she had pulled on her leather jacket. There was a dark stain near the dress' hem where, in her haste and a little jumpy, she'd knocked over a bottle of wine.

Alex Emmerich opened the door the instant the bell rang. He didn't invite her inside but simply picked up a set of keys from a table by the door and joined her in the hall. He was about her own age, maybe a bit older, with brown eyes and soft brown hair, fit-looking, wearing jeans and a baggy white tee-shirt. In the harsh glare of the overhead lights, his eyes looked deeply set in shadow, his jaw bone hard. There was a hum of lights as they walked on thick cream carpet up two short flights of stairs to the sixth floor, otherwise the building was silent. They didn't speak until Alex was unlocking the studio door. 'The spotlights aren't working,' he said. 'I'll have to turn on the kitchen light.' He crossed to the tiny kitchen, his footsteps ringing out on the bare wooden floor. The neon strip flickered on immediately, casting a long white triangle into the room.

'I haven't been here for ages,' Susan said, looking around.

It hadn't changed. Bare white walls, white venetian blinds over a wide wall of windows facing the street, two tracks of spotlights over rough wooden shelves, empty now except for a few remaining reels of film and a couple of cameras. At the far end of the room, a low table, an armchair and old leather sofa. The metal slats of the blind were half open, casting occasional strips of yellow light onto the cracked brown leather.

She remembered the first time her father had brought her here. The empty space had seemed vast to her as a child, a huge, bright vault. At one end of the room, he had stretched a plain piece of canvas from floor to ceiling. He'd made her stand against the white backdrop with her back to him. She could feel the intense heat of the studio lights on her bare legs. He'd said: 'Jump! Jump round to your right, Susie, as high as you can!' Then, 'Again – do it again!' She couldn't see her father's face, just his nose squashed against the black lens of the camera and one eye squeezed to a slit. Hear his voice – again, again! She had the photo still, a little girl in a cotton frock, laughing in mid-air.

On the table by the sofa was a glass filled with whiskey and a newly opened bottle. Jack Daniels. Her father's favourite. The whiskey he always drank. She picked up the glass, inhaled the smell of alcohol, then set it back down. Next to it, an ashtray was filled with cigarette butts. Matches and her father's tobacco pouch lay open beside it. They must have used the papers from the pouch and the stale tobacco because the cigarettes, stubbed out in the ashtray, were all hand rolled. She heard Alex Emmerich cross the room and felt, rather than saw, him stand beside her.

'He seems to have made himself at home,' he remarked, his voice echoing a little in the bare room. 'It's odd. Why would anyone go to all this trouble just to drink a glass of whiskey and smoke a roll-up? Someone breaks in here, has a drink and a smoke, uses the phone, and leaves all this valuable equipment untouched?' He shrugged. 'Perhaps they're intending to come back for it later.'

He picked up the leather tobacco pouch and pulled out two thin cigarettes. She bit back the impulse to tell him sharply to leave her father's things alone. 'Freshly rolled,' he commented, putting the cigarettes back in the pouch and setting it down.

They stood rather awkwardly round the table. Outside, the cars passing along Kensington High Street cast long shadows, rippling like tentacles over the ceiling and walls. Six floors up, the sound of the traffic was just a steady murmur. Susan walked over to the window, pushed up the slats of the blind and stared down through the gap at the street below. A couple waiting at the bus stop were embracing. Her eyes lingered on them. Two people kissing in the dark out of sight of the world. They reminded her, all too forcibly, of her mother and Nick. She let the blind drop back into place. When she turned back to the room, Alex was by the front door, examining the lock.

'Absolutely no sign of forced entry,' he remarked, straightening. 'And this isn't an ordinary lock. It couldn't have been easily opened without a key. Whoever it was either had a one already or was a real expert.' He wiped his hands on the back of his jeans. 'You're sure there isn't another key floating about?'

'Absolutely sure. It's a Banham lock. You need a letter signed by the owner to get a spare cut. I never bothered.'

'Maybe your mother did.'

'Even if she wanted to, she couldn't without my signature. It's my flat. In his will my father left the studio and everything in it to me.'

'I see.' He raked his hair off his forehead with his fingers. 'Or rather, I don't.'

He walked into the centre of the room and stood facing her, his hands in the front pocket of his jeans, clearly unsure of what to say next, or how to say it. 'About your father,' he began hesitatingly. 'I should say – well, how very sorry I am about his death. It was unbelievably bad luck.'

She nodded, not trusting herself to speak.

'I'd got to know him a little. We had lunch a few times – he showed me some of his photographs.'

'Did he? That was unusual. He must have liked you.'

'I liked him very much. He was good company.'

'Yes. Yes, he was.'

Her fingers had left four white stripes in the coating of dust on the metal surface of the blind. She rubbed the black on her fingertips off with her thumb. Looking at her hand, she asked: 'What did you think of the photographs?'

'I thought he was talented. Original and – poetic. He told me that you take photos too. Are you as good?'

'Different. Dad always said I was better.'

'Are you?'

She shrugged. 'I always assumed he was just being generous. He was a very generous man.'

She moved away from the window, looking round the room. 'It's so strange being here. I can almost feel his presence. It's like... it's like he's still around.'

She could see all the forgotten things – the old Brownie, a dusty tripod, the Nikon with its cap screwed on. Lightly, almost tentatively, she touched the metal cap with the tip of one finger. 'I still can't believe he's not here anymore. Not really,' she said, tracing a line along the camera's edge. 'I keep waiting for him to call or something. I keep on expecting him to call and say, let's go away for a few days, like he used to.'

She didn't speak for a moment, just stood, looking down at the camera. 'We weren't like father and daughter. We were more like friends. Actually even closer than that. Like people who shared the same vision in life.' Her lips curved into a secret smile. 'He always said I understood him so completely it was like having a second set of eyes. He called me,' she looked up, her eyes suddenly alive, unguarded, 'his Antigone.'

'You must miss him very much,' Alex said gently.

Her eyes clouded over. 'More than I could have ever realised. I'd have done anything for him. He was wonderful.'

Their eyes met, she slid hers away quickly. She could tell by his expression that he could see in her face what she was feeling: despair, confusion, anger.

'He taught me everything he knew about photography,' she explained, talking quickly to cover her embarrassment. 'The right exposure to use, how to change perspective, when to consider the balance between the light and dark, the shape of things…' She drew a figure of eight with her finger in the dust on the shelf. 'That's why I'd hate to be considered better than him. I mean, we're just different. It doesn't feel right to say better or worse.'

She gave Alex a quick, sidelong look, hoping she had not said too much. She'd learnt to be careful when she spoke about her father. There was a particular expression in people's eyes she'd come to recognise – the wary, triumphant look of the living when they speak of the recently dead. But Alex Emmerich didn't have that look. She dotted a full stop next to the eight. 'I'm not any better but just as good. You know.'

'I'd very much like to see your photographs – if you wouldn't mind showing them to a stranger.' He smiled. He had a nice smile, she thought. 'This probably sounds horribly poncey, but I have a friend who owns a gallery – '

She cut across him. 'Did you know he'd started working on a book?'

'Steven? No, I didn't.'

'I was helping him with it. Of course, it was nowhere near finished and won't ever be now.' A shadow crossed her face. 'A lifetime's work wasted.'

'But it wasn't wasted,' Alex said gently. 'He taught you. And perhaps you'll publish a book of your own photographs one day and dedicate it to him.'

'No.' She shook her head. 'Perhaps I'm talking like I'm planning to, but the truth is I can't imagine ever taking another picture. It all seems completely meaningless now he's not here. Empty. Like dust and ashes.' She lifted her hands in the air, fingers parted, as though ashes were falling through them to the ground. 'To be honest, there seems no point to anything.'

'But that will change, won't it? You won't feel like that forever.'

'Won't I?' She sounded unconvinced. 'I'm afraid my desire for taking photographs was murdered along with my father.' She looked at him. 'Does that sound terribly self-centred?'

'It sounds – sad.'

Her gaze shifted. She was still facing him but her eyes strayed beyond him to the door next to the kitchen which was open a crack. Inside, she knew, was a single bed covered with a plain grey blanket. Her father had sometimes let friends sleep there when they needed a place to stay. She wondered if the bed was still made up. 'I think about it a lot,' she said, gazing over Alex's shoulder. 'We're all going to die one day, though perhaps not so brutally or unexpectedly as Dad. But death – well, it's always brutal, isn't it? And if that's the way things end, what's the point to anything?'

She gave an awkward laugh. 'I don't know why I'm talking to you like this,' she said apologetically. 'I'm not usually so depressing.'

'Sometimes it's easier speaking to strangers than to people you love or know well. They don't know you either, there's nothing to get in the way.'

'Yes, I suppose so.'

'Look, do you want to come downstairs for a cup of tea? I know it's late, but we could talk some more. You could call the police, if you like, from my flat.'

'I'm afraid I've rather lost faith in the police's ability to help.'

'Come and have a cup of tea, anyway.'

'I think I'll stay here a bit longer. But thanks anyway.'

'Are you sure? There's nothing more you can do tonight.'

'I'm sure,' she decided. 'I've brought my own key. I can let myself out.'

'Another time then.' He took a card from his back pocket and handed it to her. 'If you need anything, I'm just downstairs.' She did not look at the card, just stuffed it into her leather jacket.

'Anytime,' Alex said. 'Just ring. Anytime. Really.' His eyes were still on her, warm and brown and slightly worried, as he closed the door.

For a moment she nearly changed her mind and followed him. She had a flash of herself sitting in a pleasant kitchen with both hands wrapped round a mug of steaming tea, talking desultorily to Alex Emmerich, all the images of the evening wiped temporarily from her mind by their conversation. But she didn't move. She placed the keys on the table, feeling suddenly very tired. It had been a long and difficult day. There was a sour taste at the back of her mouth, the bitter remains of the alcohol she'd been drinking earlier.

She took a glass from the cupboard in the kitchen and poured herself a drink from the open bottle of Jack Daniels. The whiskey helped a little, warming her throat, filling the emptiness, easing the pain, she thought lazily, splashing in another.

It was cold in the studio. The heating had been turned off long ago. She switched off the harsh neon light and lay full length on the cracked leather sofa, taking off her jacket and draping it over her for warmth. She had a vision of herself as she must look from outside. Wearing black and, beneath her make-up, pale as a ghost.

There was a shadow on the floor beside her in the shape of a lopsided bird. Long neck and one broken wing. 'I'm just downstairs,' Alex Emmerich had said. As she watched the shadows drift across the ceiling, Alex's flat seemed a long way away. She was in her father's place now. Contained within her father's space, held, cold and hungry, within his empty body and downstairs was a lifetime away.

She felt the weight of her body, she must have fallen asleep, she did not dream. It was still dark when she woke with a jerk and saw him. The smell of him woke her, the familiar smell of him, mingled now with something else, the smell of decomposing flesh, the rotten stench of his body. She was not sure of the time. There were no clocks in the studio and she did not wear a watch.

9

He was sitting in the armchair opposite, his head tilted back against the edge of the seat, long legs stretched out in front of him. He held a glass loosely in his hand. Most of the liquid in it had spilt onto his brown corduroy trousers – there was a dark, circular stain on the knee. He didn't seem to notice. He was wearing a raincoat, as Alex Emmerich had described. It was open and she could see that the check shirt underneath was torn and streaked with dirt. But Alex hadn't seen the eyes…

Susan wanted to scream when she first saw his face. The dull black orb where his left eye had been, the deep jagged wound that snaked like an S, still glistening with blood, underneath. She wanted to scream and scream when she saw his damaged face. But she was filled with silence. A universe of luminous silence rising up to meet her.

When she opened her eyes he was waiting, her dead father.

Waiting to speak to her, wanting to speak to her again.

'I came back to see you,' he said. 'As soon as I could.' His voice was rasping, deeper than it had been in life. He sounded tired. 'Can you hear me?' He shifted his legs and sat up a little straighter in the armchair.

'Yes,' she said, through lips that felt stiff and out of control. 'I can hear you.'

She stared into her father's empty black eye.

Carefully he leant forward and set the glass he was holding down on the floor. 'I can't drink whiskey,' he said, 'really. There's a hole in my stomach the size of a fist.' He held out a shaking hand, squeezed tight. 'Or smoke. It hurts,' he explained, 'like hell – when I move my face. I suppose it's one way to give up.' He laughed. His laugh was rasping, bitter. 'I still feel the urge though. Surprising isn't it? Death hasn't taken that away from me.' Again the bitter laugh. 'Yet,' he added. 'I've been trying to contact you without success,' he said, after a moment, 'for some time.'

He picked up the tobacco pouch from the table and pulled out one of the rolled cigarettes – his hand trembled. Slowly he lit it, took a deep drag and grimaced. The expression in his good eye was vaguer, more lost, without the warmth she remembered. But there was the same cragged nose, wide mouth and beard beginning to be flecked with grey, the same lines across the forehead and long fingers that were so surprisingly fine for such a big man, spread out on his knees in his habitual way. His hair was matted and thickened with what she now realised was dried blood.

She was shivering uncontrollably. Her limbs were heavy, her voice was stuck in her throat – she couldn't have screamed or spoken if she had wanted to. The world around them seemed to have stopped. All the normal sounds and movements had disappeared – the distant sound of traffic and shadows, all gone. There was just the beating of her body and his faint voice; the throbbing in her ears, in her throat and wrists, the pounding in her chest and her father's voice, as she sat, still and frozen with fear, on the sofa.

When he saw the look on her face he got up and walked across to the window. The toe of one of his stained leather shoes had peeled away from the sole. He was limping and the loose leather on the bottom of his shoe slapped softly against the wooden floor. He stood at the window, where she had stood earlier, staring down at the street through the metal slats of the blind, exactly as she had, both hands in the pockets of his raincoat. From this angle, she couldn't see his missing eye or the open scars on his face. His skin was white, untouched: he looked exactly as he had in life.

'There's not much time left,' he said hoarsely. 'I don't have much time. I must tell you everything.' He sounded exhausted. 'Everything.'

With an enormous effort she moved so that she was sitting upright on the sofa though her legs were still stretched out in front of her. The leather jacket that had been covering her slithered down onto her knees. I'm awake, she thought with horror. I'm alive. My eyes are wide open and I'm sitting up – this isn't a dream. There was an icy feeling in her toes, rising up through her body to her chest. This is what it must feel like when you die, she thought. Is that what's happening? Am I dying?

'You're cold,' her father said flatly, without turning his head. 'Put on the fire.'

There was a small electric fire that was always kept in the hall cupboard. But to even lift her feet off the sofa and place them on the floor would take a greater effort of will than she could imagine. She was shaking so hard either from cold or shock that she felt if she tried to stand she wouldn't be able to balance properly. There was a feeling of space between her ears, her head was pounding, her armpits were stiff with dried sweat. When she didn't move, he shrugged, lifting the slats of the blind slightly so he could lean forward and rest his forehead against the window. Outside it was still dark enough for her to see her reflection on the glass. She could make out her own panicky eyes and white face, surrounded by darkness. The red, reflected glow of the cigarette her father held was burning a hole in the centre of her forehead.

'Oh, Susie,' he said at last, turning round to face her. 'I've tried for so long to get in touch with you. You are my only hope. You're the only one who can help me – the only one.' And it was his voice again, the one she remembered from childhood.

She moved, making a great effort to stand, intending to move nearer.

'Don't!' he said, with a sharp gesture, turning his heavy, brooding one-eyed glare on her. 'Don't come too close!'

Frightened, she sank back in her seat. Her body felt weighted.

'You'd better not touch,' he said after a moment. 'Who knows what might happen if you do?'

Am I imagining this, she thought with a gleam of hope. Am I making it up? I'm making it all up, aren't I? This isn't happening. She was sure she did not speak aloud but perhaps she had, for he answered as if her mind had no walls: 'Oh, I'm here alright. You're not imagining this – I exist. In the abyss, if you can count that. What you're seeing is a projection of your own mind. Like with colours. We say something is pink or black or green but these are just words. That isn't to say colours don't exist. That cushion looks red to you, doesn't it?' Her eyes followed his arm as he pointed. 'But it looks green or orange or fluorescent to creatures who are built differently. Like myself,' he added.

She wanted to ask, What colour? What colour does it look to you? She wanted to say, what is this? A fucking philosophy lesson? But she couldn't speak.

'You forget,' he continued in the same hoarse, flat tone. 'So quickly. All the little things, the really important ones. Warm, cool, supple, turquoise. Soon they're just words for something long gone. A thread of memory clinging to an old idea. I only appear to be part of the external world.' He gave a strained smile. 'Death really does do something to you. It really changes people.' He paused. Frowned. 'We aren't so – nice.'

The cigarette he was holding had burned right down and there was a sudden sharp smell of singed flesh. He looked at his fingers as though he was surprised to find them still there, then stubbed the cigarette out in the glass ashtray on the window ledge. He misjudged the distance and it fell heavily onto his foot. He didn't seem to notice. He lit another cigarette – he had to use two matches, the first did not catch. He dropped the curled, blackened ends of the matches onto the floor. Inhaled, coughed. 'They told you that it was a burglary turned nasty, I suppose? They said it was bad luck – A tragic mistake. The wrong place at the wrong time. It wasn't bad luck,' her father said. 'Not in the way that they mean, anyway. It was a well-planned and cold-blooded murder. No one knows that except me and my killers, Susie, and I am dead.'

Her hands were clasped tightly in her lap and her fingers looked like writhing snakes. Like the letter S scarred deeply into a man's cheek. She wanted to cry, 'Planned? By whom?' but could not form the words.

'I need you,' her father said, his voice suddenly much clearer. 'You are my only chance. I cannot rest. I'm a *ruach* – a wandering soul. The stone setting is in twenty-four days and if nothing is done before then, I'll have to go on like this for all eternity. It has to be done before the stone goes down. It's my only hope – I have to get to the Nothing before then. Otherwise I'll be in Limbo forever. You have to help me die, Susie. Can you help me die?'

Her intake of breath sounded like a scream, like a piece of fine silk ripping. She must have gone very white because he asked roughly: 'Are you alright? Can you hear me?'

She nodded twice, staring into his black eye, wanting to cry, *No, no, no.*

'You must do what is – necessary,' he said, speaking slowly, enunciating each word carefully as if he were afraid she would not hear or, hearing, not understand. 'He has smeared me in blood, urine and excrement, I have lost everything, because of him. If you ever loved me – '

'Oh, God!' she sobbed, finding her voice at last.

'Avenge my murder. Allow me peace. Or he will go on, living in my house, with my wife, enjoying all the things he has stolen from me.'

'Who? Who is it?' Susan screamed, wild now, out of control.

'Open your eyes and you will see.'

'See what? See who? *Who murdered you?*'

But she had the answer before her father turned his lost eye on her and uttered the words in the hoarse, terrible voice that she loved. 'Your uncle,' he said. 'My darling brother Nick. You know it already, don't you? *Don't you?*'

10

Steven limped slowly across the room. When he sat down and put his elbows on his knees she saw that his hands were still shaking. The roll-up burned unheeded between his fingers. She looked at him in fear. His single eye upon her, he smiled. When he started talking he still had this strange little smile fixed on his face.

'They came to Nick's house, two of them,' he began, with the formal little smile. 'Real psychos. The kind of men you read about, the kind that enjoy that kind of thing. One was blond, slim. The other was older, balding. Ordinary looking. They wore tracksuits, one grey, one blue. Two ordinary men in tracksuits, with knives. It was all arranged. Nick had asked me to stay with him for the night so we could discuss the business. I knew things were bad but I never dreamed... He'd got involved with gangsters, you see, with real scum. It was an important deal and meant big money for them all – I only found out about it by accident. One evening I was working late, killing time before meeting Isabella in the West End. We were going to the theatre – she'd wanted to see *The Vortex* for weeks and I'd got tickets. I wasn't all that bothered but friends of hers were in it so – I was in Nick's office for some reason and happened to look through the Beaux-Sarr file. It's one of our East London contracts. Spelt like beautiful in French with an x at the end,' he added as if it were important. 'No reason. I just flicked through the file for no particular reason. There were a couple of sheets that had been misfiled. Put under Sales, rather than Accounts. I glanced at them as I was slipping them back in place and realised instantly that something was wrong. It was obvious as soon as I saw the figures. I stood by the filing cabinet looking down this list. Then I sat down in Nick's chair, behind his desk, and went through it more carefully. I took the sheets away with me.

'That night I couldn't concentrate in the theatre, I couldn't sleep. I got out of bed around two, leaving Isabella sleeping, and went through the figures again downstairs. There was no doubt about it. It was a fiddle involving huge sums of money. In a few days we were having our yearly audit – presumably the accounts would have looked completely different by then.

'I confronted Nick next morning, asked him what the hell was going on and he – He just laughed. He said: "OK, big brother. It's your lucky day. You can come in on the deal. Sure, you can have a cut. How much?"

'I'd asked him to come to my office. It was eleven and we were drinking coffee from the cappuccino machine. I told him I wanted nothing to do with any of it – nothing. East End gangsters! Had he gone mad?

'Nick stirred two sugars into his cup. He'd always liked his coffee sweet: "It's a lot of money, Steve. A lot of shit. Think about it. We're talking millions here. Millions! For doing nothing except keeping quiet. For that, a nice big cut. Five, six million pounds at least. I don't mind sharing it with you, I really don't. You know, it's a relief in a way that you've found out. I wished from the start I could bring you in. I wanted to say, come over to our side." He smiled but his eyes, looking sidelong into mine, were wary. "Would you have come?"

'"You bet your bottom dollar I wouldn't."

'The smile remained on Nick's lips. His voice grew almost dreamy. "Easy, easy money. Money you don't have to spend years slogging your guts out for being nice to people you despise. Money for all the things you've ever wanted. The cars, the houses in Italy and New York, trips to, I don't know, the Seychelles. You could retire and live off the interest alone. Or you could make that film you're always talking about. It's all been figured out. There are ways to cover up the sources of finance. That's the beauty of it – it never happened so no one will ever know."

'And he was right. When he explained the whole deal to me I could see he was right. No one would ever find out.

'"But I'd know," I said.

'"Can you imagine?" was all he said in response. "Can you *imagine*?"

'We had lunch at Porters in Spitalfields. The service was bad. The restaurant was packed and there was only one waiter. It was almost impossible to attract his attention. Nick was talking. He was very excited. Nine months of intense preparation was about to pay off. He was almost proud – Of his baby, he called it. And very persuasive. You know how Nick can be.

'"I don't care," I said to him finally. "I don't want to be involved in something like this."

'"You're already involved whether you like it or not."

'"This is drugs money, Nick."

'"Yeah, well, didn't you notice? The war is over and the good guys lost."

'"I'm sorry, but I won't have dirty money backing my father's business. You stop the deal or I'll go to the police, whoever gets hurt in the process. I'm not joking."

'Then Nick got nasty. He spoke in a voice I barely recognised. "*My* father's business? *My* father? Listen, big brother, I've put a lot of hard graft into this, a lot of time. It's taken years to be trusted by these men – small favours, nothing much, but always done smoothly. You're not Dad's protector, you don't own the rights to him. He was my father, too. He was smart. But who knows what he would have done, under these circumstances?"

'By this time we'd asked the waiter to bring us two steaks and a salad. Nick called him over and asked how much longer we were going to have to wait for our meal. The waiter said it wouldn't be long. Nick poured more red wine into his glass and lit another cigarette. "If you want to remain an ordinary schmuck, if you're not interested in the first big opportunity that's ever come our way, then fine. Fuck off. Fuck off out of the business and go and take your pretty pictures." He wasn't so much talking as hissing these words at me. "But don't talk to me about the police, do you understand? Just don't. Leave it alone. I'm warning you." Beads of sweat stood out on his forehead. I'd never seen him like that before. It was like – the mask was off. I knew that for the first time I was looking at the real Nick. Someone I'd known nearly all of my life and never known.

'"Pretty pictures?" I said stupidly. "Is that what you think?"

'His face as he looked at me was filled with hatred. That was more shocking to me than anything. I'd had no idea. No conception of how much he hated me. "Personally I'd prefer to have a wank," he replied with a sneer. "It's more straightforward and far more pleasurable."

'There was still some wine left in the bottle. He poured it out and swallowed it in one gulp. It calmed him a little. "It's too late," he said, back to his normal manner. "Don't you get it? *Too late*. We're in too deep. We're in up to our fucking necks. There's no going back now. We've taken the money and now we're up for more. These aren't schoolboys that we're dealing with. These men are serious – deadly serious. Get in or get out or else. Understand?"

'"Yes," I said. But I didn't understand, not really. Even then, I misunderstood my brother's character completely. I left him sitting there, waiting for the food to arrive, smoking his third cigarette, his eyes following me as I walked out. He has our mother's eyes, did you know that? Golda's eyes. That very deep brown, flecked with gold.

'When Nick was a child, when we were very young, he idolised me. He used to follow me everywhere. He was five years younger so it got on my nerves a bit at times. But we were close. Our parents were working hard building up the business and weren't around much so I saw myself as Nick's protector. Once he awoke in the middle of the night screaming. I heard him from my room, a single thin, high wail. Then a brief pause, followed by another shrill, eerie cry. I rushed to his room but when I moved towards him, he shrank away in terror and began to sob even harder. His hand clamped over his mouth, his frightened eyes never leaving my face for a second, and these tears streaming non-stop down his cheeks... After a while he grew calmer and told me he'd had a dream I was trying to kill him. Our bedrooms were at the top of the house. He'd dreamt that as we were walking upstairs in our pyjamas, ready for bed, he'd turned round and, behind him, where the stairs had once been, there was now a yawning black hole with thirty or forty thin but deadly snakes writhing around at the bottom and he knew that I meant to push him in to it.

'I did my best to settle him down again but for days afterwards I could see him remembering. And I couldn't forget the dream either. When we walked upstairs to bed in the evenings I couldn't help glancing back and thinking how easy it would be for someone to fall all the way down to his death. I imagined Nick desperately grabbing for the banisters and screaming as he couldn't catch hold. Imagined him falling, arms and legs flailing, head banging hard against each step until he reached the bottom. Heard his last piercing scream and the dull thump of his body as it finally landed…

'When I left the restaurant it was drizzling and I hadn't brought my coat. I walked the streets for hours as if I was in a strange city. What was I going to do? "Stop. Just stop now – That's all I'm asking," I'd said to Nick in the office.

'"The answer's no, big brother. No, no, no. Got it?"

'If only I could get him to change his mind, I thought. If only I hadn't looked in his filing cabinet – What if I hadn't looked? What if I was still innocent? If I hadn't gone to the theatre with Isabella that evening, if the show had started at seven instead of eight, if I hadn't confronted Nick that weekend… If, if, if.

'But I did stay with Nick when he suggested it so that we could discuss the business in greater detail. In fact, it was my idea. I still hoped I could talk him out of it, you see. Or at least get him to give up his share of the money – Something. And on Saturday night two men climbed in through the bathroom window. Nick had left it open for them before he'd gone out – on a date he couldn't cancel at such short notice, he claimed. I was deeply asleep. I didn't hear a thing. Nick had probably put something in my drink. He knew that I always have a nightcap and he must have chosen something you couldn't taste with whisky. When I first glimpsed them I was so groggy that for a moment I assumed it was a dream, a horrible dream. Then they dragged me out of bed and I knew that it wasn't.

'They took me to the bathroom. That was where my body was found, wasn't it? Dragged me down the short flight of stairs, punching me from one to the other, in the face, the stomach, the back of the neck, as if they couldn't wait until they had me. Once the bathroom door was shut they were more systematic. They took turns, they helped one another. The younger one was the worst. He started with my face. Your name's Steven, I hear, he said. Steven Savage – SS. Nice. We'll let everyone know that your name begins with an S, shall we? He carved this S on my cheek, just for the fun of it, and then he said: We'll have your eye. Out. We're just going to smash up your left arm, they said. They even discussed it between them for a while. Just smash it a little bit, break all his fingers. You can still use the other one, can't you, Steve? Oh, perhaps we should do the other one after all, what do you think?

'The blond had a very soft voice, like he was whispering: I like it when you moan Stevie, he whispered, I like it so much. They spent an hour on me, just one hour, and in the end I wanted to die; at the end of that time I didn't even *want* to live anymore. Because they were excited, you see, they were enjoying it, and when they'd finished beating me up – You'll be ours, they said, holding the knife to my face, all ours when we're through with you. You'll be our very own sweetheart, yes? *Yes?*

'Then Nick arrived. He came into the bathroom where these men had just – I was lying naked on the floor, soaking wet. I didn't know whether I was bathed in blood or piss or semen. But I did know, when my baby brother came through the bathroom door, that it was all over. Until then I'd thought I might survive, even if I lost an eye or an arm. They'd known exactly how to keep me alive, those two men, it was their profession and their delight. And I'd sensed that they weren't actually trying to kill me and it had given me hope, despite what they were doing to my body, despite the part of me that desperately wanted to let go and die.

'I don't think Nick expected what he saw – I don't think he had any idea until then what he'd set loose on me. He'd thought, a nice, clean killing and that's that. He must have been shit scared when he saw what they'd done, more scared than he'd ever been in his life. But he couldn't back out now even if he'd wanted to. They wouldn't have let him. They were like wild animals – worse. They could smell his fear from a distance. He must have seen that given half the chance they would turn on *him* – one false move and nothing would stop them. "What about you, barmitzvah boy, do you want it next?" Because he had to kill me, you see. That was part of the agreement he'd made, part of the trust they'd insisted on. And, of course, by then he was afraid for his own life so when they said, you kill your informing pig of a brother, he said – Of course.

'They pulled me to my feet, supporting my weight between them, each holding an arm. Blood filled my ears and nose. Nick stood in front of me, we were looking into each other's face. I looked into his face for what seemed like minutes, five, ten, a lifetime. He was so close I could smell the drink on his breath. The focus was odd – his features kept slipping away from me. But I could see his eyes clearly – imploring me, begging me, asking me for something – What? Love? Forgiveness? And do you know, I felt pity for him in those moments? A strange, a terrible pity. I could see only the child in Nick, the little boy who had adored his big brother. The bathroom dissolved around me and I remembered him on the day of his barmitzvah starting his speech, "Now I am a man."'

Steven stared unseeing ahead, his damaged face jagged with emotion. 'Thirteen years old and thin as a stick – "Now I am a man…"'

Her father didn't speak for a moment after he had said this. 'The funny thing was that I really did want to help him,' he said at last. 'Wanted to ease his anguish, bear his pain. In that moment I would have given almost anything to make him feel better.' He gave a laugh that made the perspiration on her body turn to ice. 'Except for what he was asking for – Myself. Except for that.'

His face was turned towards her but he wasn't really looking at her. His one good eye was blank and inward-looking. Susan was not even sure that he was aware she was in the room with him. He was alone again with his brother.

'Then Nick's eyes emptied,' her father went on, in the same eerie, relentless voice. 'I watched the life leave them. He stood before me – a dead man with his eyes open. He took the knife they were holding out to him and, closing his lifeless eyes, plunged it into my stomach. I looked down. I saw my brother plant the knife. I saw. The knife go… in. All the way – all the screaming way. Knife into flesh… Silver-white burning through flesh and blood… A hot rush pours over me, I'm seized with panic – I've lost my footing… I can't see the room anymore – I can't, you know, focus…

'I look down. Nick's hand is on the knife's handle. He has thrust the blade into me, right up to the hilt. He twists it. He is twisting the blade… Everything is bright silver and brilliant and, oh, pain… more pain…'

Steven lifted two shaking hands to his head. When he dropped them again they hung limply at his sides. Susan wanted to press her fingers into her ears and chant over his voice as she used to when she was a child and didn't want to hear any more. *No more!* she beseeched in silent terror. Perhaps she did cover her ears because his voice grew muffled – it seemed to come from the bottom of a deep well, somewhere far below water, all choked with moss and algae and seaweed.

'A flower is growing opposite me about two feet away,' Steven said in this faint, garbled voice. 'A deep purple flower made up of many tiny dots splattered on the wall. I close my eyes. Beneath my lids it is black. I inhale the sweet fragrance of the blood-red rose of death. I am falling asleep. For a few seconds I am asleep. Before death claims me from pain, I sleep. When I open my eyes, I know perfectly well what is happening to me – I know the pain is mine. But a part of me simply watches. I'm a spectator.

'For the burning pain is not burning anymore. In that weapon's slow second it has become pure pain, platonic pain, the essence of pain, moving on a scale that has no upper limit, on and on, all the way to infinity. Spinning through infinity on the end of his blade, hurtling through space to the other side of existence – four inches of steel, the length of the universe. I'm climbing and climbing and there's only darkness. I feel like nothing, I can't do anything. It's raining and hailing and I'm still climbing and… There's a sound, a horrible sound. I don't know what it is at first. Then I realise. I'm taking my last breath.'

His empty black eye searched the room and found her. Susan realised with cold horror that he could see just as well out of it as the other. 'Shall I tell you the most striking thing about my death?' her father asked. 'The thing I found most striking? It's the feeling that time has stopped. That's a more powerful experience than you can ever imagine. No past, no present, no future… Like music that has ended, distant music. It isn't silence – I mean, the same sounds go on as before. But something weighty that had been there my whole life was suddenly over – My own breathing.

'I can feel an abyss in my chest where my heart should be – the dark purple beating had gone.

'And the shadows aren't just shadows anymore. Living silhouettes lie across the walls where my blood has warmly splattered and clung to porous plaster… Spinning before me is the black bubble of time into which I'm about to be tossed. For I'm lost, I'm locked out, I'm dead – I know I am dead.

'I look down. I see Nick remove the knife from my stomach with a sharp backwards thrust. My brother has killed me. He has finished me. And now –'

Susan stared at him, petrified.

'Now,' her dead father intoned, 'he is sleeping with my wife. That bastard is alive, rich and he's got Isabella.'

He had stood up and wandered across the room as he'd been talking. His limp seemed to have disappeared. Now he turned and moved a little closer to her. She tried not to shrink back in her seat. 'Can you hear me?' he asked urgently. 'Susie? Are you there?'

He was standing only a little distance from her. She felt the cold like an aura around him. His image was wavering before her eyes. The light was beginning to turn. 'Can you stop him for me?' he asked softly. 'Susie? Please?'

Then he stretched out his hand with the slow, uncertain movement of a blind man and very lightly touched her cheek.

11

Susan sat motionless in the car, her hand still frozen in mid-air, on the way to touching the same cheek. When it started shaking, she lowered it, putting it next to the other one, stiffly curled in her lap. Her heart was acting strangely. It felt as if she'd just run a hundred miles and lived a thousand years in the last few minutes. Keep calm, she told herself. Don't panic. Just breathe – in out, in out. It's a dream, you've remembered a dream. A vivid dream. A very, very vivid dream. Just a bad dream, like the one you had last night…

But staring at her panicky eyes reflected in the car mirror, she thought – Who am I kidding? Who am I fucking kidding? It doesn't *seem* as if I'm remembering a dream. It seems much more real – it seems as if it actually happened. But it can't have, it *can't*. In out, in out… Oh God, she thought, the panic rising, I've lost my looks and now I'm losing my mind.

At the back of her consciousness, she was aware of a long, dreary hooting coming from the car behind. A face loomed suddenly at the car window startling her and making her jump. A man wearing thick black-rimmed glasses peered in. 'You are presumably aware that the lights are green?' he asked irritably. Then, more kindly, 'Are you alright?'

Susan fumbled with the handbrake. 'Oh, yes, I'm sorry… I'm just – Sorry.'

The man straightened, shaking his head. She could see him in her rear mirror, hurrying back to his car as she engaged the gears. What was she supposed to be doing after the doctor's? Oh, yes! Driving home.

She had missed the green light; they were already changing back to red. She drove slowly through, only vaguely aware of the sound of a blaring horn behind her, indicated and turned down Haverstock Hill. She felt dazed, unable to think clearly. She felt physically battered almost as if an enormous iron bar had crashed down on her shoulders and then been picked up again to smash down on the crown of her head. She felt divided between two worlds, half of her mind and body in the car on the way home from Doctor Spelling's, the other half somewhere else. In a cold, bare studio in Kensington…

She gripped the steering wheel for dear life. She didn't know how she reached home. She saw the road ahead of her, the familiar trees and railings of Primrose Hill, the two telephone boxes on the corner, the small, expensive supermarket and the café and launderette opposite. But at the same time, images formed and faded. Imprinted over the top of the ordinary world, she saw a hand lifted in warning… a broken shoe slapping against wooden boards… an empty eye… As she walked on stiff, shaky legs up the stairs to the flat, she saw a knife glinting against her father's horribly damaged face.

Her own face, she saw when she looked in the bathroom mirror, was much better, though she was white as a sheet beneath her long dark hair. There was still a slight, sneering twist to the left side of her mouth, that was all. Gently, she touched her cheek. Almost normal. Without taking off her leather jacket, she took the Ajax and a Jeye cloth from the cupboard beneath the sink and squirted thick, clear liquid into the basin. 'I'm in shock,' she said aloud to herself. 'I'm in shock and I'm cleaning the sink.'

Downstairs, she did the washing-up, dried all the plates and cups and stacked them away in the cupboards. Then she sat at the kitchen table, her head in her hands, staring down at the wine stain on the floor.

'The most likely explanation is that I went to Keyes Court and met Alex Emmerich but, after he left, I fell asleep and dreamt the whole thing,' she told herself. 'And that is why I have Alex's card in my pocket.'

It was a dream, she assured herself, a hallucination; a vision so horrible it had taken her by the throat and shaken her to the core. Her father hadn't really touched her cheek with a hand as cold as death, she'd only imagined he had. You're going bonkers, she thought, her skin crawling. You've just had a massive hallucination. Nina was right. This is all a figment of your lurid imagination. *You're having a nervous breakdown.*

There had been signs leading up to it over the past year, she couldn't deny that there had been signs. The feeling of being followed or watched, even in the most improbable places. A sense of what Nina would call persecution. Those eyes on her… All this she had imagined too… She felt too exhausted to move. She sat slumped, at the kitchen table.

Yes…

She was going crazy.

See her father? Talk with her father? Hear from his own, ruined lips what had happened to him just before the grave? It was impossible, it didn't even bear serious consideration. Because he was dead. However painful, however horrible, however unfair – he was dead. Dead and buried. She said the words aloud. Dead and gone. Everything had been an illusion borne out of her pain and grief. She hadn't wanted her father to be gone forever and so she'd pretended, for a brief while, that he was not.

Susan took her fingers out of her hair and pushed herself upright in the chair. She felt light-headed, a little dizzy. She would make herself a cup of tea. She would drink the tea and then she would mop the kitchen floor. She stood to fill the kettle. But as she held the unplugged kettle in her hand, it struck her again how undream-like it all seemed. For one thing, she remembered every detail with an absolute clarity that was quite unlike the jumbled logic of a dream. That terrible story, recalled to the last, including the smell of his decaying body and the look on her father's face when he spoke of what his brother had done, and was doing now.

That smell…

Were even wholesale delusions like that?

Susan sat down heavily at the table, the kettle forgotten in her hand. Supposing it wasn't a hallucination? Supposing that deep down she'd known all along whose eyes were on her, from exactly three months to the day after her father's murder. Even on the very day he was murdered? Suppose she had known who it was on the other end of the telephone, trying desperately to get through – 'I've been trying to contact you for some time…'

Through her open mouth she felt herself beginning to pant like a frightened dog. Oh, God, it had really happened. The story her father told had been true.

But Nick? He was bad, but was he really that bad? Had he really killed his own brother? She felt a jolt of grief. If yes… Oh, if yes…

It can't be true, she told herself. It just can't be.

She felt split in two. She could hear Nina's disdainful voice: 'It's just your imagination, Susan. What, another feeling? Seen a ghost? You must be joking.' But there was also memory – a memory of *something*… But what?

The phone rang. Probably Nina. She ignored it.

Dazedly, Susan looked down at her hand and found it still resting on the kettle. Tea? Fuck tea. She wanted whisky. She needed a drink. She jumped up and started rummaging frenziedly through the cupboard, her heart pounding. When she found the bottle, it was virtually empty, just a pathetic drip in the bottom, not even an inch. Hardly worth putting back in the cupboard at all. Unscrewing the lid, she didn't bother with a glass but swigged it straight from the bottle. As the warmth of the liquid coursed through her, she sank back down at the table and stared into space.

First things first, she told herself. You must check out the story properly. There had been nothing much said by the police at the time, only that, for a burglary, it was an especially brutal and senseless killing. They hadn't told her anything more and she hadn't asked. But was it a burglary? She took another swig. Or had Nick killed her father and made it *look* like a burglary? If the company had been used as a cover for a drugs racket and Nick had been ordered to kill Steven *at all costs*? Kill him *at any risk* before he spilled the beans? Then surely something would show up somewhere. But where? How? Susan had no experience of how a shipping business worked. She had never been the slightest bit interested.

She finished off what was left of the whisky, thinking hard. She'd need help, she decided, sitting a little straighter. She'd need help dissecting truth from fiction. Her first thought was of Nina. She was a lawyer. She might know how a business worked and would probably have the name of a good private detective. She would ask Nina. She sat straighter still. Then, if no fraud was uncovered, there was a good chance that she'd made it all up – She was stark, staring mad. But if it were true –

Oh, God, if it were true…

She drooped forwards with a groan. Help me, her father had said. Avenge my murder, he had begged her. The stone setting is in three weeks – it has to be done before then. But, even if his story turned out to be true, what was she supposed to do?

Was it only a few hours ago that she'd told Dr Spelling she'd give anything to know who'd murdered Steven?

Her head was spinning. The edges of reality and unreality seemed blurred, like a bottle of Jack Daniels, when her eyes were filled with tears. Which was worse? Her father returned from the dead to seek her help – Or madness?

Your father loved you very much they'd said to her after the funeral, meaning to comfort her. 'So why,' she'd sobbed irrationally, once she was alone, 'Why did he leave me?' She longed to have her father back; longed to speak to him one more time. She wanted to ease her pain by crying on *his* shoulder, not anyone else's. He was the only person she wanted to speak about his death, and the only one she could not.

'People who have relationships with people who can't commit, can't themselves commit,' Nina had said to her with stern eyes, was it only the day before? Well, she was committed now, Susan thought grimly. The question was, to what?

Two

REMEMBER ME

'Mourning is a reaction to the loss of a loved person. Reality-testing has shown that the loved object no longer exists, and it proceeds to demand that all libido shall be withdrawn from its attachments to that object. This demand arouses opposition [which] can be so intense that a turning away from reality takes place and a clinging to the object through the medium of hallucinatory wishful psychosis.'

Sigmund Freud, *Mourning and Melancholia*, 1917

12

Susan felt her mouth go dry as she entered the café and spotted Nina in a black velvet beret near the back. She paused for a moment by the door, waiting for her heart to stop thumping. She hadn't expected to feel like this. To have such an overwhelmingly powerful physical reaction at even the sight of Nina. For the room to spin and her legs to grow weak beneath her so that she had to rest a hand on the sloping glass counter momentarily for support. Or for the sheer weight of relief at seeing her. Next to Nina, in a red and gold tie and charcoal grey suit, was her friend, Jonathan Woolf. Susan had forgotten he was coming too. She fixed her features into a welcoming smile and began crossing the room.

The café was crowded. Squeezing past tables, she saw herself, slim, dark and serious, in the mirror covering one wall. I was here only a few days ago, she thought. In another world. She thought of her father's scarred face and a sick, incredulous feeling made her stomach lurch suddenly. 'Sorry I'm late,' she murmured, sitting down.

Nina glanced at her sharply, then tilted her face for Susan to kiss. 'You sounded terrible on the phone – I was expecting God knows what. How are you?'

'Better.'

'Actually you look fine. If you hadn't told me I wouldn't even have noticed.'

Susan wriggled her arms out of her jacket and hung it over the back of her chair, examining herself in the mirror opposite. Beneath the carefully applied make-up her left eye still had a dead look she thought. Perhaps it wasn't so noticeable to others.

Nina handed her the menu. 'She looks fine, doesn't she, Jonathan?'

Sitting half turned with one hand hanging over the back of the chair, Jonathan studied Susan across the table. 'A bit washed out. But Nina's right, it doesn't show whatever it was. What was it?'

'Bells Palsy, the doctor said.' Susan opened the menu without meeting his eye. 'What are you having?'

'Apple cake and a cappuccino,' Nina replied.

'I'll have the same,' Susan said, closing it again.

Jonathan shifted his chair closer to the table as Nina was ordering. In his expensive grey suit and flashy tie he didn't quite seem to fit into the café's plain wooden chair. He was, like Nina, a solicitor. He smiled at Susan. 'Did you get any of my messages?' he asked. 'I left a whole bunch on your answering machine.'

'I got one, I think. About three months ago.'

'Only one?'

'Maybe two. My machine's broken. You've shaved off your moustache, Jonathan. It suits you.'

'Think so?'

'You look younger.'

Clearly pleased, he stroked his bare upper lip, thrusting his chest forward slightly and opening a button of his jacket to reveal a perfectly white starched shirt. He was in his mid-thirties with straight black hair parted to one side and large, beautiful brown eyes.

'How's the business going?' she asked politely.

He heaved a theatrical sigh. 'Oh, it's all gone wrong.'

'Really? It was going so well. What happened?'

'Matthew's what happened.'

'But he's still in the practice?'

'No.'

'He's left the practice?'

'Exactly.'

'How awful – why?'

But Susan didn't really listen to his answer. Sitting with her hands in her lap, looking into Jonathan's face and nodding politely every now and then, she heard his words without taking in their meaning. A dream? she was thinking. I could as soon assert – sooner – that Jonathan isn't sitting here now, in the chair opposite me, talking about the split from his partner Matthew and the immanent collapse of his law firm.

'...*with an overdraft of ninety-seven thousand pounds...*'

As soon assert that Nina isn't sitting next to him looking suitably outraged.

'*Ninety-seven thousand? You must be worried sick.*'

'*Oh, I was, Nina, I was. But then I thought, I'm not working, I'm worrying – irritable bowel, ulcers, migraine, you name it, I had it. So then I thought...*'

It was an effort even trying to look interested. Susan wondered why she'd come. Wouldn't she have been better simply cancelling the whole thing? But she needed Nina's help, she reminded herself. Needed it to begin unraveling her experiences of the other night, one way or another. And she must do it fast, before she lost her nerve. In the meantime, whatever she felt like underneath, on the surface at least, she must appear totally normal. Totally.

'*... The trouble was the other two conveyancers suddenly stopped producing any money.*'

'*What do you mean, suddenly stopped?*'

'Just that – they weren't producing any fees. I had a business at the end of February with…'

There was no point in hiding away, helplessly replaying the night in the studio over and over again, or taking to her bed as she'd done for the first twenty-four hours. No point in going over and over the possible explanations, each as gut-wrenching a cul de sac as the other. She had to act, whatever the outcome. A faint, determined smile appeared on her face, misinterpreted by Jonathan as a deepening fascination with the story of his downfall.

'… though the problems have nothing to do with Matthew leaving, that work's been replaced, I've stopped worrying about it actually…'

For Susan their voices provided a soothing background for her ruminations. Too late, she realised that Jonathan was smiling across the table at her, clearly having just asked a question. She stared back at him blankly. Luckily Nina answered for her. 'She hasn't got one at the moment.'

One what? A boyfriend? A job?

Jonathan leaned back as far as he safely could in his chair and smiled encouragingly. 'No? The last time I saw you I think you were taking pictures for a dotcom.'

'Oh, was I?' Susan responded, realising what the question must have been. 'I'm not working for them anymore.'

'And now?'

'A bit of freelancing.'

'She's not even looking for work,' Nina stated.

'Well, it must be ages since I last saw you because I shaved off my moustache months ago. It must have been before – ' He stopped, suddenly realising.

'It was last November,' Susan confirmed. Her heart was suddenly beating fast. 'At my father's funeral.'

'The stone setting's in three weeks,' Nina put in.

Jonathan's face grew serious. 'Is it a year already?'

'Yes. It is.'

Susan's heart was still racing but she was at least outwardly calm. Over by the till she could see a man collecting his change from the waitress. He pulled on his raincoat. The woman next to him placed manicured nails on his sleeve. Long painted nails, red as blood. The door swung shut behind them sending a cold breath of air through the café.

'What time is it?' Jonathan asked.

Susan stared at him blankly. 'I'm afraid I don't wear a watch.'

He said gently: 'I meant the stone setting.'

'Oh. Eleven-thirty.'

'Where? Bushey?'

'Golders Green.'

'On Sunday the twenty-seventh,' offered Nina.

Jonathan took a fountain pen from inside his jacket, uncapped it and scribbled on a paper napkin. As he was slipping the pen back there was a dull vibrating sound. He pulled out a mobile phone so small, not even the size of his palm when it was open, that Susan only realised what it was when he said into it: 'Tell him to send it straight back again. Yes, by bike. What do you think – by carrier pigeon?' And as the waitress began setting out a piece of cheesecake and a coffee in front of him, 'Alright, e-mail him then – tell him,' he bent his arm so that the cuff drew back, exposing the gold watch on his wrist, 'tell him twelve o' clock. What? Well, he'll just have to be a bit more patient, won't he? Damn,' he groaned, snapping the phone shut. 'I'll have to get back to the office straightaway.'

'On a Saturday? Good timing,' Nina said, pulling a face. 'Drink your coffee at least.'

'Can't.' Grabbing his keys from the table, he stood up. 'An overdraft waits for no man.' He looked at the cheesecake longingly and sighed. 'I'm on a diet anyway.' He bent to kiss Nina's cheek, then Susan's. 'I'll pay on my way out.'

'Bye, Jonathan.'

They didn't talk for a moment after he left. Susan bit into the apple cake. It had a bottom layer of custard and tasted of burnt almonds and cinnamon. She picked at the pastry with her fork for a bit longer, then gave up and put the fork down. She felt too queasy to eat anything and there was a dull ache behind her temples. She reached in her bag for a cigarette. Nina pulled a face and pushed the ashtray towards her. 'What's the matter with you?' she asked, with more aggression than concern in her voice. 'You don't seem all here today.'

'I'm a bit tired, that's all.'

'You're getting up too late in the mornings. Apart from anything else, it's demoralising. I meant what I said just now, you know.'

'About what?'

'Looking for work. You have to start getting your act together. You have to find something new. How long's it been?'

'I don't know. Four, five months.'

'Much longer. You weren't working when I joined Fishburn Boxer and that was six months ago. It really isn't going to look very good on your CV, is it? You'll be lucky to get a job if you wait too long.' Nina picked up her fork, then put it down again, frowning impatiently. 'Oh, I can't eat with my hat on.' She pulled off the beret and shook out her hair. 'That's better.'

Squashing the hat in her lap, she took a forkful of cake. 'You have to begin picking up the pieces,' she said through a mouthful. 'I know it was a terrible thing about your father – terrible,' she repeated, seeing the look on Susan's face, 'but you have to start living a normal life again.'

For something to do, Susan drank the rest of her cappuccino, then swivelled round, looking for the waitress. 'Oh, it's the blonde one. I'll never get her attention. She always makes a quite deliberate point of ignoring me. Look, Nina, she's cut her hair.'

Nina glanced over. 'It looked better before. So what are you going to do?' she persisted.

'Haven't the faintest.'

'What about journalism?'

'I hated journalism. And I was a lousy journalist. You have to ask these questions all the time.'

'Well, of course you do. That's what reporting is.'

'But it's so intrusive. If you're too nice the piece is boring, if you're not, it's interesting but, oh, so cruel.'

'Can't you do something with your degree?'

'Like what?'

'Teach. I should think they'd snap you up.'

'I'm afraid it isn't really like that.'

'You should make enquiries.'

'I have. It isn't so easy.'

'Well, your photographs then. Surely you could do something with those? I could help. Talk to people – perhaps some of your father's friends? Mmm, this cake is good. You're not eating any more?'

'I will in a minute.' Susan played with her fork defensively. She makes everything sound like an accusation, she sighed inwardly, even eating cake.

'If there's anything I can do about the photographs you just need to ask.'

Nina's face, peaceful and self-absorbed as she munched, moved momentarily out of focus, then regained its normal lines. Shut up! Susan wanted to shout. The thought of even picking up a camera made her feel sick and Nina, marching in hobnailed boots over something so sensitive, made her feel even worse. 'It's very sweet of you, Nina,' she said, unable to keep a hint of irritation out of her voice, 'but not right now. Perhaps in month or so.'

'Well, don't leave it too long. There's no point in sitting at home brooding.'

'You sound like my mother,' Susan said with a faint smile.

Nina didn't answer.

'Actually there is something you can do for me,' Susan said, after a moment. 'There is something actually.' She took a deep breath. 'I need a private detective.'

'A detective?' Nina stopped eating, her fork in mid-air.

I should have been more casual, Susan thought. Not blurted it out like it was the most important thing in the universe. 'Do you know of a good one?' she inquired more lightly. 'I thought you might, being in a reputable law firm.'

'Why?'

'Why?'

'Yes, why do you want a detective? Do you want to check out Paul?'

Susan gave a startled smile. 'What would I want to check him out for?'

'Or his wife?'

'She's not his – anyway, it's nothing like that.'

'Well? What then?'

Susan hesitated, covering up the delay by making a fuss of lighting the cigarette she was holding and taking a drag. 'I need someone to investigate my father's business affairs,' she said finally, directing at Nina a look of mingled anxiety and mistrust through the smoke.

'Since when have you been interested in your father's business?'

This wasn't a good idea, Susan thought. Asking Nina was a really bad idea. Why hadn't she tried looking on the net for a detective? Or even Yellow Pages. There were probably pages and pages of agencies listed under D if only she had looked. She could have taken a chance on finding one that was any good.

She reached across for Jonathan's abandoned cup of coffee.

'I hope that this sudden interest isn't due to another feeling you have,' Nina said sternly. 'Because if so, forget it. Private investigators aren't cheap. Don't waste your money.'

A bad idea. Terrible even. Susan knew that she shouldn't say any more but she could feel the conversation dragging her in like a net. 'Let's just say I have reasons for believing that something illegal has been going on,' she said, trying to sound stern and confident in her turn but succeeding only in sounding high-pitched and querulous to her own ears. 'And I'd like to check it out.'

Nina stared at her unblinking.

'I simply want to eliminate some of the alternatives. I want proof – either yes or no,' Susan said, meeting her gaze. But her stomach lurched as she spoke. Yes or no? Either way I'm fucked, she thought. She slid the cup towards her and took a gulp.

Nina grimaced at the cup. 'That must taste perfectly revolting by now. I'll get you another one.' She gestured across the café to the waitress, then turned back to Susan. 'You've been acting very oddly all morning. Your voice sounds very strange. I suppose now you've intuited something wrong with your father's business? Got another feeling, have you?' She gave a small, unfriendly smile. 'I mean, what's the point of wasting money checking the company out now? Your father's not around to run it any longer. I know that sounds harsh, but who else is there to worry about?'

Susan only shrugged helplessly.

Nina's eyes widened. 'Oh, my God. This isn't about Paul, is it – it's Nick. You want the private detective for Nick. You think he's involved in something illegal and that – ' She stopped, an expression of dismay crossing her face. 'This is all linked in your mind, isn't it? In some strange, paranoid sort of way you've managed to twist it all round so that somehow it all seems to you connected. The phone calls, the man who's supposed to be following you, the suspicions about something nasty in the woodshed – ' She glanced up with a slight smile as the waitress put two cups down on the table. 'Thanks. Tell me,' she demanded, once they were alone again. 'Who is this investigator you're hiring supposed to be investigating?' She drank a mouthful of cappuccino, grimaced, then stirred in a spoonful of sugar.

'It isn't Nick.'

'So it is!'

'I just said that it's not! This has nothing whatever to do with Nick,' Susan said, wishing she'd never begun. She tried to pitch her voice precisely – hurt but not amazed, with a deliberate dash of indignation. 'Look, you were right – it's Paul,' she said, lying badly, and too late, she thought. 'I felt a bit silly so I said that it wasn't but, in fact, I want a detective to find out if he, or preferably Julia, have been seeing anyone else so that – '

'Bullshit!' Nina said. 'I can always tell when you're lying. You're a lousy liar – your eyes sort of shift about. You have a particular liar's look. So you think – what? That Nick's had you followed? That he's been phoning in the early hours and hanging up? Why would he *do* that, Susan? What would be the point? Even if he were engaged in something shady – which I don't for a moment believe he is – what would he gain from it?'

Susan did not answer. Let Nina believe what she wanted: it was better that way.

'This isn't amusing anymore.'

'It isn't supposed to be,' Susan replied, giving up.

'You think that Nick – Nick! Your father's brother – was involved in – This is crazy! Actually, worse than crazy. It's quite sickening, I feel quite sick. The police have already been over all this. At the time they investigated the whole damn company. Didn't they?'

'Yes, they did.'

'So why are you concerning yourself with this again now? If there was anything to find don't you think they would have found it? There was nothing. Nick was clean. They were all clean.'

'Listen –'

'No! I've listened enough. Now *you* listen to *me*! You're talking about your uncle, your father's own brother. Do you think that your father would be happy if he knew you were behaving like this?'

Susan didn't reply. What could she say – yes?

'The truth is that you don't want to eliminate anything. You simply want to *prove* Nick's crooked.'

Again Susan did not speak. Was it true? Did she? A chill ran through her. Because if Nick was guilty – then what?

'You have to let go of this,' Nina said urgently, keeping her voice low. They were, after all, in a crowded café. 'It's doing you terrible harm. It's clear that you've become obsessed with Nick because he's romantically involved with your mother –'

'No! I –'

Nina raised her hand. 'Let me finish. You have to face the fact that you're obsessed with him because he's having an affair with Isabella. Look, I know it's difficult happening so soon after your father's death. I understand.'

You don't, Susan thought.

'But the fact is,' Nina went on, 'it's all been too much for you. I'm sorry to be so blunt. But you're twisting everything, don't you see?'

'Please believe me,' Susan said desperately. 'I can't tell you what my reasons are but they're good ones, honestly.' But even to herself her voice sounded disjointed and unconvincing. Nina only stared at her. 'I'm not a bloody jigsaw puzzle,' Susan snapped.

'What?'

'Oh, forget it.'

Susan felt suddenly overwhelmingly sad. For the first time she realised fully how much what had happened had set her apart – from the whole human race, it felt like. The tables around them were filled with people who acted like the most important decision they would ever bother to make was whether to have a poppy seed pretzel or an apple slice. Susan could remember feeling the same way herself. It seemed a long time ago now. 'Oh, Nina,' she said miserably.

'Why are you so against Nick? He's so bloody *nice* to you. Why are you determined to find fault with him? Well, we know why,' Nina answered her own question, 'but it's really not a good enough reason for bringing in a detective. Having sex with your ex-in-laws isn't a criminal offence, you know.'

Susan's feeling of misery evaporated abruptly. 'Look, I don't give a shit whether you believe me or not. There's no reason on earth why you should, except a decade of friendship and trust and clearly that isn't enough.' She picked up her cappuccino and drank without tasting. 'I should go. I'd better go, there's really no point in staying any longer. We'll only argue if I do.' She put the cup down.

But before she could get to her feet, Nina said quietly, 'Did you know that Isabella phoned me?'

Susan looked startled. 'Of course I didn't know. Where? At work?'

'She's worried about you, very naturally.'

'Where?' Susan asked again. 'At Fishburn Boxer? I didn't think she had any idea you'd recently moved jobs.'

'What does it matter where? She phoned me.'

'Where?' Susan persisted.

'If you must know – at home.'

'But you're ex-directory. How did she get your number?'

Nina did not answer straightaway. 'Nick asked me for it the other night,' she replied coldly, after a moment.

Susan stared at her. 'Nick asked for your number? You gave him your telephone number? Why didn't you tell me before?'

Nina shrugged. 'I know how strongly you feel about him. You said he's a bastard. You're always saying he's a bastard. I thought,' she glanced at her sideways with a sly expression Susan hadn't seen or noticed before. 'I thought it might upset you.'

'You're damn right it upsets me!' Susan retorted furiously. It was like a hand had gripped her stomach and twisted it hard. Around her the café felt like it had shifted, slightly but significantly. The colours were a little different: the faces around her - talking, smiling, mouths open, teeth bared - looked yellower, their expressions suddenly sinister. She reached for the cup, hoping that the feel of a solid object would bring her back to earth. Her fingers closed around the handle but she did not pick it up.

'She phoned because she's worried about you,' she heard Nina say. 'Very worried. You can't really blame her, can you? She sees that you have too much time on your hands. Too much time to brood. She asked if I could help find you a job. Something in my company, she suggested.'

'Oh, great!'

'She's right, you know. You do have too much free time. After the events of the past year anyone would go crazy without the structure of work.'

'I thought you were my friend,' Susan said in a low voice.

'I *am* your friend, of course I am, that's why I spoke to her, actually.' She shot Susan a quick, darting glance. 'You see, I'm a little worried, too.'

Susan had a sudden thought that made her grow cold. 'You didn't tell her about the phone calls?'

'Oh no.'

'Or the feeling of being watched?'

Nina shifted uncomfortably in her seat. 'Not exactly.'

'You told her.'

'I kind of referred to it – but very indirectly.'

'Oh, Nina! That was all in the strictest confidence.'

'I know, I *know*. And normally I wouldn't dream… But the circumstances were a little unusual, you have to admit, and – well, I wasn't sure what to do… And yes, I told her,' Nina finished defiantly. 'I think if our positions were reversed you would have done the same.'

The waitress had taken the old cups from the table. Susan forced herself to pick up the fresh cup and her hand was fairly steady. Congratulations Susan, she thought furiously. Excellent work so far, top marks for discretion. I missed my vocation in life: I should have taken up poker. As she drank, she kept her eyes on the marble table-top. She felt the anger in them would burn a hole in Nina's face if she lifted them too soon. *Stupid, so stupid*. How stupid to think she could safely confide in Nina. Well, it's too late now, she thought. I must stay cool, I mustn't show her how upset I really am. Thank God I was wise enough to keep quiet about the rest. A walking, talking corpse? A ghost? That would have really given her a good laugh. She asked in as friendly a voice as she could manage: 'What else did my mother say?'

'That you never talk to her. She complains that you always keep her in the dark. She knows we're close so she thought perhaps she should speak to me instead.' Nina's voice was smooth but, underneath the silkiness, she was defensive. 'I wasn't sure what to say or do in response – which is unusual for me, you must admit.' She gave an edgy laugh. 'It was all extremely difficult. She was nice about it, very apologetic.'

'I bet.'

'She said how sorry she was to involve me in her family's affairs but she was at her wits' end. There were things she felt she had to know.'

'Like what?'

'She asked if you were drinking too much,' Nina continued in the same hateful, cool, condescending manner. 'Well, you are, aren't you? Ever since your father's death you've really gone at everything as if there's no tomorrow. And she wanted to know if you were seeing anyone regularly. If there was a man in the picture, as she put it.'

Susan placed her cup carefully down in the saucer.

'I didn't tell her about Paul,' Nina said quickly. 'I suggested she ask you.'

'That was good of you,' Susan said dryly.

'Well, I couldn't see the relevance to her anxieties about your – ' Nina hesitated, 'your mental state.' She stretched a hand across the table and placed it over Susan's. 'She only wants to help, you know.'

The touch of Nina's hand on her skin made Susan flinch inside but she made herself wait a few seconds before moving away. 'And Nick?' she asked, trying to keep her voice calm. 'Has he phoned you?'

'Not yet.'

'And if he does?'

Nina twisted a strand of bright hair round her finger, then began slowly flicking the ends against her cheek. 'He's just being friendly, Susan.'

She always plays with her hair in that moronic way when she's thinking of flirting with a man, Susan thought viciously. 'What about Ian?' she asked, her voice husky with suppressed disgust. 'I thought you were engaged.'

'Yes, well things aren't going so well in that department.'

'You never mentioned it before.'

'No.' Nina examined the pale polish on her nails, picking a fragment of pink from her cuticle with her thumbnail. 'He does care about you, you know. Nick, I mean. I don't think you realise how much.'

'Oh, I realize.' Susan closed her eyes. 'Nina, you have no idea…' she said huskily. 'There are certain things about Nick… things I've never told you… things I've never told anyone… ' She opened them again. 'You don't know him.'

'No, but I'd like to,' Nina replied coldly. 'I suppose you'd mind that too.'

'Mind? Nina, if you got involved with Nick in any capacity I'd – ' Susan stopped. The desire to smash her fist into her best friend's smug face was so overwhelmingly strong that she was taken aback by the power of it. She hadn't felt such pure, unadulterated rage since she was a child. Her nerves were already stretched to breaking point by the last few days but somehow she managed to resist the impulse. She gripped her hands together under the table. Forcing herself to speak quietly, she said: 'How can you? How can you take their side?'

'Oh, don't be so melodramatic. This isn't a conspiracy. It's what happens when grown-ups are brought together. No one can predict what the outcome will be, or afterwards control it. It was you who introduced us, actually. Look, your mother and Nick are genuinely concerned. And I wasn't sure what to do because – Let's face it. They do have reason to worry, don't they? I mean, having sex with every man in north London who asks isn't going to help you get over your father's death, is it?'

93

Nina's plump, pink hand was lying on the table. Her grin was small and sharp. Faced with this smug smile Susan could no longer control the strength of her anger. She grabbed the hand and squeezed so hard that her nails dug into the soft flesh. She heard Nina's sharp intake of breath, heard her protest and say her name or something. When she let go several small, bright red crescents had appeared on the skin, one bleeding slightly.

'Worry? I'll give you reason to fucking worry!' she heard herself hiss, seeing Nina's shocked face pull away from her. She stood up, knowing that she'd gone too far, that she'd passed over the line of what Nina thought of as civilised behaviour, but not caring. Pulling her jacket off the back of the chair she caught the lining – there was a slight ripping sound. She could see her own twisted features in the mirror as she stumbled out of the café, over feet, pram wheels, towards the exit. The people at the table nearest the door casually turned their heads as she rushed past and pushed the door open, the cold air striking her as she ran across the road without looking. Where had she left the car? Where was the damn car? She heard Nina's voice behind her, rising on the air. 'Su-san!'

The sight of the blue Mini was like coming home. She gave a sob of relief as she twisted the key in the lock, started the engine and shot off up the road, ignoring the small figure in the black coat and beret waving and shouting her name.

There is no such thing as friendship, Susan told herself fiercely. There are just the people you love and would do anything for, and the others. The ones that you know in your heart you wouldn't save at any risk to yourself because they are the ones who wouldn't save you. Except that sometimes you didn't know the difference until the final moment; the moment of crisis, when you are sinking beneath the water for the third time. Oh, Nina! Beautiful, golden Nina with her cheekbones and clever talk and graceful ways. With her clear blue eyes and sure hands and understanding of the workings of the world.

There are only the people you love and would do anything for, and the rest...

She was sinking, she was drowning, Nina, help...

When she reached home she sat without taking off her jacket. Then, her hands and toes tingling, she picked up the phone and stabbed in a number. At the other end the answering machine clicked on. '*This is 020 7794 6283, Isabella Savage speaking. If you'd like to leave a message, please speak after the long beep stating the time, day and date of your call...*'

Susan disconnected the call then pressed more buttons. First 141, to make sure that she couldn't be traced, then the number. Nick's message was shorter. '*This is Nick. You can leave a message or send a –* '

'Hello?' Nick's deep voice cut across his recorded message. 'Hello? Who is this?'

Susan didn't speak. She could hear him breathing down the phone. She did not say a word until she had replaced the receiver. She did it carefully as if he might otherwise guess who had been on the other end of the line. Then, staring ahead, her hands on her knees in the familiar way, she smiled. 'Hello, Nick,' she said into darkness.

The child was fair. Her hair would eventually darken into golden brown and grow straight but at this age she was still blonde with wavy hair her mother tied into pigtails. There were red ribbons in her hair, two identical pieces, one at the end of each plait, with the ends carefully snipped into V's. She had done it herself with sharp scissors, her mother had let her, two deep cuts into red so that the ribbon wouldn't fray. And tights, red tights, not black, her mother had said no to black. I don't care what the other girls do, you are not wearing black at your age, red or blue or green, if you're not careful you can wear socks.

Her legs encased in ribbed tights wriggling in front of her, her dress riding up to her waist as he tickled her, laughing, squeezing, as she sat on his lap, the rough warmth of him. His hands held her firmly against him, familiar hands, familiar skin, like Daddy's. 'My hands are like daddy's, are they?' he said teasingly, smoothing her hair. 'You love your daddy, don't you?' Daddy darling, daddy darling. She said yes, though she didn't understand the expression in his eyes, didn't much like it. But she kissed him when he asked her, licked his lips with her warm tongue, and agreed to tell no one, especially Daddy. Because it felt nice when he did that thing inside her tights with his hand. She wanted more, she wanted it to never end. She pressed round and round with flushed cheeks, her breathing laboured, searching with her body for the place where pleasure begins and ends but could not find it, did not know then, or care, that she never would. Her hot body pressing down against him, his hands moving over her, trousers rough.

'You like to be tickled, darling, don't you?' he whispered when they were alone. That look in his eyes, when they were alone. 'I know. You like it, don't you, sweetheart?' Dark eyes smiling down into hers, stroking, pinching her nipples, fondling her aching new breasts. Her hair was darker now, she wore skirts and sheer black tights. His touch made her shudder. She pretended not to understand when he pressed against her, his big bastard cock rubbing against her.

After that, she was never alone with him. She never told anyone, but she made sure she was never alone with him again.

On Tuesday morning a letter from Nina came in the post. A card with 'Compliments from Nina Shooke' printed on it and a name and phone number scrawled across the bottom in turquoise ink. Above it, Nina had written a few lines: 'I hope you can understand my motives for speaking to your mother. I understand how upsetting any interference from your family must seem to you but please try and understand my position too. I have been very worried about you over the last few weeks and I think your behavior in the café was inexcusable. I am enclosing the number of an investigator recommended by a colleague, though I still think this is a mistake. It's your life, as they say. I think it would be better for both of us if we did not see each other for the time being.' Underneath her name she had crossed something out. It looked like – You should see a doctor. The word 'urgently' remained fairly clear.

She's used 'understand' three times, Susan thought. She dropped the card straight in the bin. *Understand, understand, understand…*

Hunger, tiredness, anxiety and the dizzying events of the last week were taking their toll. Susan made herself an instant coffee but the hand that topped it up with a hefty dose of whisky was unsteady. I've blown it, she thought, wincing at the memory of Nina's plump hand with the five small red moons her nails had made on the skin. As far as she's concerned, I've gone completely off the rails. I was allowed to have problems before – actually I was supposed to. But not such strange and spooky ones. Not ones that seem so crazy.

It's my own fault, she told herself. I chose this kind of friendship – I insisted on it. Let's face it, for the past year it's suited me very well. And when the chips were down, I paid the price. She's more like my mother than I ever allowed myself to realise. Nina senses weakness then moves in for the jugular. Look out if she's wearing stiletto heels. She'll elbow me off the lifeboat to get to Nick. In the case of a desirable man, our friendship doesn't count for a bean. She'll betray me in a flash.

Susan didn't bother with coffee next time but slopped the whisky neat into a mug, balancing the bottle in front on her on the kitchen table. The good old kitchen table, she thought, pouring another drink down her throat. Where would I be without you? Ha. Sipping coffee in mid air.

'I'll drink to that,' she toasted aloud, raising the mug in the air before draining it. The bottle, bought the day before, was already two thirds empty. Or a third full, depending how you look at it, she thought, swirling the amber liquid in the air to check. She swayed pleasantly as she walked upstairs, one hand on the banister, the other holding the bottle's neck.

'Stick to the facts,' she instructed herself, talking aloud to her reflection in the bathroom mirror. 'One, she is selfish.' She held up a finger. 'Two, superficial. Three, she likes feeling superior to me. Our friendship is summed up by the fact that – ' Susan rested her hands against the edge of the sink and leant forward so that her breath left a circle of mist on the glass, 'she enjoys feeling patronising and I enjoy being patronised.'

But in the mirror her face looked suddenly sober. She could see only fear and anxiety reflected there.

And Paul? she asked herself silently, staring close-up at her anxious reflection. What about that? Just another escape route from pain?

When in doubt, have sex, Susan told herself, reaching for the phone. When he answered, she asked, her voice low: 'Can I see you?'

He hesitated. 'When?'

'Tonight?'

Another pause. 'Hang on. I'll have to check… Yes,' he confirmed after a moment. 'Yes, that's OK.'

'What time?'

'Eight o'clock. Here.'

Her breathing was too shallow and rapid as she replied: 'See you tonight then.'

'Yeah,' Paul said. 'See you later.'

During lovemaking, Paul's face and lips would grow pale, his pupils huge and black, as if the intensity of their pleasure was a violent shock to his system. Susan sometimes imagined she could see his heart beating, a quick pulse throbbing between his ribs. He was fine featured with hazel-brown eyes and thin, sensitive lips and, though tall and his hands and wrists large, the overall impression was of fragility. Good-looking in a cool English way, not a type she had particularly liked before they had met but, 'he grows on you,' she had sighed to Nina in one of their interminable conversations about Paul.

'He's a cold fish,' Nina had decided a few months on. 'He's much too old for you and he doesn't treat you well enough. Give him up.'

'But I love him.'

'You always think that.'

'No, really. This time it's – different.'

Nina looked skeptical. 'Yes?'

'And I think he's in love with me, too.'

'Oh *love*. What does that mean? It's not *whether* he loves you but how he treats you if he does.'

'Julia's supposed to be moving out,' Susan said defensively, 'but she never seems to do much about it.'

'*He* could move out, you know. He's the one having the affair.'

'It's his *house*, Nina. It was left to him by his grandmother. He can't just give it to Julia. Besides they've agreed. She's supposed to be finding somewhere.'

'Who knows what's really going on between them? You only know what he's told you. If he really loved you he wouldn't care where he lived. He would just want to be with you properly.'

'You talk like everything is black and white. It's not so easy for him. He worries about Julia. He feels guilty. He wants her to be happy.'

'And you? What about you? Oh, give him up, Susan, before it's too late.'

'It's too late already,' Susan answered miserably. 'I think about him all the time. I've tried but I *can't* give him up.'

Nina shook her head. 'Sex is a funny thing,' she replied, a little enviously.

Susan was thinking of this as she turned off Tottenham Court Road, heading briskly for Paul's design studio in Soho, but Nina's more recent voice kept on breaking into her reverie. '*I'm worried about you… we're all very worried… your mental state is of some concern. You're drinking much too much and your thinking is – well, frankly it's become really bizarre…*' Susan's pace did not falter. It was true she'd been drinking too much since her father's death. It was also true that she had no intention of talking to Paul about the events of the last few days. She'd never done before and she had no intention of starting now. She'd always shut the door firmly on what she thought of, when she was with him, as her 'other' life. That wasn't why she hurried up the street, not even glancing at the shop windows, already decorated for Christmas. To drown herself in the oblivion of Paul's arms – that's what she intended. To lose herself in sex – rid herself of all thought and memory. What were the words of the song? *Don't use sex as a weapon*? But it was the only one she felt she had, the only defence against death and loss and pain. The more fearful she became, the more she wished to lose herself, submerge herself completely in that wild and stormy sea. If anything, her desire for him over the last week had become greater. Walking quickly up the street, she knew in her heart that there was very little real satisfaction for her with Paul and that afterwards she'd only need him even more. But, for the moment, there was the promise, however false, of pleasure. For a brief ecstatic time she could be free of anxiety. The external world would simply disappear. They'd exist in their own little world, as they always did. There would be just the physical moment and her and Paul.

Tomorrow, she promised herself. She'd start thinking about it again properly tomorrow. Perhaps start looking seriously for a detective, though without any help from Nina Shooke, this time. Any worries she'd put off till then. Her stomach lurched as she remembered the finality of the argument they'd had in the cafe, and the reason why; recalled the simplicity and ease of Nina's betrayal. She'd have to get used to life without Nina but she'd miss her – yes, even her nagging.

She turned left into Soho Square. There was a smile of anticipation on her lips as she bounded up the stairs two at a time. If nothing else, Nina was right about one thing. Love? What did that mean? The chance for someone to treat you as badly as they liked? Oh, yes. Oh, yes, yes, *yes*…

16

There were 2,944 entries under 'Private Detective – London' on the net when Susan used Google the next morning. *'If you have a problem, a crisis, or just a suspicion give us a call,'* she read, scrolling through Howatt's UK Agents. *'We'll tell you exactly what action we would propose, what we would charge, and what results you can expect, and by when.'* She ruled out The Meridion Bureau Ltd. on the basis of appalling copy – *'we serving the papers, we trace the culprits, we finding the answers'* – and scrolled down Elite Investigations Ltd which offered services for *'Fraud (Ex Fraud Squad), Matrimonial, Civil and Criminal Enquiries and Process Serving,'* assuring her they were *'private and discreet'* and *'members of the Institute of Professional Investigators'*.

Susan rubbed her forehead. She was feeling a little the worse for wear after a long night with Paul. She had a throbbing pain behind her temples that had grown worse as soon as she'd switched on the computer. She felt confused, lost: what was she doing? She wasn't even sure what she was asking a detective to find *out*.

Staring indecisively at the scribbled list she'd made, she felt a momentary stab of regret that she'd thrown away the postcard from Nina and considered searching through the rubbish. Then she thought of another lawyer she could ask. She looked up a number in her filofax, picked up the phone and, after a moment's hesitation, dialled. 'Jonathan Woolf, please.'

'Who shall I say is calling?' asked a bored female voice on the other end.

'Susan Savage.'

'One moment, please.'

She sat slowly coiling the phone wire round her index finger till she heard Jonathan's voice on the other end – pleased, faintly surprised. 'Susan Savage... This is an unexpected pleasure. How nice to hear from you. How are you?'

'I'm OK. And you?'

He sighed. 'Oh, don't even ask. Look, there's someone on the other line. Can you hang on a for one second? Don't go away – I shan't be a...' The line went dead. After a minute, Jonathan's voice reappeared. 'Sorry about that. What can I do for you? Is this a business call or purely pleasure?'

'Mostly business,' Susan admitted. 'Actually I'm in the process of hiring a private detective,' she said, trying to sound as if it were the most natural thing in the world. 'The trouble is that I don't actually know any by reputation and I would hate to waste anyone's time – ' she gave a forced laugh, 'but I need some information dreadfully fast, by yesterday actually – ' She gave another high laugh. That's not a laugh, she thought, that's a neigh. I'm actually neighing. I sound like my mother – my mother at her most affected. 'So I thought of you because under the circs - ' The *circs*? Oh, come on, Susan. She finished in a more normal voice: 'I wasn't quite sure what to do.'

'What you do is, you ask me,' Jonathan replied promptly. 'Do you want me to fix up a meeting?'

'Oh, could you?'

'No trouble. How soon do you want it?'

'As soon as possible.'

'We use a firm called – oh, MCI Investigations or something. They've aways been pretty good. I'll phone you straight back.'

The phone rang five minutes later.

'This afternoon at three,' Jonathan said immediately. 'Why don't you come to the office first? You remember where we are? The intelligence agency is just round the corner. Two o' clock suit you?'

'Two would be great. Thanks. Thanks, Jonathan.'

'So why the private dick?'

She sat opposite Jonathan, her feet on his thick olive green carpet, her back pressed against the firm green leather chair. His feet were up on the polished mahogany desk in front of him, his hands behind his head, elbows wide. 'Getting married?'

Susan smiled a little tensely, taking a sip of coffee from a bone china cup. 'Oh, no.'

'Thank God for that. I'm still in with a chance.'

'You're already married.'

'Only because you wouldn't have me. We were walking along New Cavendish Street and you told me you could never feel romantically interested because I was too serious about you. Remember?'

'No, I don't actually.'

'Well, I'm hurt. Cut to the quick.'

She laughed uneasily, not quite sure whether he was serious or not. Hopefully, he was just being flirtatious.

'I thought you might be planning to marry someone dodgy and want to check him out before the big day,' he probed.

'This isn't California, Jonathan. People don't do that kind of thing here.'

'You'd be surprised. Things are changing. Even in good old Britain there's something called a 'peace of mind report'. Sounds nice doesn't it? Peace of mind… ' Legs on the desk, ankles crossed, he examined the toe of one gleaming brown shoe. 'I don't suppose it would help the victim's peace of mind though, once they learnt of it. What do you want an agency for?'

Susan looked at him, wondering if Nina had said anything to him about their last conversation. She would have said definitely not a few days ago, now she wasn't so sure. Discretion would be pointless if she had. 'This is all in the strictest confidence, isn't it?'

'I'm a solicitor – "in confidence" is my second name.' He leant back precariously in his chair. 'Well, second and third names.'

'Of course I'll pay you.'

'That won't be necessary.'

'No, really. How much do you charge for a consultation?'

'Forget it.' He tipped the chair back a little further.

'That's very kind of you, Jonathan. You know,' she pointed out after a moment, 'you look pretty silly balancing like that, especially in that incredibly smart suit. You'll fall.'

'It's a rather comfortable position actually.' But he lifted his feet off the desk and put them on the floor, letting the chair tip slowly forward and sat up, straightening his brown and cream tie.

Susan examined him critically. 'What do you wear at weekends nowadays?'

'Jeans, like anyone else.'

'But they're ironed, I bet. I bet your wife puts a crease down the front.'

'Certainly not. I look jolly cool actually.' He grinned. 'You should check me out when I'm not working one Saturday. Look, you don't have to tell me if you don't want to. But you're hiring me to help you, right? I just need to be sure that we've got the right firm for the job. I don't want to waste anyone's time. Am I mistaken or did I get the impression you're in rather a hurry?'

Susan took another sip of coffee, trying to decide how much she should tell him. She'd have to give him some idea; he was right, there wasn't much time. But how to do it without giving too much away? She felt a bit edgy about letting anything slip after the disastrous meeting with Nina. Still, she decided, he has agreed to treat this confidentially. 'I need someone to look into fraudulent activity in a company,' she said, choosing her words carefully.

'Is this your father's company?' he asked so quickly that she wondered again how much Nina had told him. She looked at him suspiciously. 'This is all in confidence?'

'Of course,' he assured her.

'Well, yes, it is.'

He picked up a pen. 'What exactly do you need investigating?'

'Fraudulent use of the company's accounts. But I don't have any details,' she added quickly.

He scribbled something on the notepad in front of him. 'Uh huh. How did you get your information?'

'My father left me a message,' she said, inventing quickly. 'A letter which only turned up a few days ago. Well, more of an unfinished note really. He told me – in this letter – that he'd discovered some discrepancies in the company records.'

Jonathan looked up sharply. 'He actually saw something?'

'Yes. But he didn't say what it was he saw or exactly where he saw it.' She pulled a face. 'Unfortunately.'

Shit, she thought, it sounded absurd. She wished, not for the first time, that her father had told her much more. Or much less. It had all been so vague. She added: 'I'm sorry I can't be more specific. It must sound pretty silly… '

'Not at all,' he said politely.

'I know that my father found evidence of a large sum of money where it shouldn't have been. I do know that.'

'Did he see the money?'

'No-o, not as such. But he saw something which showed him that it definitely existed. That's what he said anyway.' She frowned. 'In this letter.'

Jonathan grunted and wrote this down. 'You say you found the letter a few days ago,' he said, looking up. 'When was it written?'

She shook her head.

'Where did you find it? Can you show it to me?'

'Look, I don't want to go into details. And I can't show it to you. You'll just have to trust me on this, Jonathan.'

He looked thoughtfully at her.

'How long have you known me?'

'Long enough.'

'Well then,'

He looked at her for a moment longer, then shrugged. 'OK, fair enough.'

'What I *can* say is that my father saw evidence of a lot of money somewhere there shouldn't have been. But I don't know anything about how a business works so I have no idea what exactly he could have seen or where to begin looking for it. That's where I thought a good investigator could help.'

Jonathan put down his pen. 'Look, a private detective would be hopeless for this.'

She stared at him. 'What do you mean?'

'It's not like in books. In real life most of their work is really boring. They seldom get to follow people and all that stuff. They serve writs. Look into tricky dealings? They wouldn't even know how to begin.'

'I see.' Susan felt her stomach sink.

She took a gulp of coffee and, frowning, set the delicate cup carefully back in its saucer. 'But in their ads they say they'll investigate a company for fraud,' she protested after a moment.

'Well, you'd be wasting your money,' Jonathan replied firmly, putting the tips of his fingers together and regarding her dispassionately over them.

He's enjoying this, she thought, I'm sure he is. Watching me anxious, watching me squirm, knowing that he has the power to help, and withholding it. He gets me to rush all the way to his office for an instant coffee and then he turns round and says, forget it. But she gritted her teeth and forced herself to smile; gripping the arms of the chair, she asked cajolingly: 'So what do you think I should do, Jonathan?'

'I suppose it would be a little like the work we do prior to a divorce case,' he suggested, softening. 'But without the right to ask questions.'

'What do you do in a divorce case?'

'Mostly find out how much money the husband has. We get any business records out of Companies House and go through them to see what they represent, that kind of thing. Now here –' he picked up a fat pale blue folder that was lying in his tray, 'is an example. Goldman versus Goldman. We know that Mr Goldman's been dealing in land and property so we've got the title to all of his properties. Then we can find out if any of them have been bought or sold.' He flipped through the papers with interest. 'Hmm, there's a lot of money here, made by what means I know not.'

She frowned. 'I don't think that would be any good at all. It's much too public. I need to look at the stuff no one's seen before or bothered to check very thoroughly.'

'You could phone up the Inland Revenue and pretend you're the company in question, I suppose. But that would only work if you have the tax reference. You'd have to be pretty intimately acquainted with that side of the business.' He chucked the folder back in the tray. 'Are you?'

She shook her head.

'What about your mother?'

'I can't ask her.'

'Then it's no good. I mean, you can phone up the Revenue and say, can you just confirm that the accounts have come in, or something vague like that. But that's about it. You wouldn't get any detail.'

'There must be *something* I can do.'

He shrugged.

Sitting in his plush solicitor's office, Susan felt for the first time annoyed with her father. She'd felt a lot of things over the last week: despair, horror, disbelief; but not this before – frustration. If he'd had to come back from the grave to speak to her, she thought irritably, he could at least have given her something definite to go on. What did he expect from her anyway? The image of his face as she had last seen it rose before her, white, scarred, smashed beyond redemption… Her hand shook as she raised it to light a cigarette.

And all the time the nagging, unsettling thought in the background – what if none of it were true anyway? What if she'd invented the whole thing? There must be a way of finding out if there was any truth in his story, there must be.

'More coffee?' Jonathan asked, reaching for the phone.

He doesn't know what's at stake, she thought. He has no idea how terribly important this is – for my sanity, apart from anything. 'No, thanks,' she said shortly.

'Sure?'

She nodded. He picked up the phone and spoke into the receiver. 'Elaine? Got a minute? Well, when you have… Another coffee, please. White, two saccarines – yeah, it's for me. Your father owned a shipping company, didn't he?' he asked, when he'd replaced the receiver.

She nodded glumly. 'Yes.'

'Big?'

'Not especially. About fifteen or so staff.'

'Any partners?'

'One – his brother.' If he noticed the bitterness in her voice he didn't show it.

'So what do you think has been going on?'

'Drugs,' she replied, hoping to shake his indifference. She succeeded, at least in part. His eyebrows rose slightly, but his eyes didn't waver. 'In what way do you think your father's business is a cover for drugs?'

'I don't think it is. It was.'

'How?'

'Someone in the company. I don't know exactly how he did it, I just know that he did.'

'And you want to hire a detective to find out who and how?'

'Not who – I know who it is. But how.'

'How do you know?'

'What?'

'Who.'

'I'm sorry, Jonathan, but I really can't go into that.'

He shrugged. 'OK.'

'Anyway, it's unimportant. It doesn't matter how I know who. I just need to discover the way in which whoever it was who did it, did it. God, this is like a tongue twister.' She took a deep breath and said more slowly: 'What I need is the details showing exactly how it was done. I need proof. Apparently a lot of money was involved. I mean, a lot – millions.' She looked at Jonathan. 'Surely that would show up somewhere.'

'Well, as I told you, in real life a private detective would be clueless.'

'So I should give up before I even start? Is that what you're suggesting?'

'No, I'm not saying that.' His next question took her by surprise. 'Do you take drugs yourself, Susan?' he asked genially.

'What's that got to do with anything?' she said hotly. Furiously, she jumped to her feet. 'Shit! You've been talking to Nina! You're suggesting that I'm – what? Being paranoid? Or that I've imagined all this in some – some drug induced state?'

'Sit down, sit down,' Jonathan said, looking alarmed, waving his hands in a downward direction. 'For God's sake, just a question. I didn't mean to imply anything.'

'Have you been gossiping with Nina Shooke? Because if so – '

'No, no, I haven't, of course I haven't. Forget I even asked. I didn't put it very well. I'm sorry. Come on, sit down. Please.'

She stared at him with angry eyes. She wanted to storm out of the room but she knew that if she did she'd lose any chance of getting the assistance she badly needed. She simply couldn't afford to be too touchy. Running out is becoming a habit, she thought, and a bad one. Restraining herself, she took a deep breath and sat down. Her bag was by her feet. She fumbled inside for her cigarettes before realising that she had one lit already. A blue line of smoke was twisting in the air in front of her. She picked the cigarette from the ashtray and took a deep drag. 'I mean, I could ask if *you've* ever taken drugs,' she said, frowning at him through the smoke. 'Have you?'

'I'm not averse to the odd line of coke if it's offered to me – ' he began. He stopped and cleared his throat. 'But that's besides the point. Look, I only asked because if you want to find out if somebody's doing a serious drugs deal then you have to ask the people who deal in drugs because they're the only ones who would know. I was just wondering if you knew any.'

'Oh.' She relaxed slightly. 'Well, no, I don't.' She stared at him defiantly. 'Do you?'

'I know two or three serious villains into drugs. I don't know them very well because it's not my field but I've met them.'

'You mean, I should forget a private detective and try and arrange a meeting with a drugs dealer?'

'I've told you. Your average investigator would be hopeless. They wouldn't do it – they probably *couldn't* do it.'

She looked at him thoughtfully. It would be like Jonathan to boast that he'd met all the big-time villains in England. On the other hand his ex-partner was a fairly big name in criminal law and could well have some connection to organized crime. 'Could you arrange a meeting for me?' she asked as sweetly as she could manage.

But Jonathan seemed either to have changed his mind or realised that, in promising this much, he had bitten off more than he could legally chew. 'You really don't want to get into this, a nice girl like you,' he said.

Susan frowned. 'I hope that you're taking this seriously, Jonathan. Because for me, it is serious – very.'

'What reason would they have to tell you anything?' He held up his hand. 'Don't answer that. The possibilities are too horrible to contemplate.'

'I'm not thinking of becoming a gangster's moll,' she snapped. 'How much money would I need?'

'An awful lot. Serious villains are very secretive. A lot of them used to refuse to be involved in the drug rackets for moral reasons but over the last twenty years they worked out it's a better bet. It was the old East End ethic – you know, it's the spics that run the prostitution and the blacks that deal with drugs and we rob people because it's the decent thing to do.' He leant back, crossing his arms behind his head, clearly enjoying himself. 'Then they said – well, we rob people but lots of us keep getting nicked and banged up and we don't want to go out with guns anymore and risk getting shot. You used to hear about security guards being knocked off all the time. Remember the sixties and early seventies?'

'Only from films.'

'Well, that's because it *is* only in films nowadays – you don't read about it anymore in the papers and the reason you don't is that serious villains aren't doing it. Professional criminals want to do a nice, quiet drugs deal because it's reasonably safe and *very* lucrative.'

'Heroin? Crack? Cocaine?' she wondered out loud. Would Nick really have got involved with something like that?

'They're certainly not dealing in grass. You need about eight barrel loads to make three quid. No, nowadays if you're a serious villain, hard drugs is the best business. Your only real cost is transportation. And, yes, you're going to be pretty bloody secretive about it.' From his backward position in the chair, he looked thoughtfully across at her. 'I mean, compare selling drugs to other illegal activities – prostitution, for instance. It wins hands down. The distribution mechanisms are pretty self-regulating. Growing it is cheap. Your only real cost is shipping the stuff. And if you look at the law enforcement you're up against – well, basically it's Customs and Excise who are notoriously rubbish. All they're any good at is catching people in white vans bringing too many cigarettes into the country. I mean, if you had any brains and wanted to be an agent, you'd hardly go into Customs and Excise, would you? If you wanted to fight world crime, you'd choose MI5. You'd become a spook, like on the telly. So where do the best and toughest villains go these days? Drugs because it's the best and toughest business. Plenty of money, no real overheads. And where do the cleverest agents go? Not bloody Customs and Excise, that's for sure. No contest.'

Jonathan uncrossed his arms and spread his hands flat on the desk, glancing hopefully towards the door for Elaine with his cup of coffee. 'Where does Savage Associates ship from?' he asked, when the door didn't open.

'From Scotland.'

'To?'

'All over. There's a route to the West Indies, I know.'

'Possibly a cocaine deal then. Two hundred tons of Columbian cocaine gets shipped out from there each month and it's coming into the UK just as fast as the punters can stuff it up their little noses. You know – ah!' His smile widened as Elaine came in holding a cup and saucer which she set down with a flourish in front of him. Straight shiny brown hair cut in a bob, the eyes which glanced at Susan before leaving the room were strangely hostile. 'You know this is pretty serious stuff,' Jonathan said when the door had closed. He picked up the cup and took a gulp. 'If you're right.'

'That's what I've been trying to tell you.'

'You say that you have an idea who this person is?'

Her voice came out surprisingly steady. 'Yes. I know who it is.'

'There's a division of the police that targets criminals involved in drugs. If they think someone's at it, then they'll follow him around for a bit. Watch everything he does for three or four months. If you like, I could contact them on your behalf.'

The phone rang, startling her. Jonathan didn't wait for her response but picked it up, eyes still on her, brows raised questioningly. He listened briefly then put his hand over the receiver. 'Could you hold on for a second? One second. Sorry – business.' He slid his hand under his tie and flicked it gently in the air as he was talking. After a short conversation he replaced the phone. 'The trouble is that surveillance is expensive,' he carried on as if he hadn't been interrupted. 'It takes something like twelve men so the police have to be pretty sure that it's worth their while.'

'I'm not sure if he's involved in anything now. It may have been a one-off, it probably was.'

'To be perfectly frank, they don't bother much with the small fry. It's the big boys they're after.'

They didn't speak for a moment. Jonathan sipped more coffee. 'I'm sorry I can't help more,' he said politely, 'because it does sound like an interesting problem. Are you sure you wouldn't like another – ?' He tipped the cup slightly.

'Quite sure. Any ideas about what I should do next?'

'Nothing immediately comes to mind... Sorry.'

'What about MCR?'

'Oh, yes, I'd better cancel the appointment or they'll be very pissed off.' He reached for the phone. 'Elaine? Listen, Andy Farrell at three o'clock – cancel it, would you. Thanks. I'm awfully sorry,' he said again to Susan who was looking at him rather wretchedly across the desk. He looked at his watch. 'I'd ask you to lunch but I have a rather important meeting in about twenty minutes...'

When he apologised for a third time, she stubbed out the cigarette and got to her feet. 'Thanks for trying, Jonathan,' she sighed.

'Let's have lunch together soon, shall we?'

'Yes, lets.'

He picked up his brown pinstriped jacket which was carefully draped over the back of his chair and shook it out. Putting it on, he strolled with her across the hall. 'I'll call if I think of anything,' he promised.

She bit her lip. 'Actually, I am in a bit of a hurry... '

He didn't ask why, standing in the hall with Elaine's fierce eyes on them, just said with a smile: 'Then I'll think very, very hard.'

Susan kissed his cheek and nodded to the secretary. He's having an affair with her, she thought suddenly. That explains the hostile glare. She wondered why she hadn't realised it before. Averting her gaze, she walked through the door he was holding open. She could feel their eyes on her back as she passed through into the street.

17

Outside, a cold drizzle was falling. The world looked grey and bleak. Susan felt a stunning despair. That had been a total waste of time. She turned up the collar of her jacket. 'What now? Give up altogether? Accept defeat?' she asked herself despondently, beginning to walk up the street. For who? she wondered. For herself? Or her father?

It started to rain quite heavily. Several taxis shot past without stopping at her raised hand. She ended up walking all the way to Oxford Circus. It was still pouring when she got out of the tube at Chalk Farm. She bought a bottle of Rioja at the off-licence on the corner and, soaking wet and miserable, trudged home, the bottle in its plastic bag knocking against her leg with each step.

Inside the flat, there were three letters on the mat addressed to her. She stripped off her wet clothes and flung them on the floor and, in nothing but pants and a dry tee-shirt, a towel wound like a turban around her head, examined the letters. Two, in brown envelopes, were clearly bills. She dropped them straight in the bin without opening them. The third envelope was larger. She tore it open and looked at the wad of leaflets from Victim Support she was holding in her hand. Dr Spelling must have contacted the society as he'd promised.

'*I never thought I'd feel like this,*' in big letters on one; '*Hurt by violence?*' on the front of another. She shuffled quickly through. '*Rape and Sexual Assault*' in grey, '*Murder and Manslaughter*' in pale blue, others in orange, green and turquoise. She kept the orange leaflet entitled '*Going to Court*' – she might need more information later on that, you never knew – the rest she dropped straight into the bin.

'What's needed is an attractive looking leaflet in black and red entitled – How to Cope with the Effects of Seeing Someone who's Dead,' she commented aloud. 'Or perhaps,' she added miserably, 'one called how to cope with *imagining* you've seen someone who's dead. Never thought I'd feel like this?' She sighed. 'What a joke.'

The flat seemed very empty. Silence pressed on her like the weight of disappointment. She unwound the damp towel and sat cross-legged on the sofa, unsure of what to do next. An immense sense of loss filled her. Loss and failure, she thought. When she'd opened the bottle of wine and swigged back a glass she felt a little better. After another, better still. She'd think of something, she decided, pleasantly befuddled.

She made herself a cheese sandwich, put a dollop of piccalilli on the side of the plate and, taking a bite, the bottle gripped in the crook of her armpit, walked upstairs. For tonight, she'd make a new list of investigative agencies. She wasn't completely convinced by Jonathan's negative description. Why would they say they'd investigate fraud if they couldn't deliver?

Stuffing the rest of the sandwich into her mouth, she switched on the computer. When the screen lit up fully, she clicked onto Google and began searching. At two o'clock, she gave up the chase and flaked out next door on the bed.

'I've had a thought,' Jonathan said, on the other end of the phone.

Susan took a moment to register.

'What we were talking about yesterday. An idea.'

She struggled up straighter in bed. 'Great,' she breathed, wishing her head was a little clearer.

'I've made a few calls. There's someone I think you might wish to talk to,' Jonathan announced, sounding pleased with himself. 'Can you meet me for lunch? Around half-past twelve?'

'Yes. Where?' She felt suddenly so weak with relief and anxiety that she almost dropped the receiver; stupidly she felt tears pricking behind her eyes.

'Do you know La Langoustine? It's on the corner of Wigmore Street. The pedestrian bit, opposite the office?'

'I'll find it.'

'Bring the company's bank account number with you. Do you have it?'

'I can get it.'

'Good girl.'

She didn't even wince at the phrase as she would have done normally. 'Thanks, Jonathan. Thanks a lot.'

'I haven't done anything yet.' But she could hear he was smiling.

Four paracetemols and several cups of coffee later, she was sitting across the table from him, all pleasantries over, surrounded by the pale green and ivory of a small but expensive French restaurant. Around them, the murmur of subdued conversation. Waiters hovered discretely in the corners of the room.

'Something to drink?' Jonathan asked.

'Just a glass of wine.'

'Red? White?'

'Oh, white, I think.'

He examined the wine list. 'The Chablis, please. The 1985 Premier Cru. And a bottle of Perrier.' He snapped it shut and handed it to the waiter.

Susan lit a cigarette nervously. She always felt uncomfortable in this kind of atmosphere. She wished she'd worn something more suitable, a skirt not jeans, at least a decent jacket. She felt completely out of place amongst all the suits and styled hair and elegant dresses. Let's face it, she told herself, there isn't anywhere I wouldn't feel out of place right now. She took a quick drag of the cigarette.

Jonathan leant forward to pour fizzy water from the bottle the waiter had slipped on their table into two tall, gleaming glasses. 'So.' He took a sip of water. 'It's a shipping company, isn't it.'

It was a statement not a question, but she answered, 'Yes.'

'And you said that a lot of money was made from the deal.'

Again not a question. 'A lot,' she confirmed.

'Money that you were sure would show up somewhere.'

She nodded.

'You see, when I thought about it afterwards there seemed only one conclusion. A rather obvious one actually.' Another sip. 'It was staring me right in the face.'

Susan looked at him expectantly but he wasn't about to let go of this one, not yet anyway. He was leaning back comfortably. She sat forwards slightly, crossing her arms on the snow-white tablecloth. He stretched out his legs under the table; she could see the muscles in his thighs flexing beneath the material of his suit.

'You see, the thing to bear in mind,' he explained, 'is that whatever these men do with the drugs, the difficulty is always hiding the money. You said – what's the name of your father's company?'

'Savage Associates.'

'You said that your father found a discrepancy in the records of Savage Associates? Money appearing somewhere it shouldn't. Something he actually saw. Right?'

'Right.'

'Which means – ' He stopped and glanced at the label on a bottle the waiter was holding out for inspection. 'Yes, that's fine.' The waiter pulled out the cork and poured a little wine into his glass. 'Which means the money must have been somewhere visible,' Jonathan went on after he'd tasted it, swirled it round his mouth a couple of times and nodded his approval, 'at least for a time. It must have been lodged somewhere it could *be* found accidentally. You're quite sure about it? He saw something? It wasn't something he heard – like a phone message?'

'No, he definitely saw it.'

Jonathan reached forward and slid a cigarette from her pack of Marlboro Lights which were lying on the table. 'I've given up,' he said as he lit it.

'But what the hell. Helps me to think.' He smiled dreamily and took a long drag, savouring the taste. 'Do you mind?'

She shrugged. 'Of course not.'

Oh, get on with it, Jonathan, she thought. But she forced herself to smile expectantly and keep her body still. Only the hand continually moving, raising the cigarette to her lips, betrayed any impatience. Clearly he was going to string this one out as long as he possibly could.

'Now, if your villain had set up an overseas account and put his millions into it, that money isn't going to show up, is it? Your father wouldn't notice anything dodgy in someone else's offshore account, would he? Why should he have any access there?' He took another long drag of the cigarette. 'I mean, that your father actually saw something limits what it could be. Because we have to ask – what could he possibly have seen? And the only answer is that it must have been something in the company's accounts or bank accounts or in its correspondence. It has to be one of the company's *own* transaction. Of course it could it have been an e-mail,' he said thoughtfully, blowing out smoke, 'but let's hope not. Because I have to tell you, if it *was*, it could easily be destroyed. He could read it and delete it, your villain. And if it was deleted, then it's gone, I'm afraid, for good. I mean, getting an e-mail back again is always possible but it would take more expertise than I can get hold of at short notice.'

'I don't think it was an e-mail. My father never mentioned anything about a computer. He said – I mean, in this letter I found, he wrote that he held the evidence in his hands. He was definitely talking about a physical thing.'

'Still could have been an e-mail. Could have been printed out. Though why would you print out an incriminating e-mail?' Jonathan frowned. 'You would read it and delete it. No,' he picked up his glass and took a sip of wine, looking happier again, 'no, it's far more likely to be a physical letter or something in the bank accounts. Something unusual in the middle of business as usual. Conclusion?' He put down the glass. 'Your father saw something in the bank account of the company who shipped the drugs in the first place.'

'You mean,' Susan frowned, 'in Savage Associates' bank account?'

'Yes.'

'That can't be right. The police investigated Savage Associates pretty thoroughly after my father's murder. They didn't find a thing.'

'Well, they wouldn't. That's the point. What I'm guessing is that they wouldn't find anything odd,' he gave a self-satisfied smirk, 'because there would be nothing odd to find.'

'But then how the – ' she started irritably, then stopped herself. 'I don't quite follow you, Jonathan,' she said, forcing herself to control her impatience. 'Why not?'

'Because I think a quite deliberate mistake was made – and very cleverly covered up. You know all that stuff in *Father Brown* about keeping the thing you most want to conceal right out in the open?'

She shook her head.

He frowned. 'Or it could have been Sherlock Holmes... Anyway. Someone or other once said that the best way of hiding something is to leave it lying around in full view. It would never get noticed that way. The point is that the police would see only what our villain wanted them to see – an error which would have been openly acknowledged by Savage Associates and which would look perfectly normal.'

'A mistake? *That* was what my father saw?'

He smiled. 'Yes.'

'Go on.'

'Look, there are two things you know for sure – one, your father saw something dodgy and, two, that the police didn't. Given what you told me yesterday, I've been thinking. Once you left the office, I remembered a similar case that Matthew told me about. Not, in that instance, to do with drugs but also involving a deeply crooked client.'

'There *was* something about a client,' Susan said slowly. 'A client called – ' She screwed up her eyes, trying hard to remember. What had her father said they were called? What? It began with a B, she was sure it began with a B. B for – 'Beaux,' she said triumphantly. 'The client was called Beaux-Sarr. Like beautiful in French – plural with an x. Apparently there were figures in the Beaux-Sarr file that weren't right.' She took a deep breath, trying to control her excitement. 'That fits in with what you're saying, doesn't it?'

He shrugged. 'It certainly might.'

She looked at him with more respect. His voice seemed sharper; he wasn't playing games any longer, he sounded business-like, more like a solicitor. He had lost all vestige of the lazy, flirtatious quality of the day before. With a flicker of hope, she thought that he might, just might, be rather good at his job.

'Let's say Savage Associates invoice this client Beaux-Sarr in the usual way,' Jonathan suggested. 'Say for £30,000. The invoice has a number and a date and a description of the job. As all invoices do. But the client pays a much greater sum than the amount on the invoice, apparently in error. They pay Savage Associates – let's suppose, £80,000. Savage Associates is a perfectly above board company. Which realises there's been a mistake and issues a credit note to the client for the difference – £50,000 in our imaginary scenario. The credit note would be on record as 'against over-payment of £50,000 on invoice number such and such,' and Savage Associate's bank account would show that £50,000 was paid out accordingly. All quite innocent, all quite normal. Mistakes like that happen. Not all the time, but they happen. And this is what the police would see, if they're curious enough to be looking – an amount on a bank statement, an invoice for the said amount and a credit note to a client. A simple, accidental overpayment and a corresponding credit note for the amount – what are we saying, £50,000?'

'Yes.'

'The police see a credit note for £50,000 paid to Beaux-Sarr as reimbursement, followed by the correct amount leaving the account. However,' he blew out smoke through his nostrils, 'in reality, it wasn't paid to Beaux-Sarr at all. It was paid by them to the person in the company who'd arranged the dodgy deal.'

'Could they do that?'

'Easily.'

Frowning, she took a sip of wine. 'I see… I *think*.'

'Do you?' Jonathan grinned. 'Because I'm rather proud of myself actually. I think this is the same scam as Matthew described to me. Yup.' He nodded, looking pleased with himself. 'I think it just might be. Under normal circumstances, this would have come to light pretty quickly because, of course, the client would complain that they'd never received their money. But in this case, since they were part of the crime, they aren't very likely to, are they? I mean, who's the victim? A client overpays and is reimbursed. We know that the client wasn't actually reimbursed and that the money was paid directly to our villain. But since our villain is working for the client in the first place, the client is quite satisfied. For them, it's just a means of paying for a service rendered. Meanwhile, Savage Associates have been overpaid but they've issued a credit note for the amount so their accounts are in good order. If they think anything, it's that the poor schmucks at Beaux-Sarr have made a bit of a mess of things. Nothing dodgy on the client's part, nothing suspicious – after all, they've *over*paid. The police are satisfied, the client is satisfied, Savage Associates is satisfied. And the money from Savage Associates is sitting happily in the bank account of this villain of yours. He's covered his tracks.'

'You mean – the money's untraceable?'

Jonathan smiled. 'No, that's the point. If it's cash then you can hide it entirely. You can't do much with it, but you can hide it entirely. If it's not, then it's very difficult to make it untraceable. You can hide it but only as long as no one's looking. The police aren't suspicious – and why should they be, since they're not looking for that kind of crime? All he has to do, this villain of yours, is to have prepared reasons that will satisfy the Revenue. They aren't going to be looking too hard anyway. He'd be hoping he wouldn't even need to explain that much. And if he's patient and waits seven or eight years before he starts spending the money, no one will ever know he's got it in the first place. Hiding the money isn't a problem if no one knows you've got it – it's spending it that's difficult. If you steal a load of money and no one catches you and you hide it under the floorboards and don't use it, who would ever know it was there?'

'Only the person who buys the house and lifts up the boards years later, I suppose.'

'Exactly. Spending the loot, that's how people get caught. Because who wants to have a million quid they can't touch? So let's imagine your villain is patient, very, very patient. He doesn't spend it, he keeps quiet. But suppose I get hold of the bank statements and turn round and say – where did this money from Savage Associates end up anyway? Who exactly are these clients? Exactly what was in those containers Savage Associates was so kindly transporting for them from Columbia? And they go and ask him? What then?'

She looked at him expectantly. 'So what do I do?'

'You'll need bank statements. You'll want to see any unusual payments, any extraordinary payments at all or, most likely, any over-payments to Savage Associates in the account.'

She felt a sudden rush of excitement. She couldn't help smiling. She felt better than she had in days. There might be a way of getting some real, physical proof, after all. And if she hadn't made it up, if her story looked as if it might be true, not only would she be proved sane, but Nick guilty, all in one fell swoop... To calm herself she took a long gulp of chilled wine. It was delicious. The food probably would be, too, only she wasn't in the slightest bit hungry. Her stomach felt too queasy to eat. 'How would I get hold of them?' she asked in a voice that trembled slightly.

'Ah, that's more difficult. You're not a member of the company by any chance?'

'No.'

'Then you don't have lawful access. It is possible to get hold of a company's bank statements. It's illegal but – Yesterday I made a few calls. There's a private inquiry agent who will do it.'

'A private – You mean, a detective?'

Jonathan nodded.

'I thought they were all useless.'

'Just the standard ones. Actually he's a debt collector. Did you bring the account number with you?'

'It's in my bag.'

'Good. One other thing,' he said, looking serious.

Her heart missed a beat. What had he heard? Who had he spoken to since yesterday? Nina? She spoke deliberately lightly: 'Yes?'

'This is going to cost you quite a bit. You're certain you want to go ahead?'

'Oh, yes!' Susan smiled, it felt for the first time in days. 'Because if you're right then I'd have real physical proof instead of only – ' She broke off. 'Only a letter,' she finished.

'Well, hang on a minute. This person, whoever he is, isn't going to come out with his hands up – not under these circumstances. He'd be charged with conspiracy to supply drugs. For proof of any involvement on his part you'd have to be able to show that your villain deposited money originating from Savage Associates in his own account in the first place.'

Her spirits sank again. It was like being on an emotional roller-coaster. One moment she was up and everything felt possible, the next, she was down, the ground whipped from under her feet and everything looking hopeless. Jonathan, of course, was simply enjoying trying to unravel an abstract problem. How would he react if she told him the whole story? The outcome might seem a little more important to him then, she thought. Or less. 'You should have been a criminal, Jonathan, not a lawyer,' she said, trying to smile. 'You could have made millions.'

'I know,' he said sadly. 'I know.'

'So how would I prove it was him?'

'*If* you find evidence in the first place,' he reminded her.

'Yes. If.'

The waiter began setting out plates of food on the table. Jonathan shook out the folds of a heavy linen napkin before placing it in his lap. 'Let's take things one at a time, shall we?' he suggested, taking a final drag of his cigarette before stubbing it out. He picked up his knife and fork and gazed sombrely at his prawn salad.

For a moment she watched him eating. She placed her own cigarette, still burning, in the small semi-circular glass dip in the ashtray and picked at a few leaves of salad. Then, feeling much too pent-up to eat, she set down her fork and drained her glass instead.

Seeing it empty, he re-filled it. 'Eat up. We have an appointment this afternoon with Mr Wexler.'

'Mr – ?'

'Hyman Wexler – the debt collector. I'd like to give him details of your father's banking as soon as possible. Because now, with a little help, we're going to play a game of hide and seek.' He grinned. 'It always comes down to this. Whether it's divorce or fraud makes no real difference. The people who've got the money try to hide it and my job is to seek it out. Wexler's in Finchley. We'll grab a cab in the street. Hopefully the traffic won't be too bad yet.'

18

Hyman Wexler was a middle-aged man with grey hair and eyes that moved quickly and nervously behind horn-rimmed glasses. The glasses had broken where they fitted over his nose and been fixed at some point with sellotape. He wore an ill-fitting suit and a tie, both plain grey. There was a light sprinkling of dandruff on his collar. At the corners of his mouth some sticky white spittle had collected which stretched as he talked. He didn't wipe it away; he seemed unaware of it, or perhaps he didn't care. The latter, Susan decided, examining him. His eyes were the only mobile thing about him; otherwise he sat expressionless throughout the entire meeting, his body heavy and still.

The office was tiny. The desk, the grey filing cabinets and carpet, all standard office equipment. The light was hard and white, the strips of a grubby beige blind pulled very firmly flat. She could feel her hair begin to crackle with the static.

Wexler barely glanced at her, talking for the most part only to Jonathan. 'What do you need?' he asked, flipping open a small black notebook.

'Bank statements for a company called Savage Associates,' Jonathan replied crisply. 'For just over one year. Let's say eighteen months. Beginning – what? May 2003?'

Susan nodded agreement.

'Ending November 2004? There may be more than one account,' Jonathan added. 'We'll want 'em all.'

'Bank?' Wexler inquired.

Susan dragged a crumpled piece of paper from her bag and handed it to Wexler.

'Sort code? Account number?'

'They're on it.' She pointed to the paper.

Wexler made a note of the numbers in his book. His eyes flickered up. 'If you want copies of the originals, that will take a little longer and be more expensive.'

'Is there an alternative?' she asked.

'You can have a copy of the original or a printed list that simply states what monies went in and out the account.'

'I think a printed list will be enough. Or do we actually need to see the statements, Jonathan?'

'Not initially,' Jonathan confirmed.

'Just the list,' she said.

Wexler wrote this down. 'You should be aware that bank statements obtained in this way are not admissible as evidence in court and that would include any matrimonial litigation,' he informed the air in front of his notebook.

'This isn't a divorce,' Susan told him firmly. 'I'm not married.' But she needn't have bothered for all the notice Wexler took of her.

'That it?' he asked Jonathan.

'Yup.'

Hyman Wexler closed the notebook with a snap. 'My normal terms are six hundred pounds a day plus expenses. This is three days work. It will cost you eighteen hundred pounds. I require half of that in advance.'

Susan glanced at Jonathan who nodded. 'That's fine,' she said.

'For a job like this I want eighteen hundred pounds in cash with half of it up front.'

'Cash?' Susan said nervously. 'I've got a cheque book and bankers card but no – '

'Is there a cashpoint nearby?' Jonathan asked briskly, getting to his feet.

'There's a Barclays on the corner of this side of the street.'

'We'll be right back.'

' I think he fancies you,' Jonathan said, in the lift.

She stared at him in amazement.

'No, really. He's got the hots for you, I can tell.'

'If it wasn't so bizarre it would have been incredibly rude – he didn't take a blind bit of notice of me. I felt like the invisible woman. I had an urge to pinch myself to check I was really there. He completely ignored my existence.'

'That's why. He's clearly mad about you. He had to blank you, otherwise he'd have jumped you straight away.'

'Don't be silly, Jonathan. The man couldn't jump on a bus in a traffic jam. Why does he want cash anyway?'

'Put it like this, he won't exactly be handing out VAT receipts. He's breaking the law getting details of bank accounts, that's why.'

'Is that why they won't be admissible as evidence in court? Because they're illegal?'

'Not illegal exactly but then again, not strictly kosher. If I've ever used any financial statements in a divorce case, I've given the barrister any relevant information beforehand so that he could ask the right questions, but he'd never expect to refer to them directly in open court. You tread a fine line in these matters.'

'And we're just about to step over it?'

'Well, *you* are.'

'This is very nice of you, Jonathan,' she said breathlessly, hurrying up the street to keep up with him. 'To go to all this trouble.'

'Yes, isn't it,' he said carelessly. 'It's a pleasure to spend an afternoon with you. Besides, I get ten per cent of anything you pay Wexler for the recommendation, so we're quits.'

They had reached the cashpoint. She pressed in her card and then turned to Jonathan in dismay. 'Shit!'

'You haven't got the money.'

'No, I've got it. But I can't take out more than two hundred pounds in one day. What do I do now?'

He drew his wallet out of the inside pocket of his jacket and flashed a gold card in the air. 'I'll get the cash,' he said. 'You can write me a cheque. If it bounces I'm so far in the red it won't matter anyway.'

Going back down in the lift on the way out, the cash safely deposited with Wexler, Susan thought: One single day. I've gone from hope to despair and back again in one day. I've been through a hundred emotions and it's only Thursday. As the lift hit the ground she stepped out, thinking incredulously: it's Thursday, and I've just paid nine hundred pounds to a man to help me track down a killer.

The men came in through the bedroom window.

One climbed in first, the other followed a few seconds later. She could see his shadow through the blind. She was too frightened to scream.

He was the bad one, she saw that straight away. He took a carving knife out of his trousers and slit her tee-shirt down the front, one clean sweep and she was naked. She was light in their hands, like paper. She felt like paper in their hands, not flesh and blood, except...

Except paper doesn't feel pain.

They wore hoods so that she couldn't see their faces, black hoods with slits for the eyes and mouth. With their knives they ruined her, what they did to her she would never tell. They had sewn up her eyes, her mouth, they had cut out her heart. She could see the black stitches criss-crossing her body, her hands, her breasts, her genitals. Sewn right up. Stitched tight. Her screams rang out, those long silent screams that no one would ever hear. They must have climbed up a ladder and over the ledge, it wasn't wide. Though the blind was pulled down, the window was not locked. She should have locked the window, locked and bolted it. Why, oh, why had she not securely turned the key?

Susan hadn't slept well for over a week and that night was no different – the events of the day kept turning over and over in her mind. She tossed and turned for hours, lurching between optimism and extreme anxiety.

Her last thought before dropping off was of Nick. *Nick… Isabella… Nick had called her darling… Nina… Isabella… Nick…*

She woke at six-thirty after only three hours of troubled sleep and climbed sluggishly out of bed, knowing there was little she could do for the rest of the day. Wexler would be hunting out bank statements, all she could was wait for the results. She made breakfast, washed, dressed and wandered aimlessly around the flat until eight. Drank some cold coffee, took a bite of cold toast and wandered around a bit more. Then she made an impulsive decision. There was one thing she could do while she was waiting, she decided. Grabbing her bag and jacket she dashed out the door before she could change her mind. She'd go and see her mother. Isabella's affair was intolerable – she wouldn't put up with it any longer; she'd put up with too much for too long. For her father's sake she would find the courage to speak. She would not shout or scream, beg or weep: she would be calm. Calmly and kindly, she would tell her mother that it *was not on*.

In the drive, parked next to her mother's Audi, was a flamboyant red Aston Martin. The license plates read LS04 BYZ. Not brand new then, but in impeccable condition, Susan thought, peering through the side window at the wooden dashboard and sleek pale leather upholstery. 'Flash,' she murmured. 'Very flash.' Not quite her mother's taste – 'But Nick's?' she wondered aloud, before ringing the bell.

Her mother in a long red velvet dressing-gown opened the door. Without make-up and with her hair loose, she looked softer and more vulnerable. Susan saw the startled look on her face when she saw her standing on the step and realised she was annoyed at having been caught unawares.

'Can I come in?'

'Of course! How unexpected! And how very nice!' Isabella smiled, recovering herself. 'The coffee's just made. I suppose you've already had your morning cup… '

'But I'd love some.'

'Goodo,' her mother said, just a shade unconvincingly. Pulling her dressing-gown more tightly round her, her eyes flickered over to the Aston Martin, then returned to her daughter.

Susan stepped into the hall, realising that she hadn't put on any make-up that morning or even brushed her hair. Her eyes burned from lack of sleep. There were probably huge dark shadows under them.

'You're up very early,' Isabella said, glancing over. For once she did not comment on her daughter's unkempt appearance.

Remember – cool, calm and collected, Susan told herself, following her through to the kitchen. Her eyes searched the hall on the way for any signs of a new male presence but there were none, no tell-tale letters, coat or briefcase.

On the kitchen table next to a plate of cold toast and a half-used dish of marmalade was a folded copy of the *Telegraph*. Susan picked it up casually. 'Since when have you been a *Telegraph* reader?' she asked, knowing the answer. For as long as her mother had been sleeping with Nick.

'Oh, for a while…' Isabella responded vaguely. 'It's an excellent paper and, whatever your politics, a jolly good read,' she added. Nick's answer. Susan had heard him say it, almost word for word, many times. Isabella, perhaps realising this, picked up a plate on which a little fried egg still remained and turned quickly to the sink to rinse off the grease. 'Would you like something to eat?' she asked. 'I could make some more toast.' She twisted slightly to see Susan's response.

Susan shook her head.

'Or poach an egg? They're organic.'

Again Susan shook her head.

'Sure?' Isabella asked, holding the cafetiere high in the air, before pouring two mugs.

'Just coffee, thanks,' Susan said, lighting a cigarette. Her mother looked at her disapprovingly but said nothing. Susan broke off a piece of cold toast, smeared it with butter and took a bite.

'I've got some lovely fresh bread. Shall I cut some for you?'

'This is fine, mum.'

'That was made ages ago.'

'I like it cold.'

'Ugh. Do you?'

'Yes.' A note of irritation crept into Susan's voice. 'The butter doesn't melt.'

Her mother pulled a face and sat down opposite, sipping her coffee. After a moment she asked a little too cheerfully: 'Well, what have you been up to?'

Susan finished off the toast and wiped butter from her fingers on a blue napkin. 'I've got a job.'

'Oh?' Her mother looked interested. 'I'm glad to – Doing what?'

'Selling life insurance.'

'You're joking.'

'People die,' Susan said. 'Is that a joke?'

Her mother's face stiffened. She got up from the table and began stacking the dirty cups and plates in the dishwasher. When she looked up, her big eyes were sad. 'Don't you want to take off your jacket? You don't look very comfortable.'

'I'm fine. I'm not staying long.'

'You're smoking too much. Your fingers are *yellow*.'

'No, they're not.'

'Well, if you carry on like this, they will be.'

Susan shrugged but stubbed out the cigarette on one of the dirty plates that hadn't yet been cleared from the table. Her mother grimaced. Holding the plate with the very tips of her fingers she emptied the contents into the bin. 'Let's go through to the living-room, shall we?' she sighed.

The living-room had always been far more her mother's room than her father's. Long acquamarine curtains looped back, pale yellow sofas and a half-circle of chairs on the cream rug in front of the fireplace. There were flowers, delicate white freesias and blue cornflowers, carefully arranged under silk-shaded lamps. A few too many knick-knacks on the tables, Susan reflected, all a little too immaculate and clean, but otherwise, as intended, a perfectly designed English upper middle-class room. The huge portrait of Isabella dressed as Portia in a long gown of white pleated chiffon, all dark hair, white skin and dark lips, hung above the fireplace, covering almost an entire wall.

The phone rang before they could sit down. 'I won't be a minute,' Isabella muttered, hurrying out to the hall. Susan perched on one of the curved back chairs and examined the room. Nothing obviously new here either. She tucked one leg under her, sitting on her foot, and, sipping coffee, listened to her mother talking.

'...What time?... I'm not sure, I'll ring when I – yes... yes... yes, I'm going out about five... At four then.' Then, more loudly, 'Susan's here. She came for breakfast... I don't know... I'll see you later...'

She came swiftly back into the room and sat down on the edge of the yellow sofa, fiddling with the velvet sash of her dressing-gown.

'Was that Nick?' Susan asked abruptly.

'As a matter of fact, it was.'

'That's his car outside, isn't it? Is he living here yet?'

'No, he's not,' Isabel replied coldly. 'Not that it's any of your business.'

'Oh? I thought it was. You seem to think my life is yours – always poking and prying. Asking questions, giving advice.' Susan felt suddenly so angry that she could hardly get her next words out. All her good resolutions were swept away on a tide of fury that had begun mounting as soon as she'd seen the sleek, expensive red car outside. 'You spoke to Nina about me! How *dare* you?'

'Well, yes, I'm sorry, but I did – '

'So why the hell shouldn't I consider *your* life *my* business?'

'It's completely different. I'm your mother.'

'My mother?' Susan gave a bitter laugh. 'That's a joke. You don't behave like my mother. You don't act like my father's widow. Haven't you ever heard of mourning?'

'What you're doing isn't mourning, Susan. It's dwelling on the past. Drinking and probably taking drugs again.'

'It was dope, mum, not *drugs*. Cannabis. Even you must know the difference.'

'It wasn't so innocuous as I recall. The clinic didn't think so.'

'The clinic didn't – but I only went to the clinic to please you! I didn't want to go – I didn't think I needed to! I went to please *you*! You were the one that thought I needed help! You make it sound like I was injecting crack or something!'

'Whatever,' her mother said, growing cooler the more heated Susan became. 'The point is you're wallowing.'

'And you?' Susan said nastily. 'What do you call sleeping with Nick? What kind of wallowing do you call that?'

There was a stunned silence between them. Susan was as startled as her mother by what she'd just said, though she tried not to show it. With great care Isabella finished tying the bow in her belt. Then she straightened the Chinese porcelain figures on the table next to her, pushing a place mat more centrally under her mug and wiping off some invisible dust from the table's gleaming surface with her fingertips. When she responded her voice was deadly calm. 'He needs me,' she said quietly. 'Your father never did.'

'He never – ?'

'He never *needed* me. Not like this.'

'And so you'd sell Dad's memory for a cheap affair with Nick?'

'I really don't think – '

'Are you afraid of growing old on your own? Is that it? Afraid of old age and loneliness?'

'I'm not as old as you think,' her mother said stiffly.

Susan glared at her. 'You're not as young as you think, either.'

'Oh, you can be so cruel,' Isabella said, looking sadly at her daughter.

'You're scared, aren't you?' Susan said fiercely, though she could see her mother's hands trembling. But her own hands were shaking, too. 'You think, I'm fifty-four, I'm getting on, there isn't much time left. This is my last chance. The last chance I may have for love.' She gave a tight little laugh that had no humour in it, jerking her arm so that her elbow caught the two small cushions balanced on the chair behind her and sent them tumbling to the floor. Leaning forward to pick them up, she said: 'You disgust me.'

'And before this?' her mother said in a hard voice, angry now too. 'Didn't I disgust you then? You were always reproaching me for something. Your eyes were always on me, blaming me. Since you were twelve years old, you blamed me. For what? Tell me. What did you blame me for then?' She glared at her daughter, her soft lower lip protruding. 'I suppose you don't even know yourself.'

'I'm surprised you noticed the look in my eye. It's a bloody miracle if you did, since you were never there to see it.'

Isabella raised her hands in the air. 'Oh, that old complaint again,' she said, exasperated. 'It's boring, Susan. Boring, boring, boring.'

'Well, it may be boring but it's true.'

'You always exaggerate everything.'

'It's how I remember it.'

'How you remember it, *not* how it was. I was around often enough.'

'Enough? Is that what you call it?' Susan sneered, setting a pale green embroidered cushion back into place. 'Let's not pretend, Isabella. For once in our lives, let's not pretend. Photographs of you as a doting mother in magazines don't actually count. I was neglected. If it hadn't been for Dad... You neglected me – my childhood passed you by. You were too busy being glamorous.'

'I had a life,' Isabella responded sharply. 'I *have* a life. That's what you can't bear, isn't it?'

'You must be very scared of not having one,' Susan retaliated, as the truth of her mother's words struck them both. 'Of being alone.'

'You're living in the past,' Isabella said dully. 'This is all in the past.'

'It's my future,' Susan shot back. Unfolding her leg from beneath her, she realized she had pins and needles badly. She straightened the leg, jiggling her foot up and down on the floor to get rid of them. 'It's my future...' she heard herself repeating. What exactly did she mean?

Isabella was sitting very straight on the sofa, her hair loose to her shoulders. Susan, sitting opposite, still wearing her black leather jacket, could see the shadows under her mother's eyes, the little lines sketched at the corners. Though she tried to cling on to it, Susan could feel her anger draining away. Was this really why she had hurried over first thing? To argue with her mother about all the lost years? About her past and present betrayal? Isabella was right – she was just being wantonly cruel. She was behaving like a sulky adolescent. But there was more at stake than some old hurt feelings, she reminded herself, much more. She pressed her foot flat on the floor, searching for something to say that would take the downward droop from her mother's mouth.

Isabella spoke first. 'He wasn't as perfect as you think,' she said wearily.

'Your father. He was just a man, with good and bad points. Some pretty bad, actually.'

Susan felt her anger, scathing and uncontrollable, returning instantly. 'So what's Nick like?' she hissed furiously. 'Is he a better fuck?'

Isabella's mouth twisted and her eyes filled with tears. She began crying softly. Susan felt the guilt she'd tried to shrug off return as a hard lump in her throat, an ache in her chest. She went over to the sofa and sat down. Taking her mother's left hand, she played with the diamond ring on her finger. 'Break it off with him,' she urged, twisting round the ring. 'It isn't too late. Stop it now. It's wrong what you're doing, you must know that. Perhaps I *am* a little jealous – ' (Was she? Of whom? Her mother? Of Nick?) 'But you're making a mockery of Dad's memory. Break if off, mum – Please?'

Isabella fished in her dressing-gown pocket for a tissue. When she found it, she blew her nose and sat up straighter. 'I think you'd better go,' she said in a muffled voice. 'You've said enough. Perhaps you needed to get all this out – perhaps it will help. But if you say any more you'll only be sorry.' She pressed her hand to her mouth to stop her lips from trembling. 'At least, I hope to God you will be.'

'You aren't going to leave him, are you?'

Her mother didn't answer.

'Oh, I wish things could be the way they were before!' Susan burst out with passion. 'I really, really wish it!'

Isabella sat with her head bowed, her free hand with the balled-up tissue resting in her lap. 'Yes,' she said finally.

'I feel I have two lives. The life before. And the life after. But before is a dream. Now is real...'

'Yes,' her mother said again.

'And in between...' Susan broke off, coming to a sudden decision. She hadn't intended to tell her mother anything but how could she expect her to end her affair with Nick unless she explained at least some of it to her? It was out before she'd thought twice. 'There's something else,' she said impulsively. 'There's something I have to tell you. I don't know how to put this but – ' She hesitated, took a deep breath as if she were diving off a high board, then said, 'I've spoken to Dad.'

Isabella didn't move, but her hand in Susan's stiffened. Susan had the impression that she'd stopped breathing. 'What are you talking about?' she asked.

'I've spoken to Dad,' Susan repeated. 'I've seen him. In the studio. He told me everything. You see, Nick killed him. He killed his own brother!' she burst out point blank, staring into her mother's astonished face. 'He was using the business as a cover for bringing drugs into the country. Dad found out about it and they murdered him. Nick arranged the whole thing. So you really must end things with him, do you see? Or – Or you're an accessory to murder.'

Isabella drew back. She looked into her daughter's face, her eyes moving uncertainly, huge and dark and heavy. 'You aren't joking, are you?' she said. 'You mean it. Oh, Susan, oh, sweetie, please – '

'Mum, listen to me for once! For once just listen! It was the evening of Nick's birthday party – do you remember?'

'Of course I remember.'

'Afterwards, when I got home, Alex Emmerich phoned.'

'Alex Emmerich?' her mother repeated weakly.

'The man who lives in Keyes Court on the floor below Dad's studio. He told me he'd heard noises coming from upstairs, he thought it was burglars. But he'd seen a man hanging round a few nights earlier and he was confused. Because the man he'd seen looked like Dad. He said he thought for a moment that it *was* Dad, only he'd known it couldn't be. He actually said that – for a brief interval, he mistook this man for Dad. I went straight over, by then it was almost midnight. After Alex left, Dad – came. To the studio. I was asleep, he woke me up. At first I assumed it was a dream but it wasn't, it was quite different, I know that now. He told me what had happened to him. It was terrible. Terrible. He was in a terrible state. It was Nick. He told me. Nick had murdered him. He had arranged the whole thing.'

Isabella had gone very pale. One hand still rested in Susan's, the other, clutching a crumpled Kleenex she held to her chest. Her eyes, wide, dark and afraid, stared at her daughter.

'Don't you see?' Susan said with desperation. 'Don't you understand? Phone Alex Emmerich if you don't believe me.'

'The man who lives downstairs?' Her mother's voice was faint.

'Yes! He saw Dad outside the studio – I'm not imagining it. He saw him too!'

'He said – he said he saw a man he thought looked like Steven?'

'Yes. Yes!'

'He said he saw a man – He didn't say he'd seen a *ghost*. Did he say so?'

'He was confused, he thought – '

'It was a mistake, Susan. He made a mistake. Or more likely, he was humouring you, trying to please you. He probably found you attractive. But it must have put the idea into your head...' Isabella's voice had returned to its normal tone. Susan wanted to block her ears and drown it out. She wanted to scream – Please! Please, listen! Her mother continued:

'You need help, darling. You're overwrought. After the party Nick told me that you – You saw us in the hall, didn't you? It must have been terrible. To see us – like that. Later that night, you went to the studio, you fell asleep, you had a dream. It's not unnatural. One of those bad dreams you used to have as a child. Daddy and I took you to the doctor's each week, do you remember? Those terrible dreams you had as a child. It's not unnatural, you – '

'It wasn't a dream!' Susan shouted, snatching away her hand. 'I know what a *dream* is! It wasn't a fucking dream! You're not listening. You don't understand.' She felt childish and stupid. How many times had she said this in the past? 'Or is it that you don't *want* to understand?' she cried in despair. 'So you can keep your love affair with Nick going?'

'Susan, please – '

'You've never believed me. Never. Everything I say is a fantasy according to you, everything. Especially where Nick is concerned.'

'Not everything but – '

'Everything that matters! Where Nick is concerned. It's always been like that – Nothing's changed.'

'He was very good to you when you were a child. You were so fond of him then.'

'Oh, yes,' Susan said. 'Very good.'

'You sound so bitter,' Isabella said sadly.

'You want to wipe it all out! But you can't and not even you can bury it anymore! You can't wipe out memory.'

Isabella frowned. 'But what you're talking about isn't memory, is it?'

Susan drew away. 'Oh, look, I'm going,' she decided, standing up. 'I did try. I tried to make you understand. You don't understand. You can't hear. As usual you can't hear a damned thing.'

Isabella rose, too, stretching an arm out to Susan. It was a dramatic gesture. Her emotion was both theatrical and real. But that was the only way her mother could experience emotion, Susan thought sadly, by acting it, by dramatising her own life. When Isabella saw the expression on Susan's face, she let her hand fall, stammering out: 'Will you telephone… ?'

'Yes, I'll phone.' At last there was neither triumph nor hostility in her voice, though she still felt angry enough to slam the front door. On the front step, she muttered: 'I always phone, don't I?'

As she backed the blue Mini out of the drive, she could see her mother's eyes watching from the window; dark, anxious and disbelieving.

19

Was her mother right? And Nina, too? *Was* she going mad? Perhaps this was what it was like – everything seems just the same except for a few minor re-adjustments. Susan turned the car sharply into the high street and stopped at the lights behind two cars. Her mother's certainty seemed to hang over her, sharp and gleaming, threatening to smack down hard on her neck, severing all connection with reality.

Why had she gone to see Isabella? How could she have been so stupid? She'd felt so confident yesterday after talking with Jonathan. Her father's story seemed to hang together, it seemed to make sense. So why had she gone?

But even as she cursed herself, she knew why. It was because she believed her father's story. Believed he had struggled back from the grave, through smashed bones and congealed blood, to tell it to her. Which meant she was left desperately wanting her mother to break things off with Nick and be – what? A word came into her mind and hovered there, unformed. It was 'innocent'. She wanted her mother to be innocent again. For that, she had to end her affair with Nick. Or she became guilty of murder by association. Murder by sexual choice. Murder.

Or was she simply being jealous Susan wondered, confused again. Madly, wildly jealous? Of her mother? Of Nick? Did she crave her mother's attention so badly that she was prepared to invent this to get it? Would she do anything, even distort her own mind, to keep the two of them apart?

She pressed in the dashboard lighter, then forgot she had done so. The heat came on as a faint reddish glow and died away again. Was her wish to help her father just a hollow resolution covering other, more destructive, desires?

Oh, yes, the deluded believe their own delusions, she told herself bitterly. Of course they do.

No, she thought, no! The truth was different. It wasn't her invention, it couldn't be. It was a discovery, a horrible, horrible discovery. She could hear her father's voice right now, see his damaged face. She could still smell him. If only she were mad. Madness would be better than this. Far, far better. Susan pressed her foot down hard on the accelerator, overtaking the red Fiat in front of her.

And whatever her mother had said, Alex Emmerich had seen him too, she was certain. Wasn't she? She wished now that her father had spoken to him. If only he had spoken to Alex, then she would know for sure.

'*Detective Sergeant Howell, Metropolitan Police – I'm afraid I've got bad news, Miss Savage. It's your father. At seven twenty this morning his body was found. I'm sorry to have to tell you – but he's dead. Was it an accident or what? I'm afraid it's too early to say what it was, but it does not appear to be an accident, no, Miss.*'

A lorry rumbled along Fitzjohns Avenue, ahead of her. She pulled out blindly, saw a car driving head-on towards her and swerved back into lane, tyres screaming. Putting her foot down flat on the brake, she changed down a gear. The lorry driver waved a fist out the window, pressing down long and hard on his horn.

You're my only hope, Susie, my only chance…

The thoughts were going round and round her head. She sped up till she was alongside the lorry driver, then swung left into Akenside Road. She shot down Belsize Park Gardens, racing across the lights on amber. When she got back to Regents Park Road, she beat the woman ahead of her into a parking space and yanked up the handbrake, ignoring her furious hooting. Then she switched off the engine and laid her head on the steering-wheel, sobbing, great dry racking sobs that shook her body but without shedding any tears.

Her body was still heaving convulsively when she finally sat up, staring, unseeing, ahead of her, at the bare tree growing in its square patch of earth by the side of the road, and the shoe shop window beyond. Automatically, she dashed a hand over her cheek although there were no tears there to wipe away. The thoughts must stop. She wanted them to stop. Tonight she'd meet Paul at nine o'clock as planned and blank all the thoughts out of her mind. She would rid herself of feeling, drown all the love and all the hate, drown them. She would drink too much tonight, far, far too much. And tomorrow? Tomorrow she'd contact Alex Emmerich.

They met at nine outside Leicester Square tube station. Although she was expecting him to be on time her heart leapt as she caught sight of him through the shifting people. One look told him it was going to be one of those nights. There was a recklessness about her. She seemed a little wild, a little out of control. She felt an overwhelming urge to take the leash off for one night, and it showed. One perfect night, just one, before being shot at dawn, was how she put it to herself.

'You're wearing a lot of make-up tonight.'

'Too much?'

'No,' Paul said. 'You look great.'

He tucked her hand firmly under his arm as if to keep her feet, at least, on the straight and narrow. They had a bottle of wine, Susan drank most of it, then crossed to the Odeon where there was a late night film he wanted to see. In the cinema they held hands. They ate quickly afterwards, then hurried round the corner to Paul's flat.

I'll get you, she thought as she ripped off her clothes. If there's anything in it, I'll catch you. You won't escape me, she thought, flinging a black lacey top across the room. Eeny, meeny, miney, mo, I'll hold you tightly by the toe. It's only Friday and you're mine…

She yanked off her earrings as Paul began kissing her body, letting the silver hoops drop carelessly from her hand onto the wooden chair by the bed where they rolled to the floor. She allowed herself just one more thought before sinking down into the welcome oblivion of her lover's arms. Nick, you murderer…

20

'Are you there, darling? Pick up the phone if you're there. Please Susan, *pick up the phone*! It's mummy, darling. Susan? Can you hear me? Pick up the phone if you can hear me, Susan. Susan! Please!'

Beep.

'Hi, it's Jonathan Woolf. It's Saturday – ten past nine. I've received the information back from Wexler. Give me a ring, will you?'

Beep.

'Jonathan again. Um, ten o'clock. I'm leaving for a meeting in Lincoln's Inn in ten minutes. I'll probably be stuck there all day. I'm going to bike the stuff over to you. It'll be with you in a couple of hours. Please phone my secretary to confirm this is OK. She'll be in the office until lunchtime. If she doesn't hear from you within the next hour I've told her to cancel the bike. OK?'

Beep.

Susan arrived home next morning feeling depressed, guilty, edgy. Her lacey top no longer seemed slinky; it just felt stale and tight. Her head was aching from too little sleep and too much wine and yesterday's visit to her mother seemed even more ill-advised in the cold light of day. But Jonathan's message acted like a shot of adrenaline. Her head felt suddenly clear and she was smiling as she dialled his number. Yes, he was out of the office all day, his secretary confirmed, her prim voice belying the heels and short skirt. Did Miss Savage still require the bike? Yes, Miss Savage did. Susan deleted her mother's message from the answering machine, had a bath and changed her clothes. She had barely finished dressing when the door-bell rang.

Good old Wexler! she thought, racing down the stairs. A man in a red and white helmet and black leathers standing on the doorstep handed her a large envelope and asked her to sign for it. She took the clipboard and pen he offered. Clutching the envelope, she ran back upstairs. There were about twenty unlined sheets inside – the printed lists showing the money that had gone in and out of Savage Associates' bank accounts for just over a year.

The paper had been folded to fit into the envelope. Susan smoothed the crease flat and gazed at the top sheet, her stomach lurching with excitement. Slowly she sat down at the kitchen table, staring guiltily at the list of figures in her hand. She felt like a voyeur, inspecting something she wasn't meant to see. This is for your father, she reminded herself sternly, beginning to read. You're doing it for him.

By the eighth page she'd begun to relax a little. A shape was beginning to emerge. Regular sums were paid out halfway through each month – salaries for clerical staff and secretaries, larger sums for the managers and two partners. Also payments to various named companies – Apsley Mill 6, Prudential banking D/D – though these were only ever in the low thousands. Opposite the 'paid in' column the figures were still low, never for more than nineteen or twenty thousand. Presumably the amount Savage Associates had been paid for shipping goods some distance across the world. She folded the paper along the same crease. Nothing unusual there. All as expected.

The other account was only a little different. The amounts were larger, the transactions more regular. The money came in and went out again within a few months. Along both the credit and debit sides were cheque numbers, no company names. But never, anywhere to be found against her steadily moving finger, a large sum of money, a sum that had been paid in and, a slightly smaller one, paid out again a few weeks later. In fact, no puzzlingly large sums at all.

By the last page, any guilt and nervous excitement Susan had felt at first had been replaced by a sick feeling of disappointment. There was nothing here that looked in the slightest bit dodgy. What she was holding in her hand was only the very boring statements of a respectable shipping company. Tears of self-pity welled up in her eyes. What had she been so eager to learn? Two thousand pounds to find out she was mad and Nick was innocent?

Don't give up now, she told herself. There may be something you've missed. Resolutely, she began reading again. Halfway down the nineteenth page, the phone rang. Dispiritedly, she got up to answer it.

'Susan?'

'Yes.'

'It's Mummy.'

'I know.'

'Now, don't be cross but I've booked an appointment for you. With a doctor,' she explained, when Susan didn't respond. 'I think you should see a doctor, darling. I think you should – '

'Is it a psychiatrist?'

Her mother hesistated. 'Well, he *is*. But very good. He's *highly* recommended. Just tell everything to Dr Wells. Just tell him – all of it. I've made an appointment for this Monday at ten past twelve. Shall I give you the address?'

GAIL LEVY

'If you want.'

'Have you got a pen?' Her mother dictated an address off New Cavendish Street. 'Now, are you writing this down?'

'Yes.'

'And you've put the appointment in your diary?'

'Yes.'

'You won't forget, will you? He's jolly busy but he made a special effort to fit you in. Perhaps I should phone in the morning to remind you? If you like, I could come with…'

Susan's bottom lip trembled. She hoped she wasn't going to cry. Loud and violent sobs were on the verge of breaking from her lips. Her mother had been right, after all. It had all been in her imagination. A hallucination, a horrible dream. An immensely vivid delusion, however unlikely it seemed. 'I won't forget, mum,' she said in a low voice.

'You're sure you don't want me to come along?'

'Quite sure.'

'Monday at ten past twelve.'

Susan looked at the futile sheets in her hand. 'Yes. I understand.'

'Oh, by the way, do you have my umbrella? I think I left it in your flat the other night.'

'No – yes – I don't know. I expect it's here somewhere.'

'I'll pop round and collect it, shall I? On Monday morning? Then we can go to Dr Wells together.'

Susan felt too despondent to argue any further.

'Alright,' she said weakly. 'If you'd like, yes.' It was hard to absorb, but the truth was she was cracking up. Going stark, staring bonkers.

A hand shaking as it lit a roll-up, a black and empty eye. 'You're the only one who can help me, Susie. The only one…'

She'd invented a ghost. Dreamed his scarred and ruined face. Her motives? Not too hard to understand. I'm the only one who can help? Susan almost laughed aloud. Not too much hope then, is there? On automatic pilot, she vaguely heard herself saying goodbye before putting down the phone. She thought: so this is what it's like…

To her surprise, she found herself feeling better than she'd expected at the thought.

The psychiatrist turned out to be a psychoanalyst and her mother came to fetch her, ringing the doorbell long and hard several times. 'So,' with a falsely bright, confident smile, 'you won't be late for your appointment'. She sat in the waiting room reading glossy magazines for the fifty minutes Susan was inside.

The consulting room had high windows looking out from the first floor onto the street. There were two comfortable looking armchairs and a long brown couch with a linen slip-cover over a pillow. No books, only one picture, of a boat on a rough sea at Skye. They sat in the armchairs facing one another.

Susan began: 'I don't know why I'm here.'

Dr Wells didn't respond. He was in his fifties, wearing a suit and tie, with grey hair and a pleasant face. He looked down at his hands folded in his lap.

She shifted in her chair. 'I mean, I do know why. Of course I do. But I'm not sure why I agreed to come. Except that my mother came round and collected me to make certain I'd be on time.'

He didn't return her rueful smile.

'I'm not mad you know,' she said, the smile fading. 'Or I don't think I am. But my mother believes I'm psychotic.'

'Why should your mother think that?'

Susan did not answer for a moment, then she said slowly: 'She's never believed me about anything. Not even when I was a child. Especially about Nick. And there's no doubt *that* was true.'

'Nick?'

'My uncle. She's having an affair with him now.'

Dr Wells nodded. 'Tell me about Nick,' he suggested.

Susan told him, leaving out the part about the ghost and the accusations of fraud and murder. For the moment, at least.

'He was all right,' Susan said grudgingly to her mother afterwards.

'There you are. I told you he was nice.'

'I've got another appointment in a week's time, if I want. He's sending you the bill. I may not go though,' she added warningly. But actually she felt relieved, almost exonerated. Wasn't it better to be treated as if she were a little crazy than face the consequences if she were not? She felt strangely tranquil. It felt like a heavy burden had been lifted from her shoulders. The futility of the bank statements which yesterday seemed unbearable to her, she now thought of quite calmly. They already felt like something consigned to the past, along with the vision of her father that she'd had in the studio. Something she needn't ever think about again if she didn't want to.

If it's all in my imagination, I don't have to do anything, Susan thought, as they began walking up the street, except accept the anxiety, relax in a peaceful high-ceilinged room and let the current carry me where it will. And she had to admit in the sober light of day that she'd been drinking a little too much recently. She let out a long, undulating sigh. Well, who wouldn't, under the circumstances? But she'd slow down, she decided. Drink less. See a shrink once or twice a week as her mother requested. Be a good girl for once.

'And I'm not sure,' she said, the lightness of relief still upon her, 'but I didn't get the impression that he thought I was *completely* nuts.'

'Didn't he?' her mother replied smoothly, tactful for once.

Susan could taste whisky at the back of her mouth, the urge for it was so sudden and strong.

21

Alex Emmerich's flat wasn't at all what she'd expected. When Susan had rung to ask if she could come over, she had a definite picture in her mind. On the other end of the phone she'd imagined bare floorboards, a few nice if threadbare rugs and a silver racing bike propped against the wall. Instead there was deep beige fitted carpets, heavily-patterned curtains with nets, little china painted door knobs with matching flowers on the porcelain keyhole covers. The front door was painted a pale, glossy yellow. Alex answered the door.

'I'm sorry I'm late,' Susan apologised breathlessly.

'Actually you're ten minutes early,' he replied pleasantly

'Oh, am I?' Flustered, she combed her hair behind her ears with her fingers. 'What time is it?'

He checked his watch. 'A quarter to.' He looked at her curiously. 'Don't you wear a watch?'

'I do have one. But I never wear it,' she admitted, thinking of her father's old watch with its delicate hands ticking past strips of gold. Except they did not move any longer: it hadn't been wound since his death. It had a sheen, that watch, a golden sheen, like her father's face used to have in her memory.

'Well, come in.' Alex stepped back, giving her a swift, warm smile of encouragement.

When she shrugged off her jacket, he turned to hang it on a wooden hanger hooked over a rail in the hall cupboard where, a floor above, in exactly the same cupboard, her father had kept old film reels and an electric bar heater. 'Actually I have a theory,' Alex said, as they were walking up the narrow hall, 'that people who don't wear watches never own umbrellas.' He stopped by the open door to the living-room and looked down at her – only a little way, he was not as tall as Paul. They looked into each other's eyes. His were a warm friendly brown. She was a little startled by her own reaction to this compassionate gaze. Her heart began beating unnaturally quickly. Feeling confused, she followed him into the living room and looked around.

The room they were in was all too familiar – long and spacious with wide windows running along the side of the room that overlooked the street. Structurally, the flat was identical to her father's studio. There was a large main room, a small kitchen and bathroom off a long, narrow hall that had at the end of it, she knew without looking, a fair-sized bedroom.

And yet, in another way, it couldn't have been more different to the austere, empty space upstairs. Lamps, whose fringed beige shades would give out warm circles of light when they were switched on in a few hours, were placed on small tables next to heavy cut-glass bowls for fruit. A polished dark wooden sideboard with glass doors, revealing rose-patterned plates and silver bowls, was placed at one end of the room, next to a long dining table with heavy, curved legs carved of the same dark wood. At the other end, a sofa and matching armchair and a large, ornate gold-framed mirror hanging over a fireplace in which there was a modern gas fire with fake logs. The carpet was beige and deep-pile. The overall effect was plush, tasteful, and surprisingly comforting.

'So do you?' he asked, a step away.

To hide the fact that her heart was still beating rather fast, she cast her eyes down. 'Do I what?'

'Own an umbrella.'

'No, I don't as a matter of fact. Actually I hate them.'

'What do you do when it rains?'

'I don't know. Borrow my mother's.' She shrugged. 'Or wear a hat.'

They were standing rather awkwardly round a low, fake antique table that was placed in front of the sofa. 'Sit down,' he said, gesturing. 'Please.'

'Actually, I wondered – could I use the loo?'

'Yes, of course… I expect you know where it is.'

The bathroom was pale green with matching green soap and toilet paper. Susan did not know what to make of it – her impression of Alex hadn't been of a man who chose his loo paper to match his curtains. Her face in the mirror looked a little dazed but it wasn't the mess she'd dreaded.

'Have you lived here long?' she asked curiously, when she was settled back amongst plump, beige velour cushions. Alex was sitting in the armchair opposite.

'About eighteen months. It's my grandmother's flat,' he explained. 'At seventy-six she decided to go on a world cruise. Now she's in Australia staying with her younger sister, who's seventy-three, I might add. They were both Tiller Girls in earlier days. I dread to think what they're up to now, two octogenarians high-kicking their way round Sydney. They must be having fun, at any rate – I'm not quite sure when she's coming back. Any day now, she tells me.' He grinned. 'So I keep the lavatory well stocked with loo-paper of her choice, in case you were wondering.'

'Oh, no… no, I wasn't… ' Susan demurred, and then, quickly to cover her embarrassment at having asked such an obviously transparent question: 'It's a big flat. You live alone?'

'Yes.'

Their eyes met. He fancies me, she thought. Mum was right. Presumably she'd also been right about Alex's reasons for suggesting he'd seen Steven Savage. It had just been an excuse to see her again. She looked quickly away, staring with a show of interest at a small gold-framed oil painting of a bowl of fruit and a dead goose on a table. The bird's grey feathered neck hung, long and graceful, over the edge.

'Can I get you anything?' Alex asked in the stiff, formal tones of a man who finds he has an attractive woman in his flat for the first time. 'A cup of tea? Or coffee?'

'I wouldn't mind a coffee.'

'I'm afraid there's only instant.'

'Instant's fine.'

'I'll put the kettle on then,' he said, springing up.

Susan nodded and smiled. He definitely likes me, she thought. She gave him a sidelong look through her lashes, for the first time examining him properly. He hadn't shaved that morning and his soft brown hair was dishevelled. Though he wasn't as tall as Paul, his body was strong and fit-looking. He was wearing jeans and a white teeshirt, as he had the first time they'd met. With his sensitive face and muscular body he looked, she thought, like a French film star – a cross between a philosophy student and a bank robber. He was, she realised, extremely attractive.

'Biscuits?' he asked, standing before her, arms crossed over his chest.

'Why not?' she replied with a smile.

He smiled back. 'Good. Well, I'll make the coffee then, shall I?'

The only evidence of Alex's personality in the flat was a large pile of books on the dining table. She opened the top one, a volume of *Gray's Anatomy*. '*The Deep Veins of the Upper Extremity,*' she read. '*The deep veins follow the course of the arteries, forming their venae comitantes. They are generally arranged in pairs, and connected at intervals by short transverse branches...*' She could hear Alex moving round the kitchen, the clink of cups and saucers. Underneath an illustration of a heart, it said: '*Pulmonary vessels, seen in dorsal view. A part of the right lung has been cut away to display the air-ducts and blood-vessels...*'

'Do you take sugar?' he asked, putting his head round the door.

'No, thanks.'

He came back into the room a few seconds later, holding a tray.

'Are you a doctor?' she asked, as he set it down on a low table.

'Senior House Officer,' he confirmed. 'Training to be a surgeon.'

They sat down opposite each other, the tray with the cups between them on the table. The china was delicate, gold-rimmed with pink roses. She took a sip of coffee. 'What do you hope to specialise in?'

'Diseases of the rich,' he replied promptly. 'Joke,' he explained, when she looked surprised. She smiled politely. She thought, is he being silly because he fancies me and feels awkward or is he always like this? 'No, come on, really,' she said. She wasn't sure if the flush she could feel on the surface of her skin was hope or guilt. So she said, very seriously, and without the slightest hint of flirtation in her manner, 'What kind of surgeon?'

'Thoracic. From here to here,' he explained, holding his hands sideways against his throat and waist.

'Have you done any yet?'

'What? Surgery? A little.'

'I've always wondered what it feels like when a knife is pushed into skin. Is it like cutting meat?'

'You can't really compare it with that.'

'Why? Is it smoother? Easier?'

'Yes, much. Because you use a scalpel which is razor sharp. We do a gentle action – ' he made a small swaying movement with his hand in the air, 'and the skin just splits.'

'And do they bleed immediately?'

'Of course. Like a damn pig sometimes.' He laughed a little nervously, leaning forward to offer her the plate of biscuits. 'Why do you want to know?'

'Just curious.'

'A bit of a gruesome interest, isn't it?'

'Actually I'm thinking of writing a book.'

'Really? What kind?'

'Fiction,' she replied, taking a digestive. 'Thanks. A murder mystery. My heroine kills a man.'

She poured a little more milk into her coffee from a small china mug, then took a bite of the biscuit and sat back, the biscuit on her knee.

'I could get you a plate, if you like.'

'No, thanks. This is fine.' She nibbled the biscuit thoughtfully. 'Say you put a knife hard into someone's chest. Would it go straight in?'

'It depends. You could hit one of the ribs or the breast bone, in which case it would bounce straight off.'

'But if you hit – ' She made a gesture.

'Somewhere in between? Yes, it would go straight in.'

'And bleed.'

'Of course.'

'And if you knifed someone in the leg? Would he be able to move afterwards?'

Alex laughed uncomfortably. 'What does she do to this man? Carve him up?'

142

'I'm considering it,' she replied seriously.

'Sounds pretty disgusting.' But he smiled, dipping his biscuit into the coffee and eating the soggy piece. 'The book will probably be snapped up and made into a million dollar movie. I must remember never to go and see it. Yes, he'd be able to move. It depends on the person. If someone's really frightened they could run with half their leg off. It just means the muscles in one leg are disabled. They've still got the other leg. And fear is a great spur to action.'

She picked up a box of matches from the table. There was a painting of a bullfighter waving a red flag on the matchbox holder; two ordinary matchboxes fitted inside. 'So what would you have to do to actually stop someone from being able to run away?' she asked, looking at the little brightly painted box in her hand.

He thought for a moment before taking another bite. 'Cut their throat. If you cut someone's throat,' he said, forgetting his reluctance and becoming interested now, 'you cut across the windpipe.' He made a motion with one hand. 'So not only is there a lot of blood – a *lot* – but they'd also choke. At least, I assume that's what happens.' He laughed self-consciously. 'I wouldn't know since I've never done it. But one thing's for sure – without help, they'd bleed to death. Or at least lose enough blood to be unconscious.'

'Would it be quick?'

'This has nothing to do with medicine, you know. These are forensic questions.'

'I'm just curious… as research for the book…' But there isn't one, she reminded herself. He's got a point. Exactly why *am* I asking these questions?

'I should imagine – You said it's a man who gets killed in your book?'

'Yes. It's a man.'

'I should imagine he'd die quickly.' He crammed the rest of the biscuit into his mouth and drained his cup of coffee, then stretched forward to place the empty cup and saucer on the table. 'He'd have coughed up a hell of a lot of blood.'

'What would that mean?'

'He'd die of drowning,' he replied casually, brushing the crumbs from his jeans onto the carpet. 'He'd have drowned.'

She was crazy. Nina and her mother had said so. The shrink had more or less implied it. There was nothing to lose any longer.

'I want to know,' she said, 'exactly what happened when you saw my father – '

'*Thought* I saw your father.'

'Yes. What happened when you thought you saw my father?'

Alex's hands were hanging loosely between his legs. He leant forward in the armchair, picked up another biscuit from the plate on the table, broke it in half then changed his mind and put both pieces back down again. 'Nothing much,' he said. 'I spoke to him. I behaved like an idiot. That was all.'

'What did you say?'

'It was late. I wasn't thinking. I'd had a beer or two in the bar after work though I wasn't really pissed. The lift had gone up to the sixth floor though I hadn't pressed the button. Or perhaps I had. Perhaps I made a mistake. Perhaps I *was* pissed. I got out of the lift and saw this man standing at the end of the corridor, in the shadows. There was just the light from the lift.'

She thought of the hall upstairs. 'But the lights are turned on brightly in the building all the time, even in the middle of the day,' she objected.

'Yes, that's true.' Alex frowned. 'Well, for some reason they weren't that evening. A bulb must have gone and not been replaced. That sometimes happens. There were no lights, that's all I can tell you.'

'On all the floors?'

'Yes – no.' He looked confused. 'I'm not sure. I think they were working on the fifth floor when I got home.' He frowned, trying to picture it.

'Anyway, you got out of the lift.'

'Yes.'

'In semi-darkness.'

'Yes.'

'Then what did you see?'

'I saw this man standing at the end of the corridor outside sixty-nine. He was putting a key in the lock – '

'How could you tell?'

'What?'

'That he was putting it in. Not taking it out.'

'Oh. Well, he might have been. I simply saw someone – '

'Who looked like my father.'

'Yes, who looked a little like Steven, inserting a key or taking it out. So I just assumed – I said something to him.'

'What did you say? Exactly?'

'I said, Good evening Steven, or that kind of thing – I don't remember *exactly*. I remember taking a step towards him, though.'

'And he didn't answer?'

'No.'

'Do you think he heard you?'

Alex combed his fingers through his hair. His face looked strained. 'It's strange you ask that. He was half-turned in my direction but it was as if he didn't see me. He wasn't ignoring me, he just didn't seem to register I was there.'

'Why did you think that?'

'It was just the impression I had.'

'But *you* saw *him*?'

'Yes, whoever it was. Mostly in profile. I could see that he had a beard.' He paused, thinking. 'It was the way he was standing, I suppose – hands in the pockets of his raincoat, head down, shoulders slightly hunched…'

'I know.'

'That was all really. It was an impression. At that moment I didn't doubt that I was addressing Steven Savage.'

'It was only later that you changed your mind?'

'It was later that I realised it couldn't have been him. I remembered – ' His voice fell. 'I remembered he's dead.'

They didn't speak. Alex was sitting with his head down, staring at the floor.

'What was it like up there?' she asked, after a moment. 'I mean, what did you feel at the time?'

'Cold,' he answered immediately. 'Overwhemingly cold.'

He lifted his head and stared at her. 'You asked what I felt – that was it. It was like a fridge door had opened and I'd stepped inside. The drop in temperature was almost tangible. To be honest, I didn't stick around. I didn't wait for the lift to return. I don't know what got into me but for some reason I started running. I didn't exactly make a decision to do it. Just found that I was. I ran as fast as my feet could carry me and when I got home, I locked the door behind me.' He gave a pale grin. 'I'm sorry. I told you I behaved stupidly.'

Susan didn't reply. She couldn't speak. Her hands were trembling; she felt that she'd paled. The room had grown darker. Everything seemed to have turned itself over, hung heavily upside down in mid-air, then righted itself again. She sat on the sofa in a room that was the same and yet so different to the studio upstairs, staring blindly at the painted matchbox holder, at the bullfighter holding a red flag out to an invisible bull, her heart beating fit to burst, feeling absolutely shocked and horrified.

'It's funny,' she heard Alex say. 'But I thought I saw Steven once or twice before. Through two sets of folded doors on a bus – you know, when you're ready to get off and they're open? Or turning a corner in the street, that kind of thing. Of course it always turned out to be someone else.'

'What if it really were him?' she asked, looking up. 'What if it really were him that you saw?'

He stared at her.

'What if you really did see my father up there last Tuesday night?'

He went white. 'Do you mean – he's not dead?'

'No, I don't mean that,' she said softly. 'He's dead all right. But – ' She looked him straight in the eyes. 'I saw him too.'

Still pale, he gazed at her. 'I'll make some more coffee,' he decided, as if he'd known all along that was what she was going to say.

And in that moment she knew. Knew every dreadful, joyous thing. Still pale he gazed at her. 'I'll make some more coffee,' he said, getting to his feet, as if he knew it too.

She wasn't sure why she wanted to visit the flat again. She didn't really – it was the last place she wanted to go. But Susan found herself arriving at Keyes Court with plenty of time to spare before meeting Alex, so she must have decided at some point. She'd thought of her mother and Dr Wells as she strode purposefully through the heavy street doors and got into the lift. 'The rise of reason,' she'd murmured, as the lift moved up.

Smoothly past the second floor... the fifth... the sixth... Her stomach lurched as the smooth journey ended with a shudder and the doors opened soundlessly. For a moment she fought with her sense of where she was and when, and almost lost. She stepped out into the familiar hallway.

Even in broad daylight the lights in the building were full on. Little natural light came through the thick bubbled glass window that ran along one wall. It didn't feel very different up there at eleven in the morning to midnight. There was no real sense of time. Just place, Susan thought, searching in her bag for the keys. She could feel them moving around near the bottom. She dragged them out, untangling her own house keys from the bunch. Hearing the wheeze as the lift doors closed, she turned sharply back – the elevator detached itself from the landing and started its slow downward journey through the building to street level.

It was incredibly quiet on the sixth floor. Just the buzz of lights and the whirr of the lift, the faintest of bumps as it landed. There was something weird about the silence that reigned there under the brooding white glare. Perhaps that was why she was shivering as she stared, key in hand, at the numbers on the studio door. Six. Nine. Sixty-nine. Or perhaps it was because, whatever her rational intentions, she felt too afraid to venture inside.

This is it, she told herself, reaching out with a quickened pulse, this is definitely it. The key was between her fingers. She stared at the numbers on the door. She stood there, for what seemed like an age, chilled and fearful, unable to insert the key into the lock. She couldn't seem to make that everyday move. Holding a key in the air, then inserting it. She just couldn't will the movement. Or rather, when she willed it, the message did not translate into action.

Cold sweat broke out on her body. Her hand was quite steady but it was as if the lock were an enormous magnet charged with an opposing force that did not attract her hand but pushed it hard away. As if her fingers were north and it was south, or vice versa. Her fear was creating a thick, impenetrable barrier which she couldn't break through.

'Hello?' she gasped, as if she was short of air. 'Is anyone there?' She felt ridiculous, like a cheap medium at a fake séance. But despite the chill in the air, the sweat gathered under her arms and ran down her body.

She waited for as long as she could, muscles tense, ready for instant retreat, trying to ignore the icy sensation at the base of her neck and the chill in her bones, trying to inch the key closer…

Then, with a shake of her head, she let her arm fall. When she lifted it to try again, the same thing happened. Her hand was paralysed. Beyond a certain point, it was outside her control.

'Hello? Are you there?' She spoke more loudly into the silence.

No one answered. Her strained, unnatural voice died away in stillness.

'So much for reason,' she muttered.

She let her hand drop, giving up the attempt. The keys fell from her stiff, cold fingers. She didn't dare look round: she was too afraid of what she might see. Only as she began the dash down the stairs did she manage a trembling peep, a quick, fearful turn of the head before turning the corner, sneaking a look behind her.

Nothing. Just the quiet, purring hall.

Taking two or three steps at a time, Susan leapt the last few and found herself crouched on the fifth floor, still shivering with cold, outside Alex's flat. A glossy yellow door. A door-knob in the shape of a lion's head some way above her head. She was holding the keys – she must have picked them up again without thinking. She pocketed them. Panting much harder than the brief flight warranted, she rested her forehead against the yellow door until she'd recovered her breath. Her heart beating fast, she pulled herself straight and stood, her forehead damp against the paint, legs still a little wobbly, with her finger poised over the buzzer. What if – ?

But, here, there was nothing wrong with her hand.

What did you feel at the time? she had asked him.

Cold, he had answered. *Overwhelmingly cold. I didn't hang about for the lift. I ran as fast as my feet could carry me and when I got home I locked the door behind me.*

GAIL LEVY

And she knew in that instant that he really had seen her father. It hadn't just been an excuse to see her again. It wasn't all a big pretence. Whatever her mother claimed, whatever Nina had said, it wasn't only her imagination. He'd seen him too.

She told him everything, the whole story. Sitting in that secure, comfortable, too plush lounge, she told it all. Not just bits with others pieces missing, as she had with Nina and Jonathan Woolf, but all of it from start to finish. He listened to her seriously, attending without interrupting. It was a relief to talk to someone who did not stop her all the time, but just nodded encouragement when it was needed. When she finished, he didn't speak for a moment. 'You haven't told anyone else about this, have you?' he asked, when he was sure she'd said all she wanted.

She looked at him sharply. 'Meaning?'

'Only that Nick could get pretty nasty if he hears you're going about making accusations like this about him. At the very least, you're accusing him of being involved in fraud and drug-running. That's the very least.' He was smiling slightly, but beneath the apparently casual remark there was an urgency in his voice that hadn't been there before. 'Who else have you told? What about that friend of yours? The blonde?'

'You mean Nina? Well, if you count Nina, then I've spoken to Jonathan and Hyman Wexler, too.'

'That's different. They're obliged to keep what you tell them in confidence. Nina isn't. What is it?' he asked, seeing her face. He half rose from the armchair, an expression of concern on his face. 'Are you alright?'

But the room was spinning around her. She couldn't easily breathe. Isabella. She'd told it all to Isabella... What had she done? If her mother spoke to Nick – if she told him only half of it. Nick might not believe the way in which she'd learnt it, but that wouldn't matter. He'd know that she knew... Susan clutched the neck of her shirt with one hand, trying to pull it loose. 'I'm sorry,' she gasped. 'I just feel a little...'

'Loosen your collar,' Alex ordered.

She pulled open the top two buttons of her shirt. 'It's OK... I'm fine... I'm –'

'I'll get you some water.'

He left the room and returned quickly with a glass. 'Drink,' he instructed, handing it to her.

She took a couple of gulps, then wiped her mouth on her sleeve. She put the glass down on the table jerkily so that a little water splashed onto the polished wood. 'It's just that –' Still feeling a little light-headed, she stared down at the small pool. 'I did tell my mother.'

'You told your *mother*?' He tried, and failed, not to sound alarmed. He sat down beside her on the sofa. 'What did you tell her?'

'Everything,' Susan confessed.

'That you thought Nick was guilty of bringing drugs into the country?'

'Yes.'

He lowered his voice a notch. 'Murder?'

'Yes,' she replied, dropping her head to shut out Alex's worried look.

'Not your father's ghost?'

'Everything,' she affirmed. 'I was so angry with her about her affair with Nick that it all sort of popped out. I thought it only fair.'

'Fair? You told your mother you'd just held a long and meaningful conversation with your father's ghost because you thought it only *fair*?'

'I also told her you'd seen him, too.'

He took a deep, wondering breath. 'Oh, great. How did she respond?'

'She didn't believe me.'

'No. No, I don't suppose she would. You're very involved with her, aren't you?'

'Involved?' Susan looked surprised. 'Not really. Actually we're not very close at all.'

'Then why did you feel compelled to rush round and confess everything to her?'

'It wasn't a confession, I just hoped it would push her to end things with Nick.' She bit her lip, acknowledging to herself that Alex might well be right. 'Anyway, she won't tell him anything,' she declared more confidently than she felt. 'Because she thinks I'm well and truly cracking up. She won't want to talk about that. Not to Nick. Not to anyone. She's too scared it will turn out to be the truth.'

She shivered, feeling at the same time reassured by her own words. It was true. Isabella would deny anything out of the ordinary. She might take her only daughter to a shrink, but she'd hush it up afterwards.

Susan did up a button of her shirt, gazing across the room at the pile of medical books on the table, reflecting on the strangeness of the story she'd just told. Then, aware of Alex's eyes on her profile, she glanced back, wondering what exactly he thought about it all. 'You don't think I am, do you?'

'What?'

'Cracking up.'

He hesitated a fraction before replying, 'Of course not.' But his voice was so soothing that it didn't reassure her. 'All I'm saying is that whether or not it's the truth, even if there's only a grain of truth in it, Nick could get pretty nasty if he hears you've been spreading stories like this. He might start worrying that someone will take you seriously.'

'But you believe me? I mean, you must. Because you saw my father too, didn't you?'

'There's stranger things in heaven and earth than lie in your philosophy,' Alex misquoted, avoiding her eyes.

'But the overwhelming feeling of cold? You didn't make *that* up.'

When he didn't respond, she didn't push it any further. If he wants to deny it that's his business, she thought. *I* know he saw Steven. That deadly, unremitting chill in the air. Alex couldn't have imagined that. So she only smiled and said lightly, 'I had a feeling one of us would quote that sooner or later. I'm just glad it was you.' But her feeling of relief and exhilaration ebbed away slightly.

She got to her feet. 'I'd better go. Thanks for the coffee, Alex. And for listening to me babbling on.'

'Don't go,' he said impulsively. He stood up, too. 'Have another coffee. Or a beer or something.'

They looked at one another for a moment. 'I didn't think you were babbling,' he said gently. 'Please stay.'

She looked into his face a little longer, then shook her head. 'I better not. I only put two hours' worth of coins in the meter.'

'Yes,' he said, drawing back a little. He frowned, looking troubled. She reached for her bag. When she straightened his eyes were still on her. 'Look, shall I give you my phone number?' she asked, slinging the bag over her shoulder. 'In case you remember anything else.'

'I'd like that. I have a pen here somewhere...' After a short hunt he found a pencil inside one of the medical books and hastily ripped half a page from a file. She scribbled down her number on the jagged sheet and handed it back to him. He pushed the piece of paper into the front pocket of his jeans. 'I'll get your coat,' he smiled.

As he took her jacket from the cupboard and handed it to her, his face grew serious. 'What if he's innocent?' he asked.

He doesn't believe me, she thought, with a jolt of panic. He doesn't believe me either. She said: 'He's not innocent.'

He stared into her eyes, brown into brown. 'How can you know for sure?'

'I know,' she said, in sudden angry despair

22

Susan chose a table near the back of the café and ordered a tuna sandwich. Closing her eyes, she rested her head in her hands, listening to the sound of conversation around her. 'I know,' she had said to Alex with certainty. 'He's not innocent. I know.' But did she really? Even as she said the words so adamantly she could feel her stomach knotting and doubt tightening her throat. The uneasiness she could see in his eyes had unnerved her. So they'd both felt a little chilly outside the studio? So they'd both felt forced to run for their lives? Did that really mean anything? *You just can't accept you're living in a dream world*, an inner voice was saying. *You just don't want to accept it.* When the waitress brought her food she wolfed down the sandwich, suddenly realising how hungry she was. Once she'd drunk a second cup of coffee, she lit a cigarette. '*I know…*'

And so she did, she thought, breathing out smoke on a sigh. Whatever the bank statements showed, or did not show, however many psychoanalysts she saw, swept by sudden doubts, Nick was guilty: she was sure of it. More than sure – in her heart, in every fibre of her being, she *knew*. She'd seen her father's ghost. And so had Alex.

I am not mad. *I'm not mad*, she thought. Just back to square one. The food and drink had restored her a little. She had some apple cake and a third cappuccino, then paid the bill.

The phone was ringing as she opened the door to the flat. She sprinted for it, snatching up the receiver before the machine could switch itself on. It was Jonathan. They must have said all the usual stuff – How are you? Fine. And you? Don't you *ever* switch on you're mobile, Susan? But the first thing she heard him say with any clarity was: '…There's another account.'

'Another – ?'

'Yeah. Wexler's found another one. Looks like it's operating like a client account.'

Susan sat down. 'What's that?'

'A client account?'

'Yes, what is it?'

'Besides the company's own office account there's sometimes another bank account with money lodged from clients,' Jonathan rattled off glibly. 'It's not the company's money, it's the clients' money, but it's held on their behalf. Often very large sums. As, indeed, is the case in our account at present. Twelve million, I believe. ' Susan heard him taking a slurp of tea or coffee on the other end of the phone. 'The money isn't due to be paid out for another ten days and, of course, we're not allowed to touch it. However,' another loud slurp, 'say I *did*, and then paid it quickly back again, it's not going to be that obvious.'

'Why not?'

'Because there's money going in and out of the client account all the time with no one keeping tabs on it. In the company's main account everyone knows exactly what's in there and why, so large sums of money going in or out would be spotted immediately. But in the client account it's a little different. You needn't know what was in there at any one time and you wouldn't *expect* to know. Finding this interesting?'

'I never thought I'd say this about a bank account – but very.'

She could hear the smile in his voice as he went on: 'Client accounts are usually only operated by law firms. However, sometimes other businesses use them. As does Savage Associates, as it turns out. If you want to look at it, it'll cost six hundred quid. Do you?'

'Yes. Yes! Cash?'

'Of course. Look, I'm afraid I'm tied up for the next few hours. Would you mind collecting the copies yourself? Is that possible? From Hyman Wexler's office in Finchley? They close about five. You'll make it – if you hurry.'

'Give me the address.'

She hadn't even had a chance to take off her jacket. Her bag was still slung over her shoulder. Since the trip to Wexler, she'd kept cash in readiness for such a contingency. She opened the fridge where it was stored, and stuffed it in the bag. She hurried out into the street. There were no cabs in sight. Should she take the car? She stood for a second unable to decide, then started walking towards the blue Mini a few streets away. At the corner she turned swiftly on her heels. The tube would be quicker at this time of day anyway, she decided.

The secretary was a peroxide blonde and wore a turquoise two piece with matching ear-rings. She looked up blandly from her keyboard when Susan inquired: 'Mr Wexler?'

'He's out.'

'Well, maybe you can help.'

'Only if you're picking up or dropping off.'

'I am.'

'Collection or deposit?' the secretary asked wearily, reaching for her book.

'Collection.'

'Name?'

'Susan Savage.'

'Oh, yes. You're here.' The woman snapped the book shut and bent to open a drawer. She slid something out. 'I'm supposed to take the money from you before I hand this over.'

Her hand was resting on a large manilla envelope. Her nails were long and painted frosty pink. She wore a diamond cluster next to a plain gold ring. Susan fumbled with her bag. The zip stuck at the side as usual. She wrenched it open and counted out the money. Mostly fifties, some twenties: six hundred pounds in cash. 'Is that right?'

The woman nodded and scooped the notes expertly into a neat pile. The envelope was handed to Susan in return. She felt a rush of adrenaline crackle through her as her hands touched the thick buff paper. She stuffed it into her bag. After three tries, she managed to zip it up again. 'That's it then,' she said, flustered. 'Thanks.'

On the wall outside was a white melamite sign: 'H.Wexler Investigations Ltd., Second floor'. Susan turned past it and the opticians next door, then strode back along the dreary High Street to the tube station without opening her bag to look at the envelope once. Sitting on the platform bench, squashed between a sturdy woman in a smart belted coat and a girl listening to an iPod – Susan could hear the thump of the drums and the wail of guitars – she couldn't wait any longer. Her hands sweated in anticipation as she opened the envelope.

There were only six sheets inside, but this time the amounts were large. A hundred thousand pounds in January, three hundred thousand in March. February, April, July and December had the highest amounts of all, each for half a million pounds. The transactions were all pretty regular, as far as she could see. The money came in and went out again within a few months. On the third page she stopped. She scanned the figures through again, her heart beating faster. A train pulled in; she ignored it. The doors slid open and closed again. Her eyes still glued to the page, Susan remained perched on the edge of the now empty bench, staring at the numbers, only vaguely aware of the train moving off.

The transaction was clear. A cheque for the sum total of all the money in the account had been written on the twenty-fifth of April. Two days later, on the twenty-seventh, the money had been returned. She flicked quickly through. Exactly the same thing had happened in July. On the twenty-fourth, the account was wiped clean. On the twenty-sixth, all back again. On both occasions, five hundred and fifty thousand pounds. Out. Then in again. Susan stared, hands trembling, at the list of figures. She couldn't quite believe what she was holding in her hands. It's proof, she told herself. This is actual proof.

She took a deep breath and laughed uncertainly, recalling a game she had played with Nick when she was small. 'I'll show you a magic trick,' he'd said. She couldn't have been more than four or five. 'What's it called?' she asked.

'It's called – Now you see it, now you don't.'

He'd taken a 10p coin and shown it to her lying in the flat of his palm. Then he'd raised his arm in the air, mumbled a few words, lowered it and opened his hand. She'd stared at his empty palm. 'All gone,' he announced, smiling at her amazed face. Then he'd closed his fingers, mumbled a few more words and, when he opened them, 'There,' before her delighted eyes, the coin was back.

Looking at the pages in her hand, Susan shook her head in equal disbelief. Her eyes resting on the printed page, she said aloud to the empty platform: 'Five hundred and fifty thousand pounds of Savage Associates' money. Now you see it – now you don't.'

Alex was almost as shaken as she was when Susan showed him the bank statement. 'Do you realise,' he said, after a moment's reading, 'what this means?'

She nodded slowly.

'He's been taking money *out* of the company,' he said, 'it's nothing more complicated than that. Look, a huge sum goes out in April,' he pointed, 'then again in July. On the twenty-fifth, five hundred thousand pounds disappears. Only briefly, he pays it straight back in again. It's all there two days later.' He drummed a corner of the paper into his palm. 'Christ! He was borrowing the money. He wasn't part of a complicated scam. Jonathan Woolf's theory was clever, but wrong. He was simply stealing it.'

They stared at each other in excitement. They were in Susan's kitchen, the papers spread out between them on the table. She'd phoned Alex and asked him to come over, barely suppressed excitement in her voice: she'd shown him the copies as soon as he walked in the door.

'But why take such a risk?' he asked, looking at her but continuing to flick the paper quietly against his thumb.

'I've been wondering that too. Only I've had a little longer to think about it.' She stood up. 'Cup of tea, Alex?'

'Yeah, thanks.'

She filled the kettle with water, then switched it on. Elbows on the table, hands in his hair, Alex watched her. She turned round, leaning back against the countertop and took a deep breath. 'Suppose Nick had decided to buy a few kilos of cocaine to sell himself,' she said. 'Supposing he thought, why should I waste my time simply shipping the stuff? I'm in so deep already, why shouldn't I sell a load of it too, and make real money? Money I can retire on. Money that will make me rich, even without doing another day's work in my life. Nick knows the drugs' cartel aren't going to say no to him. He's providing a legitimate front for their traffic. To them, he's invaluable. And they agree. Why not? It ties him in all the tighter anyway. If he ships the stuff under cover of his reputable shipping firm they, in return, will let him buy a stack of it to sell himself.'

She sat down again opposite Alex and looked at him eagerly. 'They aren't interested in where he gets the money from. Why should they be? And he has no reason to tell them. He simply borrows a large amount of money from his own company for a few days to do a deal himself.'

'You think he stole half a million pounds of the firm's money to buy drugs.'

'He might think of it as a short term loan rather than stealing. And it's the logical place for him to get a large amount. He thinks, it's my company. It's me that's slogging my guts out. Just a few days, that's all, and I make millions.' Her eyes were bright. 'The street price of cocaine varies a little but generally it's about fifty pounds a gram.'

'Is it?'

'Yes. I checked.' She leaned forward. 'He takes the money out of the client account and no one's supposed to notice. Except someone does. Well, it's possible, isn't it?'

'It's certainly *possible*. It would be fraudulent use of the company account. But it's possible.'

'He makes a hell of a lot if he does it that way.'

'A lot,' Alex agreed.

'The drugs' cartel aren't going to pay him before he's shipped the stuff. They're not going to hand over hundreds of thousands of pounds worth of drugs on a promise. He might open an account in Switzerland or wherever in readiness for full payment but, until the job's over, it would be empty. He has to get some money in advance of the shipment. He can't borrow it from Savage Associates' main account because that would be immediately apparent. But why would it if it were from this other account? Who would notice if half a million went missing from the client account for a day? Who *did* notice? No one who's still alive to tell the tale.'

The kettle clicked itself off. She didn't move.

'This is pure hypothesis,' Alex said quietly.

'Yes,' she agreed. 'But extremely likely. Knowing Nick.'

'Risky though. Is he the type?'

'Oh yes. He'd think he was invincible.'

Alex looked at the sheet of paper in his hand. 'On Monday evening the money leaves the account,' he muttered unwillingly. 'On Wednesday morning, it's repaid. He's made a fortune and no one notices a thing.'

'No one would ever know… ' Susan murmured, recalling a phrase of her father's.

They stared at each other without speaking for a moment.

'All this proves is embezzlement,' Alex said at last. 'It doesn't show that Nick was involved.'

She bit her lip. 'Then we just have to show that he was.'

She picked up a sheet of paper and examined it, tapping her index finger against her bottom lip thoughtfully. 'There are cheque numbers by each transaction,' she said, after a moment. 'Look, here's the number of the cheque taking all the money out of the account. And there,' she dashed her finger against the page, 'is the cheque that paid it back again. The question is – where was it kept in the meantime?' She looked up. 'We need to show this money was held in Nick's account for a day.'

'Yes, but how?'

She frowned. 'That is the question.'

She stood, still frowning and clicked the kettle on again. The water was still hot. It didn't take long to boil. She dropped a teabag in each mug and poured boiling water on top. Adding milk, she squeezed the teabags out with a spoon and put the mugs on the table. Alex picked one up and blew into it before taking a sip. She picked up her tea but didn't drink, staring into the steaming brown liquid. 'Are you any good with computers, Alex?' she asked, gazing into the mug.

'Pretty good. Why?'

She looked up, her face brightening. 'Because I think I know what to do,' she said, putting the mug of tea down.

'We'll go at night,' Susan said, 'about nine-thirty. There'll only be the night-watchman then. Monty. He's known me since I was a child. I'll say – I'll say I left something in Dad's office ages ago and I've only just got round to picking it up. You've come with me for moral support. We'll be a bit merry, we've been drinking. We were nearby, we decided to drive over on the spur of the moment. I'll take something with me in my bag. A photo or something. A picture in a frame. Then when we leave, I can show it to him. Look, I can say, waving it in the air. Here it is. Found it. Thanks very much for your help. Jolly nice of you. We'll go to Dad's office and look around, open a few drawers of his desk, that sort of thing. Meanwhile you can slip down the corridor to – What's the matter? Why are you looking at me like that?'

'This won't work.'

'Yes, it will. Why shouldn't it? You can find the office where the accounts are kept, can't you? I'll give you directions.'

'They aren't going to be lying around in the open, you know. They'll be stored on computer.'

'Exactly. On the hard drive. That's where your computer skills come in.'

'There's probably a password. Do you know what it is?'

'I'm pretty sure there isn't. And if there is – well, we'll just have to play it by ear.'

'It won't work,' he repeated.

She looked into his face for a moment. 'Do you want another cup of tea?'

'I haven't finished this one.'

She slid across to the chair next to him. 'I can't do this alone. I'm crap with technology.' Elbows on the table, she leant towards him slightly. 'Alex. Alex, please.'

'It won't work,' he said, but he sounded less convincing than before. She could see he was wavering.

'It will. I'm sure it will,' she said persuasively, placing her hand on his arm. He didn't speak for a moment. She could see him struggling with himself. She could almost hear the to-and-fro ticking of his mind. 'What photo are you thinking of taking along?' he asked finally.

'We'll take the one from the hall,' she decided, sitting up straight. 'The black-and-white shot of a woman's bare feet walking in sand. It's about the right size. And it's an appropriate choice. It's the last photograph I ever took with Dad.'

Her hand was still on his arm. Slowly he shook his head.

'If this works I'll be – '

'Pleased?'

'That wasn't the word I was searching for. But, yes, I'll be very pleased indeed.'

Savage Associates had its head office in a large, red brick building in East London named Britannia House. They left the car outside in one of the parking bays. They'd gone for a drink in a pub around the corner 'to be realistic'. A glass of wine later, Susan was looking up at the silent building while Alex locked the car. Her heart was thumping hard. The shipping company's offices were mostly on the first floor. No lights were on. Except for the reception area, the building was in darkness.

This is going to be fine, she told herself as they stood on the steps outside. Just fine. We'll simply shoot in, get the info we need and shoot out again. No problem. She had been saying this to herself all evening but it seemed a little different now they were there.

An Asian man, in his forties, with several large bunches of keys on a belt around his waist appeared on the other side of the re-inforced glass when they pressed the buzzer. Not Monty. Her heart sank. She didn't recognise him. 'I'm Susan,' she mouthed into the speaker. 'Steven Savage's daughter. I wanted to collect something from his office. Would you mind?'

'Steven Savage's daughter?' The man frowned.

'Yes.' She raised her voice. 'Nicholas Savage is my uncle,' she shouted in despair.

'Oh yes! Yes!' the man said, unbolting the door. 'We have never met, I think, but I have heard all about you.' He smiled widely. 'I am,' he pointed to his chest, 'Vishram.'

She breathed a sigh of relief. 'This is Alex,' she introduced him. 'Dr Alex Emmerich.' She stepped through the doors, Alex following close behind. 'Where's Monty?'

'Monty works only two nights now,' Vishram replied, looking serious. 'And I work the other five. He is an old man, Doctor,' he explained to Alex, 'and must rest often.'

Alex nodded understandingly. 'It's Mr Emmerich actually,' he muttered to Susan under his breath as they followed Vishram into the building. 'I'm a surgeon.'

'Doctor sounds better,' she whispered back. 'Just needed to pick up something from Dad's office,' she loudly announced. 'I left a photograph behind last time I was here. A framed black-and-white pic. A woman's bare feet walking in sand. Very soft and dry. The sand, that is. Not the feet.'

You're talking too much, she told herself. Just act casually. He doesn't know your heart is beating fit to burst and your hands are sweating. They were walking into the reception area. A sofa and two armchairs were on a raised platform. Opposite, on a white laminate desk-top, a television was blaring out the canned laughter of a sit-com.

'We shouldn't be more than five minutes,' she called over the noise, marching straight ahead. 'Is that OK?' She glanced over her shoulder. Her heart missed a beat. Vishram was standing at the end of the corridor, watching them. 'Stop! Stop right now!' she heard him shout in her imagination. 'I must telephone to Mr Nicholas for permission! This cannot be allowed!' She carried on walking, expecting to hear the watchman's clear command at any moment. Alex was just a few steps behind her. She strode on, her shoulders hunched as protection against the dreaded sound.

Vishram called out: 'Would you like the lights on, Miss? I will turn them on for you. Yes?' The fluorescent strip flickered on.

'Great. Much better.' She half-turned without slowing and gave a little wave. 'Thanks.'

The hall was long with doors on either side. Even under bright lights, the corridor with its lino floor and grubby cream walls seemed lost and lonely. Susan's heart was pounding. Her mouth was dry. She felt a mixture of excitement and fear. It was strange being there without either her father or Isabella, or even Nick. She turned the corner, then stopped uncertainly. Another narrow corridor, walled with doors, stretched ahead of them.

'Which one is it?' Alex asked quietly.

'I'm not sure… This one, I think.' She reached out her hand and tried the door. It was locked. 'Shit! We'll have to go back and ask Vishram to unlock it.'

Silently, Alex handed her a bunch of keys. 'Try one of these,' he suggested.

She looked at him for a second, then began fitting the keys into the lock. Her hands were trembling. 'Shit! Shit!' she kept swearing when a key didn't work.

'Let me try,' Alex said, taking them from her. He found the right key on the third go. She let out her breath as he twisted the knob and the door swung open. It was her father's room all right. She recognised the thick blue carpet and the kilim rug on top of it.

'Where's the accounts office?' Alex asked.

'Four doors along.'

'On which side?'

'This side.'

'Keep a look out,' he warned her.

She hovered nervously in the corridor. It seemed to take forever for Alex to find the right key. She had almost given up when she saw him standing in the open doorway. He gave a quick wave and disappeared. She stepped into her father's office, pulling the framed photograph out of her bag. She set it on the desk in front of her and prepared to wait.

She wished she were wearing a watch so that she would at least know how long she'd been sitting there. She sat stiffly on her father's chair, behind his desk, staring down at the photograph she'd brought with her. After a while, she relaxed enough to stand up and wander around. The room had been stripped of anything personal. All pictures on the walls, the pots of plants and few pieces of sculpture had been removed, leaving only the bare bones of an impersonal office. Computer unplugged and covered. Telephone unplugged. Empty shelves, kept dusted. She ran a finger along to check. Her father had kept a lot of his old philosophy books here. She wondered where they were now. Grey filing cabinet, locked. Even the desk was empty when she opened the top drawer. Except for the deep-pile carpet and the rug, the room might have belonged to anyone.

There was a square mark in the pile where another filing cabinet had once stood. She walked around for a bit longer then sat down again at the desk and idly opened the middle drawer. Nothing inside this one except for a single green Bic pen rolling around. She slid the drawer shut and pulled open the bottom one.

Blank paper still in its box, a few brand new envelopes, some brown, some white. Five first class stamps. At the back of the drawer, some old cheques, held together by an elastic band. She slid off the band and examined the cheques one by one. The first few had been paid long ago and returned by the bank – each had on it a smudged red circular stamp. 'Wainright and Co,' she read on the top one. 'Two hundred and twenty-three pounds only.' Signed in black: Steven Savage on behalf of Savage Associates. She was still looking at the familiar signature when the door opened and Alex stuck his head round. 'Let's go,' he said quietly.

She shoved the cheques into the pocket of her leather jacket. 'Find anything?' she asked in a low voice as she hurried up the corridor after him. He didn't answer, just handed her the bunch of keys once they were in Reception. Her eyes met his. She could read nothing in them.

She walked over to where Vishram was watching TV and laid the keys on top of the white veneer. 'Thanks. We turned off the lights.' She waited for a second as if interested. 'Good programme?'

'Very good.'

'Really?' She peered at the screen.

'You should watch it. I can't recall now what it's called but it's on ITV at nine-thirty.'

'Maybe I will. It looks very funny.'

'Oh, yes, it is. Did you find what you were looking for?'

'Yes, thanks,' Susan said, patting her bag. At the same time she realised that she didn't have the photograph. It was still standing on the desk in her father's office in its wooden frame. For a moment her heart seemed to stop, she couldn't breathe. Well, too late to go back for it now. How would she explain what they'd been doing all this time if not searching for, and finding, the photo? She dug her fingernails into sweating palms.

'There's no need to mention I've been here,' she heard herself manage. 'Everyone's always complaining how forgetful I am as it is.' She gave a glazed smile. Vishram smiled back. 'I won't,' he assured her. 'Mr Nick rarely comes in nowadays. Maybe once a fortnight to see if things are continuing along in an orderly fashion. It was nice meeting you, Miss.'

'Send my best to Monty. Goodnight.'

She hurried after Alex. Her legs felt wobbly, especially when she thought of the picture she'd left behind on the desk. She glanced briefly back at

Britannia House. 'Well? Find anything?' she asked urgently, when she'd caught up with him.

Alex smiled over the roof of the car. 'You were right. No password.' He got in and leant across to unlock the door on the other side. She got into the car quickly. 'You got them?'

'Yup. Downloaded the lot. All the employees' bank details captured on printout.' Before clicking on his seatbelt, he lifted his shirt slightly so she could see the corner of a sheaf of paper poking out of his trousers.

'That's brilliant. Brilliant!' she cried in delight, flinging her arms round his neck.

'Hey, watch it,' he grinned. 'I'll crash the car.' He looked suddenly serious. 'That's all we need.' Before turning into the street, he gave a short laugh. 'Christ.' He shook his head. ' Who'd ever have believed I'd be persuaded to do something like this, even by you?'

Alex was due at the hospital in less than an hour so their self-congratulations had to be short. Round the next corner, he dragged the computer print-out from his jeans and handed it to her before shooting off, leaving her, standing forlornly, outside Bethnal Green station. The paper was in one long piece with holes along both sides and perforations between the pages. She rolled it up tightly, bending the roll in half so it would fit into her bag, then ducked inside the station.

In the lift, everyone's eyes seemed to be turned on her accusingly. Guiltily, she clutched her bag. She wished Alex were with her. Left alone, the terror and the fear inside swamped her. Not going back for the photograph seemed suddenly a dreadful mistake. Did she actually *want* to get caught? She seemed to be leaving a trail a mile wide behind her for Nick to find – seemed to be doing everything possible to let him see she knew what he'd done, short of accusing him directly to his face. She didn't know whether she felt more frightened or angry with herself.

Bethnal Green was on the Central line and she had to change at the Bank. To her surprise, sleep overtook her suddenly and she nodded off, almost missing her stop. Jumping out hurriedly at Chalk Farm, she handed in her ticket and walked over the bridge, the cold night air striking her face. She felt better for the short sleep on the tube, but still a little panicky when she thought of what she'd just done, and what it might mean. The bag with the list of account numbers and salaries of all Savage Associates' staff banged ominously against her hip. Now she had the numbers, what next? In the morning she'd contact Wexler with the cheque numbers that had cleared out Savage Associates' client account and ask him to find out if either had been paid into any of the bank accounts listed. For now, she wouldn't think any further ahead than that.

Crossing the bridge seemed to take forever but walking up Regent's Park Road she could see it had only been a few minutes. She walked slowly homewards. Her feet dragged a little. She knew that once she'd translated the number on the list into a name, she'd have the proof she'd been seeking and there would be no going back.

23

Attached is a list of the employees of Savage Associates with corresponding details of their bank accounts. Could you please see whether cheque no. 3634500 was paid into any of these accounts on or around the end of April 2004. Ditto cheque no. 3634527 in the last weeks of July of the same year.

Please contact me directly at the above e-mail address ASP –

Susan Savage.

Even so, she felt much better when she'd faxed the list to Wexler from the print shop in Belsize Park next morning. It seemed like a weight had been lifted from her shoulders. There was nothing more she could sensibly do for the time being except wait. The only decision she had left to make was what to wear for lunch with Alex. They'd arranged to meet at one o'clock in a Greek restaurant in Earl's Court. She decided on jeans and a black silk shirt.

'You know it's totally illegal what we did last night?' Alex said, once they were sitting opposite each other. The tablecloth was red and white checks, the menu padded black plastic. There were only two other people in the restaurant. 'We must have been mad. *I* certainly must have been.'

'You were brilliant, Alex. Much cooler than me.'

'I wasn't underneath.'

'I faxed all the details to Wexler this morning.'

'Where from?'

'There's a print shop on the corner.'

They didn't speak anymore about it. For the moment, there wasn't much more to say. Instead, over a carafe of retsina, they talked of her mother and Nick, of Nina Shooke and Jonathan Woolf, of silly things they'd done when they were younger. He told her something of his own family while they ate rice and lamb shashlik. A sister called Tanya, 'still at university', and an older brother, Mark, also a doctor. 'It's catching, you see, like measles. My father was a surgeon – '

'Was?'

'He died of a heart attack when I was twenty-four. Now both his sons are following in his footsteps and Tanya's contemplating applying to medical school after she's finished her degree.' His mother lived on her own in Norfolk, 'gardening, pottering, the usual'. Only two topics were skirted around. Susan didn't mention Paul – she'd choose the right time for that, she told herself. And, by mutual consent, they avoided talking about her father.

But she felt completely at ease in Alex's company. She had the sense, deep down, that things had fallen into their correct place. She felt this was where she was supposed to be. Desire mingling dizzily with nerves surged through her as she sat opposite him, calmly eating. She found she was smiling a lot. It wasn't the intense excitement she experienced with Paul: there was between them none of the heady exhilaration of the forbidden, or the displaced. It was the exact opposite – in this man sitting opposite her, devouring black olives, Susan felt she had truly found herself. Her smile as she looked at him held an element of fear.

And there was a bond between them so strong she felt she could almost reach out and touch it. *He has seen my father, he's seen him, I'm sure of it!* She hugged this knowledge to herself all through the meal. Only as they were sipping small cups of Turkish coffee, did she finally bring up what was really on her mind.

'Alex, there's something I want to ask you – '

'Yes?'

She picked up a powdery square of Turkish delight and considered it. 'Why exactly did you help me get the employees' bank account numbers last night? I mean, you've only known me for about a week.'

'I must find you irresistible.'

'No, really. Be serious.'

'I am being.'

'You had an irresistible urge – '

'Yup.'

'To break the law?'

'That seems to sum it up. Any time.' He grinned. 'You just have to ask.'

'Come on, why?'

He hesitated. The grin faded slightly. He looked into his coffee cup. 'Well, I like you'. He looked up. 'Quite a lot.' Then down again. 'And I suppose I thought – '

She stared at him. 'Go on.'

He still wasn't looking at her. He spoke slowly. 'Well, I suppose I thought you'd do it with or without me. And that it would be better if I were there to watch out for you if you did… '

'But the reason I needed the bank details? I mean, my father's story. You do see why it was so vital I got them? It wasn't merely robbery. Other, more serious things were at stake – Alex, tell me the truth. You don't think I'm imagining it all, do you? I mean, why else would you help me, if you didn't really *know*?'

He was staring into his cup again. His face was tight. After a moment, he replied: 'You've known Nick all your life. You don't trust him. You think he's up to no good. You believe him capable of shipping drugs. There's some proof you may be right. Anyway, there's pretty strong evidence that *something* unusual has been going on at Savage Associates. That's good enough for me. The rest doesn't really matter, does it?'

Her mouth was suddenly so dry that she had to take a gulp of coffee before she could answer. 'I think it does.' She stared at him across the table. 'Actually I think so.' The thick, sweetish grains at the bottom of the cup caught in her throat. She coughed to clear it. Realising she was still holding a piece of Turkish delight in mid-air, she put it down.

'Look, I don't think you're crazy. Whatever your mother says. You're not crazy.'

She was still staring at him. She wanted him to cry out – 'Because I saw your father too! That's why I know!' But he did not.

'You're as sane as I am,' he said. He smiled, but his mouth was tense. 'And I should know. I'm a doctor.'

She didn't smile back. She wiped the powder from the sweet off her fingers with a red cloth napkin and slowly took a pack of Marlboros out of her hand-bag. She felt suddenly aware of the distance between them, despite his helping her last night. Despite everything. She realised she was sitting so rigidly, she could scarcely breathe. Trying to keep calm, she tore the cellophane from the pack, tapped out a cigarette and offered him one. He shook his head, watching as she lit her cigarette.

'And now? What do you intend to do now?' he asked with a tight smile.

Her eyes narrowed as she inhaled, pulling smoke deep into her lungs, feeling the warm rush of smoke like a comfort. Squinting across at him, she waited till she'd blown out a thin stream before saying: 'I've faxed Wexler the account details. I'm waiting for his response. I told you.'

'Be careful, Susan. This is a dangerous game you're playing.'

Her chest felt suddenly tight and her hands clammy, but she only frowned dismissively and said a little bit too breezily: 'What? Waiting for Wexler's reply?'

'And when you get it?'

'That depends on what it is.'

'Yes. That's what I mean.'

Not replying, she took another long drag. He was slumped in his seat, his collar crooked, his eyes dark and troubled. She felt suddenly sorry for him. It can't be any fun being caught up in all this, she thought. It wasn't as if he hadn't a choice. He could just have walked away from it all. Still could. And he had helped her. The question, she supposed, was why.

Because she'd only have gone ahead and done it anyway? Did he even believe that himself? She blew out smoke, wondering what his real reasons had been.

He sighed and looked at his watch. 'I've got to go. I have to be at the hospital at four.'

Swivelling round, he gestured to the waiter for the bill. They paid and left without speaking. She knew everything had changed between them in the past few days but she wasn't sure how. Outside, she said: 'Thanks for last night, Alex. I mean it. I couldn't have done it without you. Good – '

'Don't.' He touched her lips lightly with his forefinger. 'Don't say it.'

Sweet, she thought. He almost tells me I'm crazy and then doesn't want me to say goodbye.

He looked at her. 'When do you expect to hear from Wexler?'

'Hopefully by tomorrow.'

'You won't do anything hasty? You'll let me know what you've found out first?'

She shrugged. 'OK.'

'Even if it's nothing at all?'

She nodded.

He stood there for a moment longer, looking at her. She wondered if he were about to say something else. It looked like he wanted to. She couldn't be sure what it was she could see in his eyes. Guilt, perhaps? Because if he *had* seen her father, even if it was just a glimpse, even if only for a second, he was doing a pretty convincing job of denying it.

Perhaps he didn't see anything, she thought, feeling dispirited. Perhaps he doesn't look guilty at all. Recalling his expression in the restaurant, the distance, the sudden decisiveness, she sighed.

'I'll phone,' she said, when he still didn't speak.

24

A message scribbled in purple felt-tip telling her to wait was on the drawing table when she reached Paul's office that evening. She sat on a high stool, her toes touching the floor, swinging herself from side to side, examining the drawings clipped onto the table. The room was in darkness except for three pools of light from the arched Anglepoise desk lamps. She lit a cigarette, twisting half-circle on the stool. She was on her second when Paul came up the stairs. He pulled a face. 'God, it stinks in here.'

'I'll open a window.'

'No, leave it. You'll set off the alarm. Let's go.'

They crossed into Soho and bought two large glasses of white wine in a crowded brasserie on Old Compton Street. Paul was silent and in one of his non-communicative moods. Usually these made her feel inadequate; on this occasion, she was thankful for it. There was too much else on her mind for casual conversation. She could still see Alex's troubled face.

They found a table by the window, overlooking the street. As she began sipping her wine, heavy drops struck the glass. The light rain became a downpour. From the warmth of the bar, she looked out at rain bouncing off the dark pavements. A man ran past, ineffectually shielding his head with a newspaper.

'Shit,' Paul said. 'Look at that. It's pissing down and I have to leave in a minute. I'll get soaked.'

'Leave? What do you mean?'

'I've got a meeting,' he said casually. 'Didn't I mention it? With the accounts man from HLL.'

'At twenty-past eight in the evening?'

'She couldn't make it any earlier.'

'The accounts man is a she?'

He nodded. 'Carla Meades. There's some problem with the budget and the shoot begins first thing tomorrow.'

'I thought we were spending the evening together.'

'I don't want to go either, you know. It's a drag for me, too.'

'You should have told me earlier.'

'I'm sorry,' he said coldly. 'I intended to, but I forgot.' He glanced at his watch. 'I've still got half an hour.'

Sitting with her elbows on the table, supporting her forehead with one hand, Susan looked out of the window. Her eyes followed two women who were sheltering across the road under a light awning, one holding a scarf over her head. 'I can't go on with this, Paul,' she said suddenly, turning her head slightly to face him.

'What do you mean?'

'I mean it's no good. I can't carry on like this. And – I've met someone else.'

Paul's lips went white, otherwise his face showed no emotion. 'Are you in love with him?'

'I don't know.'

'Does he love you?'

'I don't know that either. It hasn't reached that point. Nowhere near.' She shifted her eyes back to the street. 'I think he likes me. Anyway, I like *him*.' She stared through the dark glass of the window. 'It wouldn't be fair to you to continue.'

'That's up to me to decide, isn't it. How old is he?' Paul asked, his voice still deceptively calm.

'Twenty-seven, twenty-eight… What does it matter?' But it did matter; she could tell. Paul's narrow face seemed to lengthen and shrink at the same time.

'What does he do, this man?'

'What difference does it make? I shouldn't have told you – '

'I'm very glad you told me.'

'He's a doctor. A surgeon. Thoracic – from here to here.' She held her hands up against her body, at her neck and waist, as Alex had done the other day.

'What's his name?'

'Alex.'

'Alex what?'

'Emmerich.'

'Where did you meet him?'

'Oh, around,' she said, shifting uncomfortably.

'When are you going to see him again?' He was trying to be cool, but some of the hurt had crept into his voice.

'I don't know,' she said listlessly. 'I'm not sure.' Then, angrily: 'What am I supposed to do? Stay in on my own every Saturday night? Watch TV, while you snuggle up with your wife?'

'She's not my wife.'

'Don't be disingenuous.'

'I'm not. It's a brute fact.'

'Do *you* love *her*? That's the real question.'

Back on familiar territory, Paul looked more confident. Some of the colour had returned to his face. He picked up the till receipt that had arrived with their drinks and examined it. 'We've been together so long,' he answered, still reading the print, 'Julia and I. It's not a matter of love anymore. It's beyond all that.' He replaced the receipt in the saucer and looked at Susan. 'I'm not in love anymore – but I do love her.'

'You're not in love with her but you love her? What kind of bullshit is that?'

'We're beyond love or hatred,' he explained, making them sound so – so *together*, Susan thought. 'Our relationship is more like a struggle for survival. That's what remains interesting about it,' he finished coolly.

Interesting? He'd never spoken about finding Julia interesting before. He stays with her because he finds her interesting, she told herself. More interesting than me. She straightened in her seat, feeling whatever edge she'd had beginning to slip away and, at the same time, realising she didn't really care anymore. She thought of the documents residing with Wexler. What did any of this matter now? There were other, far more important things at stake. When she'd met him nearly a year ago, Paul had been her escape route from the pain of her father's brutal murder. He'd given her the chance to step outside her own damaged life for a while. But things were different now. Even if she didn't want them to be, they were. Looking into Paul's thin face, she realised the self-deception, and deception, had been mutual: he'd never had any real intention of leaving Julia for her. It wasn't love she'd felt for him, she admitted to herself; it was infatuation. A safe affair with a married man. After her father's death, she'd had no emotion left for anything else and Paul, offering nothing, had offered her that.

If he'd behaved differently, she wondered, would my feelings have deepened and grown into something more real? But he hadn't, and they hadn't. And now? She felt strangely blank. There was an ache in her chest when she breathed. Meeting Alex hasn't changed anything, she thought. Her life was a mess long before then.

'I can't carry on seeing you,' she repeated. Then, with genuine shame: 'I'm so sorry.'

'Look, if this is some sort of game to keep me interested, it's not working.'

'It's not a game. I only came this evening because – well, I wanted to tell you to your face – '

'Because you belong to me,' Paul said, his voice suddenly rough. 'You came because you love me.' He took hold of her wrist. She tried to pull it away but his grip was too strong. They stared at each other, their gaze locked.

'Let go of me,' she said coldly. 'I have to go.'

'Don't.' He didn't let go of her wrist. 'Please.'

She tried once more to free herself then, realising the impossibility without creating a scene – the couple at the next table were already eyeing them curiously – relaxed her arm. 'You're leaving to meet Carla Meades, remember?'

He kept his eyes steadily on hers. 'I'll cancel it.'

'Cancel such an important meeting?'

'Yes. This is more important to me.'

'You're a selfish shit.'

'I need you – I love you.'

She sighed. 'You're still a selfish shit.'

They saw an old black-and-white film at the Everyman, catching the Northern line to Hampstead to avoid the problem of parking. They sat in the nearly empty cinema holding hands, his finger and thumb loosely encircling her wrist. As she watched the flickering lights on the screen, she told herself she should feel happy to be spending the night with Paul, after all. But instead she felt nothing, only tired and cold and strangely guilty.

The green luminous figures on the dial said 3:02.

Susan lay for a while, listening to the sound of Paul's breathing. Once it was clear that she was not going back to sleep, she threw back the covers and sat up, half hoping her movements would wake him. He was a light sleeper. But he didn't wake.

The room was spinning slightly as she pulled on the tartan cotton dressing-gown Paul kept in his Soho flat and crossed the hall to the bathroom. She hated the light in the bathroom, a sickly, yellow light from overhead, the light of bad dreams. In the mirror, she saw that black make-up had rubbed into the hollows beneath her eyes as she'd slept. She looked like a character in a Fellini movie, all white face, tousled hair and black, black eyes. Her head was throbbing and there was a foul taste in her mouth from too much white wine. They'd drunk a lot, both before and after the film, and eaten little.

She splashed her face with water, rubbing a little soap under her eyes with the side of her finger. Then she sat on the lavatory, her head in her hands, eyes closed; yawning, she stood to press the lever. Only later did she realise she'd recognised the smell in her nostrils. A faint, rather putrid smell. There was no other warning. He appeared while she was washing her hands. She saw her own eyes widening with shock before she registered what was happening. She was looking in the mirror, he was standing behind her, she was seeing him over her shoulder. Her hands were under the running water from the taps.

'Hello, Susie,' he said.

She turned with wet hands. Her legs were trembling so much they failed her and she slid down the wall till she was sitting on the floor with her knees up, staring at him.

His face was different. One eye was still missing, but his wounds had healed and his hair was brushed and shining, thicker than she remembered. On his cheek was the long snaking scar, now scarcely visible. His hair and skin were pale, luminous, almost silvery-gold. He wore the same raincoat, now clean. If it hadn't been for the missing eye, or faint scar, he'd have looked, not as he had in life, but as he had to her in the months after his death. He looked like her perfect glowing memory of her father.

'Remember me?' her father said.

She tried to get up but her legs were too wobbly and she sunk back to the floor.

'You haven't done what we talked about,' he said, his good eye steadily on her. 'Have you?'

'Yes, yes, I have! I've got the name of a detective agency – Wexler Investigations. They specialise in financial affairs. I've sent them the number of the cheques – the ones that took all the money out of the client account. Any day now I'll hear which account they were paid into. I've paid a retainer, I'm just waiting for the results. Any day now. The ball's been set in motion. They've begun.'

'Oh, Susie,' he said, shaking his head in mock sorrow. 'Two thousand pounds? What a waste. They won't find a thing of importance. Not a damn thing. Nick's far too clever for that. I told you, remember?' He shook his head again. 'And you promised. Not to forget me. You promised.'

'I haven't forgotten you,' she said desperately. 'I *haven't* forgotten. I went to see Mum. I told her what happened. I told her what Nick had done. I told her – '

'Leave Isabella out of this!' Steven interrupted her sharply. 'Leave her out! She's innocent. Are you listening?'

He stood with his hands in the pockets of his raincoat, his skin glowing palely in the yellow light. She felt the fear in her. She was so afraid it hurt. She hadn't known it was possible for fear to make your throat contract so it was almost painful to breathe. She whispered: 'I need more time.'

'There's no more time – the time is up! They put the stone down next Sunday. After that, it's too late. I'm in the dark here!' he cried, his voice suddenly rough with anger. 'Do you understand? In the dark! I've been cut off from both worlds! I am unremembered! Do you know who I am? Do you know what they call me? I'm Steven the Silent!' When he took his fist out of his pocket to shake in the air, his hand was wrapped in clean, light gauze.

'What am I supposed to do?' she whispered, her heart beating wildly. When he remained silent, she cleared her dry throat and repeated: 'What do you want me to do?'

'You know what to do,' he said, quiet but smiling again. For the first time she noticed how cunning his smile was. 'You know.'

Her mind went black. Blood was roaring in her ears. She gave a great sob.

'Don't disappoint me. You won't disappoint me, Susie, will you?'

The spinning black pool opened at her feet. She dived in, head first. When she came round she was still sitting with her back to the sink, the thin cotton dressing-gown rucked up round her legs. She was alone. She fought dizzily for consciousness, pulling herself to her feet by holding onto the taps and got to the lavatory just in time to throw up. She stood, hunched and shivering, until she felt able to move across to the sink and splash cold water on her face. Leaning over, she pulled Paul's toothbrush from a chipped white china mug and, with shaking hands, brushed her teeth, spitting out pink bubbly liquid. Then she staggered back to bed.

Paul stirred as she slid in besides him. 'Who was that?' he murmured sleepily. 'You were talking…I heard voices… ' He mumbled in his sleep, so low she almost didn't catch it: 'You were talking to that doctor again, weren't you?'

Susan stared at his upturned face. His eyes had closed, his breathing was regular. Trying not to disturb him, she put her head on the pillow beside him, knowing sleep was impossible. Her muscles were knotted; she ached all over, her ribs, stomach, even her armpits. She was damp inside her tee-shirt. She lay stiffly, simply breathing, hoping her body would begin to relax. She was so knocked off balance, she couldn't think straight. But she knew then for sure that she wouldn't see Paul again. It really was over. Behind all the shock and fear, there was still room for self-contempt. By the time she had said, 'It was no one,' he was asleep again. She watched him as he slept.

Three

THE STONE SETTING

STONE SETTING: a simple graveside religious service marking the formal setting of a headstone at the cemetery at the end of the mourning period, or 11 months following the death, also sometimes called an 'unveiling'.

R. Brenner Smith, *Jewish Traditions*, 1987.

QBDX 06106

Application Number PAS 585892/200

CERTIFIED COPY   OF AN ENTRY

DEATH	Entry No.	60

Registration district	Administrative area
Hammersmith and Fulham	London Borough of Hammersmith and Fulham

Sub-district

1. Date and place of death	3. Sex	Male
Twenty-second November 2004 Chelsea and Westminster Hospital, Fulham	4. Maiden surname of a woman who has married	————

2. Name and surname

Steven SAVAGE

5. Date and place of birth

5th August 1949   Hackney

6. Occupation and usual address

Company director
31 Ellerdale Road, NW3

7 (a) Name and surname of informant	(b) Qualification
Certificate on inquest adjourned received from M L Smith	

7 (c) Usual address

Coroner for Inner South London. Inquest held on 29th November 2004

8. Cause of death

Ia. Haemorrhage
  b. Stab wounds to chest and arms

9. I certify that the particulars given by me above are true to the best of my knowledge and belief .... Signature .... of informant

10. Date of registration	11. Signature of registrar
Ninth January 2005	D. Nissan Deputy Registrar

QBDX Series DM 0884 13M 6/00 SPSL(280831)

*See notes overleaf

CERTIFIED to be a true copy of an entry in the certified copy of a register of Births or Deaths in the District above mentioned. Given at the GENERAL REGISTER OFFICE, under the Seal of the said Office on   **1st February 2005**

174

25

Susan climbed the hill on legs that shook under her. Reaching the top, she stared out across the park trying to focus her mind. She wasn't usually out so early: there was a raw chill in the air. When she exhaled, white vapor hung in front of her face for a few seconds before disintegrating. A few dog walkers were trundling around the paths near the bottom, their dogs following on leads. People with briefcases overtook them, hurrying to work.

She rubbed her forehead. Her head was aching terribly. What had he said? She knew what to do. Did she? *Did* she?

The wind had picked up. A discarded sheet of a newspaper was tossing over the grass. A small brown and white terrier attacked it with a fierce high bark. She pushed cold hands deeper into her pockets. *He was wonderful*, she'd said two weeks ago to Alex, speaking of her father. *I'd have done anything for him.*

Susan held her hair back with one hand, feeling the chilly air battering her. She turned towards the path with a sigh that was almost a sob. Halfway down, she stopped, opening her mouth in a long, silent scream. Throat clenched, eyes screwed shut, the tendons on her neck stiff, she stood for a moment motionless.

She'd lost her father once before. That had been bad enough. Now he was lost to her for a second time. He'd changed beyond all recognition. He wasn't the same man anymore. We shared the same vision in life, she'd once said confidently. Would she say so again as certainly now? She kept her eyes tightly closed, wincing at the force of the answer that came echoing back to her, helplessly recalling Steven's words that night in the studio and his thin twisted smile. *Death really does do something to you. It really changes people. We're different to the living. We aren't so nice. Actually, nowhere near as nice...*

She let the tears run down her face freely.

I'd do anything for him...

What the hell had she meant by that?

When she reached home, she went straight upstairs and ran a hot bath. She'd zipped her jacket right up to the neck and buttoned her jumper but she couldn't get warm. While the water was filling up, she uncapped a bottle and poured herself what was left of the brandy, a good two inches worth. The spirit burned her throat going down but the warmth spread through her body instantly. She stopped feeling so cold and her legs stopped shaking.

The images of blood and terror that filled her imagination were, for the moment, stilled. She switched on the computer but 'wireless network connection is not connected' kept popping up on the screen. Deciding to try again later, she stripped off her clothes, pinned up her hair and stepped into the bath. She lay back in the hot water and closed her eyes, trying to blank her mind.

She must have drifted off to sleep because she only became aware of her surroundings again when she realised the water she was floating in was lukewarm. The sweat on her top lip was cold and her fingers and toes were wrinkled like prunes; she wiped the back of a hand across her forehead. Dripping wet and a little chilly, she climbed out stiffly and wrapped a large towel around her The network was connected again, she saw as she switched on the computer. When she keyed in her password, the e-mail was waiting.

Dear Miss Savage,

We now possess the information referred to in your recent fax to this office. Please make an appointment to collect the relevant documentation in person.
Yours sincerely,
Hyman Wexler

Her heart leapt. There might be a way forward, just might be… She didn't bother to dress; stepping over the pile of discarded clothes, she phoned Wexler's secretary and made an appointment for later that morning.

He handed her a sealed brown A4 envelope, his dark, deep-set eyes moving quickly and nervously behind their horn-rimmed glasses around the confines of his tiny office. 'Here you are, Miss Savage,' Wexler said, with what passed for a smile. His tongue flickered over thin, dry lips. 'I think you will find what you are looking for inside.'

'Here,' she said, thrusting a thick wad of notes into his hand. 'Nine hundred pounds. The balance. Plus the other six hundred. You can count it, if you like.'

'I'm sure everything is perfectly in order,' he said. He opened a drawer in his desk and placed the money inside. 'Please contact us again if there's anything more we can do for you,' he said, sliding it shut.

But Susan was already out of the door. She walked quickly up the corridor, nodding to the secretary on the way out. In the hall, by the lift, she couldn't wait any longer. She ripped the envelope open and drew out ten or so sheets of paper, held together by a paper clip. There was the original list she'd faxed Wexler, a page of figures from a bank statement and a brief memo, typed on blank paper.

Please find confirmation that cheque no. 001086 was paid into bank account no. 78000109 on 26/4/04.

Further, that cheque no. 3634527 was paid into the same account on 27/7/04.

Her heart leapt. 'Confirmation', he had written. It was true.

She ran her eyes eagerly down the list of employees and their bank account numbers, stopping when she came to Nick's name. Nicholas Savage – account number 56743108. She frowned, disappointed. Not the same number. She checked it again. No. The cheque definitely hadn't gone into his account. Had he got another somewhere? That would make it marginally more difficult. She returned to the list of figures.

The entry jumped out at her immediately. It was on the second page. Account number 78000109. She read through the digits more slowly. Once. Twice. Then she flicked to the photocopied page of the bank statement. Her heart was pounding. There was no mistake. Now she knew why her father had told her not to bother. Now she knew what he had meant. Three thousand wasted pounds… Nick was clever, all right. Too clever by half.

On the back of the sheaf of papers Wexler had pinned two narrow slips – photocopies of cheques made out to Savage Associates. She unpinned them, staring at the signatures in disbelief. *Isabella Savage*. Her mother had signed both cheques.

Account number 78000109 was the joint account of Isabella and Steven Savage.

The lift doors had opened without her noticing. She stuffed the photocopies back into the envelope and hurriedly stepped inside. Her mind racing, she pressed the lighted button for the ground floor.

26

She stepped out of the lift. She couldn't take it in. She kept staring at the photocopies clutched in her hand, trying to absorb their meaning. *Nick… Steven… Isabella… Too clever by half…* There must be a way out of this, she thought desperately, there must be. But if there was, she couldn't imagine one.

Think, Susan, *think*. Even the smallest decision felt beyond her. Except for drinking. It was easy to decide to blot everything out for a while by pouring alcohol down her throat. There was an off-license on the corner. Susan bought a quart bottle of whisky and several cans of Guinness.

Nick… Steven… Isabella…

She would think about it carefully. But she couldn't think now. Later. She'd think it through later. Yes.

'Hello Alex.'

Alex opened the door in hastily pulled-on jeans and a tee-shirt, rubbing his eyes. 'I was on duty at the hospital all night,' he yawned, tucking his tee-shirt in. 'Didn't get to bed till six.'

She leant against the doorway. 'Did I wake you? Sorry. Got the reply from Wexler here.' She waved the large brown envelope in the air. 'Thought I'd come round and show it to you. Thought you'd like to see.' She giggled. 'I'm slightly squiffy,' she said, her face growing serious. 'Just slightly. Sorry about that.'

He examined her quickly. She'd changed into the short black dress she'd worn to Nick's birthday party. Put on a lot of make-up and lipstick. Her hair was loose and fell down her back, her eyes half closed, as if the weight of mascara was too heavy for her lids. Crumbs from a stale croissant she'd bought at a kiosk in the high street were scattered down her leather jacket. She was clearly drunk. Very. She was right about that. She still looked beautiful, he thought.

'I'll make some coffee,' he decided, finishing tucking in his tee-shirt. He stepped back. 'You'd better come in.'

She stumbled on her high heels, staggered, almost fell. 'Could I have a dash of whisky in mine?' she asked, when she'd recovered her balance.

'I think you've had enough already, don't you?'

'Just a dash.' She held a thumb and finger an inch apart in front of her face, squeezing shut one eye.

He took her arm and led her through to the living-room where she collapsed onto the sofa. The room was whirling around. She looked up at him, trying to focus.

'Stay there,' he instructed her. 'Don't move.'

'Oh, Alex,' she said, starting to cry. 'I'm fucked. I'm really fucked.'

Susan groaned. Her head was splitting. The taste in her mouth told her she'd eaten a dead rat. Perhaps several. She sat up, then regretting the movement, sank gingerly down again. Alex's flat. The sofa. A blanket draped over her. She was still dressed, except for her shoes. She groaned again. 'Water,' she croaked. She couldn't seem to raise her voice above a whisper. 'Can I please have some water?'

Alex appeared above her. 'Headache?' he inquired gently.

'Yes.'

'Take these.'

She took the tablets he was offering with the glass of water, briefly resting on one elbow to drink it, then lay back, closing her eyes. After a while she drifted back to sleep.

When she opened her eyes again, Alex was sitting in the chair opposite her, reading a newspaper. She watched him for a moment.

'Hello,' he said, noticing.

She didn't speak.

'You've been asleep.'

'Yes.'

'Take another couple of ibruprofen,' he suggested.

'What time is it?'

'Eleven-thirty.'

'In the morning?'

'Yes. Planet earth.'

She smiled. Or tried to.

She had to sit up to swallow the water. The bottle was on the large manilla envelope she'd brought with her. Why should an envelope create such a severe reaction? Anxiety, fear. She remembered as she shook out the painkillers. Her mother's name on the cheques, not Nick's. A wave of nausea swept over her. She clapped a hand over her mouth and dashed for the loo.

All the lamps were switched on. The curtains drawn. He'd put down the newspaper. 'What's this?' he asked, looking at the sheets of paper she'd handed him before collapsing gratefully back on the sofa.

'A copy of my father's bank statements. From the year he died. And two cheques. Look at the entries for April and July,' she suggested, as he flicked through the pages.

He spent a while examining them. 'I don't understand,' he said at last. 'There are hundreds of thousands of pounds going in and then out again in both April and July. But this is your father's personal account.'

'Joint account,' she corrected him.

He looked up, frowning, the copies of the cheques in his hand. 'Your mother's signature,' he said, stating the obvious.

Susan nodded.

'What does it mean?'

'Don't be dense, Alex. It means – ' She stopped with a groan, lifting her hand to her head. After moment she went on less heatedly: 'It means that Nick bamboozled Mum into borrowing the money for him. It means she put the cheque from Savage Associates into her own account and gave him the cash he needed. When he gave it back to her, having quietly made a few million meanwhile, she kindly wrote the cheque for the original amount to the company. It means that everything is in her name. Nick made sure there was nothing incriminating against him. It means,' she said quietly, 'it means, I'm fucked.'

'So even if you were able to show Nick was involved in something dodgy you can't prove a thing without incriminating your mother, too.'

'It looks that way.'

'She'd be charged with being an accessory to God knows what. She'd go to gaol.'

'Yes. I expect so.'

Alex shook his head wonderingly. 'What was she *thinking* of?'

Susan shrugged. 'Nick can be very convincing when he tries.'

'But she must have known it wasn't legal. Did she think your father wouldn't notice hundreds of thousand pounds turning up unexpectedly in his account?'

'He never, ever examined his statements. Never. He was notorious for it. Mum took care of all the financial stuff. The most he ever did was to check the balance at the end of the month to make sure they weren't over-drawn. She used to joke that if she bought anything too expensive she'd make sure she did it mid-month. Dad always said,' she smiled bitterly, 'he had enough to do with accounting at work. He didn't want to bother with it at home, too.'

Alex hesitated. 'You're sure she isn't guilty?'

Susan remembered her father's warning words: 'She's innocent – Leave her alone, Susie!' She grimaced. 'Quite sure.'

'Then why – '

'Oh, I expect Nick persuaded her to keep quiet. It's just for a few days, he'd say. Not long. And it's not so *very* naughty if I pay it back in full at the end of the week. Steven won't notice. Hide a page of the statement, pretend it's lost if necessary, anything. It's my own company, there's no harm done. That sort of thing. My mother would have been rather flattered actually. You know, that it was her he'd chosen to come to for help. She always complained Dad didn't involve her enough in the business. Nick would say – no one need ever know about this if we both keep quiet. Just the two of us.' She gave a stiff smile. 'He'd have made her feel included.'

'Even so. It's crooked.'

'He's her brother-in-law. She must have thought that if *he* asked her do it, then it was alright. Oh, I don't know why I'm arguing on my mother's behalf.' Susan rubbed her aching forehead. 'I can't understand how she could have done it, either.'

'Well, I can see why you got so drunk.'

'Yes. Yes... Look, I'm sorry about last night, Alex. I made a fool of myself. Luckily I don't remember much about it. No,' she raised a hand. 'Please don't remind me. One thing's for sure.' She looked grim. 'I'm never doing it again. That's the last time I run away from bad news. Next time – ' she took a deep breath, 'next time I face it full on.'

'Well, that's it then,' Alex said, chucking the papers onto the table. 'At least you tried.'

'So you think – you think I should just forget all about it?'

'What else can you do? This is embezzlement. Your mother's not going to get out of it by simply saying – it wasn't me, your honour, it was Nick. He told me to do it. I was just following orders. I was only trying to *help*. It doesn't look good for her. She doesn't look like an innocent party. It's her name on the cheques and her signature. Isabella Savage – three hundred and fifty thousand pounds.'

'Five hundred,' Susan corrected him miserably.

'Nick might plausibly argue that he wasn't involved at all, that she bought the drugs for her own use and for some reason – I don't know what, unrequited love, a woman scorned, that sort of thing – turned round and falsely blamed her ex-lover. Which I assume he will be, by that time.' He raked his fingers through his hair. 'Or even that, since *he* didn't lend her the money, Steven must have been in on it from the start. After all, her husband had equal access to the firm's funds. Who's around to say differently? Certainly not your father. You have to ask yourself if the courts will find your mother's story convincing. Will a jury decide in favour of her on this evidence?'

Alex searched her face. 'They might,' he went on, seeing her unhappy expression and pushing home his point, 'and then again, they might not. Is that a risk you're prepared to take?'

'I don't know. I don't know.'

'If you go ahead, Nick could remain free and your mother might end up in jail. Is that what you want?'

'Of course I don't. She's innocent. He's guilty.'

'Forget innocent or guilty,' Alex said roughly. 'There's just the law. You can't prove it's him from this evidence. You don't know yourself for sure.'

'I do.'

'How?'

'You know how.'

Alex looked down. He picked up the scattered papers from the table and shuffled them into a neat pile. 'You have to let go of this. You have to. There's nothing you can do about it. Not a bloody thing.'

'Isn't there?'

He flung out his hands. 'Christ! I can't believe that you're even *thinking* of going ahead with this now. '

Susan opened her bag and got out a packet of Marlboro Lights but felt too sick to smoke. She offered the pack to Alex and when he said no, shook out a cigarette and lit it without enthusiasm. 'He planned it this way,' she said in a low voice, the cigarette burning between her fingers. 'That's what's so horrible. He wanted a way of assuring himself of immunity if Dad ever found out. And this was it. His nasty, clever, typically sly little scheme. My father would never have done anything to hurt Isabella. He would have been forced to cover up. He'd lie, cheat, beg, borrow or steal to save her. Nothing else would have made him do that, not even any danger to himself. He is – he *was* – an incredibly honourable man. But my mother at risk? That would be another matter. And Nick knew that. This way, he didn't even have to sleep with her. He didn't even have to fuck her,' she said bitterly. 'He knew that if it ever came to this point, we'd have to let it go.'

'Well, yes. Yes, I'm afraid that's probably true.'

Digging his hands into his pockets, Alex stood up and moved across the room.

'I can't just sit by and do nothing,' Susan said desperately, following him over. 'I can't! I can't let Nick get away with murder, not now I know for sure that he did it.'

He turned, jamming his hands into his armpits, and stared at her. 'But do you? Do you really? You know he might have stolen money from the company – OK, he probably did. Perhaps even bought drugs with the money, but that's *all* you know.'

'No, you're wrong. I know he killed my father. I know it. Because if that bit of my father's story is true, then it all is. I either made it all up, or none of it. Don't you see? How would I know any of it otherwise? Guesswork?'

'Why not? You know Nick well enough.'

She looked incredulously at him. 'Do you *really* imagine I'm just surmising this from what I know of him?'

Alex didn't reply.

'Nick took the money, he bought the drugs, he made a fortune doing it,' Susan said forcibly. Too forcibly – her head began to pound again. 'He *trashed* Savage Associates – he corrupted the company and he liked doing it, you can be sure of that. An extra bit on the side, that's how he would have seen it. A bonus.' She walked back to the sofa and sank down, putting her hand across her forehead and speaking with it there. 'My grandfather built that business up from nothing. He came from Poland at the turn of the century a poor man, virtually uneducated, and – And Nick would have liked spoiling it, he would have enjoyed it. Because that's the kind of man he is. Perverting the company was just for starters. It was the hors d'ouvres. Then there was murder…'

'How dangerous is he?' Alex asked alarmed. 'Do you think he enjoyed that too?'

'No. No, I don't. I think it was – necessary.' She closed her eyes. There was a shooting pain above them and her head felt like it was going to split in half. 'He couldn't rely on this set-up, however clever it seemed. He got Isabella to bank the money for him but he still had to make doubly sure. Once he had chosen that path, once he had started down it, there was no return. At the end of it, waiting for him, was death.' Alex was staring at her when she opened her eyes. She added weakly: 'It sounds melodramatic,' she lowered her hand, 'but that's the truth.'

'It sounds crazy. Is Nick crazy?'

'I don't think so, no. I think he's – weak.'

'Which is probably even more dangerous. You've answered my question. You must keep away from him. You must stop.'

'But I have the evidence proving what he's like!' she insisted, ignoring the faint voice inside her that told her Alex was right. When he spoke, she could hear her own voice coming out of his mouth. Somehow it was so much easier to resist coming from him. 'How can I leave it alone now? Nick could go to jail for a long, long time which personally I think he deserves. Oh, I accept there's a bit of a risk since my mother is implicated. But that's why he involved her in the first place. So if it ever got to this point, we'd have to let it go. That's what his plan *was*. A bit risky?' She gave a short laugh. 'There *was* no risk – for him. But I can't let him win so easily. Not after all these terrible – these *evil* – things he's done.'

183

'So this is retribution, is it?' Alex demanded. 'With you in the guise of avenging angel?'

'Look, I'll speak to Jonathan Woolf. I'll explain the situation,' Susan said placatingly. 'Perhaps he can arrange police surveillance of Nick that will leave my mother alone.'

'Let's hope he succeeds then,' Alex said grimly.

'I can't just let Nick get away with it,' she repeated, still desperately trying to persuade Alex and, at the same time, herself, that she was right. 'I have to do *something*.'

'But what?'

She opened her mouth but did not reply. Give it up? How could she? But anything other than the entirely straightforward just wasn't a part of Alex's thinking and he couldn't imagine the strength it could have for anyone else. Nick's perverse mentality was a closed book to him, and one that he had no wish to open. That was his strength and his flaw.

Oh, convince me that you're right, Alex! she thought. Surely you can? Had she not come round to be persuaded of precisely that? She stared first at him, then at her own hand clenched on her knee and then up again at Alex. Her head was aching badly. She seemed torn and undecided.

'It's a mess isn't it?' he encouraged her gently, seeing this.

She cast her eyes down. 'Yes,' she replied.

'Look, don't do anything yet,' he said, sitting down besides her. 'You've had a shock, seeing your mother's name on the statements and realising she's been duped, too. He's a wily fox, isn't he?'

Susan nodded, her eyes still down.

'Let things settle first,' Alex urged persuasively. 'That doesn't mean you can't do something later. It just means that you'll have thought it through properly first.'

'Ye-es,' she said uncertainly.

'Things can look very different after a few days.'

She nodded meekly.

'So you'll think about it for a bit,' he said, deciding for her.

She looked down at her feet. Her knees were up and her arms around them; she was gripping her toes.

He took her chin in his hand and tilted her face up to the light. 'Promise?'

'Oh, Alex,' she said sadly. He was right about one thing – there was nothing she could do with the bank statements. That route had turned out to be a complete and total impasse. But there must be something she could do, there *must* be.

He put his arms round her. 'I'll look after you,' he said softly. 'If you'll let me.'

'Oh Alex,' she said again, wishing she could. She felt more peaceful in his arms, calm, but also trapped. Like an imprisoned bird she longed to spread her wings and break free. But where did she wish to fly? Where? She slid one leg down. Her head on his chest, she tried to block the possibilities out of her mind. She could feel the steady warmth of his breathing on the top of her scalp. Feel him against her – warm and sane and safe.

'You're beautiful,' he whispered, his mouth in her hair. 'Beautiful.'

'The image of death is in everything I do. I can't get away from it, I will never be free. There's only one way I'll ever be – ' She broke off, comprehending her own unfinished sentence with a thrill of horror. Her eyes widened. 'Only one way.' She lifted her head and looked up at him. 'I feel so confused, Alex, I – '

'Sssh,' he said.

'Every night I dream of a ghost. Every morning I remember…'

'Sssh,' he said again. She was looking into his face. He gazed down at her. Softly, he said: 'I'll put your memory to sleep.'

27

There was a black and white cartoon her father had pinned to the board in the kitchen years ago. It showed two short, stocky women in smart black laced-up shoes and little black flowerpot hats standing outside a café. In the window was a sign in bold letters which read: 'Reduced – apple pie, five pence a slice!' The two plump woman were gazing at the sign and one was suggesting hopefully to the other: 'Let's just go in and see what happens.'

'A fine description of weakness of the will in action,' her father had smiled. 'Perhaps the finest. How do you get yourself to do what you want but have already decided you shouldn't? You say – Let's just go in and see what happens. Knowing, of course, full well what will.'

So on Monday first thing, she telephoned Nick.

'Who's that?' he asked, a wary smile in his voice. 'To whom am I speaking?'

There was a short pause when she answered, 'It's Susan.'

'I was going out of the door. You just caught me. In fact, I'm late already.' He spoke mechanically, playing for time, trying to get used to the idea of her calling, and calculating what it might mean.

'I thought we might meet,' she said, barely recognising her own voice.

'And what might we meet for?'

'A drink.'

He said slowly: 'Is that so?'

She could hear the click of his lighter as he fired it, heard him inhale and breathe out smoke. Apparently he had decided on directness. 'Why now?' he asked. 'Why are you calling me now?'

'I thought it was about time,' she explained. 'And – well, perhaps I was a bit jealous before.'

'Oh yeah? Of whom?'

'Things haven't been easy lately. I called because I wanted to see you. I want to see you really badly, Nick.'

'That's a reply of sorts, I suppose,' he said, his voice still hard. There was a pause in which she could hear him smoking his cigarette. 'You've got a real chutzpah phoning me now,' he said at last. 'A real nerve after all your –'

She interrupted him. 'I thought we might meet at Romano's.'

He was silent for a minute. 'Christ,' he said. 'I don't know, it's been a long time.'

She was silent too, waiting. Would he fall for the bait? He fell. *Let's just go in…*

'This afternoon,' he said at last. 'At four.'

She put down the phone, not quite knowing what he'd fallen for.

'You see your face,' Nick said. 'In the mirror. It's no one you recognise. You wonder where you've gone. You wonder, what was I after? Some things you want so badly you're prepared to do almost anything to get them. Whatever it takes. That's how it has to be, you tell yourself. You want something, you go for it. No regrets. The world as pure striving, you know? You read Schopenhauer, perhaps a bit of Nietzsche. But it doesn't really help. Because it's wrong what you're doing, you know that. And yet you go on. You have no choice. Well, you do. Of course you do. But you tell yourself you have none, so it's almost as if you don't. It's overwhelming, the desire.' He took a long gulp of whisky. When he set it down on the table there was a crack as the glass struck the marble. 'Afterwards you're sorry. But not sorry enough to say no the next time. Not *that* sorry. Or to give back all the things you've taken. Achieved, you call it. You despise yourself, though for years you don't admit it. You're a big man in the world now, a successful man. *You're* the man with the large red nose. You recognise yourself from a distance – you are Dostoevsky's drunk. But you know you're a shit. Not even a big shit, just a pathetic one. You think that you're one person, you turn out to be another. It all seems so important at the time. But none of it's important,' he looked up, 'once the witnesses are gone.'

When he poured more whisky from the bottle he missed the edge of his glass so that a little of the liquid splashed onto the table. He mopped it up moodily with a paper napkin. 'I'm bad. Not bad, no. Rotten. You know what keeps me going?' He lifted his eyes briefly to hers. 'The thought that one day – ' He stopped in mid-sentence, looking over her shoulder at some point far away.

'What?' Susan asked softly.

He shook his head. 'Never mind.' Raising his glass, he smiled. 'To dreams – which will almost certainly never come true.'

They were sitting in Romano's. They had been drinking for nearly two hours. Susan was drinking white wine mixed heavily with Perrier; Nick, whisky. He had started talking after his second glass and had not stopped. He was always a great talker, was Nick, she thought. It was early. The bar was almost empty, just a couple of people sitting apart from them, on the other side of the room.

'And Isabella?' Susan asked, after she had taken a sip of watery white wine.

'Ah, Isabella.' Nick sat hunched over his glass which he was holding in both hands, peering in so that his nose was almost inside it. 'Is-a-bel-la…'

He drew out the name, leaving a pause between each syllable almost like he was singing it. 'Isabella is just as beautiful now as when I first set eyes on her,' he said, staring into his half-empty glass as if it, and not his own mind, were filled with memories. 'As beautiful and as desirable as when Steven first brought her home. She'd just got her first starring role in *The Doll's House*, I think it was, and she was glowing, she was on fire with success and admiration – and with love. She was so full of life, so vital. I wanted her so badly it was like a physical pain. I thought – big brother, you lucky bastard. But it was always like that. I was the good-looking one, I had the *charm*,' he used the word mockingly, 'but it was Steven who people really took to, who won the scholarships, went to Oxford and, in the end, got the girl. When we decided to enter the business he was the one our father naturally put in charge. You know how I felt?'

'How?'

Nick sat back in his chair, looking at her with drunk and cloudy eyes. 'My whole life I've felt like I've just scaled a fucking mountain. Clawed my way, struggling inch by inch up the side. And when I finally crawl to the top, when I arrive at the pinnacle, panting and exhausted, with bleeding fingers and torn nails – ' he looked at the tips of his fingers as if they really were in that state, 'there they are. Steven and Isabella with all their rich, expensive friends, relaxing in their deckchairs in their elegant clothes, having tea. "Oh, hi, Nick," they say, perfectly friendly, waving their smug, manicured hands, "jolly glad you could make it. Have a cucumber sandwich, won't you?" They hadn't even noticed my effort. Hadn't even noticed. I don't think Steven was ever aware of the force of my hatred. Oh, I loved him, of course, I did. I *loved* him alright. But, God, did I hate him, too. There must be some way, I thought. Something that will attract his attention. I couldn't bear it, you see. All those years of being shut out. In the end I got what I wanted. I usually do. In the end.' Nick's eyes were blank. 'But Isabella doesn't feel any more mine now than she did when I first saw her and she belonged to him. It's no good,' he repeated. 'When the witnesses are gone.'

'So why are you still with her?' Susan asked quietly.

He looked at her as if he had only just remembered to whom he was talking, his eyes suddenly sharp and sober. 'It's a long game, as your grandfather used to say.' He smiled, showing his teeth. 'A long life.' His smile was neither warm nor friendly. The amicability that had been on his face a moment before had vanished. For the moment, she belonged with them, at the top of the mountain, with the friends in their deckchairs and the cucumber sandwiches. 'At least for some,' he added.

'If it brings you no joy, why are you still with Isabella?' Susan persisted.

'No joy? Oh, I wouldn't say that.'

'Satisfaction then.'

'Because I want my cake and eat it, too.' He was still smiling as if this thought brought him some sort of bitter pleasure. 'Yeah,' he repeated. 'I want my cake and eat it too.'

'Well, that's honest at least.'

'Yeah, honest and true, that's me.'

He gave her an odd look before he turned away. She thought she saw tears in his eyes for a moment. If so, he'd blinked them away by the time he'd turned back to her. His eyes, when they focussed and met hers, were dark brown and flecked with gold. 'You look just like your mother when she was your age,' he murmured.

'So I've been told.'

'You are so beautiful – you are *so* beautiful.' And his words, like his eyes, were a caress, like a piece of the finest velvet drawn across her cheek. 'You were such a lovely child – a fairy, a little wild thing. And now… a woman.'

He did not stroke her hair but it felt like he had, his eyes gently following the lines of her. Feeling his gaze moving over her, she shivered. 'I thought it was all buried,' he said softly, seeing this. 'But things don't stay buried for ever.'

'No,' Susan said, a little bitter now, too. 'As it turns out, they don't.'

Very quietly, he asked: 'Do you remember the time that I bathed you?'

Her parents were away in York for the weekend. Nick was staying in the house while they were gone. He was looking after her. Susan was twelve. They had been watching a film on TV. When it ended, Nick said, as if it were the most natural thing in the world, 'Come upstairs. I'll give you a bath, shall I?'

While Nick ran the water, she took off everything except for her shirt. She stood in the bathroom with the rest of her clothes around her on the floor. Nick sat on the edge of the tub, his back to her, his hands under the running water to test the temperature. He poured in some of the bubble-bath that was kept in a heavy green bottle on the shelf.

'That's Mum's,' she told him.

'Just a drop.'

'She'll kill you if she ever finds out.'

'She won't find out. We won't tell her, so it doesn't count. Don't watch. Close your eyes.'

The room smelt of mountain paths and steam and her mother's perfumed skin. When the bath was full of green bubbles he turned off the taps. 'Come over here.' He unbuttoned her shirt very carefully and helped her to take it off. She held onto his shoulder to steady herself as she stepped into the water.

'Is the temperature alright?' he asked.

She nodded, sitting down.

'Turn round. I'll wash your hair.'

She rested her head back in his cupped hands, squeezing her eyes tight shut and blocking her ears with her fingers so that when he dipped her head under the water she didn't get too much in her eyes. She had to sit up, laughing and gasping for air, afterwards. He laughed too, waiting until she'd rubbed the water out of her eyes before he poured on the shampoo. Once he leant forward and very gently touched his mouth to hers, but she couldn't open her eyes or the soap would have got in.

There was a new bar of soap on the shelf. When Nick unwrapped it, the smell of lavender rose up, mingling with the steamy air. He dipped the bar in the water and rubbed it between his hands. Then he soaped her chest, her neck and arms, her hands and, individually, all of her fingers and toes. His hands were big on her body but his touch was very gentle. Halfway through, he removed a heavy silver wedding ring he always wore, although he had been divorced for some time, as long as she could remember.

'You're a skinny thing, aren't you,' he said, amused, holding his hand against her heart. 'Look, I can count your ribs.'

He waited for her to kneel up so that he could wash her all over, everywhere, entrancing her body with the same slow, rhythmic, slippery motion. They didn't speak much. The soap had made most of the bubbles disappear and the water had grown lukewarm by the time she climbed out.

Nick dried her just as deliberately as he'd washed her, carefully combing the tangles out of her wet hair. They went back downstairs and she sat naked in his lap for the rest of the evening, his arms around her, the damp towel on the floor in a heap. The fabric of his trousers was a little scratchy against her legs but she didn't mind. They watched a video. She couldn't remember which one.

At ten o'clock he said: 'Come on, Susie Bear, bedtime,' and took her up to the big bed in the guest-room. The curtains were made of soft blue velvet that hung in heavy folds to the floor. Susan did not wear her nightgown but Nick wore white pyjama bottoms, piped with blue. She pressed her body against his back all that night, wrapping her arms round his neck and her legs against his. She slept like that, in the double bed, both the nights her parents were away. On both nights, Nick held her in his arms.

On the day her parents were returning, she opened her eyes in the morning and Nick said: 'Would you let me kiss you?'

He lifted her up tenderly so that her body was lying across the pillows and opened her legs wide. She lay on her back and he pushed his mouth between her legs, moving his tongue round for a long time, with a slow steady motion. A long, long time.

She made no sound except at the end, when she may have cried out. She wasn't sure. It was their only weekend together. Their first and their last.

•

'What were you going to say?' Nick asked.

'Nothing. Why?'

He fumbled for his cigarettes but could not find any in his pockets. 'Give me a cigarette.'

Susan opened her pack and silently handed one to him. He searched for his lighter then, failing to find that too, used a book of matches lying on the table. After lighting it, he stared morosely through the smoke, at the floor, without speaking. People, finishing work, had been steadily coming into the restaurant. The bar was beginning to fill up, though the tables around Susan and Nick were still mostly empty.

'What do you want from me?' he asked. 'What is it that you want from me, Susie? Really?'

'Oh, I don't know,' she replied lightly. 'What does anyone want from anyone? A little loving kindness, a little reassurance that one isn't so bad, after all.' Then, more seriously: 'Actually I'd like to see you now and again like we used to.'

He glanced at her and carried on smoking. 'Do you ever think of the Saturday afternoons when I'd take you to the pictures? I took you to see *The Spirit of the Beehive*. Remember?'

'Of course.'

'One of my favourite films.'

'I didn't understand much of it.'

'You weren't supposed to. I was trying to *educate* you.'

'I remember the little girl's face. Those dark Spanish eyes with very thick, straight black lashes.' Susan closed her own eyes, trying to recapture the film. 'She'd been frightened and she was running. I can't remember any more.' When she opened them again, her eyes had a faraway look, like they were fixed on things that had happened long ago. 'Afterwards, you took me to Fortnum's for a milkshake. I had a strawberry sundae.' He saw her face tilt and the smile break out. 'You called it a filthy pink concoction. You probably don't remember.'

'I remember very well. It was. Absolutely disgusting. You wore a hat. A kind of funny knitted beret pulled down over your eyes. Your hair stuck out underneath.' He grinned in reminiscence. 'You looked sweet.'

His smile had something of the old charm. His little crooked smile. She smiled back. She had forgotten how warm and tender Nick could sometimes be. Had been… She felt confused.

'Isn't it funny, what we choose to remember?' he said, still smiling. 'Do you still have it?'

'What?'

'The hat.'

'Don't be silly. It was fourteen years ago.'

'Yes, I suppose it was.'

His face changed, losing its vivacity, slipping back into the old lines. They didn't speak for a moment, each taking a sip of their drink.

'You wore a hat, too,' she reminded him, looking into his dark, unhappy eyes. 'It was cold.'

'Freezing.' But the lines on his face did not change.

'You gave me a book by Dostoevsky. One of my very first hardbacks. *Notes From Underground.*'

'Sounds apt,' he said, his face still morose.

'I still have it somewhere.'

'After fourteen years?' he growled.

'I had a nice time,' she said in a low voice.

'Did you?' He glanced at her. He looked suddenly tired. 'Well, so did I.'

He rubbed the back of his hand across his mouth like he was aware he'd already said too much. Said and drunk too much. 'I'd better go. It's late and I told Isabella I'd be back for dinner.' His eyes, like his words, had already acquired a remote, disdainful quality.

'Nick – ' she said, as he rose to go.

He buttoned his coat and stood there for a long second, looking down at her. 'Yes?'

She looked back at him. For a moment they gazed into each other's eyes. 'Nothing,' she said, letting her eyes drop first. 'It doesn't matter.'

He didn't kiss her goodbye, just squeezed her shoulder slightly from behind. Left sitting in the now crowded bar, more sober than she'd ever been in her life, Susan slowly finished her drink, feeling in her hand the weight of the heavy gold lighter Nick had mistakenly left on the chair behind him.

28

Later, she thought again of her last glimpse of Nick. She'd looked for what seemed a very long time into those familiar brown eyes. She had known then, without any doubt, that he had killed her father. It had been his hand on the knife when it made its final thrust, she was sure. For a few seconds she'd felt the elation that comes with certainty. Then the darkened, smoke-filled bar had receded and she'd been filled with her father's terror – at that moment, she was in the bathroom staring down at the point of Nick's knife, too.

'What the hell were you thinking of?' Alex demanded. He was staring at her in amazement from the other side of the sofa. They'd been sitting close together. Now he moved away. 'You met up with *Nick*? I don't understand. Met up with – For Christ's sake – why?'

'I don't know myself,' Susan admitted.

'I thought we'd agreed – I thought that you'd promised – You were going to take things slowly. You weren't going to do anything for the time being – ' Alex could barely find the words. 'And now this! What was in your mind?'

'I really don't know,' Susan muttered again.

She stared into Alex's open, shocked face. Why had she even told him, knowing how he felt? Why had she raced straight round to Keyes Court to see him as soon as Nick had left Romano's? She didn't know that either. To regain the innocence she found in his eyes? For understanding? Forgiveness?

'You have to leave it alone, you *have* to. What can you do? There's fuck all you can do.'

Susan thought of Nick's final expression; the cool, quiet, lopsided murderer's smile. 'I'll do anything I have to,' she said, her voice still calm but her heart suddenly hammering, 'to get even with Nick.'

'What do you mean?'

'Just that.'

'And destroy a lot more than him in the process?'

'If necessary.'

'That's stupid. Worse than stupid.'

'What isn't? Letting him get away with it?'

'Yesterday you asked for my advice and I gave it to you. I thought we'd agreed that you couldn't sensibly do anything without incriminating your mother. I thought we'd agreed.'

'You didn't see the look in his eyes,' she said, in a low voice. 'I did.'

'No, I bloody well didn't see it and you shouldn't have either! Because I'd make it my business to stay as far away from him as possible and if you had any sense you would too. What you saw – *if* you did – means he dangerous. Don't you realise that? If you're right, he's a scared and dangerous man.'

'And?' she said. 'So?' She didn't bother to hide the contemptuous note in her voice.

'Does he have any *idea* what you suspect him of?'

'I don't think so, no. He's vain. He wants to believe he's irresistible which means he has to trust me. But he's got strong instincts, so he doesn't.' He watched her reach for the gold lighter on the table. 'And deep down? Underneath all the vanity and pretence?' She balanced the lighter in the palm of her hand, looking down at it, feeling the dread like a cold weight in her stomach. 'Underneath, I think he knows that I know.'

'So he does,' Alex said in dismay. 'Susan – you must keep away from him. As far away as possible.'

'So he ends up with everything?'

'It depends,' he said wearily, 'on what you mean by everything.'

'That's easy. For Nick, money, sex. Most importantly, power. He wants it all, whatever it turns out to be. He wants the beetle from everyone's box. And, preferably, crushed into little powdery pieces so that he can enjoy it slowly, bit by bit. Except of course he never really enjoys any of it. He's a destroyer.'

'Then he ends up with nothing.'

'And my father?' she said, suddenly angry. 'What's he ended up with? You want nothing? That's nothing! I can't do it, Alex. Run away from this? I've tried but I can't. I wish that I could.' She closed her eyes, shutting out the sight of him sitting there, so normal, so decent, so *sane*. 'The thought is unbearable to me,' she declared, opening them again. But was it? Or was she only angry with herself because really it wasn't and she still hoped he could convince her otherwise?

'Yes, it's unbearable,' Alex said, suddenly losing patience. 'That's life, I'm afraid. You must have lived a very sheltered existence if you don't know that yet. In the hospital children come in with leukaemia. They die. I see it all the time. I live with it. And yes, it's unbearable. It's unfair. It's all bloody unfair. Fairness isn't the point.'

'That's different. It's terrible but nobody *made* it happen. No one deliberately made those children suffer through planning and effort. There's no one to *blame*.'

'No, it's called bad luck.' He glared at her. 'And maybe that makes it even more intolerable. Facing the fact that, in some situations, there's nothing you can do.'

'Can't you?'

'I'm a doctor, not God. Sometimes people want to live, but sometimes they want to die. I tell them, it isn't my job to help with that. My job is to try to save people's lives, not make decisions about whether or not to end them. Our task has always to be protecting life, not prolonging hatred.'

'God, listen to yourself! Do you know what you sound like? You sound like a pompous twenty-eight year old doctor.'

'I'm sorry, but that's how I feel,' Alex replied with dignity. He stared down at his hands, clasped together between his legs. 'Actually, a pompous twenty-nine year old,' he said, looking dispirited.

After a moment, she slid along the sofa and moved closer to him. 'There has to be some form of retribution,' she said quietly, slipping her arm through his. 'Someone has to act sometimes, whatever the cost. Or life becomes absurd. I've thought about it a lot since we last spoke – '

'When?' he interrupted bitterly. 'In the five minutes before you rushed round to meet Nick?'

'And I believe it's courage that's important,' she carried on, ignoring this, 'not some middle-class, high-minded sense of morality. The courage to do what you believe is right – the integrity to *act*. There are some crimes that cannot be forgiven – don't you see?'

'No,' he replied. 'I don't. On the contrary. Repaying an evil simply means bringing more wickedness into the world. It's adding one evil act to another.'

'There's no simply about it,' she snapped, pulling her arm away. 'And I think *your* attitude's evil. I think it's evil to let evil deeds go unpunished. You have to face what's wrong and cruel in the world full on. You can't just sit by and do nothing.'

'What? An eye for an eye?'

'I don't think it means what you think it means – but yes. No one has the right to forgive murder – except the one who's been murdered. That's what Jews believe. That's what *I* believe – no one else has the right. It's the unforgivable crime. You believe in turning the other cheek, I suppose?'

'Loosely, yes.'

'How very Christian of you,' she said nastily. 'Well, it's fine to talk like that if you're not in the slightest bit involved!'

'Oh, you haven't learnt anything!'

'What I've learnt,' Susan responded with cold fury, 'is that my father is dead and buried and his murderer is walking the streets, free and rich and happy. Actually, he's not *walking* the streets – he's driving around them in a spanking new Aston Martin.'

'So what are you planning?' Alex asked sarcastically. 'Hiring murderers yourself?'

'Perhaps.'

'Oh, this is ridiculous!' he cried in a voice unlike his own – a hoarse, high, angry voice. He got up, turning to face her. 'You asked if I thought you were crazy. Well, you *are* crazy!'

'Oh, fuck off,' she said.

She stood, too, and walked past him to the window, standing with her back to him. 'I thought you understood,' she said in a low voice, pleating the heavy fabric of the curtains between her fingers. Head down, she was crying silently. 'Apparently I was mistaken.'

He followed her over to the window and drew her hand away from the curtain, holding it in his. 'There's nothing you can do – you have to face that,' he said gently. Her hand was cold; he held it to his mouth to warm it. 'We've agreed that you can't do anything about the drugs deal. And the murder? What can you do? You don't even know for sure that Nick was involved. You don't know he's a murderer, whatever else you believe. You don't really have any evidence for that, do you?'

'So I tried and failed, is that what you're saying?' Her hand was in his, but she still had her back to him.

'Sometimes what really matters is what we do in extreme situations,' he said evenly, his lips pressed into her palm. 'Whether we face them, or whether we run away.'

'But I'm not running away.' She turned round, wiping the tears from her face impatiently with her other hand. 'That's the point. I'm twenty-six years old and I'm not running any longer.'

'I wouldn't be too sure. There's all sorts of running and some of them come well disguised.'

'Oh, there's always a hundred reasons not to act! Good reasons – rational reasons. But there's only one good reason for doing something – because you must.' She thumped her chest with her fist, pulling her hand out of his to do it. 'Because you *feel*.'

'Oh, grow up,' he said, not unpleasantly. 'Revenge? It's – it's childish. It isn't a motive in real life. It's TV drama. What you're talking about isn't integrity. Getting your own back? Even the idea that you ever could is nonsensical. It's all child's play.'

'It's a brute fact. You can't go any deeper. It's a basic human impulse.'

'It's an animal instinct. It's *animal*.'

'Which probably makes it all the more human. What's wrong with a desire for revenge?'

'So it's OK?'

'It's unavoidable, whether it's OK or not. And it's not revenge I'm talking about – it's justice. Which is very, very different. It may seem the same –

but it's not. I'm seeking justice for my father. Oh, you understand really,' she said, looking into his face.

'No. You're wrong. I don't. I don't begin to understand.' After a moment, he said: 'I'll make some coffee.'

She could hear him in the kitchen. He must have bought some coffee beans because she heard the sound of the grinder before the whistle of the kettle. He came back holding two new dark blue mugs. She took the mug he gave her and took the first sip leaning against the window. She said, staring down into the mug: 'I once asked if you thought I was telling the truth about seeing my father but you didn't really answer.' She looked directly into his face. 'I need to know, Alex. A straight answer this time. Do you believe me or do you think it's all a figment of my twisted imagination?'

She held her breath – everything hung in the balance. Everything swayed on a tiny thread. If Alex gave the answer she hoped, then she would trust him and give it all up. But if he did not...

'It seems possible,' he answered carefully, 'that Nick was involved in a big drugs deal – even murder. Even that's possible.'

'And that night in the studio? My father's story?' she asked, her voice sounding tight.

'What does it matter what I believe?'

'It matters,' she said. 'To me.'

'Is it really important?'

'It would be nice to have someone on my side. I thought you might be.'

'I am on your side. It just isn't the side that you think it is.'

'Oh, words,' she said in disgust. He was gone, lost to her. If he said that he didn't believe her father's story, then of course he had no reason to believe Nick was a murderer. She had no proof other than her own eyes, ears and heart. If she acted on their appeal then she had to follow them, whatever Alex believed. Or seemed to believe.

Because he wasn't admitting the truth, she thought despairingly – he'd seen Steven with his own eyes, he'd told her so! He had *heard* him, in the flat above his own. What more did he want? It was all very well denying it now, but he'd seen and heard Steven and, in his heart, Alex knew that he had. She'd said that she was one hundred per cent certain Nick was guilty but she was not – she couldn't be. There was still that niggling half a per cent. For absolute certainty she needed Alex to admit what he'd seen.

They faced each other across the room like strangers, which in a way, Susan reminded herself, they were. Who was he? A man she'd let kiss her once or twice, that was all. A dissembling, weak-willed shit who could deny the evidence of his own senses when it suited him. A man she did not really know. But it felt like somebody had cut out her heart and handed it to her to hold along with a deep blue coffee mug.

'Sometimes I feel,' he said, his voice low and shaky. 'Sometimes I feel as if I'm watching you on a raft drifting out into a rough and stormy sea, powerless to save you.'

'Do you know why I came back to see you this evening, Alex?' she asked suddenly, only just realising herself.

He shook his head. She could see his hands by his side were trembling.

'Because you tell yourself you don't believe me,' she said, 'but really you do. Because you know it, too. Don't you? You can say what you like, babble on about possibilities and probabilities forever and a day – but you know. You're not like Jonathan Woolf – for you this isn't a game. It's not just some clever-clever detective work with a fat fee at the end, if you're lucky. It's not superficial for you, anymore than it is for me. You talk of not running away from the truth, however unpalatable, so why are you running away? *Why are you running*? How can I take your advice if I can't trust you to tell the truth even to yourself? Who do you think it *was* outside the studio that night?'

He didn't answer. She could read the fear in his eyes and the die was cast. 'Who?' she demanded.

'It was dark,' he replied. 'Late… I don't know.'

'There are three keys, Alex. Mine, my mother's and yours.'

'Keys are keys!' he cried.

'Who?' she insisted, not taking her eyes off him.

'Perhaps Nick borrowed your mother's keys? There's no mystery to that.'

'It didn't look like Nick to you at the time.'

'Well, maybe I was mistaken.'

'You made a mistake?'

'Possibly.'

'I see.'

Stiffly, she walked the short distance to the couch – three steps – and sat down on the edge. She felt cut up, torn into pieces, lost. She felt there was no one else out there. She bent forward over her knees, her mouth open, as if she could retch all the feelings out, all the loneliness, terror and pain. There was no point in talking anymore. He understood nothing. Because he didn't *want* to understand. There was a lump in her throat so big it was threatening to stop her breathing. She clutched her neck, feeling she was choking. She knew that she'd made an irrevocable decision. This was the beginning. Or the end. She was alone, cold and afraid: she was without friends and a future. There were no choices for her now.

'What kind of man are you?' she choked, burying her face in her hands. His denial that he'd ever seen her father turned suddenly to anger in her. Talking through her fingers so that he could barely hear, she answered her own question: 'You're a coward.'

She dropped her hands, looking into his kind, serious face and could see only weakness and lies. She felt suddenly terribly afraid. She was going to have to face whatever came next alone. 'It isn't too late for me, is it?' she said, staring up with frightened eyes.

'Of course it isn't too late. What do you mean?' He sat down next to her and put both arms round her, squeezing her fiercely. 'Of *course* it isn't. Look, don't go home tonight. Stay here. The sofa turns into a bed. It's very comfy.' He gave the springs a hard thump to show her. 'And I won't be far.' He gave a wry smile and gestured towards the bedroom. 'I'll just be sleeping inside.'

She hesitated for a moment, considering, looking like she was about to reject his offer. Then she nodded. 'If you're sure it's OK?'

'Of course.'

'Then thank you, yes, I think I'd like to. I really don't want to be on my own tonight.'

But as soon as the words were out of her mouth, she knew that, whatever he replied, she was alone, and completely now.

Next morning, as they were eating breakfast, he said thoughtfully: 'I was speaking to a friend in Forensic medicine the other day. You know there have been real breakthroughs in DNA testing lately?'

'Really?' she murmured, helping herself to a slice of toast.

'Forensic scientists can create genetic profiles from a tiny stain on the victims clothing, or a hair picked off the body, or a cigarette left at the scene of the crime. Pretty much anything. It's incredibly sophisticated. They just need a few cells. Once upon a time, they needed to find very large samples for chromosomal testing but now a tiny sample of tissue – I mean, really tiny, blood or saliva, invisible to the naked eye – can be used to reconstruct a DNA profile. And the chances of two people sharing the same profile are smaller than one in a billion.'

'Is it?'

'And it can be done for old crimes, too,' Alex said eagerly, 'if the samples have been stored properly. Murderers who got off scot free at the time are now being put away for crimes they committed *over twenty-five years ago*. So I was wondering – why don't you approach the police again? After all, you believe you know who killed Steven – if you could convince them there's a good case, they could do a simple mouth swab and compare it with the profile of things found at the crime scene. You never know – they might get lucky.' He looked at her. 'What do you think?'

He couldn't see the expression on her face. She let her hair fall over her face as she spread marmalade more thickly on her toast. I think it's too late, she thought sadly. The stone setting's on Sunday. That's five days away. Yes, Nick would go to jail, but my father? What eternal torments for him?

She looked across at Alex, only the sudden tension in her body recording her thoughts. It was all very well accusing Alex of self-deception but wasn't she fooling herself too? That hurt more than the awful sense of loneliness that filled her when he had distanced himself by denial from the whole, horrible tale. She felt suddenly ashamed of herself, of all her wavering, of the panic. How could she have thought that hiring a private detective would make any difference? How could she have wasted so much time? Her father had warned her. He had told her there wasn't much time for him left. And she'd carried on, oblivious. She'd spoken at length to Jonathan Woolf, rushed round to her mother's, talked to Nina, searched out Paul, discussed the whole thing thoroughly with Alex, even paid for bank statements before discovering their worthlessness. All a cop out, she realised now. She'd wasted two whole weeks.

Why should she care? she thought bitterly. Oh, yes, it was easy for her to have moral doubts. Because it wasn't her time that was slipping away; it wasn't her soul living in torment. She was not faced with eternal wandering – her father was. She drew a deep trembling breath. If she wanted to avenge his murder, she had to do something now. Not in a month's or a year's time, not after a drawn-out court case or a long string of tests, but now.

But what was she expected to do? What?

There was no point in talking anymore to Alex; there was no point in talking to anyone.

The stone setting was in five days.

What could she do in five days?

Aloud, she said with a faint smile: 'It's an interesting idea. I'll consider it carefully.'

She took a big bite of toast. And thought longingly – Oh, for Alex's blindness!

When she left, early on Tuesday morning, she crossed to the other side of the wide road, busy with rush-hour traffic, and stood with her hands in her pockets, examining Keyes Court. Five floors up – Alex's window. Directly above it – the studio. Susan gazed at the window for a long time as if there was something to be learnt from blank, unreflective glass. A dilemma that could be resolved on the surface of a building's smooth, flat brick walls.

It was one of those raw, grey November days that seem to go on forever. People hurried past, ignoring her in their quest for warmer places. Susan wiped her nose on her sleeve, wondering what she was really searching for. She thought of the very first conversation she'd ever had with Alex. Surely she'd known what she should do even then, whatever she said, or did not say, to him? When she'd kissed him goodbye at the block's entrance that morning, mouth open, eyes dry, she already knew. Returning his kiss, she'd known the answer. Looking at Keyes Court now through tear-filled eyes, she thought that perhaps she'd known it for a very long time.

'*Dance to your daddy, my little baby, dance to your daddy, my little lamb,*' her father had sung to her when she was little. She couldn't recall him singing this. He had told her: 'This is what I sung you to sleep with when you were small, Susie… '

She thought of the children's rhyme. It sounded both enchanting and dreadful to her at the same time, a voice chanting the melody relentlessly in her head. *Dance to your daddy. Dance to your daddy. Dance to your daddy. Dance.*

'Man trouble?' the taxi driver inquired sympathetically, glancing at her blotchy face in his mirror.

'It's an allergy.' Susan searched in her bag for the tissue she was pretty certain wasn't there.

'My wife suffers from hay fever something rotten. You wait for the summer all year, then, when it comes, it's no fun at all. Sneezing, blowing, itchy. She gets all itchy, her eyes go all red and puffy like yours. It's the rape, you know. Terrible stuff. It self-seeds. Ever since they started growing it in this country she's been bad. What do you take for it then? Clarityn?'

'Yes,' Susan smiled faintly. 'Usually.'

The cab swerved in to the kerb. 'Here we are, love. It was the corner of Gloucester Avenue you wanted, wasn't it? Fitzroy's just up there. You don't want me to turn around, do you?'

'No, this will do fine.'

'That'll be nine pounds forty, darling,' the taxi driver said, his elbow resting on the open window. He smiled at her when she handed him a ten pound note with, it seemed, suddenly shrewd and knowing eyes. 'Good luck.'

•

She found the turning pretty easily. A primary school on the corner surrounded by trees, a few houses mostly set back from the path. It was not a road exactly, too short and full of dips for that. Susan drove slowly, trying to avoid the rain-filled holes. Leaning forwards slightly, she could make out the numbers on the doors – seven… nine… eleven… A little further on, another house. Two houses, in fact – the original stone building had been divided into two. The road ended here. She came to a stop with a bump.

Fields all around her, in front and to her right. A wooden stile ahead. A sign painted in white with an arrow – 'public footpath'. Overgrown hedges against a low, overcast sky.

She switched off the engine and rolled down the window on the passenger side, examining a glossy black front door. Silver numbers were placed one slightly below the other.

15 Dancers Hill.

Susan stared at the house for almost five minutes but finally had to admit it evoked no memories in her at all. She could have been anywhere, looking at any house, not the one she'd lived in until she was seven years old. The only familiar thing was the number on the door. Perhaps there was something about the house she dimly recognised though she would have been hard pressed to say exactly what. The only thing she could say with any certainty was that it wasn't the least bit like the house she'd visualized after the car crash, just before she'd passed out in the snow besides the upturned wreckage of her father's car. In her vision, the house stood tall and solid, its walls painted a radiant, shining white. Her father had been standing outside of it, waving wildly to her. Even taken as a whole, the house was much smaller than she'd remembered. And not shimmering at all, but really rather shabby.

She shivered. Why exactly had she come? Had she hoped to find her father here, still waving? Had she really thought that he might, just possibly, appear to her once again? That the year-old vision in France had been a clear message from him, the clearest she had any right to expect, and, arriving at Dancer's Hill, she'd find him standing on the front step, smiling hopefully at her, as he had fleetingly after the car crash? *Waiting to tell her exactly what she should do…*

The thought of seeing him terrified her, it turned her insides to water, but on the other hand – Either she did something to save her father within the next five days, or she did nothing at all, ever. Either she believed in him, and all he'd told her, or she did not. Which really came down to believing in herself, she supposed. This was the end of the road, she stared around, in every sense.

It had started to drizzle. The wind blew small, sharp points of rain onto the windscreen. Susan turned up the collar of her jacket, stuffing as much of her hair as she could inside. Careful to step over the rain-filled holes, she crossed to the house.

The front garden had definitely changed. There was an old and familiar photograph, a slightly torn colour print of her father digging outside this very front door, next to a bed filled with daffodils. Young and fit, kneeling on grass with fork in hand, he had looked so happy. Over the last twenty years someone had got rid of most of the earth and grass replacing them with concrete paving stones so that only a small circle of bare soil remained in the centre. It must have been March when the photograph was taken since there were daffodils. Now it was November – no flowers, only rain which drizzled down on Susan's scalp and damp which was already seeping into her shoes. The place where the daffodils had grown was locked beneath hard grey stone and she refused to think of what else lay buried deep in the earth.

Looking down, she saw she'd stepped into a puddle. 'Shit,' she muttered, shaking her foot.

She was standing behind a low wrought iron gate. She slid back the bolt, feeling the chilled metal against her hand. Then, trying to make her back look straight and purposeful, despite the drenched shoe, walked across the paving stones to the black front door. She pressed a nervous finger on the doorbell, listening to an unfamiliar flurry of tinkling chimes. She could hear them echoing inside the house. When no one answered she pressed the bell again, then, when there was still no movement from inside, pressed it boldly, long and hard, a third time. Two empty window boxes were set against the front window. Standing between them, she cupped her hands round her face and peered through the net curtains. A fuzzy image of a sofa and a small table set next to it, a closed door through to what she knew was a dining room. A small wooden sign was attached to the wall above the table. She could just make out the words painted on it – 'You don't have to be mad to live here but if you are it helps'. Rather than listen to any more chimes, she moved round to the side of the house.

A brand new wooden gate led through to the garden. As she put her hand on the gate's catch, Susan had a sudden flash. She saw a swing made of green, rather rusty, metal standing next to a twisted apple tree; a stretch of grass winding down to the river; white roses, lots of them, covering a high wooden fence. She had fallen into them early one morning, riding a new bicycle before anyone else was up, and had to lie pinned beneath the handlebars amongst thorns, screaming for help for what seemed like hours, until her father had finally rescued her. She'd forgotten about it until now. Smiling slightly at the memory, she stood on tiptoe to peer over the gate. A cat's litter tray and a green plastic watering-can stood outside the kitchen door.

As she balanced there, she felt the hairs on her nape stand erect. A sound. Just behind her. Surely she'd heard something? Slowly, she sank to the flat of her feet and spun round, feeling dizzy with dread. For a moment she thought – she hoped – But, whatever she'd expected, there was nothing to meet her frightened gaze. Just grass and field and bare grey sky.

Susan let out her breath. Her heart slowed down again. She stood for a moment, checking all around, breathing deep lungfuls of fresh air. Then she pushed the gate open. No sudden voices called out to stop her as she stepped inside.

She was riding her new green bike round the garden, along the paved path that ran through the rose bushes. She had to be very careful – if she fell off, the bushes were full of thorns. When her father came out she laid the bike down and ran over to him, laughing. She walked round the garden at his side. He didn't take much notice of her chatter, probably he was tired. It was a Sunday after all, and he was always tired on Sunday.

'Can we play Romeo and Juliet?' she asked.

'Not now.'

She tried again after a moment. 'Dad, when I whistle look at me, OK?' She whistled. He bent to smell the fragrant interior of a creamy white rose. 'You're supposed to look at me,' she frowned.

He straightened. 'Why don't you go inside and watch TV. Your favourite's just starting. Popeye's on at four. Why don't you go in and watch it?'

'I don't want to. I want to play Romeo and Juliet with you. Can't we play?'

'Stop asking, Susie,' he said wearily. 'Or go inside.'

They carried on round the garden. She was quiet now.

'What's that?' he asked suddenly. He stopped and looked down at her face. Following his eyes, she touched her brow.

'Yes, there. On your forehead.'

'I don't know.'

'There's a mark. What on earth is it?'

She shook her head, fighting back tears. The look on his face was so strange.

'It looks like – lipstick,' he said. He took his handkerchief out of his pocket and rubbed her forehead hard.

Her forehead was burning. 'Has it gone?'

'No,' he said, frowning. 'No, it hasn't.'

He put the handkerchief back in his pocket. Then, taking her hand, he continued walking down the garden towards the river, along the path through the roses, holding her hand in his.

•

Susan sat shivering in the car while the day grew dark around her. Further down the road, the lights came on in the windows and curtains were drawn, but no one came to light up number 15. *You know what to do*, her father had said to her. *You have to do it before the stone goes down*, he'd said. *I can't get to the Nothing once the stone is set. You have to avenge my murder before the stone setting. After that it's too late. After that, I'm stuck in limbo forever. And don't fool yourself, Susie – forever is a really long time…*

It was cold in the car. She turned on the engine every now and then to keep the heater going. But she didn't want to attract too much attention so she mostly kept it off. For hours, she huddled there but he didn't come.

Five days. She only had five days. To do – what?

You know what to do…

She felt chilled and tired and more alone than she'd ever felt in her life before, lonelier than she'd ever thought possible. In the car window she could see her own reflection, pale face, big frightened eyes, surrounded by a mass of dark hair. The cigarette she was smoking seemed to burn a hole in the middle of her forehead. Her thoughts swept her back to the first night in the studio and her face reflected on dark glass then. Her father standing at the window and a spark from his hand-rolled cigarette burning on her brow. She watched herself, remembering; watched herself rubbing her eye with the back of her fist in the car window. She wished she could be sure what her father had meant. What exactly had he meant?

Daylight began streaking across the sky. At twenty five past five, when it was clear he was not coming and she only had memories to keep her company, Susan reached out her hand and turned on the ignition.

And still the buring question – *what was she going to do?*

205

29

She rang the doorbell several times. She was sure he was home. She could see his red Aston Martin across the road, outside a run-down house with silver graffiti sprayed on a dull purple door. Her throat was a hard, dry knot. She checked the address again, pulling a slip of torn paper from her bag with trembling hands. Flat 3, Number 23. And a pretty seedy looking building it was too, she thought, glancing up before pressing her finger down long and hard on the bell. She would give it another minute then... There was a click as the intercom sprung into life. 'Yes?'

She recognised Nick's voice through the crackle. 'It's Susan,' she mumbled to the wall. She waited for the buzz, her hand ready, then pushed the front door open and walked on grubby lino up a flight of stairs.

At the top, Nick was waiting. He was unshaven, his hair still tousled from sleep. He was wearing a long, cotton Japanese dressing-gown under which he was clearly naked. She could see the dark, curling hairs of his chest before he pulled the fabric tighter round him and tied the sash in a half-bow. He looked at Susan standing there in her short black leather skirt and coat, her bag slung over her shoulder. 'Come in,' he said, holding the door wide, either unsurprised or deliberately cool.

She stepped inside. Her heart was beating so hard she could barely breathe. Her bag was a dead weight on her shoulder. She was trembling from head to foot.

He yawned. 'Would you like some coffee?' Yes? Because I would.'

She nodded. The only sound she managed to produce was an odd, pitiful little bleat.

'Sit down,' he said, gesturing to one of the modern black leather sofas, set at right angles to each other, 'and I'll make some.' He looked her slowly up and down. The stance of his body was insolent even if his expression was not. 'At least you match the decor.'

He walked on bare feet from the room. Susan sat stiffly on the sofa, holding her bag close to her body, and lit a cigarette. When she took a drag, it tasted foul. But she'd relaxed enough after a couple of puffs to look around. She was sitting in a huge, dramatic space, very much done up, belying the shabby outside of the building. All on one level, it was painted in a wash of dark-green and swirling indigo blue. The wooden floor had been painted the same dark-green, flashed with gold, then highly varnished. The blinds were pulled down tightly as if it were still night, which added to the general sense of unreality.

Around the room, were three larger than life papier-mâché models. Two men knelt one either side of the opening through which Nick had disappeared, one with his hand outstretched as if in supplication, the other bowed over as if a heavy object were about to be placed on his back. A third stood by the front door.

Susan felt dislocated, lost in space and time as she sat there rigidly, on the smart leather sofa, smoking. The sculptures seemed to her to contain within them real, breathing men, contorted in agony. Only the concealed lighting hitting them revealed that the cut-out eyes were empty.

I wouldn't chose to eat breakfast here each morning, she thought, looking round the whole fantastical space. Not for a hundred pounds. Not for a thousand I wouldn't. She took in the long steel dining-table on the other side of the room. Did Nick really have his cornflakes here? Did he drink tea thirstily in front of these three spooks?

The scent of coffee drifted through the air. Somewhere in the flat a door slammed.

When Nick came back he was holding two white espresso cups and a small bowl of sugar on a silver tray. He had shaved, dressed and presumably showered – his black hair was wet and combed straight back from his face. He plonked one of the cups down on the floor beside her, then walked across the room to release a couple of the blinds – they flew up with a shimmy, revealing the light of a normal day. He settled down on the sofa opposite. The palms of her hands were sweating with an effort to appear relaxed.

'So?' he said, smiling. 'Do you like it?'

'Do I like what?' she asked, her voice coming out like someone else's.

'All this.' He made a sweeping gesture round the room without taking his eyes off her. 'Pretty cool, isn't it? Kind of unusual.'

'It's big,' she replied, glancing round, thinking that she would rather live in hell. 'Much bigger than you'd expect from outside.'

'I'm thinking of buying it. Depending on circumstances.' He stirred two sugars into his cup. 'The present owner is an art director with a penchant for interior design and money to burn. He's changed it twice already. Last year it was very white – he called it Post-Modern Deco.' The spoon clinked against the side of the cup on each circle. 'The magazines all took it up. *Interiors* was round to photograph it in a flash and *Elle Decoration* came twice. You can get away with anything if you've got the money, can't you? A tin of Dulux emulsion and a brand new aesthetic movement is born.'

He crossed his legs, relaxing back with a grin, holding the little cup and saucer in the air and assuming an air of recklessness. It was a mood that Susan had seen him in all too often. But the hate in his dark, smiling gaze she didn't quite understand.

Oh, God, she thought, he knows. Someone's told him. I told Isabella and she's told him. He wheedled it out of her after he got back from Romano's the other evening. There's no use pretending. He knows.

'What about your house in Fulham?' she asked uneasily.

'It's already sold. The market's high at the moment. I got a good price, a very good price, which is why I can afford to rent all this.' He waved his hand round the room. 'It's the interest, you see.'

'Are they included in the price?' she asked, nodding towards the papier-mâché figures.

He grinned disarmingly. 'Actually not. Which is a shame – they're by a Turner prize artist. Worth a small fortune.'

'Oh, really?'

They both sipped their coffee.

'So you've got rid of the house…' Susan said, her mind whirling, her face blank.

Nick glanced at her, his expression seeming to say, So what?

'I also hear you're selling your share of the business and taking early retirement,' Susan added, intending to wipe the smirk from his face. But her voice echoed strangely in her ears, as if someone else were saying these words for her.

Nick didn't move, even his eyes. But behind them, things watched and waited. He was still grinning, but no longer so pleasantly. 'Who told you that?'

'Oh, these things get around. You know how it is.'

'No,' he replied smoothly. The smoothness of ice. 'I don't. Tell me, how is it?'

She met his gaze steadily, forcing herself not to show any emotion.

'No one's supposed to know anything about it yet,' he said in the same even tone. 'How did you hear?'

There was something in his voice that made the short hairs on the back of her neck prickle. She said: 'Just a lucky guess,' and smiled, though fear had dried her mouth and tightened the muscles of her throat. 'Actually,' she heard herself say, 'someone at Beaux-Sarr gave me a hint.'

Something flickered in his eyes, then was gone. 'Really?' he said with icy affability.

She had done it now, she had really done it: there was no turning back. She exhaled, realising she had been holding her breath. What would he do?

But Nick simply drank the rest of his coffee in one go, tipping his head back slightly, then got to his feet, saying: 'I'll show you around, shall I?'

The rest of the flat was just as big, but less dramatic. A hallway lined with framed photographs led to a ultra modern bathroom covered from floor to ceiling with grey mosaic tiles with a sink built into the wall, the shape of the taps suggesting a left-over from the Post-Modern Deco scheme. There were several bedrooms, one clearly Nick's. Pale grey walls and thick darker grey curtains, a high brass bed roughly covered with a heavily embroidered orange and red rug that Susan recognised from the house in Fulham. She looked around, glad of the natural light.

'I haven't got round to doing it up yet,' Nick explained. 'Needs a new bed and what not.'

'I rather like this one.' She smiled. 'It reminds me of old times.'

He glanced at her quickly.

Long windows opened onto a wrought-iron balcony. 'Can I – ?' she asked, gesturing.

'Sure,' he replied. 'They're not locked.'

She opened the windows and stepped out, enjoying the feel of cool air on her flushed cheeks. He followed her. When she turned round he was standing right next to her, so close that she instinctively stepped back, then found that she couldn't move any further and that her back was jammed painfully against the iron railing.

'Let's stop pussy-footing around, shall we?' he hissed, leaning forward so that she had no option but to bend further backwards. 'What is it you're really after, Susie?'

'You asked me that once already,' she said weakly, gripping the iron rail behind her.

'To see me now and then like we used to, yeah. Well, you don't need to treat me like shit for a year then come mincing round in black leather at nine on a Thursday morning for that.' He leaned forward, his eyes narrowing. 'What the fuck do you want?'

She whispered, her throat tight with fear: 'You know.'

'Do I?'

'Yes.'

'Tell me,' he said menacingly, leaning further forward. There was no mistaking the hatred on his face now.

She licked dry lips. 'I want – '

'Go on.'

'Nick… You're scaring me…'

'Go on.'

'I want – ' She breathed in deeply. What was she doing here? What was she *doing*? Alex was right. Nick was dangerous, he was crazy, he was – But she knew that she had no choice now but to carry on. Hesitate and all was lost.

'I want you to finish what you began,' she blurted out shakily on the long breath out, 'all those years ago.' She lifted her chin and looked straight at him. 'Nothing has come close to it since for me.' She forced herself to keep her gaze direct and unblinking. 'Nothing.'

He stared unfalteringly back at her through narrowed eyes. His eyes were depthless, black and inscrutable – except that she could see everything in them, see her own accidental fall from Nick's balcony, look down at her own smashed body on the kerb below. She was scared, more scared than she had ever been in her life. He wouldn't do it, would he? He wouldn't risk it. Another dead body found in his home? He couldn't chance it. Except she could see in his eyes that he would. If it was necessary, he would do anything and sort out the consequences afterwards. *She was unbalanced, Officer. She came round to the flat and made a pass at me. Of course I turned her down, but the next thing I knew the bloody little fool had thrown herself off the balcony... said something about wanting to join her father...*

After a moment, or a decade, Nick turned away with a little laugh. A little crazy laugh. Her legs were trembling. She clutched the railing, feeling that if she let go she would collapse. 'What is it?' she asked, forcing normality into her voice.

He turned back to her. 'What is what?'

'You laughed.'

'Funny, isn't it?' he said. 'For a moment I thought – ' He broke off, his smile disappearing as quickly as it had come. 'Come inside,' he said brusquely. 'It's cold out here.'

They walked back to the room where they'd drunk coffee – it seemed a long time earlier. She thought, I could race past him up the hall, wrench open the front door and dash down the stairs into the street. But would I make it, with Nick hot on my heels? Nick the murderer, Nick the drugs dealer, Nick the thief? Wouldn't it simply be an admission of her real intentions? But what were her real intentions anyway?

What did I think I was going to accomplish by coming here, she wondered, sinking down onto the sofa. What really was my plan? Whatever it was, I can't do it. And Alex's words again, spinning round and round in her mind – *he's dangerous; if you're right, the man is crazy.* Then her own offhand reply, relying heavily on Nick's long-standing affection for her – *not crazy, no, a little weak perhaps...* Which was, of course, perfectly easy to assume when she was with Alex. Here, faced with the reality, it was different. The dark, curling hairs of his chest, the long, strong, muscular legs, the shaded, empty eyes... Someone you have known all your life and never really known...

Her heart thumped wildly. Was she making the same mistake as her father? Assuming she knew Nick better than she really did? The leather, as she moved into it, made a long, soft hiss.

'So after fifteen years you'd like to start it all up again? I'm very flattered,' Nick said, the sarcastic lilt in his voice belying his words. 'I am really. But it just isn't possible, is it?'

She thought, what isn't possible? An affair with you, Nick? You're bloody right it isn't. Then: he believes me at least. I'm safe for the time being. And then: Safe? From what? Aloud she asked: 'Why not?'

'What is this? A battle between you and Isabella with me as first prize? What am I? A fucking rosette?'

'You loved me once,' Susan said quietly. 'As you reminded me the other day.'

'I felt certain things for you,' he replied carefully. 'That's true. Though perhaps not quite what you imagined.'

'What did I imagine?' She could feel her mouth held in a curve like a dead smile. 'Tell me, Nick.'

'Look, you've grown into a beautiful woman. But strange as it may seem, I'll take Isabella any day. If I have to make a choice between you, it's no choice. Isabella makes me feel calm. She satisfies me. She *believes* in me. It's a very simple thing really. She makes me feel like I'm someone. That I'm not a totally worthless piece of shit. I'd do a lot to preserve that feeling.' His face hardened. 'Actually, quite a lot. Maybe I'm just getting older but I'm happy. For the first time in my life, I feel happy. I've got a life. Not a veneer. Not a carefully structured edifice, but a life.'

'But you said – '

'What?'

'You said that you felt – ' Susan stopped, a catch in her voice, unable to go on.

'Look,' he sighed. 'I'm sorry if I misled you in any way.'

She thought, you don't sound it.

'But you could say that I've got what I always wanted.' He smiled, with a flash of the old charm. 'It's nice, for once, envying myself.'

Despite herself, she couldn't stop herself asking: 'What about me?' sounding even to her own ears like a plaintive little girl.

He examined her white face. She watched the discovery dawning in his eyes. It was as if he had known something for a very long time but was only now fully realising just what it had been. 'To be frank,' he said at last, 'I preferred you when you were a child.'

A kind of terrified fascination held her in Nick's cool gaze. She wanted to cry – You bastard! But more than one emotion held her back. Her heart was beating very fast – she thought that he must be able to hear it, or at least see it pumping through her clothes. She didn't care what he said. Why should she mind? It was only a ruse to get close to him anyway. But she found that she did care, quite a lot.

211

'You were sweet then,' Nick continued, in the same cool, dispassionate tone. 'And you loved me, completely and without complication. I enjoyed the involuntary sparkle of hero worship that came into your eyes whenever you saw me. Those big, brown eyes looking up at me with adoration. It was very charming, that adoring look. I would have given a lot to be on the receiving end of it. I *did* give a lot. Oh, you were really something then, lover. For a few months I thought I couldn't live without you. But that feeling, like so many others, passed. Because,' his eyes rested on her without desire, without passion, without even the slightest vestige of real feeling, 'the inevitable happened.'

'What?' she whispered.

'You grew up.'

'I grew – ?'

'Why did it come as such a surprise? Why did it hurt so much? You changed, we all change.' He sighed, and glanced unlovingly at her. 'Of course you did.'

Time seemed to have slowed painfully down, like holding a breath beyond human endurance. They sat in the strange green light of Nick's flat like they were the only two people left in the world. She could see the cruel light reflected in his eyes, the icy triumph of victory: he was enjoying himself.

'So that's all I ever was to you?' she asked slowly. 'Just a figure in one of your dreams? You never really cared at all?'

'Oh, I cared,' he replied coolly. 'I just didn't care for what you thought I cared for.'

'You never really loved me?'

'You could call it love. Why not? Though, looking back, it was more like addiction. Addicts really love their fix, don't they? But like all addictions, you can lose the habit – if you try hard enough. Or at least replace it with another.' He leant back on the couch, uncrossing his legs, then crossing them in the opposite direction, away from her, and rubbed the side of his nose thoughtfully, pressing in the nostril for a second with a sharp sniff. He was probably not even aware he'd made the gesture. So that's your replacement, she thought, understanding now. Oh, Nick!

'You see, one day you looked up at me with those beautiful big brown eyes,' he went on, 'only they didn't seem quite so beautiful any longer. I saw in them something different. Something more like – contempt. Dislike even. I was quite hurt, believe it or not. You and me?' He laughed without humour. 'Oh, baby, life's too short. I'd never know, would I, exactly what was on your mind.'

When Susan had first met Paul she'd had a recurring dream. She'd found a letter on his bedside table to another woman, declaring his passionate and undying love for her. The woman was an air-hostess he'd met on one of his frequent trips to France, tall, blonde and elegant. Oh, that, he had said coldly when Susan had confronted him with the note. Yes, I love her, far more than I love you. In fact, I never loved you much at all; it was a charade, a big pretence. I was *dissembling*. 'Do you really mean this?' she asked Nick now, as she'd asked Paul in her dream.

Unexpectedly Nick smiled. He lifted his arms above his head and stretched. 'Oh, I don't know,' he replied lazily. 'Perhaps. Sometimes you say things which, when spoken aloud, sound quite different to the way they seemed when you only thought them. They become something alien and strange. I loved you once – in a way.' He let his arms drop. 'That's the truth of it.' He frowned. 'Do you understand now?'

'Of course I don't.'

'I'm sorry,' he said, but she could still hear the faint but distinct ring of pleasure in his voice. 'Not pleasant, is it, once it's out, the truth? But then I'm not a particularly pleasant man.'

'No,' she said, her voice trembling. 'You're not.'

What do I do now, she thought. Have I got the nerve to act on the truth, too?

He leant forward, his eyes like black ice, his voice changing key. 'Have you ever looked at your face in the mirror, Susie? Oh, it's a beautiful face, of course, but to me it's – dead. Your face died for me years ago. When other people grew up, you only grew older.'

'Whose fault is that, Nick?' she asked in a low voice, returning his gaze.

'I had so much to teach you once,' he said. 'You were so hungry for life. But there's nothing left for you to learn. There's nowhere left for you to go and, for sure, nowhere for me to take you.' The sneer was back on his lips. He looked at her without bothering to hide the cruelty in his eyes. She thought perhaps she could have forgiven him anything but this – his pleasure. His pleasure in the murder of innocence. His face changed again, his voice sounded flat, almost bored, though his eyes remained wary. 'Of course it was all a long, long time ago.'

'In the past,' she agreed.

'Look, you don't love me anymore than I love you.'

'I don't even like you,' Susan replied. 'What's that got to do with it?'

'And Beaux-Sarr?' he asked, after a pause, 'Whilst we're being so delightfully honest with each other, what do you know about that?'

'I know everything,' she stated flatly.

'Yeah? How did you find out? Did Steven tell you?' He saw the look on her face. 'Of course he did. Stupid. Even for him. Stupid, stupid. And telling you, of all people. He swore to me he hadn't mentioned it to any-one the night of – ' He broke off.

'The night of what, Nick?' she inquired, sweetly.

'He must have been out of his mind telling you. It's trouble, Susie, real trouble. Forget all this other stuff.' He waved his hand in the air. 'Forget I'm a bastard and all that, but remember this.' He leant further towards her until his eyes were bright and close. 'These men are nasty. Very, very nasty. I've seen it – I wish to God I hadn't. Don't get involved, for your own sake.'

'For my sake? Or yours?'

'Both.'

'And the company? Savage Associates?'

'So it changes,' he said wearily, leaning back again. 'Is that so terrible?' Whatever emotion had been in his eyes was gone. 'Just don't mess around with the Beaux-Sarr lot.'

'Is this a warning – or a threat?'

'Take it whatever way you like. But, believe me, you're biting off more than you can chew. If you decide to put something over and these men get wind of it…' His eyes narrowed a little. 'Well, I certainly won't be around to protect you.'

'You'd save your own skin?' she asked, giving him a narrow glare of hate.

'You bet your cotton socks I would. I've seen what these men can do. I saw what they'd done to – ' He stopped.

She thought, it's the second time. Twice he's come to the verge of con-fessing. Really he wants to continue to the end, he *wants* to tell me – but why? Remorse or triumph, or both? Her anger and repulsion almost welled over. She leant forward. 'Say it. Say it, Nick. You saw what they'd done to my father.' She said, very softly: 'You killed him, didn't you? You killed Steven.'

Still leaning back on the sofa, he examined her. For a moment she thought he was going to deny it, but he did not. 'Yeah, I was involved,' he admitted with a sneer. 'But you've guessed that already, haven't you? You've put two and two together and made ten. Or perhaps even done a little snooping about on your own. Though without much success, I imag-ine.' He smiled at her, his body deliberately relaxed. 'What do you want? A signed confession?'

And although she already knew it, her skin crawled at his words.

'You know, I must be one of Nietzsche's Supermen or something,' Nick said, 'because I don't feel any of that remorse they talk so much about. I feel good. I felt good. Glad I got away with it.' But when he stopped talk-ing and his veneer of triumph dropped, his face looked haggard. He looked suddenly, haunted, like a man consumed with self-hatred.

'You don't look like you feel so great,' she pointed out quietly.

'Well, I feel a whole lot better than Steven does, wherever he is now,' he said with a faint, contemptuous laugh.

Which was his mistake, she thought; his real, his last mistake. She dropped her eyes. 'As you said just now, it's all in the past. Let's forget it.'

'I'm trying,' he muttered. 'I've been trying for a long time.'

She said: 'I'd like a beer. I'll get it,' she added quickly as he moved. 'Where are they? In the fridge?'

'Yeah.'

She got to her feet, clutching her bag, giving one last glance backwards. At Steven's murderer, Steven's torturer, whether by proxy or in the flesh made no difference. Isabella's lover, Susan's uncle, Susan's seducer – Welcome. Her legs felt weak, her knees were trembling. When Nick smiled up at her, a little crooked smile, an oh so triumphant smile, she felt she had arrived back from a long, long journey and at last she knew why she was there.

30

When she returned from the kitchen, Nick was lying on his back, relaxing full-length on the sofa, his head resting on the wide leather arm, long legs stretched out in front of him. She stood before him and slowly unbuttoned her shirt. 'You remember the time that you bathed me, don't you, Nick? Come on, let's have a bath together now. For old times sake…'

He rested an arm across his face, smiling up lazily past the crook of his elbow. 'You never give up, do you? Don't you ever give up?'

'No, never,' she replied, squeezing down besides him on the sofa. She sat, squashed against his thigh, on the edge, facing him.

'Well, there's no bath here,' he murmured, his eyes on her breasts. 'Only a shower.'

She smiled. 'A shower then.'

He pushed his hand into her open shirt, taking hold of her nipple with hard fingers. 'Like it rough, Susie?' he said dreamily, squeezing her nipple till it hurt. She sucked in her breath. 'Your mother does,' he explained, his voice relaxed and mellow, eyes narrowed and smiling into her face. 'And your father – well, he could never give her what she really wanted. Or so she's always telling me. She likes to talk, does Isabella. In the middle of a fuck, she likes to tell me that – '

Susan struck.

She placed the bottle on the floor and, her eyes still fixed on Nick, his hand still on her breast, raised the knife from behind her back. It was unexpected. He was slow to react. His eyes followed the path of the bottle down to the floor, then up, along her other arm to the blade of the knife. He was still smiling as his eyes began to register surprise, fear. For a fraction of a second she saw his face turn to her, beseeching help, as if he did not recognise where danger lay. Frowning, he tried to sit up, but he was awkwardly placed for escape and her hand came down before he could move. She lifted the knife the length of her arm, then brought it down as hard as she could, hitting him in the chest. It did not go in deeply, but it was far enough. He gazed down at the wound. They both stared at it.

'Shit,' he said.

His chest looked odd, almost as if it had deflated. He looked startled: Susan looked panicky. 'This is funny,' he said in mild wonder. He put his hand over his chest. Blood began seeping out between his fingers. 'Very funny. Except – ' He looked down his body. 'This time, the joke's on me…'

She opened her mouth, wanting to speak. To say sorry, or something equally stupid, but no words came. Her mouth still open, she drew back, appalled, moving away from him, as if she could distance herself from the wound she'd just inflicted. Slowly, she backed across the room, still holding the knife, shirt flapping, her mouth a gaping hole. She was breathing fast, wheezing, as if it were her who had to squeeze in air through a gash in her chest. She was white with disbelief: she could not believe what she'd just done. If he hadn't been lying there, covered with still flowing blood, perhaps she would not have.

With difficulty, Nick rolled onto the floor, propping himself up against the sofa. He was shivering hard. After a moment, breathing heavily, he began to drag himself on his hands and knees towards the front door, leaving a long smear of blood in his trail. She knew that she couldn't leave him like that – in pain, still alive to tell the tale. To come and get her. She had to finish what she'd begun. It wasn't over yet. His movement shocked her into action. She followed on shaky legs, as he crawled across the dark, varnished floor, painfully making his way forwards, and stood over him. When he halted, gasping for air, she pushed him gently with her foot, then, taking a deep breath and closing her eyes, kicked harder so that he was forced over and lay wheezing on his back. Her eyes squeezed shut, she brought the knife down again, this time aiming for his neck. *You never really loved me? Not really. Because, you see, you grew up. You didn't get old and ugly, you just got old. You changed, we all change…* Opening them, she saw the blood and thought in disbelief – Oh my God, I have just cut Nick's throat.

She was not expecting the spurt of blood that shot out. She had to move quickly to one side to avoid it. She fell to the floor, hunched over, breathing quickly. Her own blood seemed to be pumping with particular force round her body as if in defiance – she could feel it surging in her ears, her chest, her wrists. On her hands and knees, she looked at Nick. I must have been planning this all along, she thought in surprise. This is what I intended to do from the start. It wasn't an impulse, was it? This was inevitable. But she wasn't sure; she did not really know.

After a moment she sat back onto her haunches. He wasn't moving much now. His shirt was drenched through with his blood. A black shirt soaked deep shiny purple. She was shivering. Her fingers were numb. The nails were almost blue. It was horrible. She had done it. She couldn't believe it. She was sweating, though she felt very cold. Heavy beads of sweat ran down the insides of her arms. She could smell herself. She smelt bad.

A thin line of blood had splashed on Nick's forehead, lying like a forgotten strand of red wool. He made a last attempt to turn over. Then, head rolling upwards, fell back again. There was blood in his mouth. He was coughing, gargling blood. After a while, this stopped. His eyes did not look puzzled now.

She dropped the knife and kicked it across the floor.

There must have been some noise before because, when it stopped, there was only silence.

Silence. And a terrible emptiness.

She stumbled through to the bedroom and fell onto the brass bed, sitting with her hands by her side, sobbing more than breathing, gripping the edge as if the bed might suddenly push her off, into darkness.

Something was missing.

Something vitally important.

She knew something was irrevocably lost, she was not sure what. She felt a thing beyond panic in the pit of her stomach. Something unimaginable, beyond dread or naming, far beyond terror, fear or despair. She felt she had no heart, no womb, her vital organs, all gone. She could hardly breath she was so afraid, hardly move. If she kept very still, perhaps she would be safe. But the light was gone forever and inside her body, there was only darkness.

A large black-winged moth flew in through the open window and banged wildly against the beaten metal light shade above her. She lay her head down carefully on the pillow, at the same time lifting her knees, and looked up at the insect. It circled wildly, then veered back towards the window, crashing into the glass once or twice before finally finding escape and flying out. Something rolled down her cheek – blood? She lifted a trembling hand. No, it was sweat, she saw with relief. She wiped her face on the corner of the sheet.

She was surprised to see how tidy the room was, undisturbed almost. Somehow she had expected disorder. The clothes were still in the fitted wardrobes, the brass bed neatly made with white pyjamas piped with blue, folded under the pillow.

From the street came music. Someone was playing the drums extremely loudly. She could hear raucous voices and shouts of laughter, like a carnival had started outside. On trembling legs she walked to the window and, standing behind the long blue velvet curtains, hidden in their torn and tattered folds, peered out.

The street was empty.

Susan let the curtain fall into place and stepped back into the room. Draped on the bed was her knee-length leather coat where Nick had thrown it earlier. She picked it up and slowly drew her arms through the sleeves. The lining felt cool against her skin. The moment she dreaded had come. It was time, she knew, to leave.

Outside the room, Nick's body lay in a crumpled heap. She closed the bedroom door and walked on stiff legs towards the body and the front door. Boots on the carpet. Swish of leather against her legs. Heart thumping in her ears. She did not look back. She had reached the end of the hall when she heard the voice. Two clicks, then the voice. His voice. Nick's voice.

'This is Nick.'

The walls of the universe seemed to crash open. She could hear the blood gurgling in her ears, feel the hot veins in her forehead bulging as if they might burst. There was black before her eyes, shooting red and black. Her mouth was open to scream. She couldn't scream. She couldn't breathe. Her throat clicked drily.

'You can leave a message or send a fax on this number. If you want to send a fax, start dialling now. Thanks.'

Her body did not respond, but a part of her was screaming – It's the machine! It's the answering machine! As soon as her fright was partially lifted, she sunk to the floor, straight down on her haunches, head hanging between her knees, eyes open, mouth wide, taking deep painful breaths. Her mind was empty but she knew enough to be sure that if she did not will herself to action straight away she would collapse. She crawled forward on her hands and knees, pulling herself to her feet with an effort and forced herself to continue up the hall, through bloody, green and gold cruel tiger-stripes, shaking, stumbling, gasping, lurching from side to side. The body was lying where she'd left it. A small amount of blood was still oozing steadily from his wounds.

Standing as far away as she could, Susan closed her eyes, leaning her head against the wall. He was dead. Nick really was dead. There was nothing to fear any longer. She had done it. She was safe. That body, which she knew so well, was damaged beyond repair. She looked down at him through half-closed, fluttering lids. He seemed to look back at her. A dead man with his eyes open.

As in life, she thought, so in death.

The knife had fallen near his body. She knelt down close enough to reach out her hand and slide it towards her. Straightening, keeping her eyes fixed carefully on the body with its dreadful glazed, lifeless stare, she dropped the knife into the pocket of her coat. Its metal tip stuck over the edge. Feeling its heavy sway against her side, she forced herself towards the front door.

Past the crouching papier-maché figure… past the man with his arms outstretched, begging for forgiveness… Stepping over the brown trail of almost dried blood, she detoured round to lift her bag from the sofa.

By the time the answering machine had finished taking its message, Susan had left the flat, pulling the door shut behind her until she heard the lock's final click.

31

Why did this voice keep trying to wake her?

She did not want to wake up. She wanted only to stay in this warm, cosy place where the waves lapped against the walls and she could hear the reassuring boom of the engine. Boom, clink, boom, clink. She felt heavy and numb. But the voice would not let her rest. A name repeated over and over again. *Su-san. Su-san.* It was clearer now, more urgent. *Su-san, wake up! You must wake up!* The darkness began to be filled with shooting lights. Red flash, white flash, green. Slowly she opened her eyes. Then she realised where she was, and when.

How she had finally made it back to the flat, or how long it had taken, Susan had no idea. All she knew was that she'd walked up the hall stairs and presumably unlocked the door to her flat because now, still wearing the stupid, uncomfortably short black leather skirt, she was inside. Barefoot, sitting under the window, in the living-room. She recalled crossing the room many hours before, looking out of the window and being dazzled by the daylight in the street, then sliding down the wall to the floor. She must have passed out because when she opened heavy, reluctant eyes it was no longer light. Outside, the cold night of Primrose Hill pressed heavily against the glass. The darkness had become absolute. There was no moon.

The flat was the same, yet different. Everything was different. She had killed a man. That was different. The man was called... At first she couldn't remember. Then, quite suddenly, she did. Nick. The man had been Nick. The moon had dropped out of the sky, she had killed the moon and the man was called Nick. This unbearable thought kept returning. I am Susan, he is Nick. I am Nick, I have just killed myself. Nick, Susan – Susan, Nick, I have murdered Susan. The moon has fallen out of the sky and the light has disappeared forever from the world...

At first she waited on her own, then, after this idea of the man's death had settled, grown clearer and developed certainty, she wasn't alone. She was not alone for one single second. For they came to visit her, all of them, one by one. Climbing in through the window, crawling out from under the bed, or standing, hollow-eyed, staring and silent, in the doorway. For hours, days, she did not know. Susan sat under the window in the living-room, listening.

Was this guilt, then? she wondered, hunching over her knees. These disembodied voices, these silly, squabbling, accusing shadows? Were they conscience? She sat with her knees up to her chin, hugging herself, head down; later, with eyeballs pressed hard into her knees, trying to block the images out. She could feel the wall behind her back, the cool blade of the knife against her feet.

She sat unmoving, locked into place. On and on the voices went, unrelenting, until she could taste whole world in her mouth. Her tears were black as blood, her bones were water. There was a long sliver of white cold ice in her heart. Listening, she stared down into the abyss. She stepped into the abyss. And on the floor in front of her, the knife.

There was very little in the room. Just the sofa covered in a red rug, the low Indian table and the framed Rauschenberg print, propped against the wall. Sofa, table, picture. And Nick, sitting by the door in a wheelchair.

He looked handsome, she had to admit, even with his long useless limbs and the unreflecting dark glasses. Behind them, his nose and mouth, with its jutting bottom lip, looked seductive and precisely sculpted.

Next to him stood Isabella, her hand protectively on his shoulder. She wore a demure black knee-length dress with large ivory buttons and a lace collar, elegant low-heeled black suede shoes and her dark hair was smoothed into a chignon.

And Susan, oh, so still in the corner. Susan, watching unseen.

Her mother was holding a glass of water. With a clean handkerchief she thoroughly wiped the rim. Leaning over the wheelchair, knees ever so slightly bent, legs in sheer black stockings, she held Nick's head erect so he could drink. Most of the water ended up bubbling out of his mouth and running down his chin, soaking the front of his shirt. When her mother turned to open the damp collar, Susan, seeing her from the side for the first time, realised Isabella was pregnant, quite far gone, maybe five months.

Isabella crossed the room and placed the discarded handkerchief and empty glass on the table, then sank onto the sofa with a sigh. Her dress rucked up, showing the tops of black stockings. Slowly, she undid the buttons at the front of her dress and, with a long 'ah' of relief, leant forward slightly to unfasten the hooks at the back of her bra. Her nipples were big and dark and blue veins stood out on her heavy breasts.

Then Nick stood up. He took off his dark glasses, set them down carefully on the wheelchair's flat leather seat and walked slowly across the room to the sofa. Sitting down next to Isabella, he slid his hands inside her opened dress, moving them gently over her distended belly and her breasts. He pulled the dress a little higher till Susan could see her mother's white open thighs and black lacey knickers before Nick drew them carefully off. Then he knelt in front of her, between those wide-open thighs. Isabella's head stretched back languorously, her body arched as she pressed against his tongue, her eyes closed.

And Susan, in the corner, barely breathing, in case they notice her.

After a time, Nick got up from his knees. He straightened the creases in his trousers and walked back across the room. Replacing the opaque dark glasses, he settled down in the wheelchair. His head slumped forward onto his chest. His legs returned to their state of ugly, useless immobility. At the same moment, Isabella started buttoning her dress. Leaving only the top button undone, she picked up the hankie from the table and crossed to the wheelchair by the door. Gripping her fingers in Nick's hair, she lifted his head and lovingly wiped all of the spittle from around his mouth and chin.

When she'd finished, unnoticed by her, Nick raised his head. He slid the dark glasses halfway down his nose, squeezing one eye shut in a grotesque wink. 'Dead?' he whispered, looking across the room with his open eye to where Susan crouched. 'You'll be lucky.'

When she awoke the world was dark. The walls of the room were black. When Susan woke, the walls were black, the window a tiny, far-off square of silver. Was she awake or was she sleeping? She didn't know. It didn't much matter. Except if she was dreaming, she would at least soon wake up…

He stood in the doorway, shaking his head.

Susan rubbed her eyes. 'Nick?' she croaked. 'Nick?'

When her eyes cleared, he was still standing there.

'I'm available for dreams, hauntings, weddings and barmitzvahs,' he said softly, resting his head against the door jamb. 'Just thought you'd like to know.'

'Leave me alone. Go away!'

'You don't get it, do you? You don't understand.' Nick smiled lazily. 'I ain't never goin' anywhere.'

'Go *away*,' she said desperately. 'You're dead.'

'Now you don't need to say anything if you don't want to. But a few more details would be helpful, don't you think? We all have to make choices and I've made mine – you. And yes, I'm dead. That's why I'm here, my darlin' child.'

Eyeballs pressed into her knees. Shooting red and black behind her lids. From that position, Susan couldn't see him but she could still hear him, all too well. It wasn't a dream this time, it wasn't her imagination. It was worse. Far worse. Nick. On his own. Begging.

'Give me the knife, Susie. Just put it down for while, will you? Now slide it across the floor…Don't kill me. Please. I don't want to die.'

'Give me one reason,' she said, 'not to.'

'I haven't got any reasons. Not good ones. I'm bad. I admit it. I'm rotten. I shouldn't have said what I did to you. I was cruel. I went too far. And it's true – I enjoyed hurting you. That's the kind of man I am. I regret it now of course. But is that any reason for killing me? I mean, you hurt me once, too.'

'How?'

'By growing up.'

'I can hardly be blamed for that.'

'You turned against me. Admit it. Your feelings changed. You loved me once. I was everything to you. Remember?'

'Yes, I remember.' Her tone was hard. 'I was a child. And you took advantage of my innocence and my love. That's unforgivable. A young girl's love for her uncle.'

'Was that why you wanted me dead?'

'Actually no, that wasn't the reason.'

'You wanted to murder me – '

'Stop right there.' She held up a hand. 'I didn't want to murder you.'

'Wanted to eliminate me, then. We won't use the M word,' Nick said, with something of the old sneer back in his voice. 'You wanted me eliminated because I rejected you and – '

She cut across him. 'That was not the reason.'

'Oh yes, it was. The reason was because I chose Isabella, not you. Tell me, would you have behaved any differently if I'd said yes when you offered yourself to me?'

'You misunderstood my intentions completely. Even dead, you misunderstand me so completely it's incredible. I didn't offer myself to you, as you so quaintly put it. It was a ploy, to get you off guard. I was *fooling* you!'

'Am I supposed to believe that?'

'You can believe what you want. It doesn't matter. You're dead.'

'It depends on what you mean by dead.'

'I'm not interested in one of your academic arguments,' Susan said wearily. 'Save the pin for the other angels to dance on.'

'I wasn't joking when I said I'll haunt your dreams. Don't fool yourself. Alive or dead, what I believe matters a great deal to you.' He stared at her. After a moment she lowered her eyes. He said: 'Let's get this straight – you're telling me you didn't kill me because I turned down your advances – '

'Correct.'

'But that you came round to my place with – what? Murder already in mind? I find that extremely hard to believe.'

'You're sneering again,' she said irritably.

He smiled. 'And you're lying.'

'Afraid not.'

'Well, it certainly looks that way. It looks as if – '

She interrupted him. 'I had the knife in my bag.'

'What?'

'I said, I had the knife already in my bag.'

'The bag you had slung over the little leather number?' He frowned. 'You mean, you didn't use one of the knives from the kitchen? You brought your own with you? But,' he objected, 'you went into the kitchen immediately beforehand.'

'Yes, I did. I went into the kitchen holding my bag, if you recall. To remove from it the knife I had brought with me.' She took a deep breath. 'I'm not saying that when I rang your front door I was absolutely sure what I was going to do, because I wasn't. But if I *did* make up my mind to kill you – which I hoped I would have the courage to do – there it was. A nice, sharp Sabattier. And after you taunted me with all that stuff about my mother and admitted to feeling quite cheery after my father's murder – well, there wasn't much question about it. Examine it.' She moved her foot in the direction of the knife. 'Please, take a good look. It's on the floor in front of me before I chuck it in the river. Do you recognise it? Does it look like one of yours?'

'I wouldn't know,' he said, his eyes on the bloodstained blade. 'I hardly use the kitchen. That's it? You came round to my flat carrying it?'

'Yes.'

'In your bag?'

'Yup.'

'It was all planned beforehand?' He looked up, taking his eyes from the knife for a moment. 'That's horrible.'

'That's great, coming from you.'

'Listen, darling, I'm absolved of guilt now. I've paid the price. I'm not the guilty one anymore – you are.'

She swallowed hard, acknowledging the truth of his words with a cold chill of fear, but said only a little huskily: 'So you admit you were guilty?'

'I admit nothing. I'm simply saying this new piece of evidence – '

'Evidence? Ple-ease. Are you kidding?'

'This new evidence,' he went on, ignoring her, 'throws a quite different light on what happened. It's a little shocking. I'm just trying to get things clear. I mean, it was my murder,' he said sharply. 'I think I have a right to know what I'm dealing with here. I trusted you and you – you *betrayed* me.' For a moment his brown eyes were liquid and sad. He looked like he might cry. 'I really didn't think you had it in you. You looked so upset when I turned you down. You looked – quite devastated. You see, I thought you still loved me – '

'Well, I don't.'

'Or more likely, that you were still unhealthily tied to me, a little obsessed. And that you were looking for an excuse in your own mind to get close to me again. As you once said – nothing since has been quite as good as me.' He smiled, rather nastily she thought. 'I could well believe that, still can, quite easily actually. It sounds pretty convincing. You never forget your first kiss, and all that. So, desperate for a reason to be close to me again, you accuse me of murdering Steven. You even believe it yourself. You intend to avenge his death, however unpleasant a task that turns out to be. You become involved with me again in order to do it. Ergo, your erotic obsession, thinly covered by a veneer of pique and hatred, is satisfied. Your own guilt about your father's murder is displaced onto me.'

'Guilt? Why the fuck should I feel guilty about Dad?'

'Why the fuck? You said it, sweetheart, not me. Freudian slip,' Nick crowed. 'Na, na, na-na, nah! Because you're still feeling bad about what we did when you were a child,' he finished, sobering up suddenly.

'What *we* did? You did it, Nick.'

'Oh, come on! You weren't so passive, as I recall. It takes two to tango, and all that. No, we – together – acted out your incestuous desires for your father – oh, I never fooled myself about that. I know how close you two were. I know what he meant to you. I suppose that was what partly motivated me, too. Triumphing over Steven.'

'What a load of shit you talk,' she said. 'Except for that last bit. That sounds true.'

'I'm not trying to convince you anymore. I'm just explaining to you how I saw things. It was how they looked to me at the time. Both of us were perpetrating a long, and admittedly pleasurable, attack on the internal parents. Our flirtation became a terrible, guilty secret of which you quickly became horribly ashamed.'

'For good reason,' she interjected bitterly.

'I'm not talking about good and bad. Those concepts don't apply here, anyway.'

'You can't have it both ways.'

'What do you mean?' He glared at her. 'Then your Daddy died,' he went on smoothly when she said nothing, 'and you felt bad because you had already murdered him – in an imaginary sense of course – by smiting a hefty blow, aided admittedly by me, against the parental couple. But now you're saying that when you, um, stabbed me to death,' he looked frenzied for a second but quickly recovered himself, 'it wasn't a crime of passion? It wasn't a response to my rejection or the cruel things that I'd just said to you? It wasn't because of our earlier sexual liason when you were only twelve?'

'No. Although they all helped.'

'It was a calculated and cold-blooded murder? Let me get this straight – it had nothing whatever to do with the whole Hell-hath-no-fury-like-a-woman-scorned thing?'

'And a scorned man?' she said quickly. 'You enjoyed hurting my feelings just a little too much, if I may say so.

He nodded. 'You may. You may even be right. What does it all matter now?'

'You've changed your tune.'

'I'm entitled to. I've only been dead a few hours. I'm feeling a little strange. A tad woozy-headed, not to mention the very odd sensation in my chest. I'm not even a proper ghost yet. Apparently that takes time. Contrary to popular belief, I didn't just transform into ghostly ether at the moment of death. It's a bit disappointing actually. Remember Rex Harrison in *Blithe Spirit*? He crashes the car, shoots upwards and immediately falls back to earth with his face painted white. A far more satisfactory arrangement. No, at present I'm still waiting for better things, existing only as a figment of your lurid imagination. It's a bit like the boy scouts really, only without the knots – you have to earn your stripes. I start out simply as a sad little memory.'

'That's what you are right now?'

'Yup. Just an item inside your head. One of the many little white birds within the cage of your mind – to steal Plato's image.'

'I see… Only a memory… ' She looked up sharply. 'And when these memories fade?'

He grinned. 'But they won't, I assure you. I'll make sure of that. Oh, they'll be strong and powerful enough to grant me a more lasting form of reality. Eventually, never fear, I'll become a fully-fledged ghost. I probably shouldn't have started on you yet, anyway. It would have been more effective to wait.'

'So why come and haunt me now?'

His grin faded. 'What else is there to do? Not a lot here, by the look of things. I'm bored already and there's eternity to get through. What do you think guilt is? The futile work of listless dead men. Tormenting you is going to be my primary, if not my only, pastime.'

'Perhaps it always was,' she muttered.

'Don't be bitter, Susie. I'm not feeling particularly tolerant at the moment. I'm dealing with my own cold-blooded murder right now. Do you think the ball stops here? It doesn't. Actions have consequences, as you're always telling me. This is murder. There isn't an inventory of people who don't *count* if you kill them. There isn't a list of those who, for some reason, don't fit under the umbrella term "murderee". Whatever I was like – it doesn't matter. It doesn't make a great deal of difference. It's killing that matters. And you'll have to pay the price.'

'I suppose you're going to tell me that I shouldn't have done it?'

'You shouldn't have.'

'Well, I did, and I'm glad. I couldn't be gladder.'

'You can say that looking at me in this wheelchair?' he said, sounding appalled. 'A blind man who can hardly lift his head by himself? My legs don't work, my arms don't work, for sure my prick won't work. Nothing works. If I can even urinate by myself it will be a miracle. I'm finished.'

'I'm still glad,' she said.

'You really hate me, don't you.'

'God, you're self-centred! This isn't about my hatred of you, Nick. I would have done the same whatever I felt about you. You murdered my father! I was simply claiming justice for him!' She took an angry, nervous breath. 'Anyway, I don't hate you any longer. You're dead.'

'That depends on – '

'Yeah, I know. Well, however you define dead, you're it.'

'Dead?' he snarled. 'I'm not dead, you skinny bitch. I'll haunt your fucking dreams. I'll wind you in chains. I'll hurt you in ways you never even thought of up till now. You want nasty? You'll get nasty. You won't know what fucking hit you. Oh, now the dance really begins! You'll never get away from me now! Trust me – I'm a ghost. Well, almost.'

32

' ... Where's Nick?' her mother demanded in what Susan thought was yet another imaginary voice, until she realised that she was holding the telephone in her hand and Isabella was on the other end. The phone must have been ringing for some time and she must have picked it up.

'I can't get hold of him *anywhere*. There's no answer at his flat and his mobile's switched off because I just keep reaching his answering service. He always keeps his mobile with him. He's meant to be picking me up this morning and driving me to the grounds. I'm supposed to be one of the first ones there... '

'What time is it?' Susan asked thickly.

She rubbed her eyes, feeling like she had just been woken from a long, weird, nightmarish sleep. A sleep filled with demons. She opened her eyes wider. She was awake – the tormenting figures had disappeared. For once she did not feel irritated with her mother. She felt grateful to her for phoning and dragging her into the light of a normal day.

'What's the time?' she repeated dazedly.

'Almost twenty-five to eleven,' her mother replied frantically. 'And the stone setting's at eleven-thirty.'

'The stone setting? Whose?' Susan asked stupidly, feeling confused, the fog in her mind still not quite clearing. Nick was dead, but it hadn't been a year yet, had it?

'Whose? Your father's. Who else died?'

'Is it Sunday already?'

Only two days had passed, then. Two and a half if you counted that afternoon: it seemed longer. Much.

'Yes, it's Sunday,' her mother snapped. 'Don't tell me you've forgotten?'

'I hadn't forgotten... '

No, she hadn't forgotten her father's stone setting: she had been thinking of little else for a long time. But she hadn't been certain where she was, or when. How could she tell her mother that?

'Are you alright?' her mother asked sharply. 'You sound most peculiar.'

'I'm – fine.'

'Well, you certainly don't sound it. Whose? For goodness sake.'

Susan took a deep breath and began again. 'What time was Nick supposed to be picking you up?'

'Ten o'clock,' Isabella replied edgily. 'We were going to have a coffee here before we went to Hoop Lane.'

Steven's loving widow and his even more loving brother having break-fast, then driving together to his stone setting, Susan thought. How sweet. Kill the man, steal his wife and then make sure you're on time for the prayers afterwards. Rest in peace, Steven Savage.

'He said he might come over last night,' Isabella went on anxiously. 'But he didn't turn up. It wasn't a definite arrangement or anything like that but – I couldn't get an answer from the flat or his mobile then, either. Where could he *be*? If he's got drunk and passed out somewhere I will personally – '

'I'll come and get you,' Susan decided.

'Will you? Oh, I don't know. Perhaps he's caught in traffic? Perhaps he's on his way? But he's three quarters of an hour late already… Forty-five minutes!' Isabella wailed. 'And today of all days! Why doesn't he answer his mobile? I've left a hundred messages. He could have called,' she finished, sounding suddenly annoyed.

'I'll be with you in thirty minutes,' Susan decided. 'How long will it take to Hoop Lane from your house?'

'It isn't far – fifteen, twenty minutes. Maybe less, depending on traffic.'

'We'll be on time. Are you ready?'

'Yes, yes. I just have to fix my hat properly and put on my – '

'Five-past eleven,' Susan promised, putting down the phone. She stood for a moment in the bedroom, getting her bearings. Her coat, a dress and hat. Hat? The beret would do. She was naked under her old blue dressing-gown; the silky viscose clung to the sweat on her body. She hadn't brushed her hair or had a bath in days. She could smell herself. She breathed in deeply, inhaling the pungent smell of guilt and fear, and with it normality. She looked around.

It had stopped. No ghosts of any sort. She was alone in the flat.

Susan heaved a deep wondering sigh. It was Sunday. Only two and a half days had gone by. She felt like she'd aged not three days but a lifetime.

There was not much time so she washed standing at the bathroom sink, splashing herself thoroughly with water and afterwards rolling on deodorant. She did her make-up and dressed in a dark knitted skirt and top in ten minutes flat, examining herself in the long bedroom mirror. She felt strangely calm now the moment had finally arrived – the moment for which she had killed a man. Her father's stone setting.

She stared at herself. Had she changed at all? Did it show? Amazingly, her face didn't look any different. No wrinkles, no white hairs, no stains or blotches on the outside to show what she'd been through. A little more shadowed under the eyes from lack of sleep, that was all. She raised her hand up to her cheek and gently touched it. Her skin felt the same.

This is funny, Nick had said, looking down at his bleeding wound. The wound she had made, the blood she'd deliberately spilt. *Only this time the joke's on me.*

But was it? Who was the joke on really? She'd killed a man and nothing had changed. Nothing was different. The police had not come after her. Yet, she reminded herself, grabbing her keys and hurrying down the stairs. They haven't come yet. She pulled the beret lower onto her forehead and stepped out into rain, wishing that if they were going to, they would hurry up.

She heard the sound of her footsteps clicking on the pavement. Glancing nervously over her shoulder out of habit, she saw no one. Her feet walked down the street.

It took longer than usual to walk to the car in the smart high-heeled shoes she had worn only once before, to her father's funeral, but the roads were pretty empty so that Susan reached Hampstead in good time. Her mother, hovering behind the curtains, came straight out. She wore a long, waisted black coat and boots and her hat had the tiniest of curling black feathers. She was very pale with strongly painted red lips and she looked fabulous – the perfect widow. But, beneath the clever make-up, Susan felt a genuine sadness.

'We'd better hurry, I don't want to be late,' she greeted Susan nervously, clicking on her seat belt.

'We'll be fine. It's only five past.'

They didn't speak much on the way. Susan concentrated on driving. Isabella didn't mention Nick again. 'Are you coming back to the house afterwards?' was all she asked. And when Susan replied that she was, answered abstractedly, 'Oh, good. The waitresses are at home setting up now. Bagels and smoked salmon, plava cake, that sort of thing... '

Getting out of the car at the cemetery she said only, glancing nervously at her watch, 'At least we're on time.'

Inside, Rabbi Katz was waiting to greet them. The prayers were mostly sung in Hebrew but Susan picked up a prayer book and read a few lines from a psalm in translation: 'Yea, though I walk through the valley of the shadow of death, I will fear no evil, for Thou art with me... '

'Where's Nick?' she heard someone ask.

And Isabella's murmured reply. 'A bit late... He'll be here soon I'm sure... '

'Shaul ben Isaac,' the rabbi began, 'was born to Isaac and Golda Savitsch in Bethnal Green, East London, on the ninth of Av in the year fifty-seven oh nine. He departed this world to our sorrow on the ninth of Kislev fifty-seven sixty-five, the victim of a tragic and pointless assault. We mourn for our loss and try, one year later, to set our grief to rest and say, it is time to begin letting go, it is time...'

There were no flowers on the grave; the whole cemetery looked grey and colourless. No colour, no solace, no comfort, Susan thought dully. Like death itself. Was that the intention, a year later? No wonder Jews were so afraid of dying. Even their religion told them it was a cold, hard business with no going back.

It had started to rain lightly again. Susan followed the others down the path to the graveside. Several people huddled under umbrellas, the only splash of colour in the whole, bleak scene.

'Here lies Steven Savage,' said the rabbi, reading the inscriptions on the newly set tombstone. 'Fifth of August nineteen hundred and forty-nine to the twenty-second of November two thousand and four. *Yehai navsho keshura* – May his soul be bound up in the bond of eternal life...'

It was not as bad as the funeral had been, though a few people had already started to weep. Susan felt horribly numb, like she was lost in a bad dream. It was the dream of her father's stone setting and the retribution for his murder had been a dream, too. But Isabella kept glancing round at the gates hoping Nick would show up, and Susan knew that he would not, so it was not really a dream, more like an awakening. Her mother had taken a hankie from her bag and was patting her eyes. Her friend Elsa stood besides her, holding her arm.

'... For with thee is the fountain of life: in thy light do we see light. *Ki imechoh mekor chaim be-orechoh nireh ohr,*' Rabbi Katz intoned, the service finished. 'Amen,' the people round the grave repeated after him. 'Amen,' said Isabella with them, but turning away for a last, lingering look at the entrance. As her big eyes moved sadly back again, Eva kissed her cheek. 'I wish you long life,' she sighed.

'And you, Eva – I wish you long life.'

Someone placed a pebble on the grave. 'Please, come back to the house,' Isabella requested, as people began coming up to wish her long life. 'There will be tea, coffee, there is cake...'

But Susan, turning to follow her mother's gaze, had seen something that had made her freeze. Over by the entrance hall, the rain drizzling down on his head, was a man in a dazzlingly white raincoat. His hands in his pockets, he made no pretence of being interested in any of the graves but stared over at the knot of mourners. No one else was taking any notice of him, but Susan did not need to be told who he was. For a moment, she'd taken her father for her earthly punishment in the form of a police-man. Then she saw the familiar figure beckoning and moved quickly forward. She stood as near to him as she was able. Close up, she could see the tracks of half-dry tears on his cheeks.

Her father leant forward. 'Remember me,' he breathed into her ear. 'Oh, please, Susie,' he said again, already fading fast. 'Please, remember me...'

She moved towards him, into his encircling arms. He drew her into his arms. She felt the burden lift. All hurt, all guilt, all love and sorrow, gone. She was in his arms now. She was forgiven. Her mother's pale face and dark lips drifted away, till her image was faint, as distant music. All the other mourners at her father's stone setting, far, far away... Susan could not see or hear them anymore. She stepped blindly forward, enveloped in his cold arms. With him, into eternal darkness...

33

No!

The world was slipping bright and glassy round her eyeballs. Her breath, naked over her teeth, came in as ice, went out as fire. Beating in each ear, beating in her throat, throbbing in her wrists... The grass whispered under her body, the wind sighed over her ears... Far away, below her, her toes creaked in her shoes.

I'm alive, she thought.

That feeling. Her heart pounding... That sensation. Her rib cage expanding, her lungs filling with air...

I'm alive. I'm alive to think, I'm alive.

'It's not my time yet!' She yelled it loud but silent a dozen times – 'It is *not my time!*'

Struggling forward, out of darkness, out of his arms, searching for the dim light, she cried out to her father as she fought against him, the tears streaming down her face: 'You have to let me go! Please, let me go! You're in your grave but I am not! I'm alive! I've done all I can for you. You have to let me go... '

So he left her. In that dark, lonely place. Her father. She said goodbye. Goodbye to him. She asked him to leave. As soon as he'd gone, she changed her mind – 'Come back!' she yelled, stretching out her arms, though she knew he would not. 'Daddy, come back!' she cried, though she knew he could not. Finally, she stepped away.

It was the hardest thing she had ever done – to live.

Later, back home, she lit a *Yahrzeit* candle for her father, placing it with trembling hands on the low carved wooden table in the living room. The candle for the dead, the eternal light by which to mourn a dead man. She sat cross-legged on the floor, wishing she knew the Hebrew prayers of lamentation to express what she was feeling, the ancient grief of generations of people who had lost everything.

She lit only one candle: Nick she could not mourn, only feel guilt and horror over what she had done. This guilt she would carry with her to her grave, but also a strong sense that what she had done was right. She believed in her father, and she had set him free. She'd sought justice for his murder and she had found it. Now he was free to die, and she was free to mourn him.

There, on the table in front of her, the candle flickered throughout the night. She watched it burning all the way down. It seemed to her the only light in the void of bottomless despair.

The vision of the candle's melancholy light remained with Susan. Its image was before her eyes as she entered sixty-nine Keyes Court a few days later, a bright wavering flame which seemed to imprint itself upon the door as she opened and closed it.

The venetian blinds were pulled right down, shrouding the room. Leaning back against the door, she adjusted her eyes to the dimness. Then, with a deep, resolute breath, she marched over to the window and yanked up the blinds, tying the cord in a tight, decisive knot on either side. Daylight streamed in, revealing a thick layer of dust covering everything. On the cameras, the table, the rows of empty wooden shelves, even the worn, cracked leather of the sofa.

She stood for a moment, looking around, thinking of her father who had loved this space so much. It had been his mother's flat when she was alive. Grandma Golda. Susan had come to visit her when she was small, though she couldn't remember how the flat had looked before Steven had it gutted, repainted, turned the bathroom into a blackout room and redone the green flowery kitchen in practical white, some years after his mother had died. She only remembered her grandma calling her *bubele* and kissing her. '*Leybn on your kopeleh*' she had said, with her warm, throaty chuckle. She remembered that.

And now?

Now Golda's two sons were both dead, one killed by the other's hand, the other, by her grandaughter, her *bubele*. What would she make of that? Would she wish a blessing on Susan's darling little head if she saw her now? Or would she simply scream – murderess! You murdered my baby! You killed my Nick! For what reason? To do such a thing, there could not *be* a reason!

Picking up a heavy black Nikon from the shelf, Susan wiped off the dust with her finger. The lens cap was scratched, silver metal showing through. Now that the stone setting was over, she intended to pack up the equipment and take it home with her, then contact an estate agent and arrange to sell the flat. She had no desire to keep it any longer. All sentiment for Keyes Court had been knocked out of her over the last month. It meant nothing to her now. It was just a place full of ghosts which she'd rather forget. Or at least, she corrected herself, she did not need any of this in her life for what she wished to remember.

She sighed, looking around one last time.

Empty.

Nothing remained here of her father except a few memories. She was alone, sorting out his belongings and, if the silence seemed a little strange to her, it was only because it was the silence of a normal flat. There wasn't the sense of another presence that had been so powerful when she'd been standing in this same spot with Alex three weeks earlier checking out a supposed burglary. Just several cameras, a TV and DVD player; a few memories left to bear witness, that was all.

She began packing the cameras into two large canvas bags she'd brought with her. She hadn't seen or spoken to Alex since the Tuesday before the stone setting. They had kissed goodbye outside this building and, exactly forty-eight hours later, she'd gone round to Nick's flat. Neither had contacted the other since. But that hadn't stopped her thinking about him. Superstitiously, coming up in the lift, she'd averted her eyes, hoping if she didn't look at the lighted button for the fifth floor, either on her way up or down, she wouldn't bump into Alex unexpectedly. I haven't grown any more superstitious then, she sighed to herself, crossing two fingers of one hand tightly as she packed.

It took her under an hour to put everything away, to fold the blankets and sheets from the single bed and drag the television and DVD player over to the door, next to the tripod and electric heater to be picked up later. The bed, sofa, armchair and table she would sell with the flat.

In the bedroom, she found an old jumper of her father's lying on the floor underneath the bed. She dragged it out and examined it. Smelt it. It smelt only of dust.

A shadow has passed through the flat and nothing has changed, she thought sadly. All that remains now is memory. And even memory fades. She dropped the jumper to the floor where she'd found it.

She took the broom out of the hall cupboard and began sweeping, then realised that she'd brought no dustpan to pick up the pile of fluff and dirt. She left the heap by the kitchen door, next to the upstanding broom. She did not even turn for a last goodbye glance. The bags that held her father's old cameras bumping heavily against her side, she left sixty-nine Keyes Court without once looking back.

34

MURDER HUNT

Detectives launched a muder enquiry after Nicholas Raymond Savage, 50, was stabbed to death at his flat in Notting Hill Gate.

Alex tore out the sheet of the newspaper which held the 'news in brief' section and folded it in half. He sat still for a moment, looking at the piece of paper in his hand. Then he rose and crossed the room, opening a drawer and pushing the folded sheet inside. Carefully he placed a neat pile of linen tablecloths on the top and slid the drawer shut, moving back to the sofa. He sat for quite a while, staring thoughtfully into space at nothing.

The traffic lights were the thing she remembered clearest. Traffic lights a long way up the road, at the top of a hill. It was pitch dark, no street lights, nothing. She could see only the red light in the distance, then another light appearing in its place. Then it disappeared and there was a green one.

The other thing she remembered was the stink. She had this oily stuff all over her, on her hands, her face, her hair. The more she tried to wipe it off, the more it seemed to get everywhere, like the Cat in the Hat with the ink. She was walking towards the traffic lights, getting nearer and nearer, till they were bright enough to see by. She could see the stinking stuff all over her, first in red, then orange, then green. Her mind seemed coloured by the lights, too, a great red, green and amber blank.

Then, suddenly, it started to come back to her. She knew she'd done something terrible. She trembled, thinking – What have I done? What? She couldn't remember. Her mind wouldn't let her. It couldn't. Never. But she realised what the oily stuff was. And knew that, even if she washed her hands forever, even if she scrubbed till the skin was raw, the stink of it would never come off. Never, never, never.

Susan was dreading the meeting with Alex. What should she tell him – lies? The truth? What would he say? There had been endless messages and a bitter, accusing letter from Paul, then finally a furious silence. But from Alex, there had been nothing.

What did she expect? she asked herself hopelessly. He must have seen the papers. Although Nick's murder had only been a small insert in the Sundays, he must have found it. He must know. She had stopped weeping and waking every night shaking and sweating, the smell of blood thick in her nostrils, and most times she could walk down the street without suddenly having to dart into a doorway, hand clamped over her mouth, jaw clenched to stifle a scream, but she put off the inevitable for another week. She let Christmas with all its trimmings pass. Then she called.

They met at an Italian café on Kensington Church Street. Susan tried to keep her hands still but found herself constantly fiddling – with the clasp of her bag, the dangling green glass stones of her earrings, her hair, her spoon. Alex was clearly edgy, too, but hid it better. What would they say to each other? How would they be? How *could* they be? He opened the conversation at last with a mundane, though husky: 'How are you?'

'Not bad,' she replied, a little huskily too. Playing with the ashtray, she circled it precariously on one side. 'Fine, actually. Better.'

He didn't ask, better than what? He nodded. 'I'm glad. You look well. A bit thinner but – ' He glanced at her, then, as their eyes met, shifted his away quickly.

'How's it going at the hospital?' she asked, equally bright and meaningless.

'Very well. I've passed my final exams.'

'That's great, Alex.'

She looked down at her coffee cup. Some of the pale brown liquid had slopped into the saucer. She picked up the teaspoon and held it in the air, watching it drip slowly into the cup. 'Are you going to – ?' she began, just as Alex said: 'I hear you are – '

'Go on,' he smiled.

'No – you first.'

'I was only going to say I heard you're selling the flat.'

'Who told you?'

'The people who are buying it came down and introduced themselves. They wanted to know if it was a nice block, quiet, good management, and so on. I told them it is. I also told them that the average age of the tenants is about ninety.' He grinned. But the smile only emphasised the tension in his face. 'They seem pleasant enough – for a couple of lawyers.'

'Mr and Mrs Wilson,' she confirmed, examining the spoon. 'We're hoping to complete around the beginning of March.'

'Oh, really?'

'Yes.'

'I also said that under no circumstances would I look after a spare set of keys for them.'

She looked up sharply. '*Did* you?'

'Just kidding.'

She looked down again. 'Oh.' He always jokes when he's feeling nervous, she remembered.

They didn't speak for a moment. Then Alex broached the subject that was on both their minds. 'Did they ever find out who – ?' He stopped, cleared his throat then started again. 'Did the police ever catch the murderer?'

She took a deep breath. Her hands were suddenly still. 'Of my father?'

'Well, I meant Nick, but yes. That too.'

'No,' she replied quietly, looking very straight at Alex. 'They didn't.' She looked into his eyes. Did he really want to hear the rest? She couldn't tell. She said very carefully: 'Both murders are still unsolved.'

They continued to look at each other, trying to decide whether to speak, and what to say.

Alex spoke first, picking his way very deliberately through the ordinary words. 'Do you think either of them ever will be?'

Susan hesitated, noting his careful tone. She was tempted, oh so tempted, to answer honestly, but she wasn't sure how he would react if she told him the truth. 'I don't know,' she said at last, still undecided. 'It doesn't appear so. I mean, the police don't seem to have anyone special in mind.'

She looked at him hopefully as she said this. It only needed one comment from him, a look or one casual word, the tiniest of reactions, and she would speak openly. He knew so much already, it felt only fitting to tell him the end of the story. He might not approve but he would understand, perhaps too well.

One little comment... a smile... a twitch of the eye... Even a cough that would tell her that he wished her to speak truthfully...

She sat, looking into his face for what seemed like ages.

No word. No cough.

And she felt she could read the look in his eyes as clearly as if he had spoken aloud. He knows. He knows that I know he knows but doesn't wish me to put it into words. He doesn't want the burden of responsibility, or shared complicity, which is what it becomes if I tell him outright. He doesn't want to have to decide, in that event, what to do.

After a moment, she dropped her eyes. So whatever they felt for each other was gone for good, she thought sadly. This really was to be their last meeting. But she'd known that before they'd met – hadn't she? Or had there still been a hope left – a shred of a fragment of a dream that she had not admitted even to herself, that he would, this time, after all, take her side?

He looked at her across the narrow formica table. Such warm brown eyes... She could see the desire for her in them. This did not feel like the ending had with Paul; it did not feel *right*. She wanted to smash her fist on the table and shout – 'Do what you have to do when you love someone, Alex!

239

Take their part! That's what love *is*! At least admit, if only to yourself – yes! I saw Steven Savage that night! I actually saw him too!'

But she didn't speak. She couldn't. Too much of what was left unsaid was up to him. There was a lump in her throat as she sat opposite him looking into his familiar face and thinking, as she had once before – it seemed so long ago – we are strangers to each other. Strangers in love. Isn't that sad? So close and yet so far, their hands almost touching but not quite. All it would take was for one of them to lift a finger and they would be holding each other again...

And for a moment she thought she saw in his face that he would make a move. That he wanted, desperately, against what he would call all reason, to be honest with her. *You killed him, didn't you? As retribution for Steven's murder? Your father told you to – and in the end you decided he was right. You murdered Nick in revenge for the whole damned caboodle. I may not approve of what you did – I may not think it right – but I do understand...*But, the next second, the fleeting impression was gone. She saw his expression change; the impulse faded, though not the love. The love did not leave his eyes, or the sadness.

He knows the truth but prefers evasion, she decided forlornly. He has one eye open but he keeps the other firmly shut. He has a talent for denial – he will never change. And so she inched her hand away and placed it beneath the table on her lap. We wouldn't have been happy together, not really, she told herself. We could never have been happy. Because he knows things about me that he would never be able to live with – every time he looks at me he would see Nick. And I know things about him that I couldn't respect – I know that ultimately he lacks the courage to face the truth.

So following what she took to be his lead Susan said, choosing her words with great care: 'The police questioned me after Nick's murder. I explained that it must have been shortly beforehand that I visited him and that's the reason my fingerprints were found all over his flat. I told them how we'd argued a lot over the last year – about his affair with my mother, and so forth. But that I thought it was time we patched things up. I mean, with the date for my – ' her voice cracked but she recovered, 'the date for my father's stone setting coming up.'

'What did they say to that?'

'That it was lucky I did.'

He frowned. 'Meaning what exactly?'

'Just that if I'd left it any later... he'd have been dead... '

There was a pause. 'Nothing else?' Alex asked.

She looked at him. 'No... We had an espresso together,' she added, her stomach lurching at the memory. And then, a little defiantly, as if he were about to refute her claim: 'The policeman found two cups.'

We are dancing, she thought. We both follow the steps of the dance so well. With one finger she pirouetted the ashtray. Looking down at her hand, she asked, 'Have you noticed that I'm not smoking any more?'

'Yes, I noticed.'

'I gave up almost six weeks ago.'

'Things change.'

'Yes… they do…'

But not everything, she thought sadly. Not enough. How relieved he seems at the change of subject. I swear that his body has relaxed as if he is easing out a long sigh of relief. Well, we've done it – we've met, and not a single word of the truth has been uttered between us. Denial and evasion. An uneasy combination. She couldn't bear any more. 'I'd better go, Alex,' she decided, making a show of looking at her watch.

'Can I walk you to your car?'

'I came by bus.' She stood up. 'But you can walk me to the bus stop, if you'd like.'

'I would,' he said, rising. 'It's nice to see you again. I'd been wondering… oh, you know…' His face creased unhappily for a moment, then he smoothed away the lines of worry to say lightly: 'Wondering if you'd ring and all that. I didn't like to phone you because – ' He broke off.

Because you might have heard something you didn't like, she thought. Is that it? She kissed his cheek. Sometimes a kiss is a way of creating a distance, not closing it. 'It's been nice seeing you, too,' she replied formally.

From the front seat of the bus she craned her neck to get a last glimpse of him. He lifted his arm in the air in a farewell salute, mouthing something which she couldn't quite catch, following her with his eyes for as long as he could.

The bus moved off with a lurch. She sighed, settling back in her seat and closing her eyes. He was not the man she'd hoped for. He wasn't someone she could love. She couldn't love someone who didn't have the courage to admit what was happening before his own eyes. Well, he has nothing to feel guilty about, she thought wearily. It was only a kiss, nothing more. She felt dried up inside, all feeling scooped out of her: a shell. We have wasted love, she thought. We've wasted it.

Squeezing her eyes tight, her face crumpled with the effort of holding back bitter tears. Goodbye Alex… Another goodbye… Only this one did not have any redeeming features at all, as far as she could see.

The driver sped along far too fast. The bus lurched around corners – the two elderly women sitting in the high seats near the front had to clutch hold of the vertical rail to prevent being flung forward. Susan stared out of the window, gloom and doubt seizing hold of her again, deliberating to the sound of their ordinary voices.

'... *I go to Marks on Thursdays for my chicken.*'

'*Not Sainsburys?*'

'*Not for chicken, no. But I get the bus there on a Tuesday to buy cod or perhaps a nice piece of salmon...*'

The world beyond the glass seemed just a blur. Susan gripped the metal bar in front of her, suddenly filled with desperate uncertainty. What if Alex was right and she was wrong? What if he were not a weak man racked by self doubt but a very sane man moved by compassion? What if he didn't want to know any more of the facts about the day she'd spent in Nick's flat because he didn't wish to be put in the position of having to give her up to the police? She'd jumped so eagerly on the path to murder with, what had seemed to Alex at the time, such little real physical evidence. Some might say – *With the eagerness, the oblivion to reality, of the insane.* And in that case, in a year or two, another ghost might appear to her with, oh, horrible thought, another lesson that needed teaching...

'*... Around the fish in a little foil I put half a lemon and some herbs.*'

'*Oh, my husband won't touch anything with herbs, he doesn't like the taste.*'

'*Not even in a little foil?*'

But Nick had confessed, hadn't he? she reassured herself. Beaux-Sarr, gangsters, murder, the lot. Before dying, Nick had admitted everything. And in those circumstances killing him was the right – no, wait, the *only* – thing to have done.

Those circumstances? she thought miserably. What were they exactly? If you imagined some of it, why not all? Your father's ghost, Nick's confession? There's nothing to say that it was not all a psychotic part of your mind... nothing at all. Alex seems to think so...

'*It doesn't taste the same nowadays, not even salmon.*'

'*Chicken has no taste either. Not like years ago, it was different then...*'

And the worst thought of all, the one that really made her tremble, the nagging idea she could barely allow herself to entertain even for a second, the one that really brought the bile up into her throat – What if she *had* been tipped over the edge by Nick's affair with her mother? What if that *was* the central thing for her – the rest of it just a last ditch attempt to get rid of the competition? A simple trick, played *on* her *by* her – *this time the joke's on me...* And the whole thing – the ghost, the confession, the whole damned caboodle – simply her chance, her one and only chance, of justifiably – in her own deluded eyes at least – of having a justified excuse for putting an end to him? An end to Nick, her lover, her very own paedophile darling, but who just wasn't interested in her any more?

The bus jerked to a sharp halt, making Susan bump her head on the glass window. A woman with a wheelie bag climbed off carefully, barely down the steps before the bus shot off again. Had she only held back from confessing to Alex, Susan thought drearily, rubbing her forehead, *not* because he didn't want to hear the truth, as she'd so confidently assured herself, but because she was afraid that he might run straight to the police with whatever he had heard? Was that why she'd maligned Alex? Because she wanted her crime to remain undiscovered? Would this turn out, in the end, to be only murder with a false and shallow veneer of justice?

She shook her weary head. She must have spoken aloud. Two young women in front of her briefly stopped their conversation to turn round and stare. Only for a moment – then they resumed their chatting.

Susan held onto the metal rail in front of her as the bus swung dizzily round a corner, clutching on so tightly, her knuckles showed white. She could feel the panic rising in her. Oh, she was guilty, guilty. And worse – psychotic and guilty. Alex clearly thought so. He was just too nice to tell her outright. Only his accusing silence told her...

There isn't an inventory of people who don't count if you kill them. There isn't a list of those who don't fit under the umbrella term 'murderee'. Whatever Nick was like makes no difference – it's killing that matters. And you'll have to pay the price...

By the time Susan stepped off the bus, she'd made a decision. She couldn't bear it any longer. She would give it one more day and then, if nothing had changed – and what could? – she'd go to the police and confess everything.

35

Susan was not sure what drew her back to the studio later that afternoon. She needed to take what she wanted out of the flat before completion, her solicitor told her, but that was not really it. A dash from the taxi to haul down some stuff and then off again, that was all that was needed. Not this – this sitting for a dull hour on the sofa by the window, staring out at a cloudy grey sky.

'Another goodbye?' Susan whispered aloud, talking to herself. But she didn't really think it was for her father that she was waiting. The place was as empty of his ghostly presence as it should have always been. Maybe she'd come hoping for some kind of sign that, in some form or other, he did exist, was now at peace and she'd acted for the best. But if so, she didn't get one. Nothing. Just the dust and the old sofa and the odd remaining camera or two. No, tomorrow she would turn herself in, she decided, rising with a sigh.

This time she'd brought a dustpan with her and was shovelling the pile of dirt into the pan with the brush when she heard a noise. She froze, feeling suddenly nervous. But this was what she had wanted, wasn't it? A sign? Another message from beyond the grave telling her, this time, quite clearly, that as a daughter she was *mensch*? But now it seemed to have come, she found she was strangely frightened.

A scrabbling sound. A key turning in the lock. The door opening slowly…

Susan found herself crouched on one knee, brush in hand, mouth open, throat dry, staring up into Alex Emmerich's face.

She couldn't speak for a moment. She closed her mouth and swallowed hard. When she did speak it came out as a husky whisper: 'What are you doing here?'

'I heard a noise.'

'I didn't make any noise. I even took off my shoes.' She gestured to her trainers standing neatly against the wall.

'Well, I heard *something*.'

He stepped inside and closed the door. She put down the brush. As she got to her feet and was moving towards him, she blurted out: 'I'm going to the police, Alex. I've decided to tell them it was me – I murdered Nick.'

He didn't reply, just stared at her.

'You were right about it all along. I thought the bank statements were convincing evidence. I thought the look in Nick's eyes meant he was a

244

cold-blooded killer – ' She took a deep breath. 'But the only real evidence was my father's story and I'm beginning to realise – well, that it's more than likely I imagined that, too.'

'You didn't.'

She stopped, staring at him. 'What did you say?'

There was a silence between them. A long silence in which she felt she was hurtling back in time and space only to be flung forward again in a split second. Her words echoed above them in the air, mundane sounds, their meaning filled with resonance. She could feel the pulse in her throat. She swallowed.

'I said, you didn't.'

He had replied. What had he said? He had said that –

'It wasn't just in your imagination,' she heard him saying. 'I know,' he said. This time she heard him quite clearly. 'I know for sure.'

'How?' she whispered from between dry lips.

'The obvious reason. Because I saw him too. I didn't want to admit it before, even to myself. It seemed so absurd. It *seems* so absurd. A ghost? A dead man?' He gave a shaky laugh. 'But I want you to know that you weren't the only one who saw your father's ghost. If you're crazy, then so am I. *I saw him too.*'

'Oh, Alex, oh, Alex,' was all she could say. She walked over to the sofa and sank down into it, dropping her head in her hands.

'I can hardly believe it, a part of me still doesn't believe it,' he said in a wondering voice. 'I'm a rational man, a scientist for God's sake – I don't believe in any of this stuff. I think it's absurd. If I admitted any of it, I'd have to change my whole world view – sling out my entire *weltanschnau-ung*. But I have to tell you your father came back from the dead and we both saw him. Whatever he said to you that night, whatever he told you, in some form or another he was there. He – he was. I'm sorry. I'm very sorry. I've thought about it over and over again. What would I have done in your place? What would I have felt if it had been my father? And I don't know but – ' He walked over and stood in front of her, his hands hanging loose-ly at his sides. 'I believe I would have done the same as you. At least, I'd like to think so.'

She was trembling so hard she could barely speak. 'Why didn't you say this before?' she croaked at last. 'Why are you telling me now?'

'Too cowardly?' he suggested, with a pale smile. 'As I think you once accused me being of yourself. But when I saw you this morning… after you left… I realised that I wanted you to go away so that I wouldn't have to face up to what I'd seen. I was willing to lose you – I hoped I would, rather than have to admit it was true. And worse. It was even worse than that. I knew, along with you, I would lose my self-respect. Your look. At the end, through the windows of the bus. Your sad eyes… They were like… '

He stopped, shaking his head. Taking a deep breath, he sat down on the arm of the sofa, legs spread on either side, hands gripping the brown leather. 'I've been looking everywhere for you, Susan,' he said, staring down at his knuckles. 'Telephoned the flat. Was just about to take the bus over there myself. And then, just as I was leaving I heard a sound coming from upstairs, or thought I did. I was shit scared actually. I really thought it might be – ' He gave a pale, guilty smile. 'Well, you know what I feared. You're right – murder is unforgivable.' Reaching out his hand, he leant over slightly and found one of hers. 'You mustn't go to the police. Earthly punishment wasn't what your father intended, as you know better than I.' He gave her hand a hard squeeze. 'You won't, will you?'

He slid off the seat's arm and drew her onto his lap. He wrapped his arms around her and held her. She was shivering again. 'I won't let you down again,' he said softly into her ear. 'I'll never let you down. The next crisis we come through together.'

He pulled her backwards with him onto the dusty sofa and fiercely kissed her, only stopping to ask: 'Why are you crying?' And cut off her reply with his mouth. 'Because– '

'Here we are.'

'Yes.'

'What are we?' she whispered.

'Alive,' he replied with laugh. 'We're bloody alive.'

'And kicking.'

'Too right.'

She kissed him. 'I never thought – '

'What?' he said teasingly, pushing his hair out of his eyes with one hand. 'What did you never think?'

She gave a shaky little laugh. 'That there would be a happy ending. You know, to all this mess… I never thought I'd ever be happy again. A few hours ago it all seemed so very different. And I'm sorry. I'm sorry for what I said to you. I was wrong. About you being a coward. You're not.' Wrong, too, about never being able to fall for you again, she thought. All the love had flooded over her the moment he'd spoken honestly. She looked into his face. Her breath caught in her throat. She felt a sudden rush of pure happiness.

'I'm sorry too,' he said. 'For taking so long. You know, to see…'

She kissed him again.

'I wonder...' she murmured.

'What?' he asked, his mouth against hers.

'I wonder... where he is now...'

'Who?'

She didn't reply.

'Who?' he asked again equally softly, raising himself from the sofa on one elbow.

She gave a groan. 'If you carry on doing that, I can't possibly answer...'

'What – that?' He squeezed down beside her, his hair falling back over his face.

'We should go down to your flat. Make some coffee...' she murmured, her eyes closed.

'In a minute,' he said.

The bedroom was empty of furniture and had a quite different feel to the rest of the flat. The bed was on a low wooden base and covered with a grey striped duvet. There was a chest of drawers by the window with a lamp and a stump of candle in a saucer on top, a wooden bedside table roughly painted white, that was all.

'Who – ' Alex asked, idly playing with a strand of her hair, 'were you wondering about – when we were upstairs?' With each phrase, he gave a different part of her face a stroke with the strand of hair. 'Not Paul, I hope.'

'God, no.'

They shifted their bodies, moving together so that her head lay on his shoulder and her legs were diagonally across the bed. She could feel the warmth of his breath on the top of her head. His hand was heavy on her thigh. She wriggled her toes out from under the striped duvet. Legs stretched in front of her, her feet crossed comfortably, she put her hands behind her head on the pillow. 'You know, this is when it's really hard to give up smoking,' she sighed. 'Right now, I would give my kingdom for a fag.'

'They say the longing doesn't go away but only becomes less frequent.'

'Is that supposed to be helpful?'

'It's an addiction. Addiction's a hard thing to crack.'

'Could you sound a little glibber, please? Just a bit?'

He grinned. 'I'll make some strong coffee.'

'You've been promising that for hours.'

'True. I got sidetracked.' He swung his legs out of bed. 'How do you like it? Black? Sugar?'

'Black, no sugar.'

'Enough sweet love for one day?' he teased.

247

'Of that, there's never enough.' She twisted under the sheet to watch him pad naked across the bedroom. 'I don't suppose you've got some chocolate, by any chance.'

'I think I might have a McVitie's digestive somewhere. Would that do?'

'Mmm, perfect. Actually it was Nick I was thinking of before,' she announced as he reached the door. 'I was wondering where he is and what he's thinking…'

'We'll never know,' Alex said confidently. He stopped, half turning, a look of alarm crossing his face. 'At least, I hope to God we won't.'

The dead sleep soundly. They never heard Susan whispering in the dark or watched her fall asleep, the touch of Alex's caresses still burning on her skin, his arms still tight around her. They never heard the promises that he breathed in her ear or saw her waking smile turn slowly to passion at dawn, just as the light was beginning to break over the city. For now her ghosts were truly set to rest and wouldn't bother her again. Not that night, nor the next, nor for any of the long days and nights that followed…

36

Except almost two months later, as Susan was cleaning her flat in Primrose Hill rather more thoroughly than usual in order to sell it and so pulled out the oak shelves in the hall, she found, stuck behind some books, a ghost of sorts. A rather dusty wad of cheques held together with a rubber band. She rocked back on her heels, suddenly recalling the cheques she'd found in her father's desk drawer. At the time, she'd slipped them into her pocket and later, in all the turmoil, forgotten them. They must have fallen out of her jacket and remained stuffed behind the shelves until now.

She slid off the rubber band and examined the cheques one by one. They had all been paid and returned by the bank long ago – each had on them the bank's red circular stamp. Except for the very last one. A cheque for six hundred thousand pounds, dated 2nd November, 2004. Made out in her father's handwriting to a company called Beaux-Sarr…

The room spun. Stopped. Spun.

She stared at the cheque she was holding in her hand. Stapled to it was a slip in the same writing – £600,000 as reimbursement to B-S for overp/t 30.08.04. So it's true, she thought unemotionally. I didn't imagine it. Jonathan Woolf was right, after all. I am holding in my hand the evidence my father saw shortly before his murder. Given the other details in the file, he must have guessed what it meant. Or come too close for comfort. And so he was murdered to shut him up.

In the dark of the night came sneaking doubts. Guilt and despair would seize her. Was Alex simply in love with her and telling what she needed to hear? Did he really know in his heart that she'd had a brief psychotic episode and simply imagined the whole sad story? Or was he fooling himself too? She looked down at the name written in black ink on the cheque. If she had needed anything else, here it was. A little late, but the final piece was in place. There was nothing quite like a physical, tangible thing that you could touch and see. This one I can't have imagined, she thought.

Waving the slip of paper in the air, she called out: 'Alex!' From her squatted position, still gripping the cheque, she called, happiness throbbing in her voice: 'Alex! Oh Alex, come and look at this!'

— 37—

£60M COCAINE SMUGGLER JAILED FOR THIRTY YEARS

A drug smuggler was jailed for 30 years yesterday for leading a bungled operation to bring a record £60 million consignment of cocaine into Britain.

Kevin Hughes, 55, and four of his accomplices were caught by 150 Customs officers on the Isle of Wight after their landing was hampered by storms after a 3,000 mile voyage across the Atlantic from the Caribbean. They had planned to unload 692lb of cocaine at an outlet of Hughes' shipping company near Ventnor, but bad weather forced them to deposit their cargo at a beach about a mile away. They were stopped and arrested after members of the gang had spent hours carrying large bales of the drugs along a treacherous cliff-top path to their original destination.

Sentencing Hughes and four others at Snaresbrook Crown Court in London, Judge Edward Gimson said: 'Drug smuggling is a scourge on our society. I and my colleagues deal on a daily basis with people whose lives have been ruined beyond repair by drug addiction. These are ordinary people who are moved to commit crime to feed their craving.

'The planning of this scheme had taken many weeks if not months, both in the West Indies and in this country. You were the boss, the man at the top of this operation. This was your brain child.'

Hughes, a father of three, was found guilty last month at the end of a six month trial.

The cocaine had been brought from the island of Bequia, near St Vincent, to the Isle of Wight, where Hughes had recently acquired a small shipping company, Savage Associates Limited. Hughes acquired the company for £3 million in January 2005 under the name Hugo Bennett. In November of that year, Nicholas Savage, the original owner of the shipping company, was found stabbed to death in his flat in Notting Hill Gate, London. Customs and Excise, and the National Crime Squad, had Hughes under surveillance after the discovery of the 'Notting Hill body', as it became known, up until the time the gang was caught in an operation which led to the largest seizure of cocaine in Britain. It is understood that the murdered man was a member of Hughes' organisation. The investigation into the unsolved murder of Nicholas Savage's brother, Steven, in 2004 is being re-opened.

The judge told Hughes: 'I regret that you are a British Citizen, for the welfare of the country. I wish I could recommend you to the Home Secretary for deportation.' Four of his accomplices were also jailed. Kevin Hughes was sentenced to 24 years in

250

prison. Hector Lernao, a Columbian who pleaded guilty at an earlier hearing was given 13 years, while two British men, Robert Fleet and Thomas Singer were each given 18 years.

A Home Office minister welcomed the convictions. He said, 'This is an excellent result for HM Customs and demonstrates that, by working abroad as well as at home, we can have a huge impact on the availability of Class A drugs in the UK.'

Daily Telegraph, Saturday, September 8th, 2006.

Four

THE DISPOSITIONAL THEORY OF GHOSTS

RUAKH: *n.* the spirit, soul; a ghost; supernatural being; the wandering soul. [Yiddish, *ruekh;* see *neshomme*, Yiddish for spirit, soul, from Ashkenazi Hebrew, *neshommah.*]
  The American-Yiddish Dictionary of the English Language

November 9th 2006
London, NW3. 6.20pm.

Isabella sat in the bedroom in front of her dressing-table mirror, putting the finishing touches to her hair. A few dark strands had fallen from her chignon. She pinned them up carefully before finishing off with a short burst of hair lacquer. She dropped a comb, a small Chanel lipstick and a mirror shaped like a shell into a bag and clicked it shut. Then she took one last look at her reflection. *Finito*, she thought, before standing up.

The bedroom was decorated in soft green and ivory with a delicate cream pattern of fleur de lys on the cushions and long velvet curtains. She glanced round, enjoying the green silk eiderdown draped over the silver wood bed and the Arts and Craft furniture around her. As her eyes rested on the bedside table, carved in pale oak with a little heart motif cut out of the wood, the telephone began ringing. Listlessly, she lifted the receiver and said, 'Hello.' When she realised there was no one at the other end, she tutted in irritation and slammed down the phone.

This is intolerable, she thought, it's the fifth call of that sort today. I must contact the operator and find out what to do about it.

Catching sight of her frowning reflection in the mirror, she hurried over to the dressing-table to apply lipstick. It's not a luxury anymore, it's a necessity, she told herself, applying carmine red to her lips. That's better, she thought approvingly, her mind turning for the first time in ages to Nick – for this was the colour she'd worn to his funeral, she realised, making a moue with her lips, then pressing them together so the colour was evenly spread. Was it nearly a year already? Another stone setting soon, she supposed.

She sighed. She tried not to think much about Nick now. It only made her depressed. The two brothers, both gone. How odd that both of them should have passed on in such crude and violent ways. And Nick into hard drugs, even dealing, killed by the men he had been working for. Or so the police said, anyway. Actually it was all too easy to believe. He'd been drinking such a lot the year before he died. Drinking and selling cocaine… Possibly using it himself…

She shuddered a little theatrically. How unpleasant, how dreadfully ugly. She wouldn't think about it; she would shut it all out of her mind. A moment's madness, that's what it had been. Yet why did Nick's death seem so much more painful to her than Steven's? Because she had been madly in love with him at the time, she supposed – madly being the operative word. Whereas Steven, she'd loved like a husband of twenty-five years, deeply and loyally, but without much intensity anymore. She sighed again, examining the faint lines at the corners of her eyes. Actually she missed them both, though she tried hard not to, especially Nick...

Her bottom lip, with its coating of red, trembled. The red she'd worn to Nick's funeral. But the memory of that terrible time was already fading. Even so, Isabella decided, she would chuck the lipstick in the bin. Its associations were too, too horrible. How morbid she felt, how depressed. And that bloody telephone didn't help, ringing on and on all day with no one speaking on the other end. She'd have to go back to the doctors if the anti-depressants were not working. Also, if necessary, get a face-lift, she grimaced, stretching the skin of her forehead gently upwards with her fingertips.

With a tissue she wiped off the dark red from her mouth and was applying a lovely deep rose pink when the telephone started again. Frowning, she let it ring, sitting across the room on the green satin stool with her hands folded in her lap. It went on for an incredible three minutes fifty-nine seconds – she timed it by the delicate silver hands of the bedside clock. As soon as it stopped, she picked the receiver up and dialled 100.

'Hello – Richard speaking,' the operator introduced himself. 'Which name please?'

'Do you have a number to stop malicious calls?'

'A number which – ?'

'You know, for calls you don't want to receive.'

'Do you want to stop all direct dialling or is this one particular caller that you want stopped? Someone who is phoning at unusual hours, that sort of thing?'

'Yes, yes, that's it.'

'Right. Then dial 0845 0700 707. This is a press button service which you can work yourself, or you can phone Nuisance Calls Advice Line on 0800 661 441. Do you want me to put you through?'

'No, no, not right now, thank you.'

'If this persists, do get back to us.'

'Oh, I will,' Isabella assured him. 'I certainly will.'

But the moment she put the receiver back on the stand, the phone rang again. She glared at it furiously, then shook a cream jacket from a hanger in the wardrobe and left the room. Enough! she thought. I'll be late for the theatre at this rate. She was meant to be meeting Max in Leicester Square at seven-fifteen and it was nearly a quarter to now.

Touching the delicate pearl drops hanging from her ears, she ran lightly down the stairs, past the phone still ringing loudly in the hall. She grabbed her cream pashmino and both sets of car keys, draping the shawl over her shoulders before pressing her fingers to her ears to block out the strident noise. She'd phone BT Malicious Calls department first thing in the morning. Or perhaps ask Max to do it for her? Max was a sweetie who adored performing simple tasks for her. 'Oh, thank you darling, you're a perfect *angel*,' she said to herself, rehearsing the words she would use.

Slamming shut the front door, she stepped out into the drive, swaying on her high heels as she hesitated by the car. The Audi or the Aston – which? She decided on the Aston Martin and bent low, shawl trailing, to get inside.

That's better, she thought, driving off – life felt instantly more normal without that damn ringing. She drove fast up the street, enjoying the speed and the absence of sound.

But Nick, watching her, cursed as the low red car swung round the corner. Stupid bitch, he muttered. It's me! I'm trying to telephone you – don't you realise! Don't you understand! I need you! Badly! And fast! The stone setting's next month. I'm in agony here! This is a desperate situation! He wanted to scream at her but he couldn't make a sound that she could hear. He wanted to yell into that deaf ear – I'm not passed away, not gone, I'm *dead*! D–E–A–D, dead! Do you know what that's like? Can you imagine? Whatever you imagine, you can't imagine! Whatever you've been told, it's worse! You have to help me! Help! Help me!

But she wasn't listening. She couldn't hear. Actually, did not want to hear. He turned away in disgust from the speeding red car. 'I only want her to go to the police and tell them who cut my throat,' he muttered. 'I'm not asking for much. I'm not asking her to commit murder, for Christ's sake. I only need her to ask the police to arrest her daughter. Just arrest the niece, you fuckers! Do your job. Because they believed Susan's story. Not even told with much conviction – she hadn't even bothered trying to make it sound true. The fingerprints all over the flat? Left when she came to make up after an argument, they supposed. The tiny drop of blood on the pillow? Ignored. Irrelevant. The single, long black hair beneath the body? Undiscovered. They believe all of it, the idiots! From their point of view there *is* no forensic evidence! The girl comes to my flat dressed in a brand new leather outfit which she gets rid of afterwards in a charity shop a few streets away from her flat. And leaves nothing behind, nothing! to incriminate herself – according to the police.

'But have they looked seriously? Have they even searched for the knife?

She didn't drop it in the Thames for three weeks! Three fucking weeks! They could have gone to her flat at any time and found it! If they'd asked in the second hand designer shop on the Camden Road they'd have discovered a nice, black leather Averyl Kane mini skirt, size eight, with a fucking great stain inside the hem. My blood! Type A! But did they look? Did they hell. Too busy chasing false leads across cliff-tops.'

Nick made a sound that was almost a sob. Now it was too late. All long gone, the skirt and coat bought on impulse far too small, chucked into a bin somewhere in Esher; the knife, swallowed up by mud, sucked into the murky depths – like he was.

Isabella swung the car into Avenue Road. *His* car. The car he had so generously *given* her. If only her memories were stronger then he could find a way of materialising. But as it was, ringing her on the telephone was about all he could manage. And that was hard enough. Anti-depressants and sleeping pills – how was he supposed to get through that? He could barely squeeze a voice out of that lot, however hard he tried. And he tried. Because this was important. His fate was sealed forever in the next few weeks – and it was all in her hands! Help me, Isabella! Help me, please…

He was really sobbing now. In despair, his eyes followed the car as it sped up the street, a frown of concentration on Isabella's brow, her mind blank of any thought of him. Any thought at all. It was unbelievable. Not a memory in sight. Oh, shit.

POSTSCRIPT

The Dispositional Theory of Ghosts

There are some qualities of objects which will be experienced in the same way by all intelligent creatures whatever their constitution – shape, mass and density, for example. These are known as 'primary qualities'.[1]

However, there are other qualities which are thought not to be 'in' objects in the same way – colours, smells and tastes, to name but three. They are properties, but they are relational ones[2] – that is, they exist only in relation *to* someone.

When we say, 'the postbox is red,' what we actually mean is that it looks red to the average human being under average conditions. It does not necessarily look red to a bumble bee or a bear– i.e., to a species with a quite different perceptual apparatus to ours. Another species with another type of visual apparatus may have a completely different experience when faced with the same thing. (Apparently, bees see a field of red poppies under a blue sky as yellow flowers growing in purple grass, with an ultra-violet heaven.) The same world does not appear the same colour to them as it does to us. Or even to the colour-blind, or ourselves at dusk.

In a similar way, when we assert that we shouldn't eat a mushroom for it is poisonous, what we actually mean is that it is poisonous-to-human-beings. It may taste quite delicious to pigs, but this gastromic delight is not a part of what is intended by the warning 'Watch out – it's poisonous!'

A sound may be heard by other species, but not us; a smell can be picked up by the sharp nose of a wolf, though we may not even know of its existence; a poppy will look yellow, not red, to bees seeking their pollen. In other words, *certain properties of the world are species-specific* and, although we do not usually spell it out in normal discourse, we are well aware of it on closer thought. The phenomenology is not *in* the world; it is brought *to* the world by a particular species. This is the sign of a dispositional property.

Thus, being poisonous, or yellow, or hot, are dispositional properties – which does not mean, of course, that they do not really exist. But where do colours exist? On the surface of objects? How can they, if the same objects look so very different to different creatures? Ultra-violet for blue, purple for green? We do not think of colours as somehow free-floating, attaching randomly and superficially to objects at will. There seems something more fixed in their relationship to the world. We believe dispositional properties are a part of the world, even if they are not a part of it in

259

the same way as the primary properties of shape, mass and density. We believe they are 'in' the world, even if we have also to bring along something of our own particular physical human nature to experience them.

In what form do dispositional qualities exist, then, if they are not merely imaginary, these colours, tastes, smells and sounds? We can begin by saying that they exist as dispositions – *dispositions to create certain experiences*. Let us take the case of colour as our example of a dispositional quality – the human visual apparatus is what we bring to the experience and science informs us that the other end of the relationship – the 'in the world' bit, so to speak – is the molecular structure of the surface of an object.

A molecular structure will reflect light back to a visual apparatus in a certain way. We will say 'it's red' when a certain percentage of light is reflected back to the human eye. The colour exists in the world (a surface's molecular structure) but the particular experience it produces in us – the colour we see – does not. Red is the experience a human being (with normal eyes, in normal conditions, and so on) will have, when a certain amount of light, (say, fifty per cent), is reflected back to strike his or her eye. A bee will have a different experience of the same molecular structure – yellow, perhaps.[3]

Thus, we see that the same object may produce different experiences: an object is called 'red' when its surface is of the kind that stimulates a particular experience in human beings, under normal conditions (a red one).

To sum up, there are certain properties of an object which exist in a way that means they will be experienced by all intelligent life in a similar manner – these are known as primary properties. However, there are others that are 'in the world' in a way that means they may produce a different experience in creatures with a different perceptual apparatus. These are called 'dispositional properties'. They are not imaginary – they exist in the world. The particular molecular structure of a surface, for example, is not created by us. But the experience we have of it, via our perceptual apparatus, is. The phenomenology is 'in our mind': the molecular structure is not. There is a very real sense in which a rose that is born to bloom unseen is *not* red – if by 'red' we mean the marriage of mind and molecular structure.

The argument of this essay is that Dispositional Theory applies not only to sensory qualities, like colour and taste, but to *extra-sensory experiences*, too. Thus, when a human being 'sees' a ghost, the apparition cannot be dismissed as purely imaginary. It is a part of the world, even though it is not a part of it in the same way as a living creature is part. It is *a dispositional property* – one that may cause certain people, under certain conditions, to have a certain set of visual, auditory or, less commonly, tactile experiences, through arousing certain memories, which may be more or less intense .⁴ The property exists in the Other Realm and glimmers through into this earthly one. (Refer to Harkley's inspiring discussion for more on this 'glimmering').⁵

*Thus, while we create our ghosts we do not do so entirely – they exist. They exist as dispositions. The dispositions to create in some human beings a certain set of projections – memories and images – by which the non-living can be seen.*⁶

Of course, extra-sensory dispositions are not 'in the world' like sensory dispositions, which are physical and so can easily be pinpointed by the physical sciences as such-and-such a property – as a type of molecular structure, for example. The disposition which produces an extra-sensory experience is *non-physical* for it exists on the Other Side and only 'shines through' into the physical world. For this reason, it cannot be measured by scientists – or anyone, for that matter. Grounded in memory, these properties are immeasurable in principle.

This does not make them, in any way, ontologically inferior, however. After all, what is there in the realm of emotion that can be so measured? Certain situations – being faced with a ravenous tiger or werewolf at full moon, a lack of natural light, heights, depths, cramped spaces and certain noises – the scream of a man dying in agony when his own brother has just thrust a knife into his stomach, for instance – may well be disposed to cause a feeling of fear in the average human being. Yet their disposition to cause dread cannot be measured, nor can the dread itself. We may speak of neurons firing in such and such a way, or discover a certain location of activity in the brain, but this does not explain the phenomenon in physical terms. It is to merely gesture to their accompanying neurological states which may co-exist, as a matter of contingent fact, with the irreducibly mental one. Dread cannot be reduced to the physical any more can than experiencing a ghostly apparition.⁷

Our ghosts are our creations. They appear to us out of the projection of certain emotions and memories which are themselves psychological, but they are not purely psychological – they are a reaction *to* something. Namely, extra-sensory dispositional properties.

This leads us to the following well-known problem – for a ghost to exist it must be perceived. Since apparitions are dispositional properties, both sides of the relation are needed – there must be a perceiver ('One who remembers') as well as a psychic disposition (the 'Remembered One', or sometimes simply 'the Dead'.) Of course, there is nothing in the slightest unearthly about this – the same is true of everyday qualities like colour which, as we have seen, consist of a relation between a type of molecular surface and an organ of sight. If the eye does not see, molecular structure not withstanding, the colour does not exist. ('A rose that is born to blush unseen' etc.)[8]

In precisely the same way, whereas the Dead exist whether they are experienced or not, for a *ghost* to exist the extra-sensory dispositional properties must have an effect on a living being – namely, the arousing of certain memories. For a ghost, *esse es percipe* is all too true – namely, *to be is to be seen.*[9]

The central question remains – how are the non-living able to communicate with some people but not others in exactly the same circumstances? We know that a disposition must create the right sort of memories for a ghost to come into being. What we do not understand is why the dispositional qualities sometimes succeed in this but, more often, do not. Why can we reach some people, while others ('those who seek to forget') remain blind and deaf to our most urgent exhortations?[10] This is a question of the utmost importance, and one of which most us have personal and bitter experience, since a ghost that is not seen does not exist.

Is it the fault of the extra-sensory dispositional properties themselves or, as we have mostly believed up until now, that of the insensitive and ill-disposed living man or woman? In short, how do the extra-sensory dispositional qualities produce their effects? That they do is without question, but we still remain unclear about the exact nature of a glimmering.[11]

Perhaps it is a little like trying to describe the colour red. In the end, human beings must repeat a brute, phenomenological fact and just say – 'it's like this', pointing, as it were, to a particular experience inside their own head, and assuming that it is the same experience for each person.

In our turn, we, the non-living, must accept that in the vital respect of our own ghostly existence we are in the position of the blind man who believes that red is like the sound of a trumpet – we will probably never know the truth of the matter for sure.

Steven Savage,
The Nothing.
November 2007.

Notes:

[1] John Locke (1632 -1704), *An Essay Concerning Human Understanding,* 1690.
[2] Locke calls relational, or dispositional, properties 'secondary qualities'; op. cit.
[3] We can even imagine a life form which 'sees' the sound of a bell ringing (think of

a bat and sonar);or, even more easily, one which, when faced with a red object, sees the colour blue – 'red' being the name we give to an object that causes a red experience in us: an experience of which we can only really say, 'you know, this one,' and assume others know what we are talking about.

That they do know – see Thomas Nagel 'What's it like to be a bat?' in *Mortal Questions*, 1967. The famous example of a blind man saying of the colour red that it 'looks' like the sound of a trumpet is more complex, although, even here, we believe we know what he means.

[4] For the role played by the intensity of a memory in the appearance of an apparition see Sigmund Freud (1856-1939), *Mourning and Memory*, 1998. See also the *Case Studies*, (2001) where Freud discusses the possibility of having a powerful wish *not to remember* those who exist on the other side of the grave.

[5] Harkley (1601-41), 'The Glimmering' in *How to be a Ghost*, 1643. The term 'shining through' is sometimes used – see Pursell 1776, Plato 347 BC, Farley, 1888 and, in particular, McDowell's seminal work, 'The Shining', in *The Nature of Things*,1576.

[6] Here the parallel breaks down, for the extra-sensory dispositional qualities appear to work across species to an extraordinary extent, affecting species with quite a different psychological apparatus in similar ways; cf dogs, Hadley (1869-1919) 'Things without souls' *Non-Being and Nothingness*, 1923.)

[7] We could, if we were so inclined, describe in detail the total circumstance someone is faced with when feeling fear – the precise distance of the man with the knife, the length and power of his thrust and the dire consequences of sharp pointed metal entering human flesh – but this does not sum up the emotion of fear, anymore than does describing a circumstance in full of a sighting of a ghost, along with all other brain activity. It does not explain why the same physical circumstances can be found in the world accompanied by exactly the same type of neurological activity when a person does *not* see a ghost, and a different one, when a person *has*.

[8] Of course, when I say 'we' see red, or find something warm or loud or fragrant, it is only for the purpose of this essay. Clearly, *we* don't. These kinds of qualities are long lost to us. I speak only nominally, from the point of view of the living in order to make the argument clear.

[9] Bishop George Berkely (1685-1753), *Three Dialogues*, 1709. Also, in conversation, 2005, 2006 and 2007.

[10] On the idea of having a powerful *wish not to remember*, see Freud, (1998), op cit.

[11] For the frustrations involved in trying to contact a wife or daughter existing on the other side, and the joy of success, see my own account in *Dance To Your Daddy*, (Abyss Books, 2007).

First published in Great Britain by:

Elliott & Thompson Ltd
27 John Street
London WC1N 2BX

© Gail Levy 2008

The right of Gail Levy to be identified as the
author of this work has been asserted by her
in accordance with the Copyright Designs
and Patents Act 1988.

ISBN 978 1 904027 61 4

First edition

Book design by Brad Thompson

Printed and bound in England by Athenaeum Press Ltd.